The James Dickey Reader

Edited by Henry Hart

A TOUCHSTONE BOOK
Published by Simon & Schuster

TOUCHSTONE
Rockefeller Center
1230 Avenue of the Americas
New York, NY 10020

Designed by Gabriel Levine

Manufactured in the United States of America

10 9 8 7 6 5 4 3 2 1

Library of Congress Cataloging-in-Publication Data
Dickey, James.
The James Dickey reader / edited by Henry Hart.
p. cm.
"A Touchstone book."
I. Hart, Henry, 1954– . II. Title.
PS3554.I32A6 1999
811'.54—dc21 99-23976
CIP

ISBN 0-684-86435-5

Permissions appear on page 351.

For Matthew J. Bruccoli

Contents

Introduction

Most people know James Dickey as the imposing, slow-talking Southern sheriff in the film version of his bestselling novel *Deliverance.* For his detractors—and there were vociferous ones by the time the film appeared in 1972—his role confirmed their perception of Dickey as a Southerner who stood up for the savage ways of the hinterland rather than the progressive ideals of the city. Dickey's role as Sheriff Bullard, which he had asked to play while working on the screenplay for Warner Brothers, provides a clue to the drama and the dramatis personae of his life. Born on Groundhog's Day in 1923 to a mother who identified with the Atlanta aristocracy and to a father who identified with its opposite—the north Georgia outback—Dickey was torn from the start. In Bullard, Dickey found a compatible as well as comic alter ego to express his sense of family divisions. Bullard, after all, is bipartisan, a mediator between the mountain folk who want bloody revenge and the city folk who simply want to return to the safety of their homes in Atlanta.

Dickey's famous peer and rival, Robert Lowell, once confessed in a poem: "Everything I do / is only (only) a mix of mother and father, / no matter how unlike they were" ("Mother," *History,* 115). Dickey could have said the same about himself. His mother, Maibelle Swift, was the privileged daughter of Charles Swift, a captain in the Confederate army who amassed a small fortune as the founder of the Atlanta-based Swift Southern Specific company, which made a tonic not unlike the original Coca-Cola. Like Margaret Mitchell, Maibelle Swift went to Washington Seminary, a finishing school for young women in Atlanta's social register, and then to Brenau College, where her main interests were writing, painting, and singing. As a mother of three children she was frail, but she was not the invalid with angina pectoris that her son claimed. Two bouts of rheumatic fever had left her with a leaky valve in her heart. She finally died of cancer at the age of eighty-nine.

Dickey's father, Eugene, hailed from Yankee sympathizers in north Georgia's mountainous Fannin County—a fact that did not sit well with Maibelle's family. Eugene played football, ran track, and studied law at Georgia Tech and Mercer College, but after marrying the wealthy Maibelle in 1910, he devoted most of his energy to the illegal sport of cockfighting. For the rest of his life he was a lawyer by name, but a cockfighter, gambler, and real-estate investor by desire.

As a boy, Jim Dickey found his father's blood sport repulsive. Sensitive, quiet, and shy, he was more interested in books than gaffed roosters. He constantly demanded that his private nursemaid or his mother read to him. According to his sister: "He was born with a book in his hand" (Interview, February 14, 1997). When he learned to read and write on his own, he started to "make" books. At the age of five he wrote, illustrated, and bound a slim volume about personal hygiene—toothbrushing—complete with cutout pictures of Forhan's toothpaste and a calendar to keep track of his brushing. Entitled *You and Yourself,* the book adumbrated his work as an advertising copywriter in the late 1950s and his autobiographical *Self-Interviews* composed in the late 1960s. At the age of six he wrote a more ambitious book—a five-page fantasy about himself as a combat pilot. He called it *The Life of James Dickey* and filled it with crayon drawings of planes. His introspection and his fantasies—especially of himself as a war pilot—were ingrained from the start.

One of the catalysts for Dickey's writing career was the death of his brother, Eugene, on April 4, 1921. Even though it occurred two years before he was born, it convinced Dickey that he was a substitute who had to excel in all endeavors to prove worthy of his parents' love. Imagining that his mother suffered from angina, he decided that she never would have given birth to him if his brother had lived. His life depended on his brother's death. According to his fantasy, Eugene had made the supreme sacrifice so that he could exist. If he felt guilt about supplanting Eugene, he felt anger about *being* supplanted by his other brother, Tom, who was born in 1925. Tom effortlessly won his parents' and everyone else's approval with his athleticism and easygoing disposition. As his middle name, Swift, suggested, he was a runner with phenomenal speed. In high school he broke records, in college became the third-highest point scorer in the Southeastern Conference, and in 1948 qualified for the Olympic tryouts, failing to make the team because of leg injuries. To satisfy his parents' conflicting ideals, which spanned business, art, soldiering, athletics, and the outdoors, the fiercely competitive Jim tried to excel in all fields. When he failed, he resorted to self-aggrandizing fantasies to compensate.

Dickey's success as a mature writer lay in his ability to universalize his private fantasies by imposing on them the archetypal shapes of myths. In the 1940s and 1950s, he gravitated toward what Joseph Campbell, borrowing a phrase from James Joyce's *Finnegans Wake,* called the "monomyth." In *The Hero with a Thousand Faces,* which Dickey read as a Vanderbilt student, Campbell argued: "The standard path of the mythological adventure of the hero is a magnification of the formula represented in the rites of passage: *separation—initiation—return*" (30). Dickey always attributed the plot of *Deliverance,* in which four men depart from the safety of their homeground, suffer initiations and trials in the wilderness, and return home with lessons learned, to Campbell's mythic formula. His other two novels traced similar mythic journeys, as did many of his major poems. Even his coffee-table and children's books drew on rites of passage and circular quests.

Dickey's literary career reached its zenith in the 1960s and early 1970s. Having received a Guggenheim Fellowship in 1960, in 1966 he won a National Book Award for *Buckdancer's Choice.* The poet and editor Peter Davison summed up the critical consensus in his 1967 *Atlantic Monthly* essay "The Difficulties of Being Major." Using criteria articulated by Auden, he argued that only Robert Lowell and James Dickey could be considered major poets: "If American poetry needs a champion for the new generation, Dickey's power and ambition may supply the need. His archetypal concerns are universal to all languages. . . . His sense of urgency is overwhelming" (October 1967, 121). During this period, younger poets such as Dave Smith and Henry Taylor tried both to emulate and to break free from Dickey's enchanting style. Universities clamored for him to read. He demanded and often got the highest fees of any poet on the reading circuit, and, like Dylan Thomas before him, whether sober or drunk he dazzled his audiences.

In his life and writings Dickey struggled to embody those attributes he deemed quintessentially American. In North Fulton High School and Clemson A&M College he played football and ran track. He desperately wanted to be a World War II pilot. After he washed out of pilot training at a base in Camden, South Carolina, he could never quite accept his new classification as a radar observer or the number of his missions in the Pacific—thirty-eight. After returning from the Philippines and Japan and transferring to Vanderbilt, he proved his mettle as a student by graduating with Phi Beta Kappa honors. During his senior year, he married Maxine Webster Syerson, a gracious, attractive woman who worked for American Airlines in Nashville. He spent one more year at Vanderbilt getting his master's degree (he wrote a thesis on Melville's poetry), and then in 1950 got a job teaching English at Rice Institute in Texas. He left to serve as an Air Force radar instructor on bases in Mississippi and Texas during the Korean War, and, after another disappointing stint at Rice, traveled to Europe with Maxine and his three-year-old son Christopher on a *Sewanee Review* fellowship.

In 1955 his mentor, the Southern writer Andrew Lytle, helped secure him a job at the University of Florida. Several months after his arrival he scandalized a group of elderly Pen Women in Gainesville by reading his poem "The Father's Body," which they deemed obscene. Because of the incident, the university refused to renew his contract. Disgusted by the high-handed rebuke and frustrated by the low-paying drudgery of his job, Dickey quit before the end of the spring term, leaving a stack of blue books on his desk and several classes without a professor. His sister-in-law in Atlanta arranged a meeting with a neighbor in advertising, and before long Dickey was on his way to New York to train as a copywriter at the McCann-Erickson agency. During the late 1950s, Dickey worked in Atlanta on McCann's Coca-Cola account. Maxine believed he was selling his soul to the devil of advertising during the day and trying to buy it back by writing poetry at night. Always supportive of his literary ambitions, she urged him to leave the business and find a job more conducive to his writing career. Instead, he moved to a smaller ad agency—Liller, Neal, Battle, and Lindsey—where he hoped to have more time for his poetry. Later he took another advertising job at Burke, Dowling, Adams. Because Dickey left the agency for a week without getting permission, in July 1961 his boss fired him.

Dickey's fortunes quickly changed. Having received a Guggenheim Fellowship in 1961, in February 1962 he returned to Europe with Maxine,

Chris, and his young son Kevin. It was on this trip, while residing in Positano, Italy, that he wrote many of his best-known poems and sketched out the plot of *Deliverance.* With a "first-read" contract at *The New Yorker* and two well-received poetry books—*Into the Stone* and *Drowning with Others*—Dickey was regarded as one of America's most promising poets when he came back to the United States at the end of 1962. Colleges recruited him for poet-in-residence positions, and he obliged by teaching at Reed College (1963–1964), San Fernando Valley State College (1964–1965), and the University of Wisconsin at Madison (1966). His nomadic lifestyle and frenetic "barnstorming for poetry," as he referred to his reading tours, did nothing to slow his prolific output. *Helmets, Buckdancer's Choice,* and *Poems 1957–1967* followed in rapid succession. His stature in the poetry world was acknowledged when he was elected Poetry Consultant at the Library of Congress, a title later changed to Poet Laureate. He served for two terms, from 1966 to 1968, continued to write poetry, revise his manuscript of *Deliverance,* and mesmerize audiences with his readings.

After leaving Washington, D.C., in 1968, Dickey taught creative writing for a term at Georgia Tech before taking a job at the University of South Carolina. As at his other teaching posts, he impressed most of his students as one of those rare writers whose fame did not eclipse his abilities as a professor. In the classroom, he exuded charisma as well as an encyclopedic knowledge of his subjects. Some of his writing students, most notably Pat Conroy and Charles Frazier, went on to distinguished careers. Inside and outside the university, Dickey's avocations continued to provide ready fodder for journalists. He hunted water moccasins with homemade blowguns, shot at bear with broad-head arrows (or so he said), played bluegrass on his custom-made guitars, learned to calculate latitude and longitude using sextants and chronometers, hit a tennis ball passably well, chased women like a priapic fraternity boy, and outdrank most of his iron-stomached companions. His crowning moment as a public figure came in 1977 when former Georgia governor Jimmy Carter, having been elected president, asked him to read a poem at the Kennedy Center during one of his inauguration ceremonies.

Dickey decided early in his career that he wanted to be known as a Jeffersonian Renaissance man as well as a Rabelaisian hell-raiser. As he drank and womanized, he read extensively in philosophy, anthropology, mythology, art, astronomy, music, fiction, and, of course, poetry. In 1972 his learning and contributions to literature earned him a seat in the National Institute of Arts and Letters; in 1988 he took John Steinbeck's former chair in the American Academy and Institute of Arts and Letters. As Reynolds Price pointed out in his *New York Times Book Review* eulogy, Dickey was one of those artists who felt compelled to disguise his love of books, so often considered effeminate or impractical in American culture, by acting like a Viking Berserker.

Yet Dickey was as well-read as any major poet and was blessed with an astonishing memory. He once said that of all the twentieth-century writers his memory was closest to Proust's. His ability to recall long passages verbatim from many of the books he had read lent credibility to his boast. When cirrhosis of the liver and later fibrosis of the lungs confined him to an armchair during his final years, he surrounded himself with a waist-high fortress of books. By the time he died on January 19, 1997, his house contained about 18,000 volumes.

In many ways Dickey was like the daydreamer in James Thurber's story "The Secret Life of Walter Mitty." Dickey spoke of his heroic feats so convincingly that even he seemed to believe them. In an interview for a profile in the Vanderbilt alumni magazine, Dickey spoke of his identification with Mitty and then told the story of his early life, which the journalist rendered as follows:

> Born [in] 1924 in a suburb of Atlanta, Dickey grew up with the nickname "Crabapple Cannonball," prowling the dusty roads of north Georgia on a Harley motorcycle, trysting with farm girls in auto graveyards, and bootlegging liquor in a '34 Ford. At Clemson University, he was a prize football back but left after freshman year for the War, flying almost a hundred Pacific combat missions in a Black Widow night fighter. After the War, he transferred to Vanderbilt. When he was barred from football by a Conference rule designed to prevent coaches from stealing each other's returning service athletes, he turned to track and became Tennessee state champion in the 120-yard high hurdles. He graduated *magna cum laude* in 1949 and got his master's degree the next year (*Alumnus*, 16).

Dickey loved to tell stories about his impoverished childhood during the Depression, his NFL potential as a football player, his dogfights and daring escapes during the one hundred combat missions he flew over the Philippines and Korea, his first Australian wife who died shortly after World War II, his successful business career as an advertising executive, his composition of "Dueling Banjos" for *Deliverance,* and so on. In fact, his nickname was not the Crabapple Cannonball; he did not drive around north Georgia on a motorcycle trysting with farm girls; he was never a pilot; he never bootlegged liquor; he was not an outstanding football player at Clemson; he was not prevented from playing football at Vanderbilt because of eligibility rules; and he was not a Tennessee state champion hurdler. In reinventing his life, Dickey glossed over what he considered to be his deficiencies.

Dickey never reconciled his mother's otherworldly aestheticism with his father's all-too-savage hedonism. He worshiped at the altars of Byron and Hemingway because he found his own divisions magnified in them. In his writing he projected his contradictory selves onto his personae and analyzed his compulsions to become a hero. As if speaking about his inveterate need to play roles and exaggerate his accomplishments, he wrote in his journal: "One feels so damn sorry for writers, the poor posers. People like Hemingway and Yeats spend their whole lives trying to make good a pose because they despise themselves. They put infinite time and energy into trying to make themselves come true, when they know that it's all a damn lie, anyway" (*Sorties,* 104). In public Dickey posed as Hemingway's successor; in his poems and novels he subjected his Hemingwayesque hubris to withering scrutiny. Like F. Scott Fitzgerald, Dickey romanticized traditional American heroes while scrupulously tracing the "foul dust" that floated in the wake of their dreams.

Like Fitzgerald's Gatsby, Dickey erected a mansion that will endure in our collective memory, but one made of books rather than expensive stones. His first volumes collected in *Poems 1957–1967* (1967) form the foundation, walls, and roof. The following volumes of poetry—*The Eye-Beaters, Blood, Victory, Madness, Buckhead and Mercy* (1970), *The Zodiac* (1976), *The Strength of Fields* (1979), *Puella* (1982), and *The Eagle's Mile* (1990)—are the inner, rococo chambers. His novels rise like towers, the massive *Alnilam* (1987) overshadowing *Deliverance* (1970) and *To the White Sea* (1993). His other endeavors—the coffee-table books *Jericho: The South Beheld* (1974), *God's Images* (1977), *Wayfarer* (1988), and *Southern Light* (1991); the essay collections *The Suspect in Poetry* (1964), *Babel to Byzantium* (1968), and *Night Hurdling* (1983); the children's books *Tucky the Hunter* (1978) and *Bronwen, the Traw, and the Shape-Shifter* (1986); the journals *Sorties* (1971) and *Striking In* (1996); the screenplays *Deliverance* (1972) and *The Call of the Wild* (1976); the dozens of published interviews and self-interviews—these are the outbuildings lending grandeur to the main facade.

Dickey's writing career can be divided roughly into two halves: pre-*Deliverance* and post-*Deliverance.* His bestselling novel represented the culmination of his early use of the "mythical method," as T. S. Eliot called it in a review of Joyce's *Ulysses.* Most of Dickey's poems published in the 1950s and 1960s have a strong narrative component. While their powerful rhythms derive from "Apocalyptic" poets such as Dylan Thomas and George Barker, their plots derive from the epic tales and fertility rituals that so enthralled Eliot, Joyce, and Pound. Unlike the Modernists, however, Dickey did not normally piece together his poems as if they were Cubist collages. He wanted to tell stories with beginnings, middles, and ends that would rivet rather than repel ordinary readers. In order to break new ground, in the 1970s he abandoned what he called his "anecdotal" style to experiment with free-flowing associations, bizarre syntax, and baroque rhetoric.

He had experimented with the design of his poems in the late 1960s, but now his poems looked more improvisatory. In the "block format" of "The Fiend," "Falling," and "May Day Sermon," the lines stretched across the page from margin to margin and the words appeared in clusters surrounded by spaces. He hoped this arrangement would make the reading process more dynamic. The reader would dwell on an image or phrase and then jump to the next after a pause. If he had hoped to lull readers with the anapestic flow of his early poems, now he wanted to jolt them with short linguistic bursts. In the poems he wrote during the last three decades of his life, he experimented further with spacing and design. Usually the poems had neither a left nor a right margin. The phrases were scattered over the page or arranged symmetrically around its center-line. Dickey hoped that his new formats would be even more dynamic and that the reader would take delight in leaping from one line to another down the page.

His most ambitious stylistic experiment during this period was in prose. In the 682-page novel *Alnilam,* he not only played with ordinary syntax; he also divided many of the pages into columns of light and dark print to indicate a split between the third-person narrative and the "dark" impressions of events by the blind protagonist, Frank Cahill. Many critics, including Dickey himself, judged his ambitious novel a magnificent failure. Critics were divided over his new stylistic direction in poetry as well. His coffee-table books, which he wrote in the '70s, '80s, and '90s, fared better, at least with the mass market, because of their more traditional plots and styles. *Jericho* sold more than 150,000 copies. Readers preferred his last novel *To the White Sea* to *Alnilam* because it was also more traditional.

The first half of Dickey's career was shaped largely by the predominant reactions to Modernism in post–World War II poetry, the second half by an attempt—however unsuccessful—to return to Modernism's original precepts. Dickey began writing poetry seriously in the late 1940s at Vanderbilt University, which had been a center of cultural ferment. The Agrarians, Fugitives, and New Critics had tried to codify the conservative political and poetic views that T. S. Eliot had espoused. At first drawn to their politics and poetics, Dickey soon disavowed them. His closest poetry friends in the late 1950s were the so-called Deep Imagists, Robert Bly and James Wright. Like them, he wrote poems that yoked the archetypal with the everyday, the universal myth with the private dream, the supernatural with the natural. But his epic ambitions, his warrior pose, and his occasional reactionary remarks led to a feud with Bly and an uneasy alliance with Wright in the 1960s.

As for the popular Confessional school led by Lowell, Plath, and Sexton, Dickey constantly berated the way they paraded their abysmal experiences in public. For similar reasons, he lambasted the Beat poets, especially their idol, Allen Ginsberg, arguing that they should keep their sexual preferences, nervous breakdowns, and drug use private. In his own poetry, however, Dickey imitated the Confessionals and Beats. His revelations of adulterous affairs, drunken frenzies, and bouts of despair made his poetry as sensational as theirs. The Black Mountain school presided over by Charles Olson also drew antipathy from Dickey, yet in his later poetry he imitated these followers of Pound and Williams by scattering his phrases over the page. Dickey had less in common with the abstract-expressionist aesthetics of the New York school, whose principal exponent was John Ashbery. Dickey's blendings of fact and fiction, questionings of stable identities, and stylistic experiments after 1970, however, made him seem more a student of the school than a truant rebel. From his peers as well as his precursors, Dickey borrowed what he could use and rejected the rest.

Dickey's tall tales and cavalier antics arose in part from his Southern roots. "Most Southern literature comes right off the front porch," Dickey once commented, "[it arises from] people sitting and talking, long-windedly, but always willing to listen to each other's stories because they've all got good ones to tell" (*Voiced Connections*, 164). Dickey spun yarns with similar facility. He also bowed to "the integrity of the family unit" and "the sense of kinship" he found especially Southern, adding, "I still believe in the things that Stonewall Jackson and Lee and those people felt were valuable: courage and dependability and other old-fashioned virtues that go all the way back to the

Greeks. I still think they're virtues, and the sense of them has been strong in the South. There are a lot of crooked double-dealing people here, but the good human beings in the South have a degree of commitment to honesty and reliability that I have never seen in any other people" (*Night Hurdling*, 239–40). Despite his obeisance to his region, Dickey never embraced his Southernness unreservedly. If he praised Southern art for its parochialism, he also attacked it for not being sufficiently cosmopolitan. If he pledged allegiance to Southern virtues with one hand, he swept them aside with the other. Like Stephen Dedalus in Joyce's *Portrait of the Artist as a Young Man*, Dickey tried to fly over family, religion, and social convention but ended up entangling himself—sometimes hilariously, sometimes tragically—in their nets.

Dickey's stance toward religion was typical of his paradoxical views. He inherited his father's atheism, but in high school, as if to appease his Episcopalian mother, he read the Bible from cover to cover. Later he read the sacred texts of other religions as well. In 1977 he "rewrote the Bible," as he liked to say, in his coffee-table book *God's Images*. Throughout his career he used symbols, rituals, and myths from different religious traditions to give his experience universal significance. His ambivalent response to religion resembled that of D. H. Lawrence, who, according to Dickey, "was a profoundly religious man who didn't happen to believe in God. But whoever or whatever force it was that created the universe, that caused it to be, whether blind force or determinism or the God of the Old Testament or chance, the rain of matter upon matter, as Democritus thought, is worthy of worship, even if it's indifferent to worship" (*NH*, 289). Dickey's worshipful view of the natural world and its creator had all the intensity of a mystic. To his way of thinking, it was incumbent upon the writer to act as the creator's midwife and spokesperson, re-creating the world in words that bore witness to its sublime origin.

Dickey belonged to the "tragic generation" of post–World War II poets who suffered from what he himself called "the occupational hazards" of poetry—alcoholism, mania, and suicidal depression. Dickey was not clinically manic-depressive like Lowell or Roethke, but partly because of his drinking he suffered their violent mood swings and grandiose delusions. His mysticism was often accompanied by pathological enthusiasm, his tenderness by a desire to inflict pain. He was a "dilettante of madness," his son Chris declared in *The Summer of Deliverance*, a memoir recounting how his father's alcoholic escapades hastened the alcohol-related death of his mother and abetted the drug addictions of his father's second wife. His own conduct notwithstanding, Dickey recoiled from the emotional instability of his peers and precursors. He scoffed at Sylvia Plath, Anne Sexton, John Berryman, Randall Jarrell, Hart Crane, Dylan Thomas, Delmore Schwartz, and Weldon Kees because they were all suicides, or, because of their self-destructive drinking, virtual suicides.

Nevertheless, Dickey understood the problems of his peers all too well. He told a *Playboy* interviewer in 1973:

> I think there is a terrible danger in the over-cultivation of one's sensibilities, and that's what poets are forced to do in order to be poets. You will find that poets, almost without exception, are cast into the most abject despair over things that wouldn't bother an ordinary person at all. Living with such an exacerbating mind and sensibility gets to be something that one cannot bear any longer. In order to create poetry, you make a monster out of your own mind. You can't get rid of him. He stays right with you every minute. Every minute of every day and every night. He produces terrible things—nightmare after nightmare. I'm subject to having them no less than any of the rest of them. But I don't fool myself. I know what's doing it. Writers start out taking something to aid the monster, to give them the poetry. Poets use alcohol, or any other kind of stimulant, to aid and abet this process, then eventually take refuge in the alcohol to help get rid of it. But by that time the monster is so highly developed he cannot be got rid of. (*VC,* 119).

The interviewer asked Dickey whether the poetry was worth the pain. Dickey said yes, because "the moments of intensity which do lead to delight and joy and fulfillment are so much better than those that other people have" (*VC,* 120). In his poetry and fiction, Dickey punctuated his tragedies with moments of comedy and joy. His talent and learning made him one of the most significant poets and men of letters in the post–World War II era.

Poetry

Introduction

James Dickey had to share his first book with two other poets. Charles Scribner's Sons published *Into the Stone and Other Poems* in the seventh volume of its *Poets of Today* series, along with Paris Leary's *Views of the Oxford Colleges and Other Poems* and Jon Swan's *Journeys and Return: Poems*. Wesleyan University Press published Dickey's next three books, *Drowning with Others, Helmets,* and *Buckdancer's Choice,* and then collected them with a group of new poems in *Poems 1957–1967.* In 1981 Wesleyan published the new poems in a separate volume, *Falling, May Day Sermon, and Other Poems.* During the 1970s and 1980s, Doubleday published *The Eye-Beaters, Blood, Victory, Madness, Buckhead and Mercy; The Zodiac; The Strength of Fields;* and *Puella.* During the 1990s, Dickey returned to Wesleyan with *The Eagle's Mile; The Whole Motion, Collected Poems 1945–1992;* and *The Selected Poems.*

Of the "Early Poems" included with the following selections, "The Shark at the Window" was the first poem Dickey published in a nationally circulated literary journal. It appeared in the April–June/1951 issue of *The Sewanee Review* and revealed the dense, highly figurative, "metaphysical" style he favored at the time—a style he learned from Dylan Thomas, Hart Crane, and Allen Tate, among others. "Joel Cahill Dead," which appeared in *The Beloit Poetry Journal* during the summer of 1958, represents a development toward Dickey's more accessible, mature style. It also introduces the central character and events behind his 1987 novel *Alnilam.* Dickey wrote "The

Wish to Be Buried Where One Has Made Love" and "The Wheelchair Drunk" in the late 1950s but never published them, although their style and themes—music, drink, ecstasy—foreshadow his later work. "Reading *Genesis* to a Blind Child" exemplifies his early visionary mode and the influences of Dylan Thomas and Theodore Roethke that shaped it. Although *The Wormwood Review* published the poem in 1960, Dickey did not collect it in any of his first books.

From Into the Stone

The Vegetable King

Just after the sun
Has closed, I swing the fresh paint of the door
And have opened the new, green dark.
From my house and my silent folk
I step, and lay me in ritual down.

One night each April
I unroll the musty sleeping-bag
And beat from it a cloud of sleeping moths.
I leave the house, which leaves
Its window-light on the ground

In gold frames picturing grass,
And lie in the unconsecrated grove
Of small, suburban pines,
And never move, as the ground not ever shall move,
Remembering, remembering to feel

The still earth turn my house around the sun
Where all is dark, unhoped-for, and undone.

I cannot sleep until the lights are out,
And the lights of the house of grass, also,
Snap off, from underground.

Beneath the gods and animals of Heaven,
Mismade inspiringly, like them,
I fall to a colored sleep
Enveloping the house, or coming out
Of the dark side of the sun,

And begin to believe a dream
I never once have had,
Of being part of the acclaimed rebirth
Of the ruined, calm world, in spring,
When the drowned god and the dreamed-of sun

Unite, to bring the red, the blue,
The common yellow flower out of earth
Of the tended and untended garden: when the chosen man,
Hacked apart in the growing cold
Of the year, by the whole of mindless nature is assembled

From the trembling, untroubled river.
I believe I become that man, become
As bloodless as a god, within the water,
Who yet returns to walk a woman's rooms
Where flowers on the mantel-piece are those

Bought by his death. A warm wind springs
From the curtains. Blue china and milk on the table
Are mild, convincing, and strange.
At that time it is light,
And, as my eyelid lifts

An instant before the other, the last star is withdrawn
Alive, from its fiery fable.
I would not think to move,
Nor cry, "I live," just yet,
Nor shake the twinkling horsehair of my head,

Nor rise, nor shine, nor live
With any but the slant, green, mummied light
And wintry, bell-swung undergloom of waters
Wherethrough my severed head has prophesied
For the silent daffodil and righteous

Leaf, and now has told the truth.
This is the time foresaid, when I must enter
The waking house, and return to a human love
Cherished on faith through winter:
That time when I in the night

Of water lay, with sparkling animals of light
And distance made, with gods
Which move through Heaven only as the spheres
Are moved: by music, music.
Mother, son, and wife

Who live with me: I am in death
And waking. Give me the looks that recall me.
None knows why you have waited
In the cold, thin house for winter
To turn the inmost sunlight green

And blue and red with life,
But it must be so, since you have set
These flowers upon the table, and milk for him
Who, recurring in this body, bears you home
Magnificent pardon, and dread, impending crime.

The Performance

The last time I saw Donald Armstrong
He was staggering oddly off into the sun,
Going down, of the Philippine Islands.
I let my shovel fall, and put that hand

Above my eyes, and moved some way to one side
That his body might pass through the sun,

And I saw how well he was not
Standing there on his hands,
On his spindle-shanked forearms balanced,
Unbalanced, with his big feet looming and waving
In the great, untrustworthy air
He flew in each night, when it darkened.

Dust fanned in scraped puffs from the earth
Between his arms, and blood turned his face inside out,
To demonstrate its suppleness
Of veins, as he perfected his role.
Next day, he toppled his head off
On an island beach to the south,

And the enemy's two-handed sword
Did not fall from anyone's hands
At that miraculous sight,
As the head rolled over upon
Its wide-eyed face, and fell
Into the inadequate grave

He had dug for himself, under pressure.
Yet I put my flat hand to my eyebrows
Months later, to see him again
In the sun, when I learned how he died,
And imagined him, there,
Come, judged, before his small captors,

Doing all his lean tricks to amaze them—
The back somersault, the kip-up—
And at last, the stand on his hands,
Perfect, with his feet together,
His head down, evenly breathing,
As the sun poured up from the sea

And the headsman broke down
In a blaze of tears, in that light
Of the thin, long human frame
Upside down in its own strange joy,
And, if some other one had not told him,
Would have cut off the feet

Instead of the head,
And if Armstrong had not presently risen
In kingly, round-shouldered attendance,
And then knelt down in himself
Beside his hacked, glittering grave, having done
All things in this life that he could.

The Other

Holding onto myself by the hand,
I change places into the spirit
I had as a rack-ribbed child,
And walk slowly out through my mind
To the wood, as into a falling fire
Where I turned from that strength-haunted body
Half-way to bronze, as I wished to:

Where I slung up the too-heavy ax-head
And prayed to my thunderous ear-drums
That the deep sweat fall with the leaves
And raise up a man's shape upon me,
Come forth from the work of my arms
And the great, dead tree I hit down on:
That the chicken-chested form I belabored

Might swell with the breast of a statue
From out of the worm-shattered bole,
While I talked all the time through my teeth

To another, unlike me, beside me:
To a brother or king-sized shadow
Who looked at me, burned, and believed me:
Who believed I would rise like Apollo

With armor-cast shoulders upon me:
Whose voice, whistling back through my teeth,
Counted strokes with the hiss of a serpent.
Where the sun through the bright wood drove
Him, mute, and floating strangely, to the ground,
He led me into his house, and sat
Upright, with a face I could never imagine,

With a great harp leant on his shoulder,
And began in deep handfuls to play it:
A sail strung up on its spirit
Gathered up in a ruin in his arms,
That the dog-tired soul might sing
Of the hero, withheld by its body,
Upsprung like a magical man

To a dying, autumnal sound.
As I stood in the shadow-ruled clearing,
Wind died, all over a thicket.
Leaves stood everywhere within falling,
And I thought of our taking the harp
To the tree I had battered to pieces
Many times, many days, in a fever,

With my slow-motion, moon-sided ax.
Reason fell from my mind at a touch
Of the cords, and the dead tree leapt
From the ground, and together, and alive.
I thought of my body to come;
My mind burst into that green.
My brother rose beside me from the earth,

With the wing-bone of music on his back
Trembling strongly with heartfelt gold,

And ascended like a bird into the tree,
And music fell in a comb, as I stood
In a bull's heavy, bronze-bodied shape
As it mixed with a god's, on the ground,
And leaned on the helve of the ax.

Now, owing my arms to the dead
Tree, and the leaf-loosing, mortal wood,
Still hearing that music amaze me,
I walk through the time-stricken forest,
And wish another body for my life,
Knowing that none is given
By the giant, unusable tree

And the leaf-shapen lightning of sun,
And rail at my lust of self
With an effort like chopping through root-stocks:
Yet the light, looming brother but more
Brightly above me is blazing,
In that music come down from the branches
In utter, unseasonable glory,

Telling nothing but how I made
By hand, a creature to keep me dying
Years longer, and coming to sing in the wood
Of what love still might give,
Could I turn wholly mortal in my mind,
My body-building angel give me rest,
This tree cast down its foliage with the years.

Walking on Water

Feeling it with me
On it, barely float, the narrow plank on the water,
I stepped from the clam-shell beach,
Breaking in nearly down through the sun

Where it lay on the sea,
And poled off, gliding upright
Onto the shining topsoil of the bay.

Later, it came to be said
That I was seen walking on water,
Not moving my legs
Except for the wrong step of sliding:
A child who leaned on a staff,
A curious pilgrim hiking
Between two open blue worlds,

My motion a miracle,
Leaving behind me no footprint,
But only the shimmering place
Of an infinite step upon water
In which sat still and were shining
Many marsh-birds and pelicans.
Alongside my feet, the shark

Lay buried and followed,
His eyes on my childish heels.
Thus, taking all morning to stalk
From one littered beach to another,
I came out on land, and dismounted,
Making marks in the sand with my toes
Which truly had walked there, on water,

With the pelicans beating their shadows
Through the mirror carpet
Down, and the shark pursuing
The boy on the burning deck
Of a bare single ship-wrecked board.
Shoving the plank out to sea, I walked
Inland, on numb sparkling feet,

With the sun on the sea unbroken,
Nor the long quiet step of the miracle
Doing anything behind me but blazing,

With the birds in it nodding their heads,
That must ponder that footstep forever,
Rocking, or until I return
In my ghost, which shall have become, then,

A boy with a staff,
To loose them, beak and feather, from the spell
Laid down by a balancing child,
Unstable, tight-lipped, and amazed,
And, under their place of enthrallment,
A huge, hammer-headed spirit
Shall pass, as if led by the nose into Heaven.

Into the Stone

On the way to a woman, I give
My heart all the way into moonlight.
Now down from all sides it is beating.
The moon turns around in the fix
Of its light; its other side totally shines.
Like the dead, I have newly arisen,
Amazed by the light I can throw.
Stand waiting, my love, where you are,

For slowly amazed I come forward
From my bed through the land between,
Through the stone held in air by my heartbeat.
My thin flesh is shed by my shadow;
My hair has turned white with a thought.
No thing that shall die as I step
May fall, or not sing of rebirth.
Very far from myself I come toward you

In the fire of the sun, dead-locked
With the moon's new face in its glory.
I see by the dark side of light.

I am he who I should have become.
A bird that has died overhead
Sings a song to sustain him forever.
Elsewhere I have dreamed of my birth,
And come from my death as I dreamed;

Each time, the moon has burned backward.
Each time, my heart has gone from me
And shaken the sun from the moonlight.
Each time, a woman has called,
And my breath come to life in her singing.
Once more I come home from my ghost.
I give up my father and mother;
My own love has raised up my limbs:

I take my deep heart from the air.
The road like a woman is singing.
It sings with what makes my heart beat
In the air, and the moon turn around.
The dead have their chance in my body.
The stars are drawn into their myths.
I bear nothing but moonlight upon me.
I am known; I know my love.

From Drowning with Others

The Lifeguard

In a stable of boats I lie still,
From all sleeping children hidden.
The leap of a fish from its shadow
Makes the whole lake instantly tremble.
With my foot on the water, I feel
The moon outside

Take on the utmost of its power.
I rise and go out through the boats.
I set my broad sole upon silver,
On the skin of the sky, on the moonlight,
Stepping outward from earth onto water
In quest of the miracle

This village of children believed
That I could perform as I dived
For one who had sunk from my sight.
I saw his cropped haircut go under.
I leapt, and my steep body flashed
Once, in the sun.

Dark drew all the light from my eyes.
Like a man who explores his death
By the pull of his slow-moving shoulders,
I hung head down in the cold,
Wide-eyed, contained, and alone
Among the weeds,

And my fingertips turned into stone
From clutching immovable blackness.
Time after time I leapt upward
Exploding in breath, and fell back
From the change in the children's faces
At my defeat.

Beneath them I swam to the boathouse
With only my life in my arms
To wait for the lake to shine back
At the risen moon with such power
That my steps on the light of the ripples
Might be sustained.

Beneath me is nothing but brightness
Like the ghost of a snowfield in summer.
As I move toward the center of the lake,
Which is also the center of the moon,
I am thinking of how I may be
The savior of one

Who has already died in my care.
The dark trees fade from around me.
The moon's dust hovers together.
I call softly out, and the child's
Voice answers through blinding water.
Patiently, slowly,

He rises, dilating to break
The surface of stone with his forehead.
He is one I do not remember

Having ever seen in his life.
The ground I stand on is trembling
Upon his smile.

I wash the black mud from my hands.
On a light given off by the grave
I kneel in the quick of the moon
At the heart of a distant forest
And hold in my arms a child
Of water, water, water.

The Heaven of Animals

Here they are. The soft eyes open.
If they have lived in a wood
It is a wood.
If they have lived on plains
It is grass rolling
Under their feet forever.

Having no souls, they have come,
Anyway, beyond their knowing.
Their instincts wholly bloom
And they rise.
The soft eyes open.

To match them, the landscape flowers,
Outdoing, desperately
Outdoing what is required:
The richest wood,
The deepest field.

For some of these,
It could not be the place
It is, without blood.

These hunt, as they have done,
But with claws and teeth grown perfect,

More deadly than they can believe.
They stalk more silently,
And crouch on the limbs of trees,
And their descent
Upon the bright backs of their prey

May take years
In a sovereign floating of joy.
And those that are hunted
Know this as their life,
Their reward: to walk

Under such trees in full knowledge
Of what is in glory above them,
And to feel no fear,
But acceptance, compliance.
Fulfilling themselves without pain

At the cycle's center,
They tremble, they walk
Under the tree,
They fall, they are torn,
They rise, they walk again.

A Birth

Inventing a story with grass,
I find a young horse deep inside it.
I cannot nail wires around him;
My fence posts fail to be solid,

And he is free, strangely, without me.
With his head still browsing the greenness,

He walks slowly out of the pasture
To enter the sun of his story.

My mind freed of its own creature,
I find myself deep in my life
In a room with my child and my mother,
When I feel the sun climbing my shoulder

Change, to include a new horse.

Fog Envelops the Animals

Fog envelops the animals.
Not one can be seen, and they live.
At my knees, a cloud wears slowly
Up out of the buried earth.
In a white suit I stand waiting.

Soundlessly whiteness is eating
My visible self alive.
I shall enter this world like the dead,
Floating through tree trunks on currents
And streams of untouchable pureness

That shine without thinking of light.
My hands burn away at my sides
In the pale, risen ghosts of deep rivers.
In my hood peaked like a flame,
I feel my own long-hidden,

Long-sought invisibility
Come forth from my solid body.
I stand with all beasts in a cloud.
Of them I am deadly aware,
And they not of me, in this life.

Only my front teeth are showing
As the dry fog mounts to my lips
In a motion long buried in water,
And now, one by one, my teeth
Like rows of candles go out.

In the spirit of flame, my hood
Holds the face of my soul without burning,
And I drift forward
Through the hearts of the curdling oak trees,
Borne by the river of Heaven.

My arrows, keener than snowflakes,
Are with me whenever I touch them.
Above my head, the trees exchange their arms
In the purest fear upon earth.
Silence. Whiteness. Hunting.

Between Two Prisoners

I would not wish to sit
In my shape bound together with wire,
Wedged into a child's sprained desk
In the schoolhouse under the palm tree.
Only those who did could have done it.

One bled from a cut on his temple,
And sat with his yellow head bowed,
His wound for him painfully thinking.
A belief in words grew upon them
That the unbound, who walk, cannot know.

The guard at the window leaned close
In a movement he took from the palm tree,
To hear, in a foreign tongue,

All things which cannot be said.
In the splintering clapboard room

They rested the sides of their faces
On the tops of the desks as they talked.
Because of the presence of children
In the deep signs carved in the desk tops,
Signs on the empty blackboard

Began, like a rain, to appear.
In the luminous chalks of all colors,
Green face, yellow breast, white sails
Whose wing feathers made the wall burn
Like a waterfall seen in a fever,

An angel came boldly to light
From his hands casting green, ragged bolts
Each having the shape of a palm leaf.
Also traced upon darkness in chalk
Was the guard at the rear window leaning

Through the red, vital strokes of his tears.
Behind him, men lying with swords
As with women, heard themselves sing,
And woke, then, terribly knowing
That they were a death squad, singing

In its sleep, in the middle of a war.
A wind sprang out of the tree.
The guard awoke by the window,
And found he had talked to himself
All night, in two voices, of Heaven.

He stood in the sunlit playground
Where the quiet boys knelt together
In their bloodletting trusses of wire,
And saw their mussed, severed heads
Make the ground jump up like a dog.

I watched the small guard be hanged
A year later, to the day,
In a closed horse stall in Manila.
No one knows what language he spoke
As his face changed into all colors,

And gave off his red, promised tears,
Or if he learned blindly to read
A child's deep, hacked hieroglyphics
Which can call up an angel from nothing,
Or what was said for an instant, there,

In the tied, scribbled dark, between him
And a figure drawn hugely in chalk,
Speaking words that can never be spoken
Except in a foreign tongue,
In the end, at the end of a war.

Hunting Civil War Relics at Nimblewill Creek

As he moves the mine detector
A few inches over the ground,
Making it vitally float
Among the ferns and weeds,
I come into this war
Slowly, with my one brother,
Watching his face grow deep
Between the earphones,
For I can tell
If we enter the buried battle
Of Nimblewill
Only by his expression.

Softly he wanders, parting
The grass with a dreaming hand.

No dead cry yet takes root
In his clapped ears
Or can be seen in his smile.
But underfoot I feel
The dead regroup,
The burst metals all in place,
The battle lines be drawn
Anew to include us
In Nimblewill,
And I carry the shovel and pick

More as if they were
Bright weapons that I bore.
A bird's cry breaks
In two, and into three parts.
We cross the creek; the cry
Shifts into another,
Nearer, bird, and is
Like the shout of a shadow—
Lived-with, appallingly close—
Or the soul, pronouncing
"Nimblewill":
Three tones; your being changes.

We climb the bank;
A faint light glows
On my brother's mouth.
I listen, as two birds fight
For a single voice, but he
Must be hearing the grave,
In pieces, all singing
To his clamped head,
For he smiles as if
He rose from the dead within
Green Nimblewill
And stood in his grandson's shape.

No shot from the buried war
Shall kill me now,

For the dead have waited here
A hundred years to create
Only the look on the face
Of my one brother,
Who stands among them, offering
A metal dish
Afloat in the trembling weeds,
With a long-buried light on his lips
At Nimblewill
And the dead outsinging two birds.

I choke the handle
Of the pick, and fall to my knees
To dig wherever he points,
To bring up mess tin or bullet,
To go underground
Still singing, myself,
Without a sound,
Like a man who renounces war,
Or one who shall lift up the past,
Not breathing "Father,"
At Nimblewill,
But saying, "Fathers! Fathers!"

The Hospital Window

I have just come down from my father.
Higher and higher he lies
Above me in a blue light
Shed by a tinted window.
I drop through six white floors
And then step out onto pavement.

Still feeling my father ascend,
I start to cross the firm street,

My shoulder blades shining with all
The glass the huge building can raise.
Now I must turn round and face it,
And know his one pane from the others.

Each window possesses the sun
As though it burned there on a wick.
I wave, like a man catching fire.
All the deep-dyed windowpanes flash,
And, behind them, all the white rooms
They turn to the color of Heaven.

Ceremoniously, gravely, and weakly,
Dozens of pale hands are waving
Back, from inside their flames.
Yet one pure pane among these
Is the bright, erased blankness of nothing.
I know that my father is there,

In the shape of his death still living.
The traffic increases around me
Like a madness called down on my head.
The horns blast at me like shotguns,
And drivers lean out, driven crazy—
But now my propped-up father

Lifts his arm out of stillness at last.
The light from the window strikes me
And I turn as blue as a soul,
As the moment when I was born.
I am not afraid for my father—
Look! He is grinning; he is not

Afraid for my life, either,
As the wild engines stand at my knees
Shredding their gears and roaring,
And I hold each car in its place
For miles, inciting its horn
To blow down the walls of the world

That the dying may float without fear
In the bold blue gaze of my father.
Slowly I move to the sidewalk
With my pin-tingling hand half dead
At the end of my bloodless arm.
I carry it off in amazement,

High, still higher, still waving,
My recognized face fully mortal,
Yet not; not at all, in the pale,
Drained, otherworldly, stricken,
Created hue of stained glass.
I have just come down from my father.

From Helmets

At Darien Bridge

The sea here used to look
As if many convicts had built it,

Standing deep in their ankle chains,
Ankle-deep in the water, to smite

The land and break it down to salt.
I was in this bog as a child

When they were all working all day
To drive the pilings down.

I thought I saw the still sun
Strike the side of a hammer in flight

And from it a sea bird be born
To take off over the marshes.

As the gray climbs the side of my head
And cuts my brain off from the world,

I walk and wish mainly for birds,
For the one bird no one has looked for

To spring again from a flash
Of metal, perhaps from the scratched

Wedding band on my ring finger.
Recalling the chains of their feet,

I stand and look out over grasses
At the bridge they built, long abandoned,

Breaking down into water at last,
And long, like them, for freedom

Or death, or to believe again
That they worked on the ocean to give it

The unchanging, hopeless look
Out of which all miracles leap.

Chenille

There are two facing peacocks
    Or a ship flapping
On its own white tufted sail
At roadside, near a mill;

Flamingoes also are hanging
    By their bills on bedspreads
And an occasional mallard.
These you can buy anywhere.
They are made by machine
From a sanctioned, unholy pattern
Rigid with industry.
They hoard the smell of oil

And hum like looms all night
    Into your pores, reweaving
Your body from bobbins.
There is only one quiet

Place—in a scuppernong arbor—
    Where animals as they
Would be, are born into sleep-cloth:
A middle-aged man's grandmother
Sits in the summer green light
Of leaves, gone toothless
For eating grapes better,
And pulls the animals through

With a darning needle:
    Deer, rabbits and birds,
Red whales and unicorns,
Winged elephants, crowned ants:

Beasts that cannot be thought of
    By the wholly sane
Rise up in the rough, blurred
Flowers of fuzzy cloth
In only their timeless outlines
Like the beasts of Heaven:
Those sketched out badly, divinely
By stars not wholly sane.

Love, I have slept in that house.
    There it was winter.
The tattered moonfields crept
Through the trellis, and fell

In vine-tangled shade on my face
    Like thrown-away knitting
Before cloud came and dimmed
Those scars from off me.
My fingernails chilled
To the bone. I called

For another body to be
With me, and warm us both.

A unicorn neighed; I folded
    His neck in my arms
And was safe, as he lay down.
All night, from thickening Heaven,

Someone up there kept throwing
    Bedspreads upon me.
Softly I called, and they came:
The ox and the basilisk,
The griffin, the phoenix, the lion—
Light-bodied, only the essence,
The tufted, creative starfields
Behind the assembling clouds—

The snake from the apple tree came
    To save me from freezing,
And at last the lung-winged ship
On its own sail scented with potash

Fell sighing upon us all.
    The last two nails
Of cold died out in my nostrils
Under the dance-weight of beasts.
I lay, breathing like thread,
An inspired outline of myself,
As rain began greatly to fall,
And closed the door of the Ark.

Springer Mountain

Four sweaters are woven upon me,
All black, all sweating and waiting,

And a sheepherder's coat's wool hood,
Buttoned strainingly, holds my eyes
With their sight deepfrozen outside them
From their gaze toward a single tree.
I am here where I never have been,
In the limbs of my warmest clothes,
Waiting for light to crawl, weakly
From leaf to dead leaf onto leaf
Down the western side of the mountain.
Deer sleeping in light far above me

Have already woken, and moved,
In step with the sun moving strangely
Down toward the dark knit of my thicket
Where my breath takes shape on the air
Like a white helmet come from the lungs.
The one tree I hope for goes inward
And reaches the limbs of its gold.
My eyesight hangs partly between
Two twigs on the upslanting ground,
Then steps like a god from the dead
Wet of a half-rotted oak log
Steeply into the full of my brow.
My thighbones groaningly break

Upward, releasing my body
To climb, and to find among humus
New insteps made of snapped sticks.
On my back the faggot of arrows
Rattles and scratches its feathers.

I go up over logs slowly
On my painfully reborn legs,
My ears putting out vast hearing
Among the invisible animals,

Passing under thin branches held still,
Kept formed all night as they were

By the thought of predictable light.
The sun comes openly in
To my mouth, and is blown out white,

But no deer is anywhere near me.
I sit down and wait as in darkness.

The sweat goes dead at the roots

Of my hair: a deer is created
Descending, then standing and looking.
The sun stands and waits for his horns

To move. I may be there, also,
Between them, in head bones uplifted
Like a man in an animal tree
Nailed until light comes:
A dream of the unfeared hunter
Who has formed in his brain in the dark
And rose with light into his horns,
Naked, and I have turned younger

At forty than I ever have been.
I hang my longbow on a branch.
The buck leaps away and then stops,
And I step forward, stepping out

Of my shadow and pulling over
My head one dark heavy sweater
After another, my dungarees falling
Till they can be kicked away,
Boots, socks, all that is on me
Off. The world catches fire.
I put an unbearable light
Into breath skinned alive of its garments:
I think, beginning with laurel,
Like a beast loving
With the whole god bone of his horns:
The green of excess is upon me

Like deer in fir thickets in winter
Stamping and dreaming of men
Who will kneel with them naked to break
The ice from streams with their faces
And drink from the lifespring of beasts.
He is moving. I am with him

Down the shuddering hillside moving
Through trees and around, inside
And out of stumps and groves
Of laurel and slash pine,
Through hip-searing branches and thorn
Brakes, unprotected and sure,
Winding down to the waters of life
Where they stand petrified in a creek bed
Yet melt and flow from the hills
At the touch of an animal visage,

Rejoicing wherever I come to
With the gold of my breast unwrapped,
My crazed laughter pure as good church-cloth,
My brain dazed and pointed with trying
To grow horns, glad that it cannot,
For a few steps deep in the dance
Of what I most am and should be
And can be only once in this life.
He is gone below, and I limp
To look for my clothes in the world,

A middle-aged, softening man
Grinning and shaking his head
In amazement to last him forever.
I put on the warm-bodied wool,
The four sweaters inside out,
The bootlaces dangling and tripping,
Then pick my tense bow off the limb
And turn with the unwinding hooftracks,
In my good, tricked clothes,

To hunt, under Springer Mountain,
Deer for the first and last time.

Cherrylog Road

Off Highway 106
At Cherrylog Road I entered
The '34 Ford without wheels,
Smothered in kudzu,
With a seat pulled out to run
Corn whiskey down from the hills,

And then from the other side
Crept into an Essex
With a rumble seat of red leather
And then out again, aboard
A blue Chevrolet, releasing
The rust from its other color,

Reared up on three building blocks.
None had the same body heat;
I changed with them inward, toward
The weedy heart of the junkyard,
For I knew that Doris Holbrook
Would escape from her father at noon

And would come from the farm
To seek parts owned by the sun
Among the abandoned chassis,
Sitting in each in turn
As I did, leaning forward
As in a wild stock-car race

In the parking lot of the dead.
Time after time, I climbed in
And out the other side, like

An envoy or movie star
Met at the station by crickets.
A radiator cap raised its head,

Become a real toad or a kingsnake
As I neared the hub of the yard,
Passing through many states,
Many lives, to reach
Some grandmother's long Pierce-Arrow
Sending platters of blindness forth

From its nickel hubcaps
And spilling its tender upholstery
On sleepy roaches,
The glass panel in between
Lady and colored driver
Not all the way broken out,

The back-seat phone
Still on its hook.
I got in as though to exclaim,
"Let us go to the orphan asylum,
John; I have some old toys
For children who say their prayers."

I popped with sweat as I thought
I heard Doris Holbrook scrape
Like a mouse in the southern-state sun
That was eating the paint in blisters
From a hundred car tops and hoods.
She was tapping like code,

Loosening the screws,
Carrying off headlights,
Sparkplugs, bumpers,
Cracked mirrors and gear-knobs,
Getting ready, already,
To go back with something to show

Other than her lips' new trembling
I would hold to me soon, soon,
Where I sat in the ripped back seat
Talking over the interphone,
Praying for Doris Holbrook
To come from her father's farm

And to get back there
With no trace of me on her face
To be seen by her red-haired father
Who would change, in the squalling barn,
Her back's pale skin with a strop,
Then lay for me

In a bootlegger's roasting car
With a string-triggered 12-gauge shotgun
To blast the breath from the air.
Not cut by the jagged windshields,
Through the acres of wrecks she came
With a wrench in her hand,

Through dust where the blacksnake dies
Of boredom, and the beetle knows
The compost has no more life.
Someone outside would have seen
The oldest car's door inexplicably
Close from within:

I held her and held her and held her,
Convoyed at terrific speed
By the stalled, dreaming traffic around us,
So the blacksnake, stiff
With inaction, curved back
Into life, and hunted the mouse

With deadly overexcitement,
The beetles reclaimed their field
As we clung, glued together,

With the hooks of the seat springs
Working through to catch us red-handed
Amidst the gray, breathless batting

That burst from the seat at our backs.
We left by separate doors
Into the changed, other bodies
Of cars, she down Cherrylog Road
And I to my motorcycle
Parked like the soul of the junkyard

Restored, a bicycle fleshed
With power, and tore off
Up Highway 106, continually
Drunk on the wind in my mouth,
Wringing the handlebar for speed,
Wild to be wreckage forever.

The Scarred Girl

All glass may yet be whole
She thinks, it may be put together
From the deep inner flashing of her face.
One moment the windshield held

The countryside, the green
Level fields and the animals,
And these must be restored
To what they were when her brow

Broke into them for nothing, and began
Its sparkling under the gauze.
Though the still, small war for her beauty
Is stitched out of sight and lost,

It is not this field that she thinks of.
It is that her face, buried
And held up inside the slow scars,
Knows how the bright, fractured world

Burns and pulls and weeps
To come together again.
The green meadow lying in fragments
Under the splintered sunlight,

The cattle broken in pieces
By her useless, painful intrusion
Know that her visage contains
The process and hurt of their healing,

The hidden wounds that can
Restore anything, bringing the glass
Of the world together once more,
All as it was when she struck,

All except her. The shattered field
Where they dragged the telescoped car
Off to be pounded to scrap
Waits for her to get up,

For her calm, unimagined face
To emerge from the yards of its wrapping,
Red, raw, mixed-looking but entire,
A new face, an old life,

To confront the pale glass it has dreamed
Made whole and backed with wise silver,
Held in other hands brittle with dread,
A doctor's, a lip-biting nurse's,

Who do not see what she sees
Behind her odd face in the mirror:
The pastures of earth and of heaven
Restored and undamaged, the cattle

Risen out of their jagged graves
To walk in the seamless sunlight
And a newborn countenance
Put upon everything,

Her beauty gone, but to hover
Near for the rest of her life,
And good no nearer, but plainly
In sight, and the only way.

From Buckdancer's Choice

The Firebombing

Denke daran, dass nach den grossen Zerstörungen
Jedermann beweisen wird, dass er unschuldig war.
—*Günter Eich*

Or hast thou an arm like God?
—*The Book of Job*

Homeowners unite.

All families lie together, though some are burned alive.
The others try to feel
For them. Some can, it is often said.

Starve and take off

Twenty years in the suburbs, and the palm trees willingly leap
Into the flashlights,
And there is beneath them also
A booted crackling of snailshells and coral sticks.

There are cowl flaps and the tilt cross of propellers,
The shovel-marked clouds' far sides against the moon,
The enemy filling up the hills
With ceremonial graves. At my somewhere among these,

Snap, a bulb is tricked on in the cockpit

And some technical-minded stranger with my hands
Is sitting in a glass treasure-hole of blue light,
Having potential fire under the undeodorized arms
Of his wings, on thin bomb-shackles,
The "tear-drop-shaped" 300-gallon drop-tanks
Filled with napalm and gasoline.

Thinking forward ten minutes
From that, there is also the burst straight out
Of the overcast into the moon; there is now
The moon-metal-shine of propellers, the quarter-
moonstone, aimed at the waves,
Stopped on the cumulus.

There is then this re-entry
Into cloud, for the engines to ponder their sound.
In white dark the aircraft shrinks; Japan

Dilates around it like a thought.
Coming out, the one who is here is over
Land, passing over the all-night grainfields,
In dark paint over
The woods with one silver side,
Rice-water calm at all levels
Of the terraced hill.
                    Enemy rivers and trees
Sliding off me like snakeskin,
Strips of vapor spooled from the wingtips
Going   invisible   passing   over   on
Over   bridges   roads for nightwalkers
Sunday night in the enemy's country   absolute

Calm   the moon's face   coming   slowly
About
          the inland sea
Slants   is woven with wire thread
Levels out   holds together like a quilt
Off the starboard wing   cloud flickers
At my glassed-off forehead   the moon's now and again
Uninterrupted face going forward
Over the waves in a glide-path
Lost into land.

Going: going with it

Combat booze by my side in a cratered canteen,
Bourbon frighteningly mixed
With GI pineapple juice,
Dogs trembling under me for hundreds of miles, on many
Islands, sleep-smelling that ungodly mixture
Of napalm and high-octane fuel,
Good bourbon and GI juice.

Rivers circling behind me around
Come to the fore, and bring
A town with everyone darkened.
Five thousand people are sleeping off
An all-day American drone.
Twenty years in the suburbs have not shown me
Which ones were hit and which not.

Haul on the wheel   racking slowly
The aircraft blackly around
In a dark dream   that   this is
That is like flying inside someone's head

Think of this   think of this

I did not think of my house
But think of my house now

Where the lawn mower rests on its laurels
Where the diet exists
For my own good   where I try to drop
Twenty years, eating figs in the pantry
Blinded by each and all
Of the eye-catching cans that gladly have caught my wife's eye
Until I cannot say
Where the screwdriver is   where the children
Get off the bus   where the fly
Hones his front legs   where the hammock folds
Its erotic daydreams   where the Sunday
School text for the day has been put   where the fire
Wood is   where the payments
For everything under the sun
Pile peacefully up,

But in this half-paid-for pantry
Among the red lids that screw off
With an easy half-twist to the left
And the long drawers crammed with dim spoons,
I still have charge—secret charge—
Of the fire developed to cling
To everything: to golf carts and fingernail
Scissors as yet unborn   tennis shoes
Grocery baskets   toy fire engines
New Buicks stalled by the half-moon
Shining at midnight on crossroads   green paint
Of jolly garden tools   red Christmas ribbons:

Not atoms, these, but glue inspired
By love of country to burn,
The apotheosis of gelatin.

Behind me having risen the Southern Cross
Set up by chaplains in the Ryukyus—
Orion, Scorpio, the immortal silver
Like the myths of king-
insects at swarming time—

One mosquito, dead drunk
On altitude, drones on, far under the engines,
And bites between
The oxygen mask and the eye.
The enemy-colored skin of families
Determines to hold its color
In sleep, as my hand turns whiter
Than ever, clutching the toggle—
The ship shakes   bucks
Fire hangs   not yet fire
In the air above Beppu
For I am fulfilling

And "anti-morale" raid upon it.
All leashes of dogs
Break under the first bomb, around those
In bed, or late in the public baths: around those
Who inch forward on their hands
Into medicinal waters.
Their heads come up with a roar
Of Chicago fire:
Come up with the carp pond showing
The bathhouse upside down,
Standing stiller to show it more
As I sail artistically over
The resort town followed by farms,
Singing and twisting
All the handles in heaven   kicking
The small cattle off their feet
In a red costly blast
Flinging jelly over the walls
As in a chemical war-
fare field demonstration.
With fire of mine like a cat

Holding onto another man's walls,
My hat should crawl on my head

In streetcars, thinking of it,
The fat on my body should pale.

Gun down
The engines, the eight blades sighing
For the moment when the roofs will connect
Their flames, and make a town burning with all
American fire.
Reflections of houses catch;
Fire shuttles from pond to pond
In every direction, till hundreds flash with one death.
With this in the dark of the mind,
Death will not be what it should;
Will not, even now, even when
My exhaled face in the mirror
Of bars, dilates in a cloud like Japan.
The death of children is ponds
Shutter-flashing; responding mirrors; it climbs
The terraces of hills
Smaller and smaller, a mote of red dust
At a hundred feet; at a hundred and one it goes out.
That is what should have got in
To my eye

And shown the insides of houses, the low tables
Catch fire from the floor mats,
Blaze up in gas around their heads
Like a dream of suddenly growing
Too intense for war. Ah, under one's dark arms
Something strange-scented falls—when those on earth
Die, there is not even sound;
One is cool and enthralled in the cockpit,
Turned blue by the power of beauty,
In a pale treasure-hole of soft light
Deep in aesthetic contemplation,
Seeing the ponds catch fire
And cast it through ring after ring

Of land: O death in the middle
Of acres of inch-deep water!   Useless

Firing   small arms
Speckles   from the river
Bank   one ninety-millimeter
Misses   far down   wrong petals   gone

It is this detachment,
The honored aesthetic evil,
The greatest sense of power in one's life,
That must be shed in bars, or by whatever
Means, by starvation
Visions in well-stocked pantries:
The moment when the moon sails in between
The tail-booms   the rudders nod   I swing
Over   directly over the heart
The *heart* of the fire. A mosquito burns out on my cheek
With the cold of my face   there are the eyes
In blue light   bar light
All masked but them   the moon
Crossing from left to right   in the streams below
Oriental fish form quickly
In the chemical shine,
In their eyes one tiny seed
Of deranged, Old Testament light.

Letting go   letting go
The plane rises gently   dark forms
Glide off me   long water   pales
In safe zones   a new cry enters
The voice box of chained family dogs

We buck   leap over something
Not there   settle back
Leave it   leave it clinging and crying
It consumes them in a hot
Body-flash, old age or menopause

Of children, clings and burns
eating through
And when a reed mat catches fire
From me, it explodes through field after field
Bearing its sleeper another

Bomb finds a home
And clings to it like a child. And so

Goodbye to the grassy mountains
To cloud streaming from the night engines
Flags pennons curved silks
Of air myself streaming also
My body covered
With flags, the air of flags
Between the engines.
Forever I do sleep in that position,
Forever in a turn
For home that breaks out streaming banners
From my wingtips,
Wholly in position to admire.

O then I knock it off
And turn for home over the black complex thread worked through
The silver night-sea,
Following the huge, moon-washed steppingstones
Of the Ryukyus south,
The nightgrass of mountains billowing softly
In my rising heat.
Turn and tread down
The yellow stones of the islands
To where Okinawa burns,
Pure gold, on the radar screen,
Beholding, beneath, the actual island form
In the vast water-silver poured just above solid ground,
An inch of water extending for thousands of miles
Above flat ploughland. Say "down," and it is done.

All this, and I am still hungry,
Still twenty years overweight, still unable
To get down there or see
What really happened.
But it may be that I could not,
If I tried, say to any
Who lived there, deep in my flames: say, in cold
Grinning sweat, as to another
Of these homeowners who are always curving
Near me down the different-grassed street: say
As though to the neighbor
I borrowed the hedge-clippers from
On the darker-grassed side of the two,
Come in, my house is yours, come in
If you can, if you
Can pass this unfired door. It is that I can imagine
At the threshold nothing
With its ears crackling off
Like powdery leaves,
Nothing with children of ashes, nothing not
Amiable, gentle, well-meaning,
A little nervous for no
Reason a little worried a little too loud
Or too easygoing nothing I haven't lived with
For twenty years, still nothing not as
American as I am, and proud of it.

Absolution? Sentence? No matter;
The thing itself is in that.

Buckdancer's Choice

So I would hear out those lungs,
The air split into nine levels,
Some gift of tongues of the whistler

In the invalid's bed: my mother,
Warbling all day to herself
The thousand variations of one song;

It is called Buckdancer's Choice.
For years, they have all been dying
Out, the classic buck-and-wing men

Of traveling minstrel shows;
With them also an old woman
Was dying of breathless angina,

Yet still found breath enough
To whistle up in my head
A sight like a one-man band,

Freed black, with cymbals at heel,
An ex-slave who thrivingly danced
To the ring of his own clashing light

Through the thousand variations of one song
All day to my mother's prone music,
The invalid's warbler's note,

While I crept close to the wall
Sock-footed, to hear the sounds alter,
Her tongue like a mockingbird's break

Through stratum after stratum of a tone
Proclaiming what choices there are
For the last dancers of their kind,

For ill women and for all slaves
Of death, and children enchanted at walls
With a brass-beating glow underfoot,

Not dancing but nearly risen
Through barnlike, theatrelike houses
On the wings of the buck and wing.

Pursuit from Under

Often, in these blue meadows,
I hear what passes for the bark of seals

And on August week ends the cold of a personal ice age
Comes up through my bare feet
Which are trying to walk like a boy's again
So that nothing on earth can have changed
On the ground where I was raised.

The dark grass here is like
The pads of mukluks going on and on

Because I once burned kerosene to read
Myself near the North Pole
In the journal of Arctic explorers
Found, years after death, preserved
In a tent, part of whose canvas they had eaten

Before the last entry.
All over my father's land

The seal holes sigh like an organ,
And one entry carries more terror
Than the blank page that signified death
In 1912, on the icecap.
It says that, under the ice,

The killer whale darts and distorts,
Cut down by the flawing glass

To a weasel's shadow,
And when, through his ceiling, he sees
Anything darker than snow
He falls away
To gather more and more force

From the iron depths of cold water,
His shadow dwindling

Almost to nothing at all, then charges
Straight up, looms up at the ice and smashes
Into it with his forehead
To splinter the roof, to isolate seal or man
On a drifting piece of the floe

Which he can overturn.
If you run, he will follow you

Under the frozen pane,
Turning as you do, zigzagging,
And at the most uncertain of your ground
Will shatter through, and lean,
And breathe frankly in your face

An enormous breath smelling of fish.
With the stale lungs staining your air

You know the unsaid recognition
Of which the explorers died:
They had been given an image
Of how the downed dead pursue us.
They knew, as they starved to death,

That not only in the snow
But in the family field

The small shadow moves,
And under bare feet in the summer:

That somewhere the turf will heave,
And the outraged breath of the dead,
So long held, will form

Unbreathably around the living.
The cows low oddly here

As I pass, a small bidden shape
Going with me, trembling like foxfire
Under my heels and their hooves.
I shall write this by kerosene,
Pitch a tent in the pasture, and starve.

Sled Burial, Dream Ceremony

While the south rains, the north
Is snowing, and the dead southerner
Is taken there. He dies with the top of his casket
Open, his hair combed, the particles in the air
Changing to other things. The train stops

In a small furry village, and men in flap-eared caps
And others with women's scarves tied around their heads
And business hats over those, unload him,
And one of them reaches inside the coffin and places
The southerner's hand at the center

Of his dead breast. They load him onto a sled,
An old-fashioned sled with high-curled runners,
Drawn by horses with bells, and begin
To walk out of town, past dull red barns
Inching closer to the road as it snows

Harder, past an army of gunny-sacked bushes,
Past horses with flakes in the hollows of their sway-backs,

Past round faces drawn by children
On kitchen windows, all shedding basic-shaped tears.
The coffin top still is wide open;

His dead eyes stare through his lids,
Not fooled that the snow is cotton. The woods fall
Slowly off all of them, until they are walking
Between rigid little houses of ice-fishers
On a plain which is a great plain of water

Until the last rabbit track fails, and they are
At the center. They take axes, shovels, mattocks,
Dig the snow away, and saw the ice in the form
Of his coffin, lifting the slabs like a door
Without hinges. The snow creaks under the sled

As they unload him like hay, holding his weight by ropes.
Sensing an unwanted freedom, a fish
Slides by, under the hole leading up through the snow
To nothing, and is gone. The coffin's shadow
Is white, and they stand there, gunny-sacked bushes,

Summoned from village sleep into someone else's dream
Of death, and let him down, still seeing the flakes in the air
At the place they are born of pure shadow
Like his dead eyelids, rocking for a moment like a boat
On utter foreignness, before he fills and sails down.

The Fiend

He has only to pass by a tree   moodily walking   head down
A worried accountant   not with it   and he is swarming
He is gliding up the underside light of leaves   upfloating
In a seersucker suit   passing window after window of her building.
He finds her at last, chewing gum   talking on the telephone.

The wind sways him softly   comfortably sighing   she must bathe
Or sleep.   She gets up, and he follows her along the branch
Into another room.   She stands there for a moment   and the teddy bear
On the bed feels its guts spin as she takes it by the leg and tosses
It off.   She touches one button at her throat, and rigor mortis
Slithers into his pockets, making everything there—keys, pen
and secret love—stand up.   He brings from those depths the knife
And flicks it open   it glints on the moon one time   carries
Through the dead walls   making a wormy static on the TV screen.
He parts the swarm of gnats that live excitedly at this perilous level
Parts the rarified light high windows give out into inhabited trees
Opens his lower body to the moon. This night the apartments are sinking

To ground level   burying their sleepers in the soil   burying all floors
But the one where a sullen shopgirl gets ready to take a shower,
Her hair in rigid curlers, and the rest.   When she gives up
Her aqua terry-cloth robe the wind quits in mid-tree   the birds
Freeze to their perches round his head   a purely human light
Comes out of a one-man oak   around her an energy field   she stands
Rooted   not turning to anything else   then begins to move like a saint
Her stressed nipples rising like things about to crawl off her   as he gets
A hold on himself.   With that clasp she changes   senses   something
Some breath through the fragile walls   some all-seeing eye
Of God   some touch that enfolds her body   some hand come up out of roots
That carries her as she moves   swaying   at this rare height. She wraps
The curtain around her and streams.   The room fades.   Then coming
Forth magnificently   the window blurred from within   she moves in a cloud
Chamber   the tree in the oak currents sailing   in clear air keeping pace
With her white breathless closet—he sees her mistily part her lips
As if singing to him   come up from river-fog   almost hears her as if
She sang alone in a cloud   its warmed light streaming into his branches
Out through the gauze glass of the window.   She takes off her bathing cap
The tree with him ascending   himself and the birds all moving
In darkness together   sleep crumbling the bark in their claws.
By this time he holds in his awkward, subtle limbs the limbs

Of a hundred understanding trees.   He has learned what a plant is like
When it moves near a human habitation   moving closer the later it is

Unfurling its leaves near bedrooms   still keeping its wilderness life
Twigs covering his body with only one way out   for his eyes into inner light
Of a chosen window   living with them night after night   watching
Watching with them at times their favorite TV shows   learning—
Though now and then he hears a faint sound: gunshot, bombing,
Building-fall—how to read lips: the lips of laconic cowboys
Bank robbers   old and young doctors tense-faced   gesturing savagely
In wards and corridors   like reading the lips of the dead

The lips of men interrupting the program at the wrong time
To sell you a good used car on the Night Owl Show   men silently reporting
The news out the window.   But the living as well, three-dimensioned,
Silent as the small gray dead, must sleep at last   must save their lives
By taking off their clothes. It is his beholding that saves them:
God help the dweller in windowless basements   the one obsessed
With drawing curtains this night. At three o'clock in the morning
He descends   a medium-sized shadow   while that one sleeps and turns
In her high bed in loss   as he goes limb by limb   quietly down
The trunk with one lighted side. Ground upon which he could not explain
His presence he walks with toes uncurled from branches, his bird-movements
Dying hard. At the sidewalk he changes   gains weight   a solid citizen

Once more.   At apartments there is less danger from dogs, but he has
For those a super-quiet hand   a hand to calm sparrows and rivers,
And watchdogs in half-tended bushes lie with him watching their women
Undress   the dog's honest eyes and the man's the same pure beast's
Comprehending the same essentials. Not one of these beheld would ever give
Him a second look   but he gives them all a first look that goes
On and on   conferring immortality while it lasts   while the suburb's leaves
Hold still enough   while whatever dog he has with him holds its breath
Yet seems to thick-pant   impatient as he with the indifferent men
Drifting in and out of the rooms   or staying on, too tired to move
Reading the sports page   dozing   plainly unworthy   for what women want
Dwells in bushes and trees: what they want is to look outward,

To look with the light streaming into the April limbs   to stand straighter
While their husbands' lips dry out   feeling that something is there
That could dwell in no earthly house: that in poplar trees or beneath

The warped roundabout of the clothesline   in the sordid disorder
Of communal backyards   some being is there in the shrubs
Sitting comfortably on a child's striped rubber ball filled with rainwater
Muffling his glasses with a small studious hand against a sudden
Flash of houselight from within   or flash from himself   a needle's eye
Uncontrollable   blaze of uncompromised being. Ah, the lingerie
Hung in the bathroom! The domestic motions of single girls living together
A plump girl girding her loins against her moon-summoned blood:
In that moon he stands   the only male lit by it, covered with leaf-shapes.
He coughs, and the smallest root responds   and in his lust he is set
By the wind in motion. That movement can restore the green eyes
Of middle age   looking   renewed   through the qualified light
Not quite reaching him where he stands again on the usual branch
Of his oldest love   his tie not loosened   a plastic shield
In his breast pocket full of pencils and ballpoint pens given him by salesmen
His hat correctly placed to shade his eyes   a natural gambler's tilt
And in summer wears an eyeshade   a straw hat Caribbean style.
In some guise or other he is near them when they are weeping without sound
When the teen-age son has quit school   when the girl has broken up
With the basketball star   when the banker walks out on his wife.
He sees mothers counsel desperately with pulsing girls face down
On beds full of overstuffed beasts   sees men dress as women
In ante-bellum costumes with bonnets   sees doctors come, looking oddly
Like himself   though inside the houses   worming a medical arm
Up under the cringing covers   sees children put angrily to bed
Sees one told an invisible fairy story   with lips moving silently as his
Are also moving   the book's few pages bright. It will take years
But at last he will shed his leaves   burn his roots   give up
Invisibility   will step out   will make himself known to the one
He cannot see loosen her blouse   take off luxuriously   with lips
Compressed against her mouth-stain   her dress   her stockings
Her magic underwear.   To that one he will come   up frustrated pines
Down alleys   through window blinds   blind windows   kitchen doors
On summer evenings. It will be something small that sets him off:
Perhaps a pair of lace pants on a clothesline   gradually losing
Water to the sun   filling out in the warm light with a well-rounded
Feminine wind as he watches   having spent so many sleepless nights
Because of her   because of her hand on a shade always coming down

In his face not leaving even a shadow stripped naked upon the brown paper
Waiting for her now in a green outdated car with a final declaration
Of love pretending to read and when she comes and takes down
Her pants, he will casually follow her in like a door-to-door salesman
The godlike movement of trees stiffening with him the light
Of a hundred favored windows gone wrong somewhere in his glasses
Where his knocked-off panama hat was in his painfully vanishing hair.

From Falling, May Day Sermon, and Other Poems

Falling

A 29-year-old stewardess fell . . . to her death tonight when she was swept through an emergency door that suddenly sprang open. . . . The body . . . was found . . . three hours after the accident.

—*New York Times*

The states when they black out and lie there rolling   when they turn
To something transcontinental   move by   drawing moonlight out of the great
One-sided stone hung off the starboard wingtip   some sleeper next to
An engine is groaning for coffee   and there is faintly coming in
Somewhere the vast beast-whistle of space. In the galley with its racks
Of trays   she rummages for a blanket   and moves in her slim tailored
Uniform to pin it over the cry at the top of the door. As though she blew

The door down with a silent blast from her lungs   frozen   she is black
Out finding herself   with the plane nowhere and her body taking by the throat
The undying cry of the void   falling   living   beginning to be something
That no one has ever been and lived through   screaming without enough air
Still neat   lipsticked   stockinged   girdled by regulation   her hat

Still on her arms and legs in no world and yet spaced also strangely
With utter placid rightness on thin air taking her time she holds it
In many places and now, still thousands of feet from her death she seems
To slow she develops interest she turns in her maneuverable body

To watch it. She is hung high up in the overwhelming middle of things in her
Self in low body-whistling wrapped intensely in all her dark dance-weight
Coming down from a marvellous leap with the delaying, dumfounding ease
Of a dream of being drawn like endless moonlight to the harvest soil
Of a central state of one's country with a great gradual warmth coming
Over her floating finding more and more breath in what she has been using
For breath as the levels become more human seeing clouds placed honestly
Below her left and right riding slowly toward them she clasps it all
To her and can hang her hands and feet in it in peculiar ways and
Her eyes opened wide by wind, can open her mouth as wide wider and suck
All the heat from the cornfields can go down on her back with a feeling
Of stupendous pillows stacked under her and can turn turn as to someone
In bed smile, understood in darkness can go away slant slide
Off tumbling into the emblem of a bird with its wings half-spread
Or whirl madly on herself in endless gymnastics in the growing warmth
Of wheatfields rising toward the harvest moon. There is time to live
In superhuman health seeing mortal unreachable lights far down seeing
An ultimate highway with one late priceless car probing it arriving
In a square town and off her starboard arm the glitter of water catches
The moon by its one shaken side scaled, roaming silver My God it is good
And evil lying in one after another of all the positions for love
Making dancing sleeping and now cloud wisps at her no
Raincoat no matter all small towns brokenly brighter from inside
Cloud she walks over them like rain bursts out to behold a Greyhound
Bus shooting light through its sides it is the signal to go straight
Down like a glorious diver then feet first her skirt stripped beautifully
Up her face in fear-scented cloths her legs deliriously bare then
Arms out she slow-rolls over steadies out waits for something great
To take control of her trembles near feathers planes head-down
The quick movements of bird-necks turning her head gold eyes the insight-
eyesight of owls blazing into hencoops a taste for chicken overwhelming
Her the long-range vision of hawks enlarging all human lights of cars
Freight trains looped bridges enlarging the moon racing slowly

Through all the curves of a river   all the darks of the midwest blazing
From above. A rabbit in a bush turns white   the smothering chickens
Huddle   for over them there is still time for something to live
With the streaming half-idea of a long stoop   a hurtling   a fall
That is controlled   that plummets as it wills   turns gravity
Into a new condition, showing its other side like a moon   shining
New Powers   there is still time to live on a breath made of nothing
But the whole night   time for her to remember to arrange her skirt
Like a diagram of a bat   tightly it guides her   she has this flying-skin
Made of garments   and there are also those sky-divers on TV   sailing
In sunlight   smiling under their goggles   swapping batons back and forth
And He who jumped without a chute and was handed one by a diving
Buddy. She looks for her grinning companion   white teeth   nowhere
She is screaming   singing hymns   her thin human wings spread out
From her neat shoulders   the air beast-crooning to her   warbling
And she can no longer behold the huge partial form of the world   now
She is watching her country lose its evoked master shape   watching it lose
And gain   get back its houses and people   watching it bring up
Its local lights   single homes   lamps on barn roofs   if she fell
Into water she might live   like a diver   cleaving   perfect   plunge

Into another   heavy silver   unbreathable   slowing   saving
Element: there is water   there is time to perfect all the fine
Points of diving   feet together   toes pointed   hands shaped right
To insert her into water like a needle   to come out healthily dripping
And be handed a Coca-Cola   there they are   there are the waters
Of life   the moon packed and coiled in a reservoir   so let me begin
To plane across the night air of Kansas   *opening my eyes superhumanly*
Bright   *to the dammed moon*   *opening the natural wings of my jacket*
By Don Loper   *moving like a hunting owl toward the glitter of water*
One cannot just *fall*   *just tumble screaming all that time*   *one must* use
It   she is now through with all   through all   clouds   damp   hair
Straightened   the last wisp of fog pulled apart on her face like wool revealing
New darks   new progressions of headlights along dirt roads   from chaos

And night   a gradual warming   a new-made, inevitable world of one's own
Country   a great stone of light in its waiting waters   hold   hold out
For water: who knows when what correct young woman must take up her body

And fly   and head for the moon-crazed inner eye of midwest imprisoned
Water   stored up for her for years   the arms of her jacket slipping
Air up her sleeves to go   all over her? What final things can be said
Of one who starts out sheerly in her body in the high middle of night
Air   to track down water like a rabbit where it lies like life itself
Off to the right in Kansas? She goes toward   the blazing-bare lake
Her skirts neat   her hands and face warmed more and more by the air
Rising from pastures of beans   and under her   under chenille bedspreads
The farm girls are feeling the goddess in them struggle and rise brooding
On the scratch-shining posts of the bed   dreaming of female signs
Of the moon   male blood like iron   of what is really said by the moan
Of airliners passing over them at dead of midwest midnight   passing
Over brush fires   burning out in silence on little hills   and will wake
To see the woman they should be   struggling on the rooftree to become
Stars: For her the ground is closer   water is nearer   she passes
It   then banks   turns   her sleeves fluttering differently as she rolls
Out to face the east, where the sun shall come up from wheatfields she must
Do something with water   fly to it   fall in it   drink it   rise
From it   but there is none left upon earth   the clouds have drunk it back
The plants have sucked it down   there are standing toward her only
The common fields of death   she comes back from flying to falling
Returns to a powerful cry   the silent scream with which she blew down
The coupled door of the airliner   nearly   nearly losing hold
Of what she has done   remembers   remembers the shape at the heart
Of cloud   fashionably swirling   remembers she still has time to die
Beyond explanation. Let her now take off her hat in summer air the contour
Of cornfields   and have enough time to kick off her one remaining
Shoe with the toes   of the other foot   to unhook her stockings
With calm fingers, noting how fatally easy it is to undress in midair
Near death   when the body will assume without effort any position
Except the one that will sustain it   enable it to rise   live
Not die   nine farms hover close   widen   eight of them separate, leaving
One in the middle   then the fields of that farm do the same   there is no
Way to back off   from her chosen ground   but she sheds the jacket
With its silver sad impotent wings   sheds the bat's guiding tailpiece
Of her skirt   the lightning-charged clinging of her blouse   the intimate
Inner flying-garment of her slip in which she rides like the holy ghost
Of a virgin   sheds the long windsocks of her stockings   absurd

Brassiere   then feels the girdle required by regulations squirming
Off her: no longer monobuttocked   she feels the girdle flutter   shake
In her hand   and float   upward   her clothes rising off her ascending
Into cloud   and fights away from her head the last sharp dangerous shoe
Like a dumb bird   and now will drop in   SOON   now will drop

In like this   the greatest thing that ever came to Kansas   down from all
Heights   all levels of American breath   layered in the lungs from the frail
Chill of space to the loam where extinction slumbers in corn tassels thickly
And breathes like rich farmers counting: will come among them after
Her last superhuman act   the last slow careful passing of her hands
All over her unharmed body   desired by every sleeper in his dream:
Boys finding for the first time their loins filled with heart's blood
Widowed farmers whose hands float under light covers to find themselves
Arisen at sunrise   the splendid position of blood unearthly drawn
Toward clouds   all feel something   pass over them as she passes
Her palms over *her* long legs   *her* small breasts   and deeply between
Her thighs   her hair shot loose from all pins   streaming in the wind
Of her body   let her come openly   trying at the last second to land
On her back   This is it   THIS

All those who find her impressed
In the soft loam   gone down   driven well into the image of her body
The furrows for miles flowing in upon her where she lies very deep
In her mortal outline   in the earth as it is in cloud   can tell nothing
But that she is there   inexplicable   unquestionable   and remember
That something broke in them as well   and began to live and die more
When they walked for no reason into their fields to where the whole earth
Caught her   interrupted her maiden flight   told her how to lie   she cannot
Turn   go away   cannot move   cannot slide off it and assume another
Position   no sky-diver with any grin could save her   hold her in his arms
Plummet with her   unfold above her his wedding silks   she can no longer
Mark the rain with whirling women that take the place of a dead wife
Or the goddess in Norwegian farm girls   or all the back-breaking whores
Of Wichita. All the known air above her is not giving up quite one
Breath   it is all gone   and yet not dead   not anywhere else
Quite   lying still in the field on her back   sensing the smells
Of incessant growth try to lift her   a little sight left in the corner
Of one eye   fading   seeing something wave   lies believing

That she could have made it at the best part of her brief goddess
State to water gone in headfirst come out smiling invulnerable
Girl in a bathing-suit ad but she is lying like a sunbather at the last
Of moonlight half-buried in her impact on the earth not far
From a railroad trestle a water tank she could see if she could
Raise her head from her modest hole with her clothes beginning
To come down all over Kansas into bushes on the dewy sixth green
Of a golf course one shoe her girdle coming down fantastically
On a clothesline, where it belongs her blouse on a lightning rod:

Lies in the fields in *this* field on her broken back as though on
A cloud she cannot drop through while farmers sleepwalk without
Their women from houses a walk like falling toward the far waters
Of life in moonlight toward the dreamed eternal meaning of their farms
Toward the flowering of the harvest in their hands that tragic cost
Feels herself go go toward go outward breathes at last fully
Not and tries less once tries tries AH, GOD—

The Sheep Child

Farm boys wild to couple
With anything with soft-wooded trees
With mounds of earth mounds
Of pinestraw will keep themselves off
Animals by legends of their own:
In the hay-tunnel dark
And dung of barns, they will
Say I have heard tell

That in a museum in Atlanta
Way back in a corner somewhere
There's this thing that's only half
Sheep like a woolly baby
Pickled in alcohol because
Those things can't live his eyes

Are open but you can't stand to look
I heard from somebody who . . .

But this is now almost all
Gone. The boys have taken
Their own true wives in the city,
The sheep are safe in the west hill
Pasture but we who were born there
Still are not sure. Are we,
Because we remember, remembered
In the terrible dust of museums?

Merely with his eyes, the sheep-child may

Be saying saying

I am here, in my father's house.
I who am half of your world, came deeply
To my mother in the long grass
Of the west pasture, where she stood like moonlight
Listening for foxes. It was something like love
From another world that seized her
From behind, and she gave, not lifting her head
Out of dew, without ever looking, her best
Self to that great need. Turned loose, she dipped her face
Farther into the chill of the earth, and in a sound
Of sobbing of something stumbling
Away, began, as she must do,
To carry me. I woke, dying,

In the summer sun of the hillside, with my eyes
Far more than human. I saw for a blazing moment
The great grassy world from both sides,
Man and beast in the round of their need,
And the hill wind stirred in my wool,
My hoof and my hand clasped each other,
I ate my one meal

Of milk, and died
Staring. From dark grass I came straight

To my father's house, whose dust
Whirls up in the halls for no reason
When no one comes   piling deep in a hellish mild corner,
And, through my immortal waters
I meet the sun's grains eye
To eye, and they fail at my closet of glass.
Dead, I am most surely living
In the minds of farm boys: I am he who drives
Them like wolves from the hound bitch and calf
And from the chaste ewe in the wind.
They go into woods   into bean fields   they go
Deep into their known right hands. Dreaming of me,
They groan   they wait   they suffer
Themselves, they marry, they raise their kind.

Power and Light

. . . only connect . . .
—E. M. Forster

I may even be
A man, I tell my wife: all day I climb myself
Bowlegged up those damned poles   rooster-heeled in all
Kinds of weather   and what is there when I get
Home? Yes, woman trailing ground-oil
Like a snail, home is where I climb down,
And this is the house I pass through on my way

To power and light.
Going into the basement is slow, but the built-on smell of home
Beneath home gets better with age   the ground fermenting
And spilling through the barrel-cracks of plaster   the dark

Lying on the floor, ready for use   as I crack
The seal on the bottle   like I tell you it takes
A man to pour whiskey in the dark   and CLOSE THE DOOR between

The children and me.
The heads of nails drift deeper through their boards
And disappear. Years in the family ark have made me good
At this   nothing else is so good   pure fires of the Self
Rise crooning in lively blackness   and the silence around them,
Like the silence inside a mouth, squirms with colors,
The marvellous worms of the eye float out into the real

World   sunspots
Dancing as though existence were
One huge closed eye   and I feel the wires running
Like the life-force along the limed rafters   and all connections
With poles   with the tarred naked belly-buckled black
Trees I hook to my heels   with the shrill phone calls leaping
Long distance   long distances through my hands   all connections

Even the one
With my wife, turn good   turn better than good   turn good
Not quite, but in the deep sway of underground   among the roots
That bend like branches   all things connect   and stream
Toward light and speech   tingle   rock like a powerline in wind,
Like a man working, drunk on pine-moves   the sun in the socket
Of his shoulder   and on his neck dancing like dice-dots,

And I laugh
Like my own fate watching over me night and day   at home
Underground   or flung up on towers walking
Over mountains   my charged hair standing on end   crossing
The sickled, slaughtered alleys of timber
Where the lines loop and crackle on their gallows.
Far under the grass of my grave, I drink like a man

The night before
Resurrection Day. My watch glows with the time to rise

And shine. Never think I don't know my profession
Will lift me: why, all over hell the lights burn in your eyes,
People are calling each other   weeping with a hundred thousand
Volts   making deals   pleading   laughing like fate,
Far off, invulnerable   or with the right word pierced

To the heart
By wires I held, shooting off their ghostly mouths,
In my gloves. The house spins   I strap crampons to my shoes
To climb the basement stairs, sinking my heels in the tree-
life of the boards. Thorns! Thorns! I am bursting
Into the kitchen, into the sad way-station
Of my home, holding a double handful of wires

Spitting like sparklers
On the Fourth of July. Woman, I know the secret of sitting
In light   of eating a limp piece of bread   under
The red-veined eyeball of a bulb. It is all in how you are
Grounded. To bread I can see, I say, as it disappears and agrees
With me   the dark is drunk   and I am a man
Who turns on. I am a man.

Adultery

We have all been in rooms
We cannot die in, and they are odd places, and sad.
Often Indians are standing eagle-armed on hills

In the sunrise   open wide to the Great Spirit
Or gliding in canoes   or cattle are browsing on the walls
Far away   gazing down with the eyes of our children

Not far away   or there are men driving
The last railspike, which has turned
Gold in their hands. Gigantic forepleasure lives

Among such scenes, and we are alone with it
At last. There is always some weeping
Between us   and someone is always checking

A wrist watch by the bed to see how much
Longer we have left. Nothing can come
Of this   nothing can come

Of us: of me with my grim techniques
Or you who have sealed your womb
With a ring of convulsive rubber:

Although we come together,
Nothing will come of us. But we would not give
It up, for death is beaten

By praying Indians   by distant cows   historical
Hammers   by hazardous meetings that bridge
A continent. One could never die here

Never die   never die
While crying. My lover, my dear one
I will see you next week

When I'm in town. I will call you
If I can. Please get hold of   please don't
Oh God, Please don't any more I can't bear . . . Listen:

We have done it again   we are
Still living. Sit up and smile,
God bless you. Guilt is magical.

Encounter in the Cage Country

What I was would not work
For them all, for I had not caught
The lion's eye. I was walking down

The cellblock in green glasses   and came
At last to the place where someone was hiding
His spots in his black hide.

Unchangeably they were there,
Driven in as by eyes
Like mine, his darkness ablaze

In the stinking sun of the beast house.
Among the crowd, he found me
Out   and dropped his bloody snack

And came to the perilous edge
Of the cage, where the great bars tremble
Like wire. All Sunday ambling stopped,

The curved cells tightened around
Us all   as we saw he was watching only
Me. I knew the stage was set, and I began

To perform   first saunt'ring   then stalking
Back and forth like a sentry   faked
As if to run   and at one brilliant move

I made as though drawing a gun from my hip-
bone, the bite-sized children broke
Up   changing their concept of laughter,

But none of this changed his eyes, or changed
My green glasses. Alert, attentive,
He waited for what I could give him:

My moves   my throat   my wildest love,
The eyes behind my eyes. Instead, I left
Him, though he followed me right to the end

Of concrete. I wiped my face, and lifted off
My glasses. Light blasted the world of shade
Back under every park bush   the crowd

Quailed from me   I was inside and out
Of myself   and something was given a life-
mission to say to me hungrily over

And over and over   *your moves are exactly right*
For a few things in this world: we know you
When you come, Green Eyes, Green Eyes.

May Day Sermon to the Women of Gilmer County, Georgia, by a Woman Preacher Leaving the Baptist Church

Each year at this time I shall be telling you of the Lord
—Fog, gamecock, snake and neighbor—giving men all the help they need
To drag their daughters into barns. Children, I shall be showing you
The fox hide stretched on the door   like a flying squirrel   fly
Open   to show you the dark where the one pole of light is paid out
In spring by the loft, and in it the croker sacks sprawling and shuttling
Themselves into place as it comes   comes   through spiders dead
Drunk on their threads   the hogs' fat bristling   the milk
Snake in the rafters unbending through gnats to touch the last place
Alive on the sun with his tongue   I shall be flickering from my mouth
Oil   grease cans   lard cans   nubbins   cobs   night
Coming   floating   each May with night coming I cannot help
Telling you how he hauls her to the centerpole   how the tractor moves

Over as he sets his feet and hauls   hauls   ravels her arms and hair
In stump chains: Telling: telling of Jehovah come and gone
Down on His belly   descending   creek-curving   blowing His legs

Like candles, out   putting North Georgia copper on His head
To crawl in under the door in dust red enough to breathe
The breath of Adam into: Children, be brought where she screams and begs
To the sacks of corn and coal   to nails   to the swelling ticks
On the near side of mules, for the Lord's own man has found the limp
Rubber that lies in the gulley   the penis-skin like a serpent
Under the weaving willow.
                                        Listen: often a girl in the country,
Mostly sweating   mostly in spring, deep enough in the holy Bible
Belt, will feel her hair rise up   arms rise, and this not any wish
Of hers, and clothes like lint shredding off her   abominations
In the sight of the Lord: will hear the Book speak like a father
Gone mad: each year at this time will hear the utmost sound
Of herself, as her lungs cut, one after one, every long track
Spiders have coaxed from their guts   stunned spiders fall
Into Pandemonium   fall   fall   and begin to dance like a girl
On the red clay floor of Hell   she screaming   her father screaming
Scripture   CHAPter and verse   beating it into her with a weeping
Willow branch   the animals stomping   she prancing and climbing
Her hair   beasts shifting from foot to foot about the stormed
Steel of the anvil   the tractor gaslessly straining   believing
It must pull up a stump   pull   pull down the walls of the barn
Like Dagon's temple   set the Ark of the Lord in its place   change all
Things for good, by pain. Each year at this time you will be looking up
Gnats in the air   they boil   recombine   go mad with striving
To form the face of her lover, as when he lay at Nickajack Creek
With her by his motorcycle   looming   face trembling with exhaust
Fumes   humming insanely—each May you hear her father scream like God
And King James as he flails   cuds richen   bulls chew themselves whitefaced
Deeper into their feed bags, and he cries something the Lord   cries
Words! Words! Ah, when they leap   when they are let out of the Bible's
Black box   they whistle   they grab the nearest girl and do her hair up
For her lover in root-breaking chains   and she knows she was born to hang
In the middle of Gilmer County   to dance, on May Day, with holy

Words all around her   with beasts with insects   O children NOW
In five bags of chicken-feed the torsos of prophets form   writhe
Die out as her freckled flesh   as flesh and the Devil twist and turn
Her body to love   cram her mouth with defiance   give her words
To battle with the Bible's in the air: she shrieks sweet Jesus and God
I'm glad   O my God-darling   O lover   O angel-stud   dear heart
Of life put it in me   *give*   you're killing   KILLING: each
Night each year at this time I shall be telling you of the snake-
doctor drifting from the loft, a dragonfly, where she is wringing
Out the tractor's muddy chains   where her cotton socks prance,
Where her shoes as though one ankle were broken, stand with night
Coming   and creatures drawn by the stars, out of their high holes
By moon-hunger driven   part the leaves   crawl out of Grimes Nose
And Brasstown Bald: on this night only I can tell how the weasel pauses
Each year in the middle of the road   looks up at the evening blue
Star   to hear her say again   O again   YOU CAN BEAT ME TO DEATH
And I'll still be glad:
                                        Sisters, it is time to show you rust
Smashing the lard cans more in   spring after spring   bullbats
Swifts   barn swallows   mule bits clashing on walls   mist turning
Up white out of warm creeks: all over, fog taking the soul from the body
Of water   gaining   rising up trees   sifting up through smoking green
Frenzied levels of gamecocks sleeping from the roots   stream-curves
Of mist: wherever on God's land is water, roads rise up the shape of rivers
Of no return: O sisters, it is time   you cannot sleep with Jehovah

Searching for what to be, on ground that has called Him from His Book:
Shall He be the pain in the willow, or the copperhead's kingly riding
In kudzu, growing with vines toward the cows   or the wild face working over
A virgin, swarming like gnats   or the grass of the west field, bending
East, to sweep into bags and turn brown   or shall He rise, white on white,
From Nickajack Creek as a road?   The barn creaks like an Ark   beasts
Smell everywhere the streams drawn out by their souls   the flood-
sigh of grass in the spring   they shall be saved   they know as she screams
Of sin   as the weasel stares   the hog strains toward the woods
That hold its primeval powers:
                                                    Often a girl in the country will find herself
Dancing with God in a mule's eye, twilight drifting in straws from the dark
Overhead of hay   cows working their sprained jaws sideways at the hour

Of night all things are called: when gnats in their own midst and fury
Of swarming-time, crowd into the barn   their sixty-year day consumed
In this sunset   die in a great face of light that swarms and screams
Of love.
          Each May you will crouch like a sawhorse to make yourself
More here   you will be cow chips   chickens croaking for her hands
That shook the corn over the ground   bouncing   kicked this way
And that, by the many beaks   and every last one of you will groan
Like nails barely holding   and your hair be full of the gray
Glints of stump chains.   Children, each year at this time you shall have
Back-pain, but also heaven   but also   also this lovely other life-
pain between the thighs: woman-child or woman in bed in Gilmer
County   smiling in sleep like blood-beast and Venus together
Dancing the road as I speak, get up   up in your socks and take
The pain you were born for: that rose through her body straight
Up from the earth like a plant, like the process that raised overhead
The limbs of the uninjured willow.
                                        Children, it is true
That the kudzu advances, its copperheads drunk and tremendous
With hiding, toward the cows   and wild fences cannot hold the string
Beans as they overshoot their fields: that in May the weasel loves love
As much as blood   that in the dusk bottoms young deer stand half
In existence, munching cornshucks   true that when the wind blows
Right   Nickajack releases its mist   the willow-leaves stiffen once
More   altogether   you can hear   each year at this time you can hear
No   Now, no   Now   Yes   Again   More   O   O my God
I love it   love you   don't leave   don't   don't stop O GLORY
Be:
      More dark   more coming   fox-fire crawls over the okra-
patch   as through it a real fox creeps to claim his father's fur
Flying on doornails   the quartermoon on the outhouse begins to shine
With the quartermoonlight of this night   as she falls and rises,
Chained to a sapling like a tractor   WHIPPED for the wind in the willow
Tree   WHIPPED for Bathsheba and David   WHIPPED for woman taken
Anywhere   anytime   WHIPPED for the virgin sighing   bleeding
From her body   for the sap and green of the year   for her own good
And evil:
          Sisters, who is your lover? Has he done nothing but come
And go?   Has your father nailed his cast skin to the wall as evidence

Of sin?   Is it flying like a serpent in the darkness   dripping pure radiant venom
Of manhood?

Yes, but *he* is unreeling in hills between his long legs
The concrete of the highway   his face in the moon beginning
To burn   twitch   dance like an overhead swarm   he feels a nail
Beat through his loins far away   he rises in pain and delight, as spirit
Enters his sex   sways   forms   rises with the forced, choked, red
Blood of her red-headed image, in the red-dust, Adam-colored clay
Whirling and leaping   creating   calling: O on the dim, gray man-
track of cement flowing into his mouth   each year he turns the moon back
Around on his handlebars   her image going all over him like the wind
Blasting up his sleeves. He turns off the highway, and

Ah, children,

There is now something élse to hear: there is now this madness of engine
Noise in the bushes   past reason   ungodly   squealing   reverting
Like a hog turned loose in the woods   Yes, as he passes the first
Trees of God's land   game-hens overhead   and the farm is ON
Him   everything is more   *more*   MORE as he enters the black
Bible's white swirling ground   O daughters   his heartbeat great
With trees   some blue leaves coming   NOW   and right away fire
In the right eye   Lord   more   MORE   O Glory   land
Of Glory: ground-branches hard to get through   coops where fryers huddle
To death, as the star-beast dances and scratches at their home-boards,
His rubber stiffens on its nails: Sisters, understand about men and sheaths:

About nakedness: understand how butterflies, amazed, pass out
Of their natal silks   how the tight snake takes a great breath   bursts
Through himself and leaves himself behind   how a man casts finally
Off everything that shields him from another   beholds his loins
Shine with his children forever   burn with the very juice
Of resurrection: such shining is how the spring creek comes
Forth from its sunken rocks   it is how the trout foams and turns on
Himself   heads upstream, breathing mist like water, for the cold
Mountain of his birth   flowing   sliding in and through the ego-
maniacal sleep of gamecocks   shooting past a man with one new blind
Side   who feels his skinned penis rise like a fish through the dark
Woods, in a strange lifted-loving form   a snake about to burst
Through itself on May Day   and leave behind on the ground   still

Still the shape of a fooled thing's body:
he comes on, comes
Through the laurel, wiped out on his right by an eye-twig now he
Is crossing the cow track his hat in his hand going on before
His face then up slowly over over like the Carolina moon
Coming into Georgia feels the farm close its Bible and ground-
fog over him his dark side blazing something whipping
By, beyond sight: each year at this time I shall be letting you
Know when she cannot stand when the chains fall back on
To the tractor when you should get up when neither she nor the pole
Has any more sap and her striped arms and red hair must keep her
From falling when she feels God's willow laid on her, at last,
With no more pressure than hay, and she has finished crying to her lover's
Shifting face and his hand when he gave it placed it, unconsumed,
In her young burning bush. Each year by dark she has learned

That home is to hang in home is where your father cuts the baby
Fat from your flanks for the Lord, as you scream for the viny foreskin
Of the motorcycle rider. Children, by dark by now, when he drops
The dying branch and lets her down when the red clay flats
Of her feet hit the earth all things have heard fog, gamecock
Snake and lover—and we listen: Listen, children, for the fog to lift
The form of sluggish creeks into the air: each spring, each creek
On the Lord's land flows in two O sisters, lovers, flows in two
Places: where it was, and in the low branches of pines where chickens
Sleep in mist and that is where you will find roads floating free
Of the earth winding leading unbrokenly out of the farm of God
The father:
Each year at this time she is coming from the barn she
Falls once, hair hurting her back stumbles walking naked
With dignity walks with no help to the house lies face down
In her room, burning tuning in hearing in the spun rust-
groan of bedsprings, his engine root and thunder like a pig,
Knowing who it is must be knowing that the face of gnats will wake
In the woods, as a man: there is nothing else this time of night
But her dream of having wheels between her legs: tires, man,
Everything she can hold, pulsing together her father walking
Reading intoning calling his legs blown out by the ground-

fogging creeks of his land: Listen listen like females each year
In May O glory to the sound the sound of your man gone wild
With love in the woods let your nipples rise and leave your feet
To hear: This is when moths flutter in from the open, and Hell
Fire of the oil lamp shrivels them and it is said
To her: said like the Lord's voice trying to find a way
Outside the Bible O sisters O women and children who will be
Women of Gilmer County you farm girls and Ellijay cotton mill
Girls, get up each May Day up in your socks it is the father
Sound going on about God making, a hundred feet down,
The well beat its bucket like a gong: she goes to the kitchen,
Stands with the inside grain of pinewood whirling on her like a cloud
Of wire picks up a useful object two they are not themselves
Tonight each hones itself as the moon does new by phases
Of fog floating unchanged into the house coming atom
By atom sheepswool different smokes breathed like the Word
Of nothing, round her seated father. Often a girl in the country,
Mostly in spring mostly bleeding deep enough in the holy Bible
Belt will feel her arms rise up up and this not any wish
Of hers will stand, waiting for word. O daughters, he is rambling
In Obadiah the pride of thine heart hath deceived thee, thou
That dwelleth in the clefts of the rock, whose habitation is high
That saith in his heart O daughters who shall bring me down
To the ground? And she comes down putting her back into
The hatchet often often he is brought down laid out
Lashing smoking sucking wind: Children, each year at this time
A girl will tend to take an ice pick in both hands a lone pine
Needle will hover hover: Children, each year at this time
Things happen quickly and it is easy for a needle to pass
Through the eye of a man bound for Heaven she leaves it naked goes
Without further sin through the house floating in and out of all
Four rooms comes onto the porch on cloud-feet steps down and out
And around to the barn pain changing her old screams hanging
By the hair around her: Children, in May, often a girl in the country
Will find herself lifting wood her arms like hair rising up
To undo locks raise latches set gates aside turn all things
Loose shoo them out shove pull O hogs are leaping ten
Million years back through fog cows walking worriedly passing out

Of the Ark   from stalls where God's voice cursed and mumbled
At milking time   moving   moving   disappearing   drifting
In cloud   cows in the alders already lowing far off   no one
Can find them each year: she comes back to the house and grabs double
Handfuls of clothes

and her lover, with his one eye of amazing grace
Of sight, sees her coming as she was born   swirling   developing
Toward him   she hears him grunt   she hears him creaking
His saddle   dead-engined   she conjures one foot whole from the ground-
fog to climb him behind   he stands up   stomps   catches   roars
Blasts the leaves from blinding twig   wheels   they blaze up
Together   she breathing to match him   her hands on his warm belly
His hard blood renewing like a snake   O now   now as he twists
His wrist, and takes off with their bodies:

each May you will hear it
Said that the sun came as always   the sun of next day burned
Them off with the mist: that when the river fell back on its bed
Of water   they fell from life   from limbs   they went with it
To Hell   three-eyed   in love, their legs around an engine, her arms
Around him.   But now, except for each year at this time, their sound
Has died: except when the creek-bed thicks its mist   gives up
The white of its flow to the air   comes off   lifts into the pinepoles
Of May Day   comes back as you come awake in your socks and crotchhair
On new-mooned nights of spring   I speak   you listen and the pines fill
With motorcycle sound as they rise, stoned out of their minds on the white
Lightning of fog   singing   the saddlebags full of her clothes
Flying   snagging   shoes hurling away   stockings grabbed-off
Unwinding and furling on twigs: all we know   all we could follow
Them by was her underwear   was stocking after stocking where it tore
Away, and a long slip stretched on a thorn   all these few gave
Out. Children, you know it: that place was where they took
Off into the air   died   disappeared   entered my mouth   your mind
Each year   each pale, curved breath   each year as she holds him
Closer wherever he hurtles   taking her   taking her   she going forever
Where he goes   with the highways of rivers   through one-eyed
Twigs   through clouds of chickens   and grass with them bends
Double   the animals lift their heads   peanuts and beans exchange
Shells in joy   joy like the speed of the body and rock-bottom

Joy: joy by which the creek bed appeared to bear them out of the Bible
's farm   through pine-clouds of gamecocks where no earthly track
Is, but those risen out of warm currents   streams born to hang
In the pines of Nickajack Creek: tonight her hands are under
His crackling jacket   the pain in her back enough to go through
Them both   her buttocks blazing in the sheepskin saddle: tell those
Who look for them   who follow by rayon stockings   who look on human
Highways   on tracks of cement and gravel   black weeping roads
Of tar: tell them that she and her rider have taken no dirt
Nor any paved road   no path for cattle   no county truck or trail
Or any track upon earth, but have roared like a hog on May Day
Through pines and willows: that when he met the insane vine
Of the scuppermong   he tilted his handlebars back and took
The road that rises in the cold mountain spring from warm creeks:
O women in your rayon from Lindale, I shall be telling you to go
To Hell   by cloud   down where the chicken walk is running
To weeds   and anyone can show you where the tire marks gave out
And her last stocking was cast   and you stand as still as a weasel
Under Venus   before you dance   dance yourself blue with blood-
joy looking into the limbs   looking up into where they rode
Through cocks tightening roots with their sleep-claws. Children,
They are gone: gone as the owl rises, when God takes the stone
Blind sun off its eyes, and it sees   sees hurtle in the utter dark
Gold of its sight, a boy and a girl buried deep in the cloud
Of their speed   drunk, children   drunk with pain and the throttle
Wide open, in love   with a mindless sound   with her red hair
In the wind streaming gladly for them both   more than gladly
As the barn settles under the weight of its pain   the stalls fill once
More with trampling like Exodus   the snake doctor gone the rats beginning
On the last beans   and all the chicks she fed, each year at this time
Burst from their eggs as she passes:

Children, it is true that mice
No longer bunch on the rafters, but wade the fields like the moon,
Shifting in patches   ravenous   the horse floats, smoking with flies,
To the water-trough   coming back less often   learning to make
Do with the flowing drink of deer   the mountain standing   cold
Flowing into his mouth   grass underfoot   dew   horse or what
ever he is now   moves back into trees where the bull walks

With a male light spread between his horns   some say screams like a girl
And her father yelling together:
                                        Ah, this night in the dark laurel
Green of the quartermoon I shall be telling you that the creek's last
Ascension is the same   is made of water and air   heat and cold
This year as before: telling you not to believe every scream you hear
Is the Bible's: it may be you or me   it may be her sinful barn-
howling for the serpent, as her father whips her, using the tried
And true rhythms of the Lord.   Sisters, an old man at times like this
Moon, is always being found   yes found with an ice-pick on his mind,
A willow limb in his hand.   By now, the night-moths have come
Have taken his Bible and read it   have flown, dissolved, having found
Nothing in it for them.   I shall be telling you at each moon   each
Year at this time, Venus rises   the weasel goes mad at the death
In the egg, of the chicks she fed for him by hand: mad in the middle
Of human space he dances   blue-eyed   dances with Venus rising
Like blood-lust over the road   O tell your daughters   tell them
That the creek's ghost can still   O still can carry double
Weight of true lovers   any time   any night as the wild turkeys claw
Into the old pines of gamecocks   and with a cow's tongue, the Bible calls
For its own, and is not heard   and even God's unsettled great white father-
head with its ear to the ground, cannot hear   know   cannot pick
Up where they are   where her red hair is streaming through the white
Hairs of His centerless breast: with the moon   He cries with the cow all
Its life penned up with Noah in the barn   talk of original
Sin as the milk spurts   talk of women   talk of judgment and flood
And the promised land:
                                Telling on May Day, children: telling
That the animals are saved without rain   that they are long gone
From here   gone with the sun   gone with the woman taken
In speed   gone with the one-eyed mechanic   that the barn falls in
Like Jericho at the bull's voice   at the weasel's dance   at the hog's
Primeval squeal   the uncut hay walks when the wind prophesies in the west
Pasture   the animals move   roam, with kudzu creating all the earth
East of the hayfield: Listen: each year at this time the county speaks
With its beasts and sinners   with its blood: the county speaks of nothing
Else each year at this time: speaks as beasts speak to themselves
Of holiness learned in the barn: Listen   O daughters   turn   turn

In your sleep   rise with your backs on fire   in spring   in your socks
Into the arms of your lovers: every last one of you, listen one-eyed
With your man   in hiding   in fog where the animals walk through
The white breast of the Lord   muttering   walk with nothing
To do but be   in the spring laurel in the mist and self-sharpened
Moon   walk through the resurrected creeks   through the Lord
At their own pace   the cow shuts its mouth and the Bible is still
Still open at anything   we are gone   the barn wanders over the earth.

From The Eye-Beaters, Blood, Victory, Madness, Buckhead and Mercy

The Eye-Beaters

[for Mary Bookwalter]

A man visits a Home for children in Indiana, some of whom have gone blind there.

Come something   come blood sunlight   come and they break
Through the child-wall, taking heart from the two left feet
Of your sound: are groping for the Visitor in the tall corn
Green of Indiana. You may be the light, for they have seen it coming
From people: have seen it on cricket and brick have seen it
Seen it fade   seen slowly the edge of things fail   all corn
Green fail   heard fields grind   press with insects and go round
To the back of the head. They are blind. Listen   listen well

A therapist explains why the children strike their eyes.

To your walking that gathers the blind in bonds   gathers these
Who have fought with themselves   have blacked their eyes wide
Open, toddling like dolls and like penguins   soft-knotted down,
Protected, arms bound to their sides in gauze, but dark is not
To be stood in that way: they holler   howl till they can shred
Their gentle ropes   whirl and come loose. They *know* they should see
But *what,* now? When their fists smash their eyeballs, they behold no
Stranger giving light from his palms. What they glimpse has flared

In mankind from the beginning. In the asylum, children turn to go back
Into the race: turn their heads without comment into the black magic
Migraine of caves. Smudge-eyed, wide-eyed, gouged, horned, caved-
in, they are silent: it is for you to guess what they hold back inside
The brown and hazel   inside the failed green   the vacant blue-
eyed floating of the soul. Was that lightning   was that a heart-
struck leap   somewhere before birth? Why do you eat the green summer
Air like smoky meat? Ah, Stranger, you do not visit this place,
You live or die in it   you brain-scream you beat your eyes to see
The junebug take off backwards   spin   connect his body-sound
To what he is in the air. But under the fist, on the hand-stomped bone,
A bison leaps out of rock   fades   a long-haired nine-year-old clubs
Her eye, imploding with vision   dark   bright again   again again
A beast, before her arms are tied. Can it be? Lord, when they slug
Their blue cheeks blacker, can it be that they do not see the wings
And green of insects   or the therapist suffering kindly   but a tribal light old
Enough to be seen without sight? There, quiet children stand watching
A man striped and heavy with pigment, lift his hand with color coming
From him. Bestial, working like God, he moves on stone he is drawing
A half-cloud of beasts on the wall. They crane closer, helping, beating
Harder, light blazing inward from their fists   and see   see leap
From the shocked head-nerves, great herds of deer on the hacked glory plain
Of the cave wall: antelope   elk: blind children strike for the middle
Of the brain, where the race is young. Stranger, they stand here
And fill your mind with beasts: ibex   quagga   rhinoceros of wool-
gathering smoke: cave bear   aurochs   mammoth: beings that appear
Only in the memory of caves   the niches filled, not with Virgins,
But with the squat shapes of the Mother. In glimmers of mid-brain pain
The forms of animals are struck like water from the stone   where hunger
And rage   where the Visitor's helplessness and terror   all
Move on the walls and create.

The Visitor begins to invent a fiction to save his mind.

He tries to see what they see when they beat their eyes.

(Look up: the sun is taking its stand on four
o'clock of Indiana time, painfully blazing   fist of a ball of fire
God struck from His one eye).

No; you see only dead beasts playing
In the bloody handprint on the stone where God gropes like a man
Like a child, for animals   where the artist hunts and slashes, glowing
Like entrail-blood, tracking the wounded game across the limestone

As it is conceived. The spoor leads his hand changes grows
Hair like a bison horns like an elk unshapes in a deer-leap emerges
From the spear-pitted rock, becoming what it can make unrolling
Not sparing itself clenching re-forming rising beating
For light.

Ah, you think it, Stranger: you'd like that you try hard
To think it, to think for them. But what you see, in the half-inner sight
Of squinting, are only fields only children whose hands are tied away
From them for their own good children waiting to smash their dead
Eyes, live faces, to see nothing. As before, they come to you smiling,
Using their strange body-English. *But why is it* this *they have made up*
In your mind? Why painting and Hunting? Why animals showing how God
Is subject to the pictures in the cave their clotted colors like blood
On His hands as the wild horse burns as the running buck turns red
From His palm, while children twist in their white ropes, eyes wide,
Their heads in the dark meat of bruises?

His Reason argues with his invention.

And now, blind hunters,
Swaying in concert like corn sweet-faced tribe-swaying at the red wall
Of the blind like a cooking-fire shoulder-moving, moaning as the cave-
artist moaned when he drew the bull-elk to the heart come ring
Me round. I will undo you. Come, and your hands will be free to fly
Straight into your faces, and shake the human vision to its roots
Flint-chipping sparks spring up: I can see feel see another elk
Ignite with his own becoming: it is time.

Yes, indeed I know it is not
So I am trying to make it make something make them make me
Re-invent the vision of the race knowing the blind must see
By magic or nothing. Therapists, I admit it; it helps me to think
That they can give themselves, like God from their scabby fists, the original
Images of mankind: that when they beat their eyes, I witness how
I survive, in my sun-blinded mind: that the beasts are calling to God
And man for art, when the blind open wide and strike their incurable eyes
In Indiana. *And yet, O Stranger, those beasts and mother-figures are all*
Made up by you. They are your therapy. There is nothing inside their dark,
Nothing behind their eyes but the nerve that kills the sun above the corn
Field no hunt no meat no pain-struck spark no vision no pre-history
For the blind nothing but blackness forever nothing but a new bruise
Risen upon the old.

The children retire, but he hears them behind their wall.

They have gone away; the doors have shut shut on you
And your makeshift salvation. Yet your head still keeps what you would
put in theirs
If you were God. Bring down your lids like a cave, and try to see
By the race alone. Collective memory stirs   herd-breathes   stamps
In snow-smoke, as the cave takes hold. You are artist and beast and
The picture of the beast: you are a ring of men and the stampeded bones
Tumbling into the meat-pit. A child screams out in fury, but where,
In the time of man? O brother, quiver and swear: It is true that no thing
Anyone can do is good enough for them: not Braille not data
Processing   not "learning TV repair" not music   no, and not not being
"A burden": none of these, but only vision: what they see must be crucial

He accepts his fiction.

To the human race. It is so; to let you live with yourself after seeing
Them, they must be thought to see by what has caused   is causing us all
To survive. In the late sun of the asylum, you know nothing else will do
You; the rest is mere light. In the palm of the hand the color red is calling
For blood   the forest-fire roars on the cook-stone, smoke-smothered and
lightning-
born   and the race hangs on meat and illusion   hangs on nothing
But a magical art. Stranger, you may as well take your own life
Blood   brain-blood, as vision. Yes; that hammering on the door is not
Your heart, or the great pulse of insects; it is blind children beating
Their eyes to throw a picture on the wall. Once more you hear a child yell
In pure killing fury   pure triumph pure acceptance   as his hands burst
Their bonds. It is happening. Half-broken light flickers with agony
Like a head   throwing up the beast-paint the wall cannot shake
For a million years.

Hold on to your fantasy; it is all that can save
A man with good eyes in this place. Hold on, though doctors keep telling
You to back off   to be what you came as   back off from the actual
Wall of their screaming room, as green comes all around you with its ears
Of corn, its local, all-insect hum, given junebugs and flies wherever
They are, in midair. No;

by God. There is no help for this but madness,
Perversity. Think that somewhere under their pummeled lids they gather
At the wall of art-crazed beasts, and the sun blazing into the blackout
Of the cave, dies of vision. A spell sways in. It is time for the night
Hunt, and the wild meat of survival. The wall glimmers that God and man

Never forgot. I have put history out. An innocent eye, it is closed
Off, outside in the sun. Wind moans like an artist. The tribal children lie
On their rocks in their animal skins   seeing in spurts of eye-beating
Dream, the deer, still wet with creation, open its image to the heart's
He leaves the Home. Blood, as I step forward, as I move through the beast-paint of the stone,
Taken over, submitting, brain-weeping. Light me a torch with what we
  have preserved
Of lightning. Cloud bellows in my hand. God man hunter artist father
Be with me. My prey is rock-trembling, calling. Beast, get in
My way. Your body opens onto the plain. Deer, take me into your life-
lined form. I merge, I pass beyond in secret   in perversity and the sheer
Despair of invention   my double-clear bifocals off   my reason gone
Like eyes. Therapist, farewell at the living end. Give me my spear.

From The Zodiac

This poem is based on another of the same title.

That one was written by Hendrik Marsman, who was killed by a torpedo in the North Atlantic in 1940.

It is in no sense a translation, for the liberties I have taken with Marsman's original poem are such that the poem I publish here, with the exception of a few lines, is completely my own.

Its twelve sections are the story of a drunken and perhaps dying Dutch poet who returns to his home in Amsterdam after years of travel and tries desperately to relate himself, by means of stars, to the universe.

—homage to Hendrik Marsman, lost at sea, 1940—

The Zodiac (Section I, excerpt; Section XII)

(i)

The Man I'm telling you about brought himself back alive
A couple of years ago. He's here,
Making no trouble
over the broker's peaceful
Open-bay office at the corner of two canals
That square off and starfish into four streets
Stumbling like mine-tunnels all over town.
To the right, his window leaps and blinds
and sees
The bridges shrivel on contact with low cloud
leaning to reach out
Of his rent-range
and get to feudal doors:
Big-rich houses whose thick basement-stones
Turn water into cement inch by inch
As the tide grovels down.
When that tide turns
Hé turns left his eyes back-swivel into his head
In hangover-pain like the flu the flu
Dizzy with tree-tops
all dead, but the eye going
Barely getting but getting you're damn right but still
Getting them.
Trees, all right. No leaves. All right,
Trees, stand
and deliver. They stand and deliver
Not much: stand
Wobble-rooted, in the crumbling docks.
So what?
The town square below, deserted as a Siberian crater, lies in the middle
Of his white-writing darkness stroboscoped red-stopped by the
stammering mess
Of the city's unbombed neon, sent through rivers and many cities
By fourth-class mail from Hell.
All right, since you want to, look:

Somebody's lugged a priest's failed prison-cell
Swaybacked up the broker's cut-rate stairs. He rents it on credit.
No picture
nothing but a bed and desk
And empty paper.
A flower couldn't make it in this place.
It couldn't live, or couldn't get here at all.
No flower could get up these steps,
It'd wither at the hollowness
Of these foot-stomping
failed creative-man's boards—
There's nothing to bring love or death
Or creative boredom through the walls.
Walls,
Ah walls. They're the whole place. And any time,
The easting and westing city in the windows
Plainly are not true
without a drink. But the *walls*—
Weightless ridiculous bare
Are there just enough to be dreadful
Whether they're spinning or not. They're there to go round him
And keep the floor turning with the earth.
He moves among stars.
Sure. We all do, but he is star-*crazed*, mad
With *Einfühlung*, with connecting and joining things that lay their meanings
Over billions of light years
eons of time—Ah,
Years of light: billions of them: they are pictures
Of some sort of meaning. He thinks the secret
Can be read. But human faces swim through
Cancer Scorpio Leo through all the stupefying design,
And all he can add to it or make of it, living or dead:
An eye lash-flicker, a responsive
light-year light
From the pit of the stomach, and a young face comes on,
Trying for the pit of his poem
strange remembered
Comes on faintly, like the faint, structural light
Of Alnilam, without which Orion

Would have no center the Hunter
Could not hunt, in the winter clouds.
The face comes on
Glowing with billions of miles burning like nebulae,
Like the horse-head nebula in Orion—
She was always a little horse-faced,
At least in profile she is some strange tint
Of second-order blue: intensity she is eternal
As long as *he* lives—the stars and his balls meet
And she shows herself as any face does
That *is* eternal, raying in and out
Of the body of a man: in profile sketched-in by stars
Better than the ones God set turning
Around us forever.
The trees night-pale
Out. Vacuum.
Absolute living-space-white. Only one way beyond
The room.
The Zodiac.
He must solve it must believe it learn to read it
No, wallow in it
As poetry.
He's drunk. Other drunks, it's alligators
Or rats, their scales and eyes
Turning the cold moon molten on the floor.— With him, it's his party-time army
Of soldier ants; they march over
His writing hand, heading for the Amazon Basin.
He can take *them* . . .
He bristles itches like a sawdust-pile
But something's more important than flesh-crawling
To gain an image
line by line: they give him an idea. Suppose—
Well, let's just suppose I . . .
No ants. No idea. Maybe they'll come back
All wildly drunk, and dance
Into the writing. It's worth a try.
Hot damn, here they come! He knows them, name for name
As they surround his fingers, and carry the maze
Onto the paper: they're named for generals.

He thinks
That way: of history, with his skin
with everything
He has, including delirium tremens
staring straight
Into the lamp. You are a strange creature,
Light,
he says to light. Maybe one day I'll get something
Bigger than ants maybe something from the sea.
Keep knocking back the *aquavit*. By the way, my man, get that *aqua*!
There's a time acoming when the life of the sea when

The stars and their creatures get together.
Light
is another way. This is when the sun drifts in
Like it does in any window, but this sun is coming
From the east part of town. Shit, I don't know where I am
This desk is rolling like the sea
Come home come to my home—

I'll never make it to land. I am alone:
I am my brother:
I look at my own decoration
Outside of the page:
three rods: they're turning modern
A mobile he's got up
Above the bed, from splintered bottle-bits and coat-hangers:
You know they are, they really *are*
Small, smashed greens revolving
In a room.
It all hangs together, and *you* made it:
Its axis is spinning
Through the Zodiac.
He flicks it and sets the model
For a universe of green, see-through stars
Going faster. The white walls stagger
With lights:
He has to hold onto the chair: the room is pitching and rolling—

He's sick seasick with his own stars,
seasick and airsick sick
With the Zodiac.
Even drunk
Even in the white, whiskey-struck, splintered star of a bottle-room dancing,
He knows he's not fooling himself he knows
Not a damn thing of stars of God of space
Of time love night death sex fire numbers signs words,
Not much of poetry. But by God, we've got a *universe*
Here
Those designs of time are saying *some*thing
Or maybe something or *other*.
Night—
Night tells us. It's coming—
Venus shades it and breaks it. Will the animals come back
Gently, creatively open,
Like they were?
Yes.
The great, burning Beings melt into place
A few billion-lighted inept beasts
Of God—
What else is there? What other signs what other symbols
Are *any*thing beside these? If the thing hasn't been said
This way, then God can't say it.
Unknown. Unknown.
His mobile made of human shattering-art
Is idling through space, and also oddly, indifferently,
Supremely, through beauty as well. Yes,
Sideways through beauty. He swirls in his man-made universe,
His room, his liquor, both the new bottle and the old
Fragmented godlike one.
He never gets tired. Through his green, moving speckles,
He looks sideways, out and up and there it is:
The perpetual Eden of space
there where you want it.
What animal's getting outlined?
All space is being bolted
Together: eternal blackness

studded with creatures.
Stars.
Beasts. Nothing left but the void
Deep-hammering its creatures with light-years.
Years made of light.
Only light.
Yes.
But what about the damned *room*?
God-beast-stars wine-bottle constellations jack-off dreams
And silence. That's about it.
They're all one-eyed—
The Lion the Scorpion the others coming—
Their one-eyed eyesight billions of years
In the making, making and mixing with his liquor-bottle green
Splintered shadows *art*-shadows, for God's sake:
Look, stupid, get your nose out of the sky for once.
There're things that are *close* to you, too. Look at *them*!
Don't cringe: look right out over town.
Real birds. There they are in their curves, moving in their great element
That causes our planet to be blue and causes us all
To breathe. Ah, long ghostly drift
Of wings.
Well, son of a bitch.
He sits and writes,
And the paper begins to run
with signs.
But he can't get rid of himself enough
To write poetry. He keeps thinking Goddamn
I've misused myself I've fucked up I haven't worked—
I've traveled and screwed too much,
but but by dawn, now NOW
Something coming through-coming down-coming up
To me ME!
His hand reaches, dazzling with drink half alive,
for the half-dead vision. That room and its page come in and
out
Of being. You talk about *looking:* would you look at *that*
Electric page! What the hell did I say? Did *I* say that?
You bastard, you. Why didn't you know that before?

Where the hell have you been with your *head*?
You and the paper should have known it, you and the ink: you write
Everybody writes
With blackness. Night. Why has it taken you all this time?
All this travel, all those lives
You've fucked up? All those books read
Not deep enough? It's staring you right in the face. The
secret—
Is whiteness. You can do *anything* with that. But no—
The secret is that on whiteness you can release
The blackness,
the night sky. Whiteness is death is dying
For human words to raise it from purity from the grave
Of too much light. Words must come to it
Words from *any*where from from
Swamps mountains mud shit hospitals wars travels from
Stars
From the Zodiac.
You son of a bitch, you! Don't try to get away from yourself!
I won't have it! You know God-damned well I mean you! And you too,
Pythagoras! Put down that guitar, lyre, whatever it is!
You've driven me nuts enough with your music of the spheres!
But I'll bet you know what to know:
Where God once stood in the stadium
Of European history, and battled mankind in the blue air
Of manmade curses, under the exploding flags
Of dawn, I'd put something else now:
I'd put something overhead something new: a new beast
For the Zodiac. I'd say to myself like a man
Bartending for God,
What'll it be?
Great! The stars are mine, and so is
The imagination to work them—
To create.
Christ, would you tell me why my head
Keeps thinking up these nit-witted, useless images?
Whiskey helps.
But it does. It does. And now I'm working
With *constellations*! What'll it *be,* Heaven? What new creature

Would you *like* up there? Listen, you universal son-of-a-bitch,
You're talking to a poet now, so don't give me a lot of shit.
My old man was a God-damned astronomer
Of sorts
—and didn't he say the whole sky's *invented*?
Well, I am now in*vent*ing. You've *got* a Crab:
Especially tonight. I love to eat them: They scare me to death!
My head is smashed with *aquavit,*
And I've got a damn good Lobster in it for for
The Zodiac. I'll send it right up.
And listen now
I want *big* stars: some red some white also blue-white dwarves—
I want *everybody* to see my lobster! This'll be a *healing* lobster:
Not Cancer People will pray to him. He'll have a good effect
On Time.
Now what I want to do is stretch him out
Jesus Christ, I'm drunk

* * *

(xii)
A day like that. But afterwards the fire
Comes straight down through the roof, white-lightning nightfall,
A face-up flash. Poetry. Triangular eyesight. It draws his
fingers together at the edge
Around a pencil. He crouches bestially,
The darkness stretched out on the waters
Pulls back, humming Genesis. From wave-stars lifts
A single island wild with sunlight,
The white sheet of paper in the room.
He's far out and far in, his hands in a field of snow.
He's making a black horizon with all the moves
Of his defeated body. The virgin sheet becomes
More and more his, more and more another mistake,
But now, *now*
Oh God you rocky landscape give me, Give
Me drop by drop
desert water at least.
I want to write about deserts

And in the dark the sand begins to cry
For living water that not a sun or star
Can kill, and for the splay camel-prints that bring men,
And the ocean with its enormous crooning, begs
For haunted sailors   for refugees putting back
Flesh on their ever-tumbling bones
To man that fleet,
for in its ships
Only, the sea becomes the sea.
Oh my own soul, put me in a solar boat.
Come into one of these hands
Bringing quietness and the rare belief
That I can steer this strange craft to the morning
Land that sleeps   in the universe on all horizons
And give this home-come man who listens in his room
To the rush and flare of his father
Drawn at the speed of light to Heaven
Through the wrong end of his telescope, expanding the universe,
The instrument   the tuning-fork—
He'll flick it with his bandless wedding-finger—
Which at a touch reveals the form
Of the time-loaded European music
That poetry has never really found,
Undecipherable as God's bad, Heavenly sketches,
Involving fortress and flower, vine and wine and bone,
And shall vibrate through the western world
So long as the hand can hold its island
Of blazing paper, and bleed for its images:
Make what it can of what is:
So long as the spirit hurls on space
The star-beasts of intellect and madness.

From The Strength of Fields

The Strength of Fields

. . . a separation from the world,
a penetration to some source of power
and a life-enhancing return . . .
—*Van Gennep: Rites de Passage*

Moth-force a small town always has,
Given the night.

What field-forms can be,
Outlying the small civic light-decisions over
A man walking near home?

Men are not where he is
Exactly now, but they are around him   around him like the strength

Of fields.   The solar system floats on
Above him in town-moths.

Tell me, train-sound,

With all your long-lost grief,

what I can give.

Dear Lord of all the fields

what am I going to *do*?

Street-lights, blue-force and frail
As the homes of men, tell me how to do it   how
To withdraw   how to penetrate and find the source
Of the power you always had
light as a moth, and rising
With the level and moonlit expansion
Of the fields around, and the sleep of hoping men.

You? I? What difference is there? We can all be saved

By a secret blooming. Now as I walk
The night   and you walk with me   we know simplicity
Is close to the source that sleeping men
Search for in their home-deep beds.

We know that the sun is away   we know that the sun can be conquered
By moths, in blue home-town air.
The stars splinter, pointed and wild. The dead lie under
The pastures. They look on and help. Tell me, freight-train,
When there is no one else
To hear. Tell me in a voice the sea
Would have, if it had not a better one: as it lifts,
Hundreds of miles away, its fumbling, deep-structured roar
Like the profound, unstoppable craving
Of nations for their wish.
Hunger, time and the moon:

The moon lying on the brain
as on the excited sea   as on
The strength of fields.   Lord, let me shake
With purpose.   Wild hope can always spring
From tended strength.   Everything is in that.
That and nothing but kindness.   More kindness, dear Lord
Of the renewing green.   That is where it all has to start:
With the simplest things. More kindness will do nothing less
Than save every sleeping one
And night-walking one

Of us.
My life belongs to the world. I will do what I can.

The Voyage of the Needle

The child comes sometimes with his mother's needle
And draws a bath with his hand.   These are your fifty years
Of fingers, cast down among
The hard-driven echoes of tile
In the thresholding sound of run water.   Here the sun divides light
From the Venetian sector of the dark
Where you sink through both,
and warmly, more slowly than being
Smoothed and stretched, your bodying barge-ripples die.
A gauze of thin paper upholds
The needle, then soaks like an eyelid
And falls, uncontrolling, away.
The hung metal voyages alone,
Like the trembling north-nerve of a compass,
On surface tension, that magic, like a mother's spell
Cast in sharp seed in your childhood, in scientific trickery rooted
And flowering in elation. It is her brimming otherworld
That rides on the needle's frail lake, on death's precarious membrane,
Navigating through all level latitudes,
Containing a human body
She gave, and saved to bear, by a spell
From physics, this fragile cargo.   "Mother," you say,
"I am lying in a transference
Of joy and glory: come to me
From underground, from under the perilous balance
Of a thicket of thorns.   I lie
As unmoving. Bring the needle to breathless harbor
Somewhere on my body, that I may rise
And tell. My sex is too deep,
My eyes too high for your touch. O let it reach me at the lips'
Water-level, the thorns burst
Into rain on your wooded grave, the needle plunge
Through the skin of charmed water and die, that I may speak at last
With up-bearing magic
Of this household, weightless as love."

From Puella

Deborah Burning a Doll Made of House-wood

I know, I know it was necessary
for us to have things of this kind,
which acquiesced in everything
—*Rainer Maria Rilke*

I set you level,
Your eyes like the twin beasts of a wall.

As a child I believed I had grown you,
And I hummed as I mixed the blind nails
Of this house with the light wood of Heaven—
The rootless trees there—falling in love
With carpenters—their painted, pure clothes, their flawless
Bagginess, their God-balanced bubbles, their levels.
I am leaving: I have freed the shelves

So that you may burn cleanly, in sheer degrees
Of domestic ascent, unfolding
Boards one after the other, like a fireman

His rungs out of Hell

or some holocaust

whelmed and climbing:

You only now, alone in the stepped, stripped closet, staring
Out onto me, with the guaranteed kiss
Off-flaking, involvedly smiling,
Cradling and throning,
With the eyes of a wall and two creatures:

Ungainly unbroken hungering
For me, braving and bearing:
Themed, intolerable, born and unborn child
Of this house—of table and floorboard and cupboard,
Of stranger and hammering virgin—
At the flash-point of makeup I shadow
My own eyes with house-paint, learning
From yours, and the shelves of Heaven-wood

take fire from the roots

Of earth, dust bodies into smoke
The planks of your pulverized high-chair,
Paint blazes on the eyelids

Of the living in all colors, bestowing the power to see
Pure loss, and see it
With infinite force, with sun-force:

you gesture

Limply, with unspeakable aliveness,
Through the kindling of a child's
Squared mess of an indoor wood-yard

and I level

Stay level

and kneel and disappear slowly

Into Time, as you, with sun-center force, take up the house
In Hell-roaring steps, a Heaven-beaming holocaust
Of slats

and burn burn off

Just once, for good.

Deborah and Deirdre as Drunk Bridesmaids Foot-racing at Daybreak

Dawn dust.   We were right.   Haze of open damp
In levels beaded and barrelling   sleep mingling with speed
and straining

Of no heat-shadow   nowhere to be left
Behind   time-sparks over the grass   sunrise

From blade to blade splaying in muscle-light
Gone to tracks tattering and shimmering

All over   beggar-lice   brierbrambles
Picked off in consuming abandon

By these long clothes: open-browed on the blood-road,
Dawn mist just crossing us backward

Into passionate burn-off—pokeweed   oakenshaw
No end to the entrance—

Footloose in creature-glow   we rose
With us we were right

In there, with our hats in our hands
Together we blew the night roadblock

Plunging and reaching   flinging, redoubling
Flat-out in sprung dust and not dying, yet dying

Of devil and sawtooth of laughter—
Where can we belong   how can we

Eye-witness except in this rambling
And beginning through shadblow and firebrush

In level-out and stride-out and sing-out,
Good draggle and time-sparks?   Look up: look out

From the overdrive-side of free-floating—
O next blaze of Liberation Fence-rails

O flat stretch of wood-lot and hazel
And all that wide-open dust,

That winging of hedgerows and stump-blasting
Freshness, what's headlong to us now?

From The Eagle's Mile

Daughter

Hospital, and the father's room, where light
Won't look you in the eye. No emergency
But birth. I sit with the friend, and listen
To the unwounded clock. Indirectly glowing, he is grayer,
Unshaven as I. We are both old men
Or nearly. He is innocent. Yet:
What fathers are waiting to be born
But myself, whom the friend watches
With blessed directness? No other man but a worker

With an injured eyeball; his face had been there
When part of an engine flew up.
A tall nurse blotted with ink
And blood goes through. Something written
On her? Blood of my wife? A doctor with a blanket
Comes round a blind corner. "Who gets this little girl?"
I peer into wool: a creature
Somewhat strangely more than red. Dipped in fire.

No one speaks. The friend does not stir; he is innocent
Again: the child is between
Me and the man with one eye. We battle in the air,
Three-eyed, over the new-born. The doctor says,
"All right, now. Which one of you had a breech baby?"
All around I look: look at the possible
Wounded father. He may be losing: he opens his bad eye.
I half-close one of mine, hoping to win
Or help. Breech baby. I don't know. I tell my name.
Taking the doctor by his arms
Around her, the child of fire moves off. I would give one eye for her

Already. If she's not mine I'll steal her.
The doctor comes back. The friend stirs; both our beards
Quicken: the doctor is standing
Over me, saying, "This one's yours."
It is done: I set my feet
In Heavenly power, and get up. In place of plastic, manned rubber
And wrong light, I say wordlessly
Roll, real God. Roll through us. I shake hands

With the one-eyed man. He has not gained
A child, but may get back his eye; I hope it will return
By summer starlight.
The child almost setting
Its wool on fire, I hold it in the first and last power
It came from: that goes on all the time
There is, shunting the glacier, whirling
Whole forests from their tops, moving

Lava, the flowing stone: moving the hand
Of anyone, ever. Child of fire,
Look up. Look up as I lean and mumble you are part
Of flowing stone: understand: you are part of the wave,
Of the glacier's irrevocable
Millennial inch.
"This is the one," the friend repeats
In his end-of-it daze, his beard gone

Nearly silver, now, with honor, in the all-night night
Of early morning. Godfather, I say

To him: not father of God, but assistant
Father to this one. All forests are moving, all waves,
All lava and ice. I lean. I touch

One finger. Real God, roll.

Roll.

The Olympian

—False Youth: Spring—

Los Angeles back-yarding in its blue-eyed waters
Of empty swim, by my tract-house of packaged hard-candy
I lay in wait with the sun
And celebrity beer
for the Olympian,
Now my oldest boy's junior
High school algebra teacher, who had brought back the black-magic gold
Of the East, down the fast lane,
Freewaying, superhuman with rubberized home-stretch,
The four hundred meters from Tokyo
To Balboa Boulevard, leaving in his wake
All over the earth, the Others, the nation-motley doom-striped ones,
Those heart-eating sprinters, those Losers.
With Olympia Beer I was warming
Warming up with the best chill waters
Of the West Coast, cascading never-ending
Down out of Washington State. Now is your moment of truth
With me at last, O Champion! for I had laid a course as strange
To him as to me. Steeplechase! I had always leapt into water
Feet first, and could get out
Faster than in. I was ready for the Big One:

For the Water Jump in the corner
Of the lax, purfled pool, under the cemented palm
Where at night the shrewd rat climbed
And rustled and ruled the brown fronds over the underlit
Blue oval, surveying Sepulveda,
And in its color and kind, suffered
World recognition.
With a slide-rule in his shirt-pocket,
His bullet-proof glasses drawing
Into points—competitive points—and fish-eye-lensing,
Crossflashing on my hogged, haggard grassplot
Of slapped-down, laid-back Sepulveda, just after he'd Won It All,
He came lankily, finely drawn
Onto my turf, where all the time I had been laying
For him, building my energy-starches,
My hilarious, pizza-fed fury. My career of fat
Lay in the speed-trap, in the buckets and tools of the game-plan,
The snarls of purified rope. Then dawned the strict gods of Sparta,
The free gods of Athens! O lungs of Pheidippides collapsing in a square
Of the delivered city! O hot, just hurdlable gates
Of deck-chairs! Lounges! A measured universe
Of exhilarating laws! Here I had come there I'd gone
Laying it down confusing, staggering
The fast lane and the slow, on and over
And over recliners, sun-cots, cleaning-poles and beach-balls,
Foiled cans of rusty rat-poison bowing, split casks
Of diatomaceous earth corks spaced-out like California
On blue-and-white dacron cords lost-and-found swim-fins
Unmatched and pigeon-toed half-hearted air
In blazing rings doughnuts and play rafts dragons and elephants
Blown-up by mouth, now sighing most of life
Away the lawful No-Running signs
Turned to the wall. And all the time, all the time,
Under the brown-browed, rose-ash glower
Of the smog-bank, the crowd, long gone
Gray with the risen freeways, were thronging and hawing
To be Doves of Peace to be turned
Loose, displaying and escaping, over the jolted crowds

Of Unimart, the rammed Victory Stand,
and in the rose-ash
Of early dusk, we called our wives, gray as crows
In their golf-hats, to the secret Olympics, laid down in my laws
Within laws, where world champions, now mad with the moon
Of moonlighting, sold running shoes. This so, we insisted
On commercials, those all-comers'
Career-dreams of athletes: "We are brought to you by the Bringers of the Flame,
The double-dry double martini," those women said. "Get set!
Get set! You're being born
Again, in spite of everything!" James Bond and my smallest boy
Blazed with one cap-pistol together. We hove like whales from the line.

Twice around

We were going for, cursing and cruising like ghosts, over dog-food bowls,
Over sprinklers passed-out from their spin-off
Of rainbows and I was losing
But not badly, and even gained a little, coming out
Of the water-jump and over the jump-rope, and out of him or maybe
Me surely me burst a mindless deep
Belching blindsiding laugh down the backstretch
Of earth-kegs and dirty cleansing-tools that skinned the dust
From the under-blue, and for one unsettling moment left it
Blazing and mattering. I blazed I felt great I was a great
Plaster stadium-god lagging lolloping hanging
In there with the best: was running pale and heavy
With cement-dust from two wives running
Then coming around coming back
Down the slow lane lurching lorry-swaying:
Now toward two wives making up for —making
The gelatin-murmur of crowds, I pounded, wet and laboring,
And then, half a pool
Behind, went into the bell-lap.
I was holding my own
Back there, as we rounded
Past the stands he a long first and I
A world-class second and counting

On my finish or something   Yes! My finish to come
From the home turf like an ascension   all-seeing
World-recognized   poison-proof   smoke-proof   time-proof
Out of the pool, a rat's climb grappling
Half-a-lap half-a-lap   still alive
In mid-stride, louring, lumbering, crow-hopping
Behind the athlete's unhurried
Slack, unearthly footling lope:
I stepped low and heavy
Over the last light rope, smashed water with my sole
Flat   climbed, lurched, legged it and duck-footed
For home   a good not shameful
Second   this was all right and everything
But no! My weave   my plan   the run
Of my knots had caught up with him   caught
Him where he lived
—in his feet—
and he was down
In styrofoam, and on a bloated blessèd doughnut-ring
Of rubber rolled: the finish-line leapt   exploded
Into Reality, shot-through with deathless flame, crossed with white paper:
Swam illicitly, aboundingly
Like wind-aided glory. With courage to do credit
To any rat, I cornered and turned
It on. He came back instantly, but instantly was not soon
Enough, for I charged past like a slow freight
All over the earth, and had got it
And gone   long gone   and burst

Through the living tissue: breasted and blanked
The Tape and can feel it

Bannering, still, on my chest
Like wing-span, that once was toilet-paper, torn epically
Where the true Olympian slurred
His foot and fell, and I felt my lungs collapsing in a square
Of the City, like Pheidippides dying of the sheer
Good of my news.

Far off, still rising at rose dusk
And night, free under the low-browed smoke, and grayer
Than any fake peace-bird,
Like a called crow I answer
Myself utterly, with a whole laugh —that body-language one-world
One word of joy —straight into the ruining tons
Of smoke that trash my head and doom it
And keep it recognized
in the age
And condition of my kind, and hear also, maybe not entirely
From myself, the Olympian's laugh
Coming from somewhere
Behind, blindsidedly, getting the point
At last, sighing like ghosts and like rubber, for fat
And luck, all over the earth, where that day and any and every
Day after it, devil hindmost and Goddamn it

To glory, I lumbered for gold.

For a Time and Place

A South Carolina inauguration of Richard Riley as governor

May we be able to begin with ourselves
Underfoot and rising,
Peering through leaves we have basketed, through tendrils hanging
Like bait, through flowers,
Through lifted grave-soil: peering
Past the short tree that stands
In place for us, sawed-off, unbendable: a thing
Pile-driven down
And flowering from the impact—such weaving
Consuming delicacy in the leaves, out of such
Up-wedged and pine-appled bark! We look alive
Through those petals in the censer-swung pots: through

That swinging soil, and the split leaves fountaining out
Of the mauled tree, to the east horizon vibrant
With whole-earth hold-down, past a single sail pillowing
From there on out.

We peer also from the flat
Slant sand, west from estuary-glitter,
From the reed-beds bending inland
At dawn as we do, to the high-ground hard-hurdling
Power of the down-mountain torrent: at a blue-ridged glance
From the ocean, we see all we have
Is unified as a quilt: the long leaves of the short tree,
The tough churchly feathers, dance rice-like this side of
The far-out wave-break's lounging
Curved insolent long sparking thorn, and
The gull's involving balance, his sweeping-through shuttle-run
Downwind; his tapestry-move
Is laid on our shoulders, where the unspilled dead
Are riding, wild with flowers, collision-colors
At the hairline, tended, sufficient, dead-level with us
From now on out.

What visions to us from all this lived
Humidity? What insights from the blue haze alone? From kudzu?
From snake-vine? From the native dog-sized deer
From island to island floating, their head-bones
Eternal and formal,
Collisionless? We are standing mainly on blends
Of sand, red-rooted, in dark
Near-fever air, and there is a certain weaving
At our backs, like a gull's over-the-shoulder
Peel-off downwind. Assuming those wings, we keep gazing
From goat-grass to the high
Shifts, splits, and barreling
Alcohol of the rocks, all the way from minnows flashing whole
The bright brittle shallows, waiting for our momentum
From here on out.

It is true, we like our air warm
And wild, and the bark of our trees
Overlapping backward and upward
Stoutly, the shocks of tough leaves counter-
balancing, with a flicker of lostness. Beside the dead,
The straw-sucking marsh, we have stood where every blade
Of eelgrass thrilled like a hand-line
For the huge bass hanging in the shade
Of the sunken bush, and have heard the unstuffed moss
Hiss like a laundry-iron. This point between
The baskets and the tree is where we best
Are, and would be: our soil, our soul,
Our sail, our black horizon simmering like a mainspring,
Our rocky water falling like a mountain
Ledge-to-ledge naturally headlong,
Unstoppable, and our momentum
In place, overcoming, coming over us
And from us
from now on out.

Early Poems

The Shark at the Window

(for my brother's marriage)

i

Driving home from your wedding in light-
blunting fog, the road I inchmeal held
Dropt instantly, I could not guess it, great
White sail-settled and drew, and I gained there
A sanctum of midnight cloud, a float of trusts.

More than the reparations of the womb, my brother,
That pilgrim-place has cast our centered bloods:
Renewal, oneness are there; our semblances fail.
We enter to find ourselves the same in love,
In kinship, as the tussled cloth about
A river-reed's needle, a stitching snag, can
Never alter, but renders Platonist and caddis
Fly the selfsame cordonnet, as of point-laced, ancient,
Vital hair, though the water move
More calmly than the waters of a grape, or mull

Sienna-spread and vastly wild
Under ephemerae of mule and leaf.

ii

Brother in the window welcome,
Welcome brother at the seatrap
Glass. Near ghost, your lacquered
Shade drops off and waits—
Aqueous, breathclouded, seeming.
Our centers meet.

iii

Flesh that would have stood in finished grainfields
(The round hard thumb, the eye, the wheaten hair)
In the pollened, trampled fore of Tartar horse,
And to the slung and sighflown spin of blade have
Sung, as it brownly, brightly cropped
Matted and cruel lives
stood off from you once
In aquarium glass. We watched it from our uncertain place,
And watched its next-to, brotherly image, and the fraught
Protected waters for a sign.
Balanced,
A huge and casual leaf
Fall, through shivered trays of stacked
Autumnal light
Our symbol subsided to us.
We marked behind our shapes of breath
The smeared and old man's mouth, the slatted
Gills, the absolute and unknown terror,
The closest conch that might be trembled into.

It was fear first pressed
Us through that pearled and helical threshold where
No adumbrations pass.

Expecting the dark, we found the shapen cupping
Resplendent with the light we made.

Gray and pink volution wore
Our whispers back in rounds.

A single voice became in those one-weltered sounds.

In the shell of the bridal
Chamber, in the still sump of midnight,
Know without fear

This with her.

Joel Cahill Dead

The farmer, fighting busily for his home,
Heard, in the pouring sound of fire,
From the blackened bushes something run
Straight up the back of his neck into the air.
Through smoke, he saw a stiff-winged shape
Smash into earth, and a great flame come from flame.

Like a man sent for, he ran,
Waving his arms, and yelled through his sooty kerchief
In a curving voice around
The boy who stood, amazed, beside the plane,
Exhaled in fire, his shirt at the shoulders smoking,
Who got then down upon one ragged knee.

The farmer threw his hat away
As if it would take fire, and knelt beside the boy,
Who then, by opening his own,
Opened the farmer's champing mouth
To speak. Between them, missing their hands,
Blood fell, and seemed to splash up from the heart

Of stone. The wind around them changed.
Over and through them, invisible in midair,

Fire leapt, from leaf to leaf.
From the other side of the house, the farmer's wife,
Expressionless, came. They picked the boy between them
Up, and stumbled him inside, where he lay down.

He lay on top of a peacock quilt
And gave off a fragile steam. Above him,
A lantern on a nail
Showed him nothing but the toothy edge of light.
He smiled, not having to breathe,
But stiffened, then, remembering the Colonel,

To whom he must affirm
That he had less than no excuse to lie
Alone, in a carven bed, to hear a woman weep,
To fade in and out of his open eyes,
And see a forest, blazing, in the teeth
Of a cock's-combed, motionless flame,

Turning down, to bother no one while he slept
In its fluted veil of glass.

The Wish to Be Buried Where One Has Made Love

At dawn, in one move, a trout
Drew his body out the length of the river;

The sun smote the rocks into view.
We walked with the earthless footsteps

Of children about to be born.
We lay on the rocks, strangely flaming;

The trees from across the river
Came, in their next shadows, slowly;

A wind sprang out of their leaves
And broke, as I touched the guitar.

At dusk the boulders arose
Until they stood shafting in moonlight.

A curved muscle shook in the river,
As I stung the last note from the string,

And we lay, looking up through the stones
As through time, and saw there

A fish like a new current swimming,
A reflexing tree on the water.

We lie here, responding forever.

The Wheelchair Drunk

I never had arms before
Those five martinis swooped into my room,
And I can tell you now that the thing I am in will dance,

Dancing not against but with
The bricks of the building, and whatever
Holds the glazed floors still while the elevator drops through.

Those doors I double-burst
And jolt down the footless stairs
Looking anywhere for a bar. Who brought that chilled pitcher

To the foot of my throne now stares
Open-mouthed out the window as I reel
The spokes forward faster than they ever intended

And unwind myself,
A horseless sulky, an old-fashioned ashcan,
Top-heavily happy, spinning my wheels in the sun

With light chopped to bits around
My center of gravity. This is where I bump
Down off the sidewalk, crossing a street where drivers

Blanch at the thought
Of running me down, even though they have
The light and the law on their side—and now must find

A driveway somewhere
To come in off the street and join
Wire carts full of soap-flakes and babies. I have forgotten

Why I can't rise and walk,
Stand on the lawns, push my self-starting chair
Out under a truck and let them smash-stop each other,

Holding up delivery
Of the U.S. mail, Grandma Foster's Pies,
Clothing store dummies, toilet seats or rose-dozens,

But it's certain I can't,
And so must go as I am, in my dressing gown,
Toward the dark neon alive in the middle of morning,

Unrolling an endless rail
On either side of me out of my powerful palms.
But it will be hard, hard to get through those two blocks:

I desire to hear
At every crossroads all the unhandled other
Wheels scream helplessly dead, for suddenly I love nothing

So much as to whirl
In the middle of traffic, holding up like a thief
Of delight those bread-trucks, those frustrated bridge-players:

To sit here like money
Lost and found in the perilous streets, and spin
Myself on a magical dime, getting better and brighter and better.

Reading Genesis to a Blind Child

I am hiding beside you to tell you
What the world itself cannot show,
That you walk with an untold sight
Beyond the best reach of my light.
Try as you can to bear with me
As I struggle to see what you see
Be born of the language I speak.

Claw, feather, fur, and beak,
The beasts come under your hand
As into the Ark, from a land
That a cloud out of Hell must drown,
But for you, my second-born son.
The sheep, like your mother's coat,
The bear, the bird, and the goat

Come forth, and the cunning serpent.
I am holding my right arm bent
That you may take hold of the curve
Of round, warm skin that must serve
For evil. Now, unbreathing, I take
A pin, for the tooth of the snake.
You gravely touch it, and smile

Not at me, but into the world
Where you sit in the blaze of a book
With lion and eagle and snake
Represented by pillow and pin,
By feathers from hats, and thin

Gull-wings of paper, loosed
From pages my fingers have traced

With the forms of free-flying birds;
And these are the best of my words.
If I were to ask you now
To touch the bright lid of my eye
Might I not see what you see?
Would my common brain not turn
To untellable vision, and burn

With the vast, creative color
Of dark, and the serpent, hidden forever
In the trembling right arm of your father,
Not speak? Can you take this book
And bring it to life with a look?
And can you tell me how
I have made your world, yet know

No more than I have known?
The beasts have smelled the rain,
Yet none has wailed for fear.
You touch me; I am here.
A hand has passed through my head,
And this is the hand of the Lord.
I have called forth the world in a word,

And am shut from the thing I have made.
I have loosed the grim wolf on the sheep;
Yet upon the original deep
of your innocence, they lie down
Together; upon each beast is a crown
Of patience, immortal and bright,
In which is God-pleasing delight.

Your grace to me is forbidden,
Yet I am remembering Eden
As you sit and play with a sword

Of fire, made of a word,
And I call through the world-saving gate
Each word creating your light:
All things in patient tones,

Birds, beasts, and flowering stones,
In each new word something new
The world cannot yet show.
All earthly things I have led
Unto your touch, have been fed
Thus on the darkness that bore them,
By which they most mightily shine,

And shall never know vision from sight,
Nor light from the Source of all light.
The sun is made to be hidden,
And the meaning and prospect of Eden
To go blind as a stone, until touched,
And the ship in a greenwood beached
Not rise through the trees on a smoke

Of rain, till that flood break,
The sun go out in a cloud
And a voice remake it aloud,
Striving most gently to bring
A fit word to everything,
And to come on the thing it is seeking
Within its speaking, speaking.

Fiction

From Deliverance

Houghton Mifflin published Deliverance *in the spring of 1970, and the book quickly reached the bestseller lists. It was nominated for a National Book Award and won France's prestigious Prix Medicis. John Boorman's movie version of* Deliverance *(1972) competed for the Academy Award for Best Picture with another bestselling-novel–turned-film:* The Godfather. The Godfather *ultimately won.*

The following excerpt describes the incidents that set the tragedy of Dickey's novel in motion. Lewis Medlock, Ed Gentry, Bobby Trippe, and Drew Ballinger have left Atlanta for the wilds of North Georgia and spent their first night on the Cahulawassee River. Ed and Bobby have paddled ahead of Lewis and Drew.

September 15th (excerpt)

I looked back. The other canoe was just coming around. Lewis had lagged behind us because, I suppose, he wanted us in sight in case we got into trouble. Anyway, they were about half a mile back and disappeared as we rounded another curve, and I pointed with my paddle to the left bank. I didn't know whether they saw me or not, but I figured to flag them in when they came by.

I wanted to lie up in the shade and rest for a while. I was hungry, and I sure would've liked to have had another beer. We dug in and swung over.

As we closed in on the left bank, a pouring sound came from under the trees; the leaves at a certain place moved as if in a little wind. The fresh green-white of a creek was frothing into the river. We sailed past it half-broadside and came to the bank about seventy-five yards downstream. I put the nose against it and paddled hard to hold it there while Bobby got out and moored us.

"This is too much like work," Bobby said, as he gave me a hand up.

"Lord, Lord," I said. "I'm getting too old for this kind of business. I suppose you could call it learning the hard way."

Bobby sat down on the ground and untied a handkerchief from around his neck. He leaned down to the river and sopped it, then swabbed his face and neck down, rubbing a long time in the nose area. I bent over and touched my toes a couple of times to get rid of the position that had been maiming my back, and then looked upstream. I still couldn't see the other canoe. I turned to say something to Bobby.

Two men stepped out of the woods, one of them trailing a shotgun by the barrel.

Bobby had no notion they were there until he looked at me. Then he turned his head until he could see over his shoulder and got up, brushing at himself.

"How goes it?" he said.

One of them, the taller one, narrowed in the eyes and face. They came forward, moving in a kind of half circle as though they were stepping around something. The shorter one was older, with big white eyes and a half-white stubble that grew in whorls on his cheeks. His face seemed to spin in many directions. He had on overalls, and his stomach looked like it was falling through them. The other was lean and tall, and peered as though out of a cave or some dim simple place far back in his yellow-tinged eyeballs. When he moved his jaws the lower bone came up too far for him to have teeth. "Escaped convicts" flashed up in my mind on one side, "Bootleggers" on the other. But they still could have been hunting.

They came on, and were ridiculously close for some reason. I tried not to give ground; some principle may have been involved.

The older one, looming and spinning his sick-looking face in front of me, said, "What the *hail* you think you're doin'?"

"Going downriver. Been going since yesterday."

I hoped that the fact that we were at least talking to each other would do some good of some kind.

He looked at the tall man; either something or nothing was passing between them. I could not feel Bobby anywhere near, and the other canoe was not in sight. I shrank to my own true size, a physical movement known only to me, and with the strain my solar plexus failed. I said, "We started from Oree yesterday afternoon, and we hope we can get to Aintry sometime late today or early tomorrow."

"*Ain*try?"

Bobby said, and I could have killed him, "Sure. This river just runs one way, cap'n. Haven't you heard?"

"You ain't never going to get down to Aintry," he said, without any emphasis on any word.

"Why not?" I asked, scared but also curious; in a strange way it was interesting to cause him to explain.

"Because this river don't go to Aintry," he said. "You done taken a wrong turn somewhere. This-here river don't go nowhere near Aintry."

"Where does it go?"

"It goes . . . it goes . . ."

"It goes to Circle Gap," the other man said, missing his teeth and not caring. "'Bout fifty miles."

"Boy," said the whorl-faced man, "you don't know *where* you are."

"Well," I said, "we're going where this river's going. We'll come out somewhere, I reckon."

The other man moved closer to Bobby.

"Hell," I said, "we don't have anything to do with you. We sure don't want any trouble. If you've got a still near here, that's fine with us. We could never tell anybody where it is, because you know something? You're right. We don't know where we are."

"A *stee*-ul?" the tall man said, and seemed honestly surprised.

"Sure," I said. "If you're making whiskey, we'll buy some from you. We could sure use it."

The drop-gutted man faced me squarely. "Do you know what the *hail* you're talkin' about?"

"I don't know what you're talking about," I said.

"You done said something about makin' whiskey. You think we're makin' whiskey. Now come on. Ain't that right?"

"Shit," I said. "I don't know whether you're making whiskey or hunting or rambling around in the woods for your whole fucking life. I don't know and I don't care what you're doing. It's not any of my business."

I looked at the river, but we were a little back from the bank, and I couldn't see the other canoe. I didn't think it could have gone past, but I was not really sure that it hadn't. I shook my head in a complete void, at the thought that it might have; we had got too far ahead, maybe.

With the greatest effort in the world, I came back into the man's face and tried to cope with it. He had noticed something about the way I had looked at the river.

"Anybody else with you?" he asked me.

I swallowed and thought, with possibilities shooting through each other. If I said yes, and they meant trouble, we would bring Lewis and Drew into it with no defenses. Or it might mean that we would be left alone, four being too many to handle. On the other hand, if I said no, then Lewis and Drew—especially Lewis—might be able to . . . well, to do something. Lewis' pectorals loomed up in my mind, and his leg, with the veins bulging out of the divided muscles of his thigh, his leg under water wavering small-ankled and massive as a centaur's. I would go with that.

"No," I said, and took a couple of steps inland to draw them away from the river.

The lean man reached over and touched Bobby's arm, feeling it with strange delicacy. Bobby jerked back, and when he did the gun barrel came up, almost casually but decisively.

"We'd better get on with it," I said. "We got a long ways to go." I took part of a step toward the canoe.

"You ain't goin' nowhere," the man in front of me said, and leveled the shotgun straight into my chest. My heart quailed away from the blast tamped into both barrels, and I wondered what the barrel openings would look like at the exact instant they went off: if fire would come out of them, or if they would just be a gray blur or if they would change at all between the time you lived and died, blown in half. He took a turn around his hand with the string he used for a trigger.

"You come on back in here 'less you want your guts all over this-here woods."

I half-raised my hands like a character in a movie. Bobby looked at me, but I was helpless, my bladder quavering. I stepped forward into the woods through some big bushes that I saw but didn't feel. They were all behind me.

The voice of one of them said, "Back up to that saplin'."

I picked out a tree. "This one?" I said.

There was no answer. I backed up to the tree I had selected. The lean man came up to me and took off my web belt with the knife and rope on it. Moving his hands very quickly, he unfastened the rope, let the belt out and put it around me and the tree so tight I could hardly breathe, with the buckle on the other side of the tree. He came back holding the knife. It occurred to me that they must have done this before; it was not a technique they would just have thought of for the occasion.

The lean man held up the knife, and I looked for the sun to strike it, but there was no sun where we were. Even so, in the intense shadow, I could see the edge I had put on it with a suburban grindstone: the minute crosshatching of high-speed abrasions, the wearing-away of metal into a murderous edge.

"Look at that," the tall man said to the other. "I bet that'll shave h'ar."

"Why'ont you try it? Looks like that'n's got plenty of it. 'Cept on his head."

The tall man took hold of the zipper of my coveralls, breathing lightly, and zipped it down to the belt as though tearing me open.

"Good God Amighty," said the older one. "He's like a goddamned monkey. You ever see anything like that?"

The lean man put the point of the knife under my chin and lifted it. "You ever had your balls cut off, you fuckin' ape?"

"Not lately," I said, clinging to the city. "What good would they do you?"

He put the flat of the knife against my chest and scraped it across. He held it up, covered with black hair and a little blood. "It's sharp," he said. "Could be sharper, but it's sharp."

The blood was running down from under my jaw where the point had been. I had never felt such brutality and carelessness of touch, or such disregard for another person's body. It was not the steel or the edge of the steel that was frightening; the man's fingernail, used in any gesture of his, would have been just as brutal; the knife only magnified his unconcern. I shook my head again, trying to get my breath in a gray void full of leaves. I looked straight up into the branches of the sapling I was tied to, and then down into the clearing at Bobby.

He was watching me with his mouth open as I gasped for enough breath to live on from second to second. There was nothing he could do, but as he looked at the blood on my chest and under my throat, I could see that his position terrified him more than mine did; the fact that he was not tied mattered in some way.

They both went toward Bobby, the lean man with the gun this time. The white-bearded one took him by the shoulders and turned him around toward downstream.

"Now let's you just drop them pants," he said.

Bobby lowered his hands hesitantly. "Drop . . . ?" he began.

My rectum and intestines contracted. Lord God.

The toothless man put the barrels of the shotgun under Bobby's right ear and shoved a little. "Just take 'em right on off," he said.

"I mean, what's this all . . ." Bobby started again weakly.

"Don't say nothin'," the older man said. "Just do it."

The man with the gun gave Bobby's head a vicious shove, so quick that I thought the gun had gone off. Bobby unbuckled his belt and unbuttoned his pants. He took them off, looking around ridiculously for a place to put them.

"Them panties too," the man with the belly said.

Bobby took off his shorts like a boy undressing for the first time in a gym, and stood there plump and pink, his hairless thighs shaking, his legs close together.

"See that log? Walk over yonder."

Wincing from the feet, Bobby went slowly over to a big fallen tree and stood near it with his head bowed.

"Now git on down crost it."

The tall man followed Bobby's head down with the gun as Bobby knelt over the log.

"Pull your shirt-tail up, fat-ass."

Bobby reached back with one hand and pulled his shirt up to his lower back. I could not imagine what he was thinking.

"I said *up*," the tall man said. He took the shotgun and shoved the back of the shirt up to Bobby's neck, scraping a long red mark along his spine.

The white-bearded man was suddenly also naked up to the waist. There was no need to justify or rationalize anything; they were going to do what they wanted to. I struggled for life in the air, and Bobby's body was still and pink in an obscene posture that no one could help. The tall man restored the gun to Bobby's head, and the other one knelt behind him.

A scream hit me, and I would have thought it was mine except for the lack of breath. It was a sound of pain and outrage, and was followed by one of simple and wordless pain. Again it came out of him, higher and more carrying. I let all the breath out of myself and brought my head down to look at the river. Where are they, every vein stood out to ask, and as I looked the bushes broke a little in a place I would not have thought of and made a kind of complicated alleyway out onto the stream—I was not sure for a moment whether it was water or leaves—and Lewis' canoe was in it. He and Drew both had their paddles out of water, and then they turned and disappeared.

The white-haired man worked steadily on Bobby, every now and then getting a better grip on the ground with his knees. At last he raised his face as though to howl with all his strength into the leaves and the sky, and quivered silently while the man with the gun looked on with an odd mixture of approval and sympathy. The whorl-faced man drew back, drew out.

The standing man backed up a step and took the gun from behind Bobby's ear. Bobby let go of the log and fell to his side, both arms over his face.

We all sighed. I could get better breath, but only a little.

The two of them turned to me. I drew up as straight as I could and waited with the tree. It was up to them. I could sense my knife sticking in the bark next to my head and I could see the blood vessels in the eyes of the tall man. That was all; I was blank.

The bearded man came to me and disappeared around me. The tree jerked and air came into my lungs in great gratitude. I fell forward and caught up short, for the tall man had put the gun up under my nose; it was a very odd sensation, funnier than it might have been when I thought of my brain as thinking of Dean and Martha at that instant and also of its being scattered, material of some sort, over the bush-leaves and twigs in the next second.

"You're kind of ball-headed and fat, ain't you?" the tall man said.

"What do you want me to say?" I said. "Yeah. I'm bald-headed and fat. That OK?"

"You're hairy as a goddamned dog, ain't you?"

"Some dogs, I suppose."

"What the *hail* . . ." he said, half turning to the other man.

"Ain't no hair in his mouth," the other one said.

"That's the truth," the tall one said. "Hold this on him."

Then he turned to me, handing the gun off without looking. It stood in the middle of the air at the end of his extended arm. He said to me, "Fall down on your knees and pray, boy. And you better pray good."

I knelt down. As my knees hit, I heard a sound, a snap-slap off in the woods, a sound like a rubber band popping or a sickle-blade cutting quick. The older man was standing with the gun barrel in his hand and no change in the stupid, advantage-taking expression of his face, and a foot and a half of bright red arrow was shoved forward from the middle of his chest. It was there so suddenly it seemed to have come from within him.

None of us understood; we just hung where we were, the tall man in front of me unbuttoning his pants, me on my knees with my eyelids clouding the forest, and Bobby rolling back and forth, off in the leaves in the corner of my eye. The gun fell, and I made a slow-motion grab for it as the tall man sprang like an animal in the same direction. I had it by the stock with both hands, and if I could pull it in to me I would have blown him in half in the next second. But he only gripped the barrel lightly and must have felt that I had it better, and felt also what every part of me was concentrated on doing; he jumped aside and was gone into the woods opposite where the arrow must have come from.

I got up with the gun and the power, wrapping the string around my right hand. I swung the barrel back and forth to cover everything, the woods and the world. There was nothing in the clearing but Bobby and the shot man and me. Bobby was still on the ground, though now he was lifting his head. I could understand that much, but something kept blurring the clear idea of Bobby and myself and the leaves and the river. The shot man was still standing. He wouldn't concentrate in my vision; I couldn't believe him. He was like a film over the scene, gray and vague, with the force gone out of him; I was amazed at how he did everything. He touched the arrow experimentally, and I could tell that it was set in him as solidly as his breastbone. It was in him tight and unwobbling, coming out front and back. He took hold of it with both hands, but compared to the arrow's strength his hands were weak; they weakened more as I looked, and began to melt. He was on his knees, and then fell to his side, pulling his legs up. He rolled back and forth like a man with the wind knocked out of him, all the time making a bubbling, gritting sound. His lips turned red, but from his convulsions—in which there was something comical and unspeakable—he seemed to gain strength. He got up on one knee and then to his feet again while I stood with the shotgun at port arms. He took a couple of strides toward the woods and then seemed to change his mind and danced back to me, lurching and clog-stepping in a secret circle. He held out a hand to me, like a prophet, and I pointed the shotgun straight at the head of the arrow, ice coming into my teeth. I was ready to put it all behind me with one act, with one pull of a string.

But there was no need. He crouched and fell forward with his face on my white tennis shoe tops, trembled away into his legs and shook down to stillness. He opened his mouth and it was full of blood like an apple. A clear bubble formed on his lips and stayed there.

I stepped back and looked at the whole scene again, trying to place things. Bobby was propped up on one elbow, with his eyes as red as the bubble in the dead man's mouth. He got up, looking at me. I realized that I was swinging the gun toward him; that I pointed wherever I looked. I lowered the barrel. What to say?

"Well."

"Lord God," Bobby said. "Lord God."

"You all right?" I asked, since I needed to know even though I cringed with the directness.

Bobby's face expanded its crimson, and he shook his head. "I don't know," he said. "I don't know."

I stood and he lay with his head on his palm, both of us looking straight ahead. Everything was quiet. The man with the aluminum shaft in him lay with his head on one shoulder and his right hand relaxedly holding the barb of the arrow. Behind him the blue and silver of Lewis' fancy arrow crest shone, unnatural in the woods.

Nothing happened for ten minutes. I wondered if maybe the other man wouldn't come back before Lewis showed himself, and I began to compose a scene in which Lewis would step out of the woods on one side of the clearing with his bow and the tall man would show on the other, and they would have it out in some way that it was hard to imagine. I was working on the details when I heard something move. Part of the bark of a big water oak moved at leg level, and Lewis moved with it out into the open, stepping sideways into the clearing with another bright-crested arrow on the string of his bow. Drew followed him, holding a canoe paddle like a baseball bat.

Lewis walked out between me and Bobby, over the man on the ground, and put his bow tip on a leaf. Drew moved to Bobby. I had been holding the gun ready for so long that it felt strange to lower the barrels so that they were pointing down and could kill nothing but the ground. I did, though, and Lewis and I faced each other across the dead man. His eyes were vivid and alive; he was smiling easily and with great friendliness.

"Well now, how about this? Just . . . how *about* this?"

I went over to Bobby and Drew, though I had no notion of what to do when I got there. I had watched everything that had happened to Bobby, had heard him scream and squall, and wanted to reassure him that we could set all that aside; that it would be forgotten as soon as we left the woods, or as soon as we got back in the canoes. But there was no way to say this, or to ask him how his lower intestine felt or whether he thought he was bleeding internally. Any examination of him would be unthinkably ridiculous and humiliating.

There was no question of that, though; he was furiously closed off from all of us. He stood up and backed away, still naked from the middle down, his sexual organs wasted with pain. I picked up his pants and shorts and handed them to him, and he reached for them in wonderment. He took out a handkerchief and went behind some bushes.

Still holding the gun at trail, as the tall man had been doing when I first saw him step out of the woods, I went back to Lewis, who was leaning on his bow and gazing out over the river.

Without looking at me, he said, "I figured it was the only thing to do."

"It was," I agreed, though I wasn't all that sure. "I thought we'd had it."

Lewis glanced in the direction Bobby had taken and I realized I could have put it better.

"I thought sure they'd kill us."

"Probably they would have. The penalty for sodomy in this state is death, anyway. And at the point of a gun . . . No, they wouldn't have let you go. Why should they?"

"How did you figure it?"

"We heard Bobby, and the only thing we could think of was that one of you had been bit by a snake. We started to come right in, but all at once it hit me that if it was something like snakebite, the other one of you could take care of the one that was bit just as well as three of us could, at least for a little while. And if there were other people involved, I told Drew I had just as soon come in on them without them knowing it."

"What did you do?"

"We turned in that little creek and went up it about fifty yards. Then we shoved the canoe in some bushes and got out; I strung up and nocked an arrow, and we came on up to about thirty yards from where you were. As soon as I saw four people there, I began to shift around to find a place I could shoot through the leaves. I couldn't tell what was going on at first, though I thought it was probably what it was. I'm sorry I couldn't do anything for Bobby, but at least I didn't make a mismove and get his head blown off. When the guy started getting back up on his feet, I drew down on him, and waited."

"How did you know when to shoot?"

"Any time that the gun wasn't pointed at you and Bobby would have been all right. I just had to wait till that time came. The other guy hadn't had any action yet, and I was pretty sure they'd swap the gun. The only thing I was worried about was that you might get in between me and him. But I was on him all the time, looking right down the arrow. I must have been at full draw for at least a minute. It would've been a much easier shot if I hadn't had to hold so long. But it was fairly easy anyway. I knew I was right on him; I tried to hit him halfway up the back and a little to the left. He moved, or that's just where it would have caught him. I knew I had him when I let go."

"You had him," I said. "And now what're we going to do with him?"

Drew moved up to us, washing his hands with dirt and beating them against the sides of his legs.

"There's not but one thing *to* do," he said. "Put the body in one of the canoes and take it on down to Aintry and turn it over to the highway patrol. Tell them the whole story."

"Tell them what, exactly?" Lewis asked.

"Just what happened," Drew said, his voice rising a tone. "This is justifiable homicide if anything is. They were sexually assaulting two members of our party at gunpoint. Like you said, there was nothing else we could do."

"Nothing else but shoot him in the back with an arrow?" Lewis asked pleasantly.

"It was your doing, Lewis," Drew said.

"What would you have done?"

"It doesn't make any difference what I would have done," Drew said stoutly. "But I can tell you, I don't believe . . ."

"Don't believe what?"

"Wait a minute," I broke in. "What we should or shouldn't have done is beside the point. He's there, and we're here. We didn't start any of this. We didn't ask for it. But what happens now?"

Something close to my feet moved. I looked down, and the man shook his head as though at something past belief, gave a long sigh and slumped again. Drew and Lewis bent down on him.

"Is he dead?" I asked. I had already fixed him as dead in my mind, and couldn't imagine how he could have moved and sighed.

"He is now," Lewis said, without looking up. "He's mighty dead. We couldn't have saved him, though. He's center-shot."

Lewis and Drew got up, and we tried to think our way back into the conversation.

"Let's just figure for a minute," Lewis said. "Let's just calm down and think about it. Does anybody know anything about the law?"

"I've been on jury duty exactly once," Drew said.

"That's once more than I have," I said. "And about all the different degrees of murder and homicide and manslaughter I don't know anything at all."

We all turned to Bobby, who had rejoined us. He shook his fiery face.

"You don't have to know much law to know that if we take this guy down out of these mountains and turn him over to the sheriff, there's going to be an investigation, and I would bet we'd go on trial," Lewis said. "I don't know what the charge would be, technically, but we'd be up against a jury, sure as hell."

"Well, so what?" Drew said.

"All right, now," said Lewis, shifting to the other leg. "We've killed a man. Shot him in the back. And we not only killed a man, we killed a cracker, a mountain man. Let's consider what might happen."

"All right," Drew said. "Consider it. We're listening."

Lewis sighed and scratched his head. "We just ought to wait a minute before we decide to be so all-fired boy scoutish and do the right thing. There's not any right thing."

"You bet there is," Drew said. "There's only *one* thing."

I tried to think ahead, and I couldn't see anything but desperate trouble, and for the rest of my life. I have always been scared to death of anything to do with the police; the sight of a police uniform turns my saliva cold. I could feel myself beginning to breathe fast in the stillness, and I noticed the sound of the river for a moment, like something heard through a door.

"We ought to do some hard decision-making before we let ourselves in for standing trial up in these hills. We don't know who this man is, but we know that he lived up here. He may be an escaped convict, or he may have a still, or he may be everybody in the county's father, or brother or cousin. I can almost guarantee you that he's got relatives all over the place. Everybody up here is kin to everybody else, in one way or another. And consider this, too: there's a lot of resentment in these hill counties about the dam. There are going to have to be some cemeteries moved, like in the old TVA days. Things like that. These people don't want any 'furriners' around. And I'm goddamned if I want to come back up here for shooting this guy in the back, with a jury made up of his cousins and brothers, maybe his mother and father too, for all I know."

He had a point. I listened to the woods and the river to see if I could get an answer. I saw myself and the others rotting for weeks in some county jail with country drunks, feeding on sorghum, salt pork and sowbelly, trying to pass the time without dying of worry, negotiating with lawyers, paying their fees month after month, or maybe posting bond—I had no idea whether that was allowable in a case like this, or not—and drawing my family into the whole sickening, unresolvable mess, getting them all more and more deeply entangled in the life, death and identity of the repulsive, useless man at my feet, who was holding the head of the arrow thoughtfully, the red bubble at his lips collapsed into a small weak stream of blood that gathered slowly under his ear into a drop. Granted, Lewis was in more trouble than the rest of us were, but we all had a lot to lose. Just the publicity of being connected with a killing would be long-lasting trouble. I didn't want it, if there was any way out.

"What do you think, Bobby?" Lewis asked, and there was a tone in his voice which suggested that Bobby's decision would be final. Bobby was sitting on the same log he had been forced to lean over, one hand propping up his chin and the other over his eyes. He got up, twenty years older, and walked over to the dead man. Then, in an explosion so sudden that it was like something bursting through from another world, he kicked the body in the face, and again.

Lewis pulled him back, his hands on Bobby's shoulders. Then he let him go, and Bobby turned his back and walked away.

"How about you, Ed?" Lewis asked me.

"God, I don't know. I really don't."

Drew moved over to the other side of the dead man and pointed down at him very deliberately. "I don't know what you have in mind, Lewis," he said. "But if you conceal this body you're setting yourself up for a murder charge. That much law I *do* know. And a murder charge is going to be a little bit more than you're going to want to deal with, particularly with conditions like they are; I mean, like you've just been describing them. You better think about it, unless you want to start thinking about the electric chair."

Lewis looked at him with an interested expression. "Suppose there's no body?" he said. "No body, no crime. Isn't that right?"

"I think so, but I'm not sure," Drew said, peering closely at Lewis and then looking down at the man. "What are you thinking about, Lewis?" he said. "We've got a right to know. And we damned well better get to doing something right quick. We can't just stand around and wring our hands."

"Nobody's wringing his hands," Lewis said. "I've just been thinking, while you've been giving out with what we might call the conventional point of view."

"Thinking what?" I asked.

"Thinking of what we might do with the body."

"You're a goddamned fool," Drew said in a low voice. "Doing *what* with the body? Throwing it in the river? That's the first place they'd look."

"*Who'd* look?"

"Anybody who was looking for him. Family, friends, police. The fellow who was with him, maybe."

"We don't have to put him in the river," Lewis said.

"Lewis," Drew said, "I mean it. You level with us. This is not one of your fucking games. You killed somebody. There he is."

"I did kill him," Lewis said. "But you're wrong when you say that there's nothing like a game connected with the position we're in now. It may be the most serious kind of game there is, but if you don't see it as a game, you're missing an important point."

"Come on, Lewis," I said. "For once let's not carry on this way."

Lewis turned to me. "Ed, *you* listen, and listen good. We can get out of this, I think. Get out without any questions asked, and no troubles of any kind, if we just take hold in the next hour and do a couple of things right. If we think it through, and act it through and don't make any mistakes, we can get out without a thing ever being said about it. If we connect up with the law, we'll be connected to this man, this body, for the rest of our lives. We've got to get rid of him."

"How?" I asked. "Where?"

Lewis turned his head to the river, then half lifted his hand and moved it in a wide gesture inland, taking in the woods in a sweep obviously meant to include miles of them, hundreds of acres. Another expression—a new color—came into his eyes, a humorous conspiratorial craftiness, his look of calculated pleasure, his enthusiast's look. He dropped the hand and rested it easily on the bow, having given Drew and me the woods, the whole wilderness. "Everywhere," he said. "Anywhere. Nowhere."

"Yes," Drew went on excitedly, "we could do *something* with him. We could throw him in the river. We could bury him. We could even burn him up. But they'd find him, or find something, if they came looking. And how about the other one, the one who was with him? All he's got to do is to go and bring . . ."

"Bring who?" Lewis asked. "I doubt if he'd want anybody, much less the sheriff or the state police, to know what he was doing when this character was shot. He may bring *somebody* back here, though I doubt it, but it won't be the law. And if he does come back, so what?"

Lewis touched the corpse with his bow tip and put his eyes squarely into Drew's. "He won't be here."

"Where'll he be?" Drew asked, his jaw setting blackly. "And how do you know that other guy is not around here right now? It just might be that he's watching everything you do. We wouldn't be so hard to follow, dragging a corpse off somewhere and ditching it. He could find some way to let the police know. He could bring them right back here. You look around, Lewis. He could be anywhere."

Lewis didn't look around, but I did. The other side of the river was not dangerous, but the side where we were was becoming more and more terrifying to stand on. A powerful unseen presence seemed to flow and float in on us from three directions—upstream, downstream and inland. Drew was right, he could be anywhere. The trees and leaves were so thick that the eye gave up easily, lost in the useless tangle of plants living out their time in this choked darkness; among them the thin, stupid and crafty body of the other man could flow as naturally as a snake or fog, going where we went, watching what we did. What we had against him—I was shocked by the hope of it—was Lewis. The assurance with which he had killed a man was desperately frightening to me, but the same quality was also calming, and I moved, without being completely aware of movement, nearer to him. I would have liked nothing better than to touch that big relaxed forearm as he stood there, one hip raised until the leg made longer by the position bent gracefully at the knee. I would have followed him anywhere, and I realized that I was going to have to do just that.

Still looking off at the river, Lewis said, "Let's figure."

Bobby got off the log and stood with us, all facing Lewis over the corpse. I moved away from Bobby's red face. None of this was his fault, but he felt tainted to me. I remembered how he had looked over the log, how willing to let anything be done to him, and how high his voice was when he screamed.

Lewis crouched down over the dead man, a wisp of dry weed in his mouth. "If we take him on the river in the canoe we'll be out in the open. If somebody was watching he could see where we dropped him in. Besides, like Drew says, the river's the first place anybody'd look. Where does that leave us?"

"Upstream or down," I said.

"Or in," Lewis said. "Or maybe a combination."

"*Which* combination?"

"I'd say a combination of in and up. Suppose we took him downstream along the bank. We're heading downriver, and if we wanted to get rid of him as fast as possible, we'd bury him or leave him somewhere along the way."

Again, his idea fitted. The woods upstream became more mysterious than those downstream; the future opened only on that side.

"So . . . we take him inland, and upstream. We carry him to that little creek and up it until we find a good place, and then we bury him and the gun. And I'd be willing to bet that nothing will ever come of it. These woods are full of more human bones than anybody'll ever know; people disappear up here all the time, and nobody ever hears about it. And in a month or six weeks the valley'll be flooded, and the whole area will be hundreds of feet under water. Do you think the state is going to hold up this project just to look for some hillbilly? Especially if they don't know where he is, or even if he's in the woods at all? It's not likely. And in six weeks . . . well, did you ever look out over a lake? There's plenty of water. Something buried under it—*under* it—is as buried as it can get."

Drew shook his head. "I'm telling you, I don't want any part of it."

"What do you mean?" Lewis turned on him sharply and said, "You *are* part of it. *You* want to be honest, *you* want to make a clean breast, *you* want to do the right thing. But you haven't got the guts to take a chance. Believe me, if we do this right we'll go home as clean as we came. That is, if somebody doesn't crap out."

"You know better than that, Lewis," Drew said, his glasses deepening with anger. "But I can't go along with this. It's not a matter of guts; it's a matter of the law."

"You see any law around here?" Lewis said. "We're the law. What we decide is going to be the way things are. So let's vote on it. I'll go along with the vote. And so will you, Drew. You've got no choice."

Lewis turned to Bobby again. "How about it?"

"I say get rid of the son of a bitch," Bobby said, his voice thick and strangled. "Do you think I want this to get around?"

"Ed?"

Drew put the tense flat of his hand before my face and shook it. "Think what you're doing, Ed, for God's sake," he said. "This self-hypnotized maniac is going to get us all in jail for life, if he doesn't get us killed. You're a reasonable man. You've got a family. You're not implicated in this unless you go along with what Lewis wants to do. Listen to reason, don't do this thing. Ed, *don't.* I'm *begging* you. Don't."

But I was ready to gamble. After all, I hadn't done anything but stand tied to a tree, and nobody could prove anything else, no matter what it came to. I believed Lewis could get us out. If I went along with concealing the body and we got caught it could be made to seem a matter of necessity, of simply being outvoted.

"I'm with you," I said, around Drew.

"All right then," Lewis said, and reached for the dead man's shoulder. He rolled him over, took hold of the arrow shaft where it came out of the chest and began to pull. He added his other hand and jerked to get it started out and then hauled strongly with one hand again as the arrow slowly slithered from the body, painted a dark uneven red. Lewis stood up, went to the river and washed it, then came back. He clipped the shaft into his bow quiver.

I handed the shotgun to Bobby and went and got my belt and the knife and rope. Then Drew and I bent to the shoulders and lifted, and Bobby and Lewis took a foot apiece, with their free hands carrying the gun and the bow and an entrenching tool from the loaded canoe. The corpse sagged between us, extremely heavy, and the full meaning of the words *dead weight* dragged at me as I tried to straighten. We moved toward the place where Lewis had come from.

Before we had gone twenty yards Drew and I were staggering, our feet going any way they could through the dry grass. Once I heard a racheting I was sure was a rattlesnake, and looked right and left of the body sliding feet-first ahead of me into the woods. The man's head hung back and rolled between Drew and me, dragging at everything it could touch.

It was not believable. I had never done anything like it even in my mind. To say that it was like a game would not describe exactly how it felt. I knew it was not a game, and yet, whenever I could, I glanced at the corpse to see if it would come out of the phony trance it was in, and stand up and shake hands all around, someone new we'd met in the woods, who could give us some idea where we were. But the head kept dropping back, and we kept having to keep it up, clear of the weeds and briars, so that we could go wherever we were going with it.

We came out finally at the creek bank near Lewis' canoe. The water was pushing through the leaves, and the whole stream looked as though it was about half slow water and half bushes and branches. There was nothing in my life like it, but I was there. I helped Lewis and the others put the body into the canoe. The hull rode deep and low in the leafy water, and we began to push it up the creek, deeper into the woods. I could feel every pebble through the city rubber of my tennis shoes, and the creek flowed as untouchable as a shadow around my legs. There was nothing else to do except what we were doing.

Lewis led, drawing the canoe by the bow painter, plodding bent-over upstream with the veins popping, the rope over his shoulder like a bag of gold. The trees, mostly mountain laurel and rhododendron, made an arch over the creek, so that at times we had to get down on one knee or both knees and grope through leaves and branches, going right into the most direct push of water against our chests as it came through the foliage. At some places it was like a tunnel where nothing human had ever been expected to come, and at others it was like a long green hall where the water changed tones and temperatures and was much quieter than it would have been in the open.

In this endless water-floored cave of leaves we kept going for twenty minutes by my watch, until the only point at all was to keep going, to find the creek our feet were in when the leaves of rhododendrons dropped in our faces and hid it. I wondered what on earth I would do if the others disappeared, the creek disappeared and left only me and the woods and the corpse. Which way would I go? Without the creek to go back down, could I find the river? Probably not, and I bound myself with my brain and heart to the others; with them was the only way I would ever get out.

Every now and then I looked into the canoe and saw the body riding there, slumped back with its hand over its face and its feet crossed, a caricature of the southern small-town bum too lazy to do anything but sleep.

Lewis held up his hand. We all straightened up around the canoe, holding it lightly head-on into the current. Lewis went up the far bank like a creature. Drew and Bobby and I stood with the canoe at our hips and the sleeping man rocking softly between. Around us the woods were so thick that there would have been trouble putting an arm into it in places. We could have been watched from anywhere, any angle, any tree or bush, but nothing happened. I could feel the others' hands on the canoe, keeping it steady.

In about ten minutes Lewis came back, lifting a limb out of the water and appearing. It was as though the tree raised its own limb out of the water like a man. I had the feeling that such things happened all the time to branches in woods that were deep enough. The leaves lifted carefully but decisively, and Lewis Medlock came through.

We tied the canoe to a bush and picked up the body, each of us having the same relationship to it as before. I don't believe I could have brought myself to take hold of it in any other way.

Lewis had not found a path, but he had come on an opening between trees that went back inland and, he said, upstream. That was good enough; it was as good as anything. We hauled and labored away from the creek between the big water oak trunks and the sweetgums standing there forever, falling down, lurching this way and the other with the corpse, thick and slick with sweat, trying to make good a senselessly complicated pattern of movement between the bushes and trees. After the first few turns I had no idea where we were, and in a curious way I enjoyed being *that* lost. If you were in something as deep as we were in, it was better to go all the way. When I quit hearing the creek I knew I was lost, wandering foolishly in the woods holding a corpse by the sleeve.

Lewis lifted his hand again, and we let the body down onto the ground. We were by a sump of some kind, a blue-black seepage of rotten water that had either crawled in from some other place or came up from the ground where it was. The earth around it was soft and squelchy, and I kept backing off from it, even though I had been walking in the creek with the others.

Lewis motioned to me. I went up to him and he took the arrow he had killed the man with out of his quiver. I expected it to vibrate, but it didn't; it was like the others—civilized and expert. I tested it; it was straight. I handed it back, but for some reason didn't feel like turning loose of it. Lewis made an odd motion with his head, somewhere between disbelief and determination, and we stood holding the arrow. There was no blood on it, but the feathers were still wet from the river where he had washed it off. It looked just like any arrow that had been carried in the rain, or in heavy dew or fog. I let go.

Lewis put it on the string of his bow. He came back to full draw as I had seen him do hundreds of times, in his classic, knowledgeable form so much more functional and accurate than the form of an archer on an urn, and stood, concentrating. There was nothing there but the black water, but he was aiming at a definite part of it: a single drop, maybe, as it moved and would have to stop, sooner or later, for an instant.

It went. The arrow leapt with a breathtaking instant silver and disappeared at almost the same time, while Lewis held his follow-through, standing with the bow as though the arrow were still in it. There was no sense of the arrow's being stopped by anything under the water—log or rock. It was gone, and could have been traveling down through muck to the soft center of the earth.

We picked up the body and went on. In a while more we came out against the side of a bank that shelved up, covered with ferns and leaves that were mulchy like shit. Lewis turned to us and narrowed one eye. We put the body down. One of its arms was wrenched around backwards, and it seemed odd and more terrible than anything that had happened that such a position didn't hurt it.

Lewis fell. He started to dig with the collapsible GI shovel we had brought for digging latrines. The ground came up easily, or what was on the ground. There was no earth; it was all leaves and rotten stuff. It had the smell of generations of mold. They might as well let the water in on it, I thought; this stuff is no good to anybody.

Drew and I got down and helped with our hands. Bobby stood looking off into the trees. Drew dug in, losing himself in a practical job, figuring the best way to do it. The sweat stood in the holes of his blocky, pitted face, and his black hair, solid with thickness and hair lotion, shone sideways, hanging over one ear.

It was a dark place, quiet and almost airless. When we were finished with the hole there was not a dry spot anywhere on my nylon. We had hollowed out a narrow trench about two feet deep.

We hauled the body over and rolled it on its side, unbelievably far from us. Lewis reached his hand and Bobby handed him the shotgun. Lewis put the gun in and pulled back his hands to his knees, looking. Then his right hand went back into the grave, and he gave the gun a turn, arranging it in some kind of way.

"OK," he said.

We shoveled and scrambled the dirt back in, working wildly. I kept throwing the stuff in his face, to get it covered up quick. But it was easy, in double handfuls. He disappeared slowly, into the general sloppiness and uselessness of the woods. When he was gone, Lewis smoothed out the leaf mold over him.

From Alnilam

Dickey began what he always claimed to be his most significant novel—the 682-page Alnilam*—in the 1950s. His notebooks from the time are filled with discussions of its plot and characters. After the success of* Deliverance*, Dickey signed a lucrative contract for the novel with Doubleday in 1971. Although his original deadline was 1975, Dickey published his book in 1987.*

Alnilam*'s main character, Frank Cahill, has gone blind from diabetes. Nevertheless, he runs the Willow Plunge amusement park in Atlanta with his helper, a young Mexican-American man named Ruíz. With his ferocious dog Zack at his side, Frank travels to the wintery Peckover Army Air Corps Base in North Carolina in order to find out more about his estranged son, Joel, the charismatic pilot who died in a crash after flying over a brushfire. Among other things, Frank discovers that a group of zealous apostles—the Alnilam cult—has formed around his dead son to perpetuate his ideals. The first excerpt is from the novel's beginning, the second from the end where the Alnilam cadets (*Alnilam *refers to the central star in the belt of Orion) show off their apocalyptic tendencies at Peckover's graduation ceremony.*

Frank Cahill's Journey to Peckover Army Air Corps Base (excerpt)

From the first, living with the dog had not been at all hard. Cahill could still see well enough to shop and otherwise look after himself, and it was not much extra trouble to buy cheap meat, including horse meat—which Zack particularly favored, and Cahill himself came to like—to keep a pan of water in the kitchen, and to take the dog out a couple of times a day. Zack slept on a mat of newspapers near the front door: newspapers from which the print was being withdrawn, fading from the war, even in its largest headlines relayed from the deserts of northern Africa. His coming life in darkness, in the total explosion of the sun, was the only condition in which Cahill took interest. Zack's body and face—especially the hazel eyes that might have been tipped up from gazing over endless tundras and through the needles of lost forests of spruce, on the migrations of caribou through deep valleys to barren ground, toward but never reaching Asia—were the center of the world which was enclosing him more and more each day in storms of stars: storms of a centerless universe through which the dog prowled and prisoner-paced, full not of longing but alert patience, lying at night and bristling—Cahill's pulse quickened when his palm felt Zack's back-fur do this, and he slept more deeply whenever it happened—or delicately pawing the door whenever Cahill approached it from the other side. At first when they went out together Cahill had used a chain, and had let Zack range and explore, but pulled him back when he felt like it. Before long, though, he found that the dog stayed close to him naturally, and would come back if he went off. Since he needed a name to serve as a command, or as the alert to a command, Cahill reasoned that the name should be short and sharp, like a gunshot. Though he had never shot a gun, the idea pleased him, and at first he had shouted a simple "Crack" at the dog, who came quickly to respond to it and the force of Cahill's harsh voice. The command had gradually changed into Zack; there had been a local politician, much on the radio denying implication in graft, who had that middle name, and it did well enough.

When the pool and the rest of Willow Plunge closed, Ruíz usually came by and together they would work with the dog. From the beginning Ruíz had insisted on Zack as a protective force, and Cahill was not reluctant to attempt his "training" in this way, although two or three of the retired couples in the building were terrified by the situation and complained of it. But Cahill was going blind, blind beyond all help except what he could give himself, and that placed him beyond or to one side of the law; he knew that everyone who came into contact with him, from acquaintances to strangers, would sense this to be the case; it was proveable, and he was living it.

They began with the horse meat, sold by groceries for pet food, and with any scraps of animal matter that Cahill did not eat. Ruíz would have to be the villain and the victim, and their parts were always cast that way: Ruíz as the tormenter and frustrater, snatching the meat from the dog, teasing him with it, kicking him, at first lightly and later with more and more force, hiding from him and leaping over the gutted gray furniture of the apartment with Zack crashing over stools and ottomans to corner him, snarling and craving, and Cahill always as the benefactor, the rewarder and comforter, the being who spoke in sharp, explosive commands, and, producing food, dropped his voice and sighed, throaty with false compassion, as Zack ate, letting the meat fall from his jaws and snatching it up again, his eyes narrowed for Ruíz's first move in the sweaty light. At first Ruíz wore only his veined T-shirt, but as his forearms showed more and more cuts and scratches he put on a light jacket of artificial silk; after a weekend when the sleeves were left spotted with teeth of blood, he went to denim. The night sky of Cahill's vision packed its hurtling sparks closer and closer together, Ruíz snatched, grappled and fled day after day, and the summer heat began elsewhere to fail, though it still poured like stone-channeling water from Ruíz's cheeks and forehead, for by this time Zack was after him in earnest. Laughing quietly, Ruíz adjusting new garments on himself and, Cahill helping, discovering unexpected resources in fingers and palms, they swathed the Mexican boy in old blankets and ragged oil-dense mats, pulled from under cars in the apartment garage.

Now, feeling the highway curves waver and lodge in Zack's spine, Cahill thought of Ruíz and the muffled beating he had taken in the shredded blankets as he fended off Zack's rushes. A few days before his blindness was completed, they had finished Zack's indoctrination, not because of neighbors disturbed by the floor-shaking savagery of sound, but because Cahill—though not Ruíz—was afraid that Zack's jaws would really close with the strength of the full-grown dog, and no such proof was needed. It was better to wait, now, in a new calm in which Ruíz became a friend once more, cautiously taking off the weeks of bullying and mocking at the same time that he unwound the chenille blankets from himself, and the oil mats slid back beneath the cars.

It was time: time to pull loose the necktie and breathe more. "What's the matter with this damned thing?" Cahill said.

Tim's sleep failed as his armpits dampened. The bus was much hotter than it had been; the others were writhing. "Somebody open a window," he said. Then, "I'll do it."

A form rose from beside him and thumped and cursed at something beyond. There was a sudden grating slide, a slotting, stopped noise, and

"Good Jesus! JESUS! Now I've sure done it. I've *done* it! God damn *Almighty*.

"What is it?" Cahill said, drawing back.

"I caught my fucking thumb in the fucking window," Tim said in a low, choked-back scream. "I sure did. God DAMN! Look! Ripped it up pretty good."

"Sit down, son," Cahill said. He could say it. "How bad . . . ? I mean . . ."

"No bone," Tim said with underpowered control, but assessing. "Just about, though. It's filling up and starting to run. Pretty soon my hand's gonna be all over the place."

"Why don't you go ask the driver if he's got some kind of first-aid kit? They ought to carry those things."

"No," Tim said. "I'll be all right. You got a handkerchief?"

"Sure. Two of 'em. Let me see, son."

Tim put his hurt hand, clasped by the fingers of the good one encircling the hump-boned wrist, carefully on Cahill's thigh. Beginning at Tim's wrist, Cahill felt cautiously toward the base of the thumb. When he first reached blood, he stopped and began to feel in the pockets of his coat. From among coins and a crush of paper money he brought up the handkerchiefs.

"One clean, one sort of clean. All right with you?"

"Got to be."

"The clean one first. Washed it in my kitchen sink yesterday, and ain't had my nose in it yet," Cahill said. The cloth passed twice around the webbed V, and Cahill did what he could to draw it tight. When Tim's leg tensed against his, he stopped pulling, and held what he had. "I think we caught the fellow," he said. "At least most of him. I don't believe any more of him's gonna get out. Now if we can just hold him, we'll all be fine. You can see the base doctor, soon as you get in."

"You're fucking-A I will. That's good duty. There's been many a Purple Heart give to some joker over something that ain't this bad. They tell me the war's full of 'em."

Cahill tied the used handkerchief over the other, his fingers moving in the small moves that the knot required. These little operations are the rough ones, he thought: and here's going to be a rule about *that:* when my sense of feeling gets better than this, that's when I'm going to have a real advantage: that and the way I hear things. And they're both coming to me with everything I do, everything I listen to. There's not any end to the new way: anybody who can't feel and hear like a blind man just can't do what he can do, or know what he can know.

They rode that way, the boy's hand in Cahill's lap, the blind man projecting himself into the future, coming to stand in a room at first empty, then with people, where he could hear the distances on all sides, the echoes of ordinary sounds taking on their own kind of measurement as they reversed themselves at walls, bodies, and objects and came back to tell him—and no one else in the same way—where they were, what they had for him. Or he might find himself one day in some woods that hung on him a thin smother of rain, and a limb would fall, somewhere: would he hear it? He would hear that sound; he and the developing power of his ears would make it good: the tree it fell from and the woods themselves. The hand now on his leg would contribute, he was sure, to the sharpness and the correct imagination of his sense of touch; he had hidden its blood, buried it in his own cloth, and now he was keeping it safe, moving somewhere toward noon. His guess of time must be true, for into the stifling bus, through the tooth-hissing wheedle of the stuck window with its splinter of an opening, another kind of warmth, a down-shining one, rested on the back of his hands and wrists, delicate as the hairs that must be—used to be—growing out of them. The glass heat on his skin and the clothed ball of blood he held were now and again passed over, like a chance flutter of space-dark, by nervous fleeting shade, an intermittent reasonless shadow, and in this slatted and shuttering dance of temperatures he dozed off, sometimes alive in a dream of performing surgery or undoing complicated knots, and again in the deepest and thinnest rain of woods, listening for the limb to fall, in his hearing, into its only place in the world.

"This is you," Tim said. "Peckover. And don't ask me what side of the road it's on. I might as well tell you, though. It's on the door side."

"How's your thumb feel?" Cahill asked, lifting Tim's hand from his lap to the boy's.

"Numb. But it'll be all right."

"Sure. Keep the handkerchiefs. Dip 'em in the Rising Sun."

"I will, if they let you fight with pliers."

"Fight with what you got."

Cahill and Zack went forward unhurriedly, down and then out. The driver handed him his straw bag.

"Thanks," Cahill said. "I hope I get you next time."

"You just might. I'll look for you. When will it be, you think?"

"I don't know. Two or three days. Maybe a couple more."

"Like I say, I'll look out."

"Don't make a point of it. I'll know you."

He and Zack stood quietly, waiting for the way in which the town would say it was surrounding or facing them, and for the engine to die. When it did they still did not move, and stayed waiting in the cold, sunny silence that might have been that of one of the fields they had come through. No hinges, no doors, no metal-clank, no voice, though they faced a small two-story hotel that was also the bus terminal. Still they waited, four ears, going outward and alert, breaths steaming and eddying. After the doze of his images, Cahill half expected a far, discreet crash, or a near object crunching in snow. Surely if they stood long enough, something, a step or a branch, would reach the ground. If nothing did, they would take steps in whatever direction was forward from where they stood.

He took these, and whistled, hoping for the walls of a building. Instead of the banked-off return of sound he had hoped for, music appeared in his ears where he had expected something solid; this was part of "The Beer-Barrel Polka," and not from the open.

A press of warm air, already chilling as it reached his face, held a few voices not concerned with him. A slushy shuffle of movement ground underfoot, then gritted hesitantly before him on ice and

On both sides of the bus about equally, the town stretched out to its visible ends. The point that Tim had brought up about the side of the

concrete. "Hello," Cahill said, for the mixed voices had been closed off as the cold settled back, and there now must be someone outside with him, ready for what he would say.

He listened, on and on. No one said anything to him, and he thought it was probably because of his dog, pressed now against his leg with no feeling of impatience in him, waiting for Cahill to move.

road the town was on was one that this town could answer with no trouble: on the right if you're going north, on the left if you're heading south. Except for a feed store and a deserted, poorly steaming filling station, its two levels of gasoline caged in the wire of its pump tops, there was no town across the highway. On the station side, for three blocks apiece up and down, were a café, a palmist's, a small jewelry store, a dry-goods store, a grocery, and a pawnshop. When he turned his head to the north to listen with his better ear, Cahill's dark glasses flashed and glittered with the nervousness of bayonets and knives stuck through the pawnshop glass by the low sun concentrating there. Through the station door a civilian in a red-and-white mackinaw came forward and stood before the blind man, the suitcase, and the dog, whose breath was heavier and more composed in the air than that of the men.

"Hello," Cahill said again. "Who are you? *Where* are you?"

"Well," the other said, "I'm right here. This is the bus station and the hotel, and the rest of Peckover, North Carolina, is up and down from here but not back and forth. What can I do for you?"

"I'd like to stay with you for a few days."

"You can. We got three upstairs rooms, and you can have the one with the bathroom. You just look after that big dog, and you can have anything I've got for five dollars a day."

"He'll be all right," Cahill said. "He'll eat just about anything. I'd like to get him some meat every couple of days, if I could do that."

"We could fix that up, for sure. How long you plannin' to be here?"

"I'm not quite sure. No more than three days. Maybe four."

"The reason I asked you is that they're having class graduation out at the base on Sunday, and some people'll be coming up to see their boys take off and fly out of this froze-up chicken track of a town for good. But don't worry. You come on in, and I'll take care of them when the time gets here."

They went in, and, though no one or nothing touched him, Cahill felt himself crowded; there were a lot of voices. "Farmers and soldiers," the other man said. At the counter Cahill spread the pages of the book placed under him and followed his name across the paper, writing, he believed, very legibly. A boy, not a Southerner, was arguing short-temperedly with a woman's slow, self-righteous, and sullen tongue, which told him that his money would take him only to New Mexico but not to California; he reckoned that he'd risk it and hitchhike the rest of the way, because anybody these days would pick up a soldier, especially if he was carrying a guitar, wasn't that so.

The room had a big sagging bed, like the one he had just come from. He sat on the edge of it, talking and listening for spaces and objects.

"I got to apologize for the smell downstairs," the manager said. "Seems like nobody ever takes a bath no more. It's just awful in the wintertime. Can you smell 'em up here? I can."

"No, I can't," Cahill said. "I didn't pay no attention." He touched his nose at the bent bridge, which looked as though it had been sideswiped by a large, unremembered object, or pushed aside, but not contemptuously. "My smell's in and out. Sometimes it's damn good, when I pay attention. But mainly, too many car wrecks. Too much bad luck in the mills; once I got hit in the face with a seven-hundred-pound swingin' crane. Too many fights; too many fists comin' at me, all right at my nose. You can keep your soldier-stinks, your barracks and latrines, you can keep your frozen mule turds. What do *they* smell like, anyway?"

"They don't smell."

Cahill grinned. He liked this; the guy didn't embarrass. "Good," he said. "That's one thing I learned today."

"You done been playing in bad luck, buddy."

"Not so bad," Cahill said. "I can still taste. Some, anyway. I'm gonna work on my smell. I can hear good, and I can guess. And I can feel." He flexed his right-hand fingers. "Come here."

In the space above his lap he held out his hand and turned the palm up. The midsummer sun of Willow Plunge warmed it, burning from memory. "Put your hand in here," he said. And, "What's your name?"

The manager became conscious of the size of his tongue, which was larger than he had thought, and the relation between it and the whole act of eating and smelling. "My name is McLendon," he said. "Boyd McLendon. Some of those people you couldn't smell downstairs call me Boysie. Some but not all." He looked down into Cahill's big half-opened hand and its tracks; another's existence and whatever had made it. "What do you want me to do?" he asked.

"Just hold on," Cahill said. "Hold on for a second or two." He took the other hand, almost as large as his, and came slowly together on it. The sense of his physical strength, an undeniable thing, first given but mostly made, struck every vein in his body like snake poison; the barbells and spring grips of his park fed into his arm, and that arm alone.

McLendon's hand began to give back force against Cahill's. "I see what you mean," he said, offering to pull away. "You ain't ready to give down yet, old man."

"No, I ain't," Cahill said, another kind of strength, equally calm and equally deep, in his voice. He bore down; there were no limits; the huge sun filled his muscles as though they were Ruíz's after a workout of bench-presses and curls and a swim, his arm solid with meaning, world authority. A low sound came from Zack; dazed with himself, Cahill was startled to recall that one growl was all that the dog would give. He let up his grip. "No, Zack. No, boy. Get down. Down. Down. We're just playin'. Down, big boy. Take it easy."

McLendon threw all of the force he had in his body, all he had ever had, into his hand offered first as an act of accommodation, then of pride, but now of survival. Nothing helped. The knuckle-sinews quit bracing; they popped and gave up as McLendon gasped and struggled to get away. "Wait, now . . . good God, that's . . . THAT'S . . .

"That ain't so," McLendon said, holding his hand and feeling it in several positions with the other. "Playin', my ass. How come you to bear down on me like that? I don't see no reason. You do that every time you meet somebody?"

"No," Cahill said. "I'm sorry; it's not somethin' I do very much. And I'm sorry Zack scared you, if he did."

"I ain't gonna die," said McLendon, putting Cahill's bag by the scaling dresser.

"No, we won't die," Cahill said. "At least not today. Can you get sugar?"

"Sure I can." McLendon hesitated and said, "As much as I get rationed. Enough for me and my family and the soldiers and field hands down at the fountain. Maybe a little more. Why?"

"Cubes?"

"Yeah, I can get cubes. How many do you need?"

"Above a dozen would be all right. I only got two with me." He pulled the syringe box from his pocket and opened it. "I need sugar to fight this thing with. The needle and the sugar fight it out in my blood, see? Every day I can't let neither one win." Suddenly he shivered and clasped his elbows to his sides. "New match coming up pretty soon; I'm starting to sweat."

"Maybe it was the shit-assing around we was doin'."

"No; it's a different kind of sweat."

"If you want to stick yourself, I'll go on downstairs, and check back with you later on. Or you could call, whenever you want me."

"Stay on, if you've got a minute. I don't mind if you don't."

McLendon stood respectfully as Cahill went through the ritual of sterilizing the needle, filling the syringe, pulling up his shirt tail and injecting himself in the stomach, his head turned slightly as though it were looking into the hard, pale sky of the window.

"How can you tell when you've got the right shot?" McLendon asked, mildly interested.

"I can't always," Cahill said. "Have to wait a little while. That's where the sugar comes in. Or it might."

"How do you feel?"

"Feel OK. How far is it to the base?"

"Ten, fifteen minutes."

"Good. I might as well get on out there."

"I think you owe me something. If you can't give me back my fingers, you can at least tell me what you're doin' here. Then I'll drive you myself."

Cahill put a hand to his throat, held it there for a moment, facing McLendon's sound-position and the middle of him, then reached into the breast pocket of his coat and drew out a telegram. "This is what I'm doin' here," he said.

McLendon took the warm paper and unfolded it.

NEXT OF KIN JOEL WESLEY CAHILL PFC AVTN CADET
A/C 2027858 MISSING PSMD KILLED TRAINING ACCIDENT
ONE THIRTEEN NINETEEN HUNDRED FORTY THREE STOP
PLEASE CONTACT STOP DEEPEST REGRETS STOP

HOCCLEVE, COL USAAC RES
COMMANDING
LATHAM AAC PRIMARY TRAINING
PECKOVER, NC

McLendon gave him back the telegram. "So that was him, huh?" he said with a constraint he seldom used.

"It was. You-all must'a heard, around here. What happened? I guess they done found his body by now. This is the fifth day."

"I don't know what happened. Somebody said he went down in a fire; there was a big one twenty-five or thirty miles from here, just before it snowed. I don't know whether they found him. Nobody said anything to me about it. They'll tell you out there, whatever they can. But I sure do feel for you, big man. I sure do. He your only boy?"

"He was. The only live one; the only dead one."

"Let me know when you're ready to go."

"I'm ready now," Cahill said, as though this should have been obvious. "Why not?"

"Don't you want to hang up your stuff?"

"No need; it looks better baggy, they tell me."

"OK, come on, then."

"Come on, Zack," Cahill said. "Let's git 'em. Ho."

The three of them made their way down the stairs, leaving Cahill's door unlocked, and came out flat among the small group gathered at the ticket counter.

"Just a minute; I'll get you some sugar," McLendon said. He came back and nudged Cahill. "Where do you want to keep these?"

Cahill took the envelope and shoved it into his overcoat pocket.

"Let's go on around out back," McLendon said. "Won't take a minute. I want to sh . . . I'll introduce you to something you may not know about."

They went out and moved along the building. McLendon made as if to take Cahill's arm, but Cahill shook him off. "No," he said. "I'm with you; just go on."

They turned the corner and left the highway as a pickup truck pulled out onto it.

The air was perfectly still, and as Cahill passed it through his nostrils it drew itself very fine, as though being made into wire. Instead of holding his usual contact against Cahill's leg, Zack drew apart; Cahill half crouched and felt for him; the dog's hair was rising, and his body was tense with the vibration that came before a growl.

They were moving toward a kind of hood, a galvanized shed. Like many buildings in the country it had a kind of slapdash mystery about it: something of the garage, something of the storehouse, something of a place where an object or event had been long hidden and either forgotten or had ceased to matter. Anything at all could have been inside; without knowing, one would most likely have thought of bales of rusted barbed wire, old highway signs full of bullet holes, two work shoes that were not matched nor of the same size, and, somehow, a ruined hat from another climate.

"What is it, boy? What's getting to you?" There was a faint jangle of cold keys, then an uncertain slide, a grinding rotation, a click, a withdrawing, and a dangling thunk against larger metal.

"Come into my house," McLendon said. "This is where I *really* live; this is where *it* lives: what I want you to meet."

Cahill stepped forward into a closed chill not like the wired air he had become used to. This was an underground feeling; he thought of stone, and around that, deep earth. Zack swayed now against his leg, growling with hard, arched shud-

ders, and barked sharply once; twice. It was not stone that the sound returned, but the less deepseated resonance of steel or tin.

"I've been hunting all my life, and I've heard about these things but I've never seen one before this. Here, feel."

His hand aided by a light touch, Cahill groped downward: the back of the head of something. Cautiously he explored, losing the head for a descending maze of curving forms, graceful but sharply pointed at the ends. Following them now with both hands, Cahill traced a stiff, branching web in the air, and then stood up. "That's a right big buck," he said. "Eight points? Ten?"

"You ain't through yet. Feel this here other'n's mouth, now."

His touch again guided, Cahill ran the tips of his fingers along a ridge of hard bristle, then, directed more closely, reduced his hand to the forefinger and traced out a vicious, hooking semicircle of what must surely have been bone. Cahill stood in a testing crouch, forming the animal in his mind. "Lord," he said, "What is it?"

"Now, right here," McLendon said. "Feel this other jaw. How'd you like to get your balls caught betwixt them things?" Holding Cahill's finger on the tooth, he put the blind man's back on the antlers.

"You ever heard of a jackalope? Combination of a jackrabbit and a antelope?"

"No," Cahill said, grinning a little. "This is a mighty big rabbit."

"It ain't a jackalope. This is a wild doar."

"Door?"

"Combination of a deer and a boar. Some call it the original North Carolina Buddy'ro. You and me are the only ones ever seen one." He broke off. "I shot the buck in a cornfield day before yesterday. The hog was in a whole swamp of ice. Two other fellows was running him with dogs, and he come right by me. Sun was going down, and I couldn't tell what he was, but there was an awful lot of shooting at him, and so I shot at him, too. Before I dressed him out, he weighed four hundred and fifty pounds. If your big dog can wait, he can eat on him in peace." He paused, looking at Zack. "I'd sure like to have him for a catch dog. He'd run him down and hold him good, I'd be bettin'. But I reckon you wouldn't want to take a chance on your dog getting chopped up."

"There's not many things around that would want to try," Cahill said. "You better not live to see the day when he gets after somethin'. You wouldn't like to see it, even if it wadn't you he was after."

"I see what you mean," McLendon said, for Zack had put his head inside the gutted body cavity of the boar, and his muffled growls, still at the point of exploding but not yet quite out of control, gave the interior of the shed the choked and savage fury of a thunderous anger no one could expect to stand against.

With some trouble dragging him by the side hairs, Cahill backed the dog away from the boar, voice last. McLendon locked the shed, and they went back to the highway and the car.

"Don't play with no echoes," Cahill said to Zack, as McLendon opened the rear door for him.

"What? You talkin' to me?"

"Don't pay no attention; I was just mumblin'."

It was warmer now, as they drove. The lifting and falling fields around them were thawing; the snow would probably be off the ground, or mostly, by sunset. Now and then there was a stand of trees near the road that Cahill could hear in a quick solid whoosh, but there was mainly the sound of space, and once an aircraft engine that vied briefly with the car-sound and faded. But in the above-noise there had been something like a flurry of menace, a suggestion of pursuit, even.

"That's what we don't like," McLendon said. "Nobody's used to the noise. Same as with deer, you know: they never look up; they don't have no enemies above 'em, like in trees. Since they put in the base five months ago, everybody's been a little scared; the whole thing's so new. This town is just *here*. Nobody likes it especially, but we use it and we're used *to* it. All that's changed now. Everybody's nervous. The people at the base, the Corps of Engineers and the Air Corps, told us that all this would be fine for the town, but we don't really want their money, and we can make do without all them kids in uniforms. All we want to do is what we've always done—farm tobacco, go to church, go to Fayetteville shopping every now and then, drink a little, hunt a little, look at the fields, look at each other, and sleep whenever we feel like it, especially in the wintertime. Now all we do is keep lookin' up, and waitin'." He paused. "The accident with your boy was the first thing like that we've had. Now . . . I don't know where it's all gonna end. Some of the town ladies'a tried to set up a kind of cadet club back a ways from the station, and the boys come in and drink beer on the weekends. But there's only a few girls here in the high school and some more that work in the cotton mill back between here and Union City. That's about all the social life there is. It ain't good; none of it is any good. I'm more or less stuck here with high blood pressure, my restaurant, and my rent-rooms. I hunt, I sell bus tickets, listen to the planes at the base warm up in the morning, and look up when I go out, and sometimes when I don't."

"Well," Cahill said, thinking slowly, "your huntin' must do a lot for you."

"I like to go out by myself," McLendon replied. "I'm sorry I—well, took advantage of you about my deer and pig. And I'm sorry it bothered your dog, too; I shouldn't'a done that."

"There's nothin' to worry about," Cahill said. "Tell you the truth, it worked out fine; it was friendly, and that's how I took it. A little out of the way, maybe, but when you're blind, you get used to things like that. At first, everything that you thought you knew, and could use without no trouble, has got another side to it that you got to learn. But what goes out with colors, and all that, comes back in your ears and your hands, mainly. You start to put things together in another way and, just a little at a time, but more and more, you come to the notion that you can have the world be anything you want it to be, because it's all in your head anyway. You're all right, as soon as you tell yourself that you'll keep on drawin' the line between what you can use and what's liable to hurt you and this other place in your head that could be anything and *can* be anything; then you've got yourself a pretty good situation."

He sat forward and turned toward the other man. "You just gave me a new animal. I can still feel his horns and his tushes, and, far as I'm concerned, they go together and make up the same critter. If you hadn't told me, I would have throwed out my old seeing-eye judgment and wouldn'ta had no trouble believin' that the thing was what you said it was—some critter with big horns and long teeth. I can make a whole world for that thing, and put him in there with the others I've got. I like this . . . this doar partic'ly because, even when I could see, I believed that there was animals like that. Down home in Georgia there's somethin' people claim leaves a crazy track in the mud alongside of rivers; they call it a hog-bear. He's with me, too, but I've never felt him, so he's not as much with me as that thing you got hangin' up in your shed. The doar has just been made up, and made; he's true, now."

"Well," McLendon said uncertainly, "that's one way to look at it, I guess."

"Yeah," Cahill said, nodding. "It's the way I've got. I'll be ramblin' around in it and buildin' it up for the rest of my life."

They rode silently for perhaps another five minutes. Cahill was not a talkative man, but since his blindness he had felt, much against his will, the necessity of conversation. His usual tone was one of sullen banter; it would not have occurred to him that his continual bad-humored teasing was a means of self-protection, for he actually feared nothing, certainly not physical pain. But a great deal of the life of the blind is lived through talk, and must be; information is crucial, and Cahill had come to find that his truculence, by irritating his informants, interfered with his knowing what needed to be known, and made his day-to-day survival that much harder. He welcomed the boredom of riding silently, for by now he was tired of the defensive muttering that he still used with strangers, not wanting pity or any show of it. Dislike was better. For that reason he was a little surprised at the way he had just opened up to McLendon—all that about the creation of a new and private animal. Had he meant it? The bumps and irregularities of the highway became both comfortable and strange to him as he concluded that he could very well have meant it: that suddenly he was right about his situation and its possibilities, its forms of secrecy and power. He pulled his latissimus and trapezius muscles tightly about him, and gave himself with new confidence to the hidden flow of concrete.

Peckover Graduation Ceremony (excerpt)

"Now," he said to Zack, turning carefully to face the other way. "Now we're gonna go. We're gonna go there, big boy. Stay right with me, and don't run me into no ditches."

Slowly, one foot following the other, a hand in front of him, he moved forward toward the music, which blew in and out of hearing, and then came more strongly, little by little. At knee level there was a bush that stopped him, and he felt for the air around it, where there were none of the sharp small limbs that caught at him surprisingly, one prodding through his pants leg as though on purpose. "Where are the fuckin' trees?" he asked Zack. "Where are all them trees, supposed to be here?"

He hit one with his shoulder; his hand, fending off whatever might be there, must have gone past it. He stopped and felt the bark, and prized loose a piece, thin and brittle. "It's a damn pine tree," he said. "That means all the rest of 'em'll be pine trees, and won't be real close together." He patted the tree, worked around it with his hand on the trunk, making the shape, and went on from the other side.

He worked forward that way, from tree to tree, untangling his legs from the low growth, making mistakes he could not help, but moving toward the music that grew until the changes of air were not able to keep any of it from him.

But there were other things than the trees and bushes, and, because he knew, now, that he would not lose the music, he listened to the air for the echo of McLendon's rabbit cry which had been so piercing that it should still be there in some way. Had anything else heard it beside himself? Had the sound reached anything that would answer it? Foxes and weasels, threading through the brush where he moved cautiously, were nothing to worry about, or even to think about, while he had Zack with him. But above him, what was there? What might be there? What might be coming? He found himself listening for wings. Between the trees, when he had nothing to get hold of, when his only contact with anything solid was through his feet, he listened hardest. McLendon had said you never heard the wings until that one beat, right at your head, that seemed like it took the air apart. One; just that one. An eagle, hawk, whatever might be there, that might be coming to him, especially when he was in the open; when he was supposed not to know that anything was near him: then it would come, if it had heard the scream. The scream had been made, had gone out, was up there above him, and around him. Whatever might answer, level with him, at his feet or above him, had been spoken to. He tried not to feel the explosion of feathers, the one split of air, the claws locking into his head. In the silence between trees his fear and anticipation, his excitement, became astounding.

But the music was closer, and he came back to it. He could make out, now, the shunting blat of trombones, oddly funny, forthright and devious at the same time, and two kinds of drums, one steady and dependable and the other nervous, higher, small and aggressive. The drums, the larger drums, took over more and more; it was impossible for Cahill not to adjust his body to them in some way; not to move in time with them. "Shit," he said. "You'd think I was marchin' in a parade, out here, bustin' my ass on these goddamn trees." But that was not all there was to it. He thought of lines of boys: those that were somewhere in front of him, and others besides them, wherever they might be doing the same thing, or something like it. He would be there soon, he was sure, across from the ones that were in the same place as he would be.

"You can't expect the damn trees to do what you want," he told himself, moving where there were none, and in the full open sound of the band. "You might'a run out of trees," he said. "And you're gonna fuck yourself if you go past 'em, and end up out where everybody and his brother can see you. Don't do that. Don't do that, Cahill. Go back a little. Find what you done left, and stay there." He turned carefully once more, and worked forward with the music at his back. A trunk came to his hand—the knuckles of his fist, actually—and when he groped to one side of it there was another. He put himself between them, propped, and settled his back. "I ain't lost," he said. "I ain't lost." He leaned a little out into the music-filled space that the backs of his hands, while he had been there, had told him was sunny; there must be sun everywhere you could look.

There was still the music, steady and forthright; the instruments making the tune were loud enough, near enough to cut, even to hurt a little, the drums were striding with them. He wondered if the cadets were in line, maybe marching. Or were they standing still? He had only Shears's description of the movie, the other graduation, to

Directly in front of the closed main hangar, on either side of the small sturdy band, the cadets were grouped. In platoon formation, two lines one behind the other, the two classes were drawn up; the under-

make up what he could of this one. He worked his mind to make the picture stronger. He had his version of the other one, and it had more power now, given by the time since he had been in the shed with the cadets; it had colors, very bright reds and blues, sharp-cut, like the ones in a flag. Maybe this formation was like the one he had, the one he was watching as the real music, the music of this one, played. Yes, maybe this was like the other one; maybe it was not something like it, but exactly. Why not? Exactly; it must be exactly, as it was there, beyond the curving violent gold, the slashing shots of his disease.

He ran his finger under his collar. It could not possibly be hot out here, but the inner cloth was wet. Between his legs was wet, as if he hadn't had a bath in a week. He tried to concentrate again.

Why was he tilting his head back? He was through with his neck; no, he could still feel it: his neck was still with . . . still part . . . it was wet, his shirt was wet, his face was unbreathable. There is something in this tree. There is. We . . . I . . . somebody told it to . . . Right over me. It has come it is there something out of the air something from a long way off . . . feet . . . claws . . . it will shit on me . . . out of the air you can't tell it is there until . . . until it is . . . like I say until

graduate class, in olive drab, had its guidon-bearer almost against the corner of the mess hall; the boy could have touched it. On the other side of the band, under a large clean American flag, was the graduating class, in cracked and oiled leather flying gear, helmets and raised goggles, the sheepskin lining of their collars clean, but still not all the same color. There was a reviewing stand of fresh lumber, but not enough room between the hangar and the parked aircraft for a parade. A small group of civilians, mainly middle-aged or older, stood awkwardly bunched, past where the ranks of helmeted boys gave out.

Colonel Hoccleve stepped onto the stand, erectly climbing the three steps, and faced outward to the aircraft. He tapped the microphone. It squealed electrically as someone tuned, the sound very high and then fading off.

it is out . . . out of the air . . . everything is wet the inside of my mouth is filling up what is making . . . why is there so much spit I don't need it what is it for . . . Good God, what have I done to myself what do I have what don't I have what do I need . . . I need . . . it's not what I need but what I've got . . . the dark form swimming . . . the music from underground not this music maybe this music in the light green light . . . the gold light from the sides . . . shading the side of . . . shading green . . . the sides of . . . of under . . . the sides of under . . . Now . . . now what was it? No music: there were some words . . . somewhere . . . somebody was saying something . . . coming to him . . . coming out of . . . not far . . . not far away . . . not about the air . . . were they . . . were they for him . . . were they anywhere . . . were they everywhere? The fox? Dark body . . . green light . . . the moon balancing? The bubble in his hands? The eagle? Nails? One minute . . . one minute now . . . one minute in the air I think we can get it . . . over the lake . . . water . . . coins scattering . . . and words: words now. They were loud, but what were they? What language was it? He should know . . . he should be able to tell: he was not in a foreign country . . . a country a fence girls hitting another girl with a ball . . . a

"I hope you can all hear me," he said, and motioned to the technician to turn the volume up. It came up; too much. "Welcome to the graduation exercises . . ." the colonel roared, then signaled again impatiently. "Welcome," he said again in a steady, carrying voice, "to the graduation exercises of the second class to be certified by Latham Field, the Peckover facility of the Air Corps; of the United States Army Air Corps.

"This should be a good occasion," the colonel went on, friendly and respectable, the loudspeaker giving out his voice without variation, "a good occasion for all of us. We've got a nice day for flying, and we're going to do something that I'm sure you good people have never seen before, in this area . . . or anywhere else, for that matter." The speaker system did what it could to convey his humor; some of the civilians responded and relaxed. "The graduating class is going to do a full-scale flyover for you. Every operational plane we've got will be up. Up and over. Over the field, and over you. That's the main course, you might say. Later, though, I'll do some aerobatics, and you can get some idea of what the planes that these cadets will eventually be flying, in the last part of their training ca-

girl in the middle . . . a girl with one leg . . . a mirror and a rattlesnake: he was in another . . . he was . . . he was where? He was not lost . . . not lost. Music from underground. No more. No more. Underground . . . singing from . . . come from . . . sent . . . coming to him from . . . from green . . . from under . . . No more. No more.

Cahill slapped himself, trying to hit it and stop it, to strike down his running mind. He pulled his muscles up desperately, all over him. I stuck myself, he said. I must've done too much . . . too deep . . . too much of that stuff: too much in me. With all his strength he went into his pockets, overcoat pocket, jacket, pants. Good God Almighty, Jesus Christ in hell, he said, the images in his mind radiant with terror as they showed and fled. I got no sugar. I forgot to get it, God *damn* I forgot it McLendon forgot it I don't have none I'm going . . . I'm going to die I can't help it: no sugar I can't help it can't get it where will I get it. And then, showing almost clearly to his mind among the night swimming pool and its black figure, the swirl of blood in the pale sunny water, the one-leggèd girl, the new flag-colors that were part of everything, the moon and the carpenter's bubble, he saw the airbase as Shears had described it to him from the film, the rows of standing boys, the planes parked next to the mess hall.

reers, will be able to do." The colonel took a half step backward, and then returned to the mike, speaking more slowly. "These boys," he said, "these cadets in formation here, are like the boys you *were*, and like the boys that some of you, perhaps, have known, *do* know, as their parents; as their grandparents and cousins and friends. The fact that they are in uniform, the fact that they are learning to fly aircraft in preparation for wartime service, does not make them any different from the boys you know: those who farm, who go to school, who play on your football team here . . ." He broke his line of thought and raised both hands . . . ". . . and now, while I'm at it, how *'bout* them Rattlers! I saw every home game, I'll have you know!

"Zack," he said, down from himself. "Zack. Come on, big boy. We can't stay here . . . we got . . . we might could . . ."

He stumbled forward toward the words, whichever ones were there . . . wetness from his head . . . his mouth maybe . . . stringing from him. He knocked it away, ropes of it away, with his hand, slashing in front of him, going through it.

The ground is . . . the ground is mixing . . . my sweat has all this power, now . . . no airplanes in their sounds . . . no long one wing with snow all the way out of sight . . . no window where the snow . . . where the sound . . . where the engine . . . the wing . . . the long wing all the way . . . out . . . out of . . . "Come on, Zack," he said. "Come on big boy . . . get your head out of your . . . get out of . . . get out of town they don't . . . get out . . . come on boy, let's get out, you and me . . . they can't . . . them others can't . . . soft ground. Now . . . now hard. Why? Hard now under . . . different."

He held himself; stamped his feet on the hardness. His mind focused for an instant. Under the rac-

"So, I want you to think about these boys that're going to be over your heads in just a few minutes: I want you to think about them as"—he paused and the drama was real; the civilians knew it—"as though they came from here, from your schools and your farms, from your stores and filling stations, from your mills and churches." He paused again. "It's your boys who are going to be up there." The colonel got ready to step back.

"Remember, now," he said, "that what you will see is part of a war: a total war, a world war, and remember that we're in it together. Some of these boys you see here will die." He hesitated, then pulled up and surged. "But not today. Today they're going to show you what the Japanese and the Germans are up against; they're going to show you what Hitler is up against." He stepped back, and some of his words, the important ones, were lost, though he said them. "You and me and these boys, these cadets of the United States Army Air Corps. Here they go."

ing strikes of self-flame through his eyes he saw the field again; the still aircraft, the mess hall next to them, seeming to be part of their line. He raised his arm and struck a vector through the air. "We've got it, Zack," he said, and then again, nearly screaming. "We got it, Hoghead; we're gonna get it. Right yonder it is; it's just right over yonder." He started forward again, in the direction of his arm, trying to stumble as he had been doing, but now there was nothing to stumble over except his feet, and he started to do his best to keep them apart.

Stathis Harbelis, in the rear cockpit of his aircraft, raised as on a porch, concentrated on his instruments, his preflight procedures. He went over everything again; he cracked the throttle a hair with his left hand; with his right on the ignition switch he waited for the underclassman—some new boy, a fat kid—to wind the inertia crank up to a pitch where the engine would take it. He listened outside also, for the others, but there was only the concentration of the other crank-whines centering on his, discordant, mechanical, more and more a sound that could not be stopped, that could not stop or lower of itself, but must be broken off, broken into by something more violent, with more strength and purpose, more authority.

He was on bad ground again he was on soft . . . he was on dirt he must have been wrong . . . he should go to his left no he should not . . . right he must go back he must get more to his right he might be going around . . . just around he had not lifted his arm . . . he had not lifted his arm in the right . . . his right arm . . . go back . . . there is not any way back . . . what was in the trees now what might be over

his head had the bird . . . had the eagle the hawk come . . . had the owl . . . the bird come out of the night . . . come forward from the next night? . . . and now . . . and now it was not mixed . . . his feet . . . his feet were one thing again . . . on one thing: hard. Hard. He could go on: just keep the thing hard . . . keep his feet hard . . . keep going he was going . . . keep going . . . he must he would . . . "I will," he said, "I'm going to . . . I'll . . ."

There is this whine made by the fire . . . by my head . . . by the . . . the fire . . . by flying . . . by eyes . . . by fire flying . . . by underground . . . by . . .

A blast, a roar took him, an explosion in one ear, and others behind it, backing it, joining.

He stopped, and swung his head, centering the new sound nearly taking him off his feet, brought it face on, and stood holding it there, as he could. "We can't go that way," he said, he hollered above the roar to Zack. "We got to go . . . we can't go there we can't go straight at it . . . whatever . . . wherever it is . . . we got to go . . . we got to go to one side." Again he lifted his right arm, and pointed, he was sure, to one side of the noise. That was it. That was the way. It must be the way. With his hand out, but not a fist, he started. The dog

Though he did not want to be the first, though he did not want to be the one to break the concentration of high desolate sound, Harbelis turned the switch; his own sound was already tuned; the fat boy's weight hit the ground and he wrung the switch more, ready with the throttle when the engine bucked. It did, and caught, and almost simultaneously another, and then several, and then a whole eruption of machinery in both ears, before and behind and all around.

The engine—his engine—was set in his hands; the brakes were in his feet. But he was afraid—a fear that found him easily—to look outside, where control was . . . where there would be no con . . .

Inside the brain-shaking roar of his and the other engines, a blasting impact, an impact that had begun as a tearing, a pull-through or shearing rip he thought was part of the one-sound of machinery, struck in from his right, and close: closer than any engine, he was sure, just after its searing scream and BLAM hit him not through the ear but through the shoulder. The aircraft to his right was tail on to him; it shook and stood:

brushed his leg. He felt and had the fur somewhere. He nudged again with his leg side for the body, and to the side . . . along the deafening side of it he was right he was dead right, he moved again.

He was not farther from the sound it was worse . . . there was a central mass of it clashing . . . a whicker and sizzle over it and through it . . . something touched . . . something a whiff or flick something else at his side at his leg pressed against him it was gone another whiff at his arm another at his neck he grabbed his collar and tore it loose the rest of the way and was hit not hard but glancing a hard lick but he had been hit harder he would not go down stumbling trying to go forward . . . went . . . to one knee went he was down he must get up Zack he called in the roar Zack come here come on boy I need you . . . where . . . everything came over . . . he was crawling where his open hand flat hand was under . . . crushing . . . crushing itself . . . weight is off it . . . weight off pain . . . bad . . . very bad . . . he rolled the sound and what was in it rolled him over he spun he tried to spin on his back find his . . . tried to reach his knees found them in air that was . . . in air whirling straight into his face . . . he could not he would not let . . . on his from around it came another, and with wounded and hysterical power, its whole left side gutted, Harbelis saw in a shot of sight as it turned and came straight at him, engine to engine. He gasped without hearing himself, but flooding with air, breath, he kicked loose the brakes, stood on the left pedal by reflex, and gunned the engine. His body leaped—what he was in leaped—having nothing to do with him but carrying him, and the oncoming engine slanted it would not come would not meet his, would not: he jarred, the other engine hit . . . had hit, caught his wingtip, turned, he turned—was turned—he had the thing though, it would turn with him, he could move it with his hands . . . his feet would move it everything he had would move it. The slam and shear of metal and fabric changed in every direction: at one side of his front view one aircraft turned over another and seemed to want to squat on it, the propeller beating back light. His cool heart pounding, Harbelis maneuvered around it. From the other side another plane bore down. Harbelis slewed, changed where he was going and was at the edge, looking in, his brakes on, engine cut back. Nothing came to him, nothing came at him from the locking, stammering yard, the unfocused deafening clutter of metal moving into itself, trapped and assaulting.

knees on one knee now getting up . . . on his legs full of strength he stood there and now he had he had his fists with him they had to come to him God damn you, he screamed into the roar, God damn you, you mother-fucker, come to me, God damn you into the wild whickering and blasting, Come to *me* God damn you let me get at you let me get *at* you.

He was there; he was still standing. He could scream anything he wanted, and keep on: he could scream louder, a little louder; maybe more than that.

He would not fall, no matter . . . he would not. He flooded through himself, and fell.

He got up.

An enormous wind was in his face. He would not fall, would not go down again, they could not make him.

He would not fall it was closer, great with air, almost solid he had

He looked out, where he could easily go: onto the athletic field, where a single plane chased a running figure, bowled it over, went past it. Harbelis turned back into the other planes, and charged.

In: he was back in: *in* it, here: he slewed and gunned toward what would be, would go across him, head toward. Swerving, he slung his tail section into the wing of another plane, staggered, whirled in place, gunned again almost to full power—going for enough to take off—and rolled toward another aircraft waddling slowly, quartering away, already slatted and gilled with rips, helpless with escape; Harbelis closed on it, sighting through his prop, centering on the rudder wagging with indecision, had it, smashed into it with the gray circle of his prop, scraps blowing past him now like sparks, chewed into the other craft until it almost stopped him, took almost all his forward motion, pulled free with power and one brake, and rammed the throttle forward again; full forward. He hunkered, then sprang . . . into . . . into a space forward of him where he could . . . No: something else: a figure: someone not in an airplane . . . out of . . . not in . . . somebody had got out . . . was trying . . . was in front of . . . a black shape . . . head and body down . . . went down . . . gone and another, lower form he could barely see . . .

better . . . he had better fall. He went down. Unfair but down. Unfair Zack he said, come here come here Zack where . . . ? He got up, groping right and left around him, trying to feel in a circle around his knees. He had it but not still it was not still it was going something went from him past . . . away from him for good past him and gone. Zack, God damn it, he screamed, Zack come on don't . . . don't do it you can't . . .

I won't go down *this* time I won't. He was hit again he was touched, he was down he rolled over and was on a knee again . . . the same knee, feeling for the low air around him for Zack he said he screamed now: Zack he yelled in the clashing and ramming noise, feeling for the dog head.

Ground, cement, and gravel. One place like another. Around himself this way . . . that way around himself . . . nothing . . . cement . . . little rocks . . . sand. Now

see for an instant just under him, came to him with a speed great as his, and could have been on him, a fury past anything human, teeth set in other black: in a stamp-print of vision there and gone. Harbelis screamed; jerked back the throttle: a slash of red across the windscreen and over him went as he ducked into the cockpit to awaken but could not as another body hit his, behind him and he fought to get clear, swiveled the ship to get out; this time truly out.

. . . he had . . . he had Zack by the . . . by the lips, had him by the teeth, the teeth even and long his head was sideways in his hand . . . his hands but it was Zack the long teeth locked come on big boy, he said I got you now they can't they can't do he pulled the head to him and felt for the fur the thick fur of the back let's get on up from here he said, let's get up, Anvil-head, you big fuckin' Hog-head, let's get on out of here gravel and sand wet this way not over here back to where the wet was found it and trailing backward strung from the head there was something, wet the head on his chest in his arm was wet he was wet his chest was wet his pants were wet he got up with the head the head with him he got and stumbled on himself he lurched he was going the noise was to one side of where he was . . . one side that's right it should be right it should still be right . . . going . . . going with it . . . come on big boy I got you we're going with one hand I got you I ain't goin' to turn loose of you I'm right with you we're gonna get there I know where . . . we're gonna . . . come on I'm with you.

His hand hit something solid. Board. Board. Board, Zack, he gasped: the thing's standin' up. With his free hand he found a corner, the corner of a building it could not be anything else. He had it, he could go around it he had done it before he could do it: his hand on it, he had it, and followed, followed.

Colonel Vernon Hoccleve, in his silver AT-6 with the canopy open, watched from the place where he had just seen two aircraft that had seemed to fight over a man's prone body kicking on the ground, the propellers a weave of blades over him, and had seen the man get to his knees and then to his feet, cradling something, and lurch clear, while one of the aircraft that had stood over him, its engine wide open, made what looked like an attempt to guide the man . . . the figure . . . away from the mass of conflict, the berserk wilderness of aircraft, herded him, nudged him at least once with a wingtip, and was now sitting beside him at the prescribed forty-five-degree angle to the runway for preliminary warm-up, his PT-17 streaming with fabric, part of which was under its wheels. He and the cadet glanced once at each other, and not again. Neither raised a hand above cockpit level; neither showed a hand to the other.

Inside the mess hall, Pfc. Robert Sorbo, Permanent Party, permanent KP, from behind his GI bucket, still holding his mop, went to the door that was pounding and shaking, and the screaming that was there, saying over and over, sugar, sugar, you son-of-a-bitch. Sugar, I done come for it. Sorbo pulled the lock. The door burst in on him and a man covered with blood, his legs wet as if he had been wading in a creek, his eyes rolling crazily, carrying the head of a dog with a long blood vessel twined halfway around him, as he took one more step and went down said Sugar again, pleadingly, almost apologetically, as Sorbo turned loose the mop and caught him.

From To the White Sea

Houghton Mifflin published Dickey's last novel in 1993, a little over three years before he died. Dickey again revisited his military experience, this time by way of Muldrow, a tail gunner who is shot down during a firebombing raid over Tokyo in the latter part of World War II. The novel, like his previous two, describes an epic journey. Muldrow travels north from Tokyo to the snowy island of Hokkaido in the Japanese archipelago. Having departed from his home in Alaska's Brooks Range to fight in the war, in his own mind he is going home because Hokkaido reminds him of the frozen wastes of north Alaska.

Dickey once again traces a questing hero's—or antihero's—rites of passage into the sort of violent, predatory, "adult" world that shocked Dickey when he confronted it during World War II. His protagonist, who was deliberately modeled after the serial killer Ted Bundy, is as crafty as he is demonic. The two excerpts come from the first part of the novel when Muldrow parachutes into burning Tokyo and learns how to camouflage himself and kill in order to survive.

The Firebombing of Tokyo (excerpt)

A little after fifteen hundred the trucks came for us, and I climbed in with the rest of the crews. As it turned out, only nine planes were making the strike, which meant there was likely to be more fighter concentration. I told the Florida boy, who was riding with me, that we'd have more to shoot at, but it didn't seem to make him feel any better. As for me, I was pretty well rested, and ready for whatever might be up there. The mission would take around fourteen hours, which is a lot of time to sit and think, with nothing going on most of the time. When we got to the ship I stretched and loosened up, and felt over myself for my gear. I had a .45 and two clips, my emergency kit and a can of C rations, and my knife, down there where it should be. I stretched some more and said hello to Major Sorbo.

"Ready for 'em, Ace?" the Major asked me.

"Not an ace yet," I said. "Maybe tonight."

Along with the others I got in, then went back to my station to see if everything was exactly like I had left it. It was, except that somebody had put a tarp cover over the pile of chutes, and I couldn't think of any reason I might need to take it off, though I would've liked to check the one chute that was taped down. I was more or less sure it was all right, and I got in behind my guns, hooked my suit up to the electrical system, and plugged my headset into the jack. After a while Major Sorbo started the engines, and we wheeled out to take off.

The back end of an airplane is not one of the worst places in it. There were at least a couple of yards between me and anybody else, and it was like I had all that section of the plane to myself. When I called in on the preflight check, Major Sorbo might have been back in the States, he seemed so far away, off in another part of things.

We took off, and I settled in against the side of the plane until we got up past the Jap picket boats, and the night fighters scrambled and got after us.

That new gunner, the Florida boy, had got me thinking with his questions, and there was not any reason I couldn't just go along on the same track, just to have something to do. I had left off when I was telling him about the icebergs, and I started in now, thinking about them like I remembered. I looked out through my plexiglass, and it came to me that clouds and icebergs were a lot alike, because they were beautiful just like they were, and there was no use to them at all. There was no reason for them to be like they were, and have the shapes that they did, except that that was the way they happened to be, for nothing.

Where my father and I had lived was on the lower side of the north slope of the Brooks Range, in a kind of a draw that kept off most of the wind. It was easy to follow the draw on down to the flat country at the bottom of the mountains, and it was also easy, more or less, to stay on the slope where you could see more, down under you. We had most of the traps along the slope, in different places from the flat up until it got too steep. We had our best luck where there was some slant, but not too much. My mother died before I ever knew anything about her, and my old man, who was originally from Virginia, got hold of the land up there for almost nothing, learned to make out with weather and the traps, and as soon as he could he brought me over from Barrow, where I was born, to the cabin. I never did go to school, at least not when I was young. My father taught me to read and write and what he'd been able to learn about staying alive up in that country. He had his own reasons for being there, which he never did get around to telling me, or that I ever really understood. It may have been he got into some kind of trouble, back in Virginia or somewhere in the States, though I don't think it had anything to do with the law. But something had happened to him that made him want to be by himself; or maybe he was just that way all the time. Like I say, he never did give me the straight of it. But he liked it up there in that place, where you hardly ever heard anything but the wind, and where anybody who didn't know how things were could get lost as quick as he could take five steps.

But I was brought up in the snow. Until the time I was fifteen, I used snowshoes more than I used my natural feet; my feet felt wrong when I took off the shoes. My father used to tell me I was half snow goose and half wolverine, and before I was more than ten or eleven I was showing him stuff that I'd picked up by myself, rambling around all over, as much as I could, from Teshekpuk Point to the Colville River and back. In all that time I never saw but one wolverine, and my father never did see one; he'd just heard the stories about them, like the other trappers. But I was proud of mine, which I saw on the gut pile of a down caribou, because I knew then that the wildest animal in the world, the one with the most stories about him, the most bad and strong magic of any of them, had looked at me—looked right at me, for a good half a minute, through the feather snow. That was enough. I'm glad my old man thought of me like that.

It bothered me that I had told the Florida boy anything. He had probably already forgotten everything I'd said, in the time-wasting time before the mission. But what I knew, I knew. Wherever it's cold enough, I can get along. Snow and wind are right for me. Dark weather is right. Nearly everything about the cold is good. The cold-weather birds are the best to eat and the prettiest by far; there's not a bird in any jungle that can compare with them. The cold-water fish are better, and stronger, and taste like fish ought to taste; the cold water makes the meat good and firm. And I love fur, and the animals that grow it. I like to sleep in a fur parka with ice all around me. Eskimos, the Nanamuit in our range, at a town there, Anaktuvuk, showed me how to cut the slabs of snow and ice, fit them, and seal them, so that you've got yourself a real quick strong house. When you get in there, you don't need anything but your parka. It's all good; you're OK.

I nodded back against the airplane, took off my glove, and felt the aluminum. But it was the wrong cold. The cold of high air is not real, it's not honest. Cold should be connected to the ground, even if it's at the top of a mountain.

I eased back again and started to move with the caribou from the tundra through the tree line into their winter range.

I looked at my watch. It had moved some, more than I would have thought. We were probably past the picket ships by now. I got into position behind the guns, and as soon as I did, the Major called and told us we were over the Kanto Plain, and that we could expect fighters. We all knew the Kanto area could scramble a lot of them.

I charged both guns and fired off a few rounds, and then leaned forward and watched and waited. I had a way of doing things that was about half the Air Force's and half mine. When I came into gunnery school, it took me time to adjust to the way you set up the lead when you're in an airplane and the target is another airplane. I had shot with a lead all my life: birds, caribou, rabbits, you name it. But I had never shot at anything that was moving when I was in something moving myself, and for a while it threw me, threw me off. But there's really not all that much to it. If you're in the tail of a plane, you've got real good visibility.

In the daytime you can see anything that's close enough to shoot at you. At night it's a little different, because the other aircraft has to shoot first, before you can tell where he is by his guns. That bothers some people, but there's no need for it to. Usually the fighter will open up before he really gets into the range where his guns will do him any good, and when he does that you've got him, because when you see those gun glitters, you put together a couple of things and set him up. According to which side of you he's on, he's got to put his inside wing down and the other wing up to get his guns on you. If he's on the right side of your plane, the starboard side, he's got to put his right wing down; if he's on the port side, it'd be his left wing. When that happens you've got the situation you want, because the line that maneuver puts him on is all in your favor. It's like the fighter was sliding down a string, and he is; he can't shoot at you unless he is on it. All you have to do is put your sight in front of him, according to where he is on the curve, track with him, and let him have it. My favorite shot is two widths of the sight ring—two rads—down to one. I let him have a three-second burst, right in there. But zero rads is not bad, either, when he's dead behind you, and usually under you, before he breaks off and down. When he's at zero rads, you go right at him, right into his teeth with the fifties, and you can make him live hard.

So I waited for that. We were close to the bomb line, I was sure. The bombardier didn't have the plane yet, and the bomb bay doors were not open, but there was that tension you always feel all over the ship when the time comes close to drop. There should have been fighters, and there weren't any. The part before the bomb run felt all right, but the rest of the situation didn't.

Then something hit us from underneath. Or, more like it, something hit *at* us, like it blew up the air right below us. "Hold on," Major Sorbo said, real loud; I believe I could have heard him without the intercom. "We got to leave this altitude. Hold on."

The 90 millimeter had never been on us this early before, not with the first crack of ground fire; it usually took them a lot longer to get us bracketed. We began to lose altitude, and I sucked on my tongue to clear my ears. We leveled out, and even before the half G of pull left me, I saw the sparkle of a fighter. Like always, he was too far off. He had showed on the port side of us, and I kept that in mind, and swung the guns. Then he was close to us, much closer than I would have thought, and firing. I fired back, but wasn't on him. I didn't think he hit us, though—at least not bad.

Another fighter showed on the same side, and this time I was ready for any rate of closure he might have. He fired again, and was in range, and hit us a little somewhere up the fuselage, as near as I could tell. He fired again, and this time he was on his curve. I led what I figured was two rads and cut loose. Nothing happened. I waited a second, until I judged he was point-blank line astern and below, and cut loose again, all three seconds.

The whole sky lit up. I must have hit his tanks, because the explosion was all over the place, and he was gone. I asked the Major if he had seen the plane blow, and he said yes, everybody did, and get off the horn. I went back to watching for guns, but I was not really satisfied with myself, because I had been wrong on one or two points, and I never had before. The two fighters I had credit for had been knocked down in daylight, but the other three, which I know damn well I got, were at night. I know, because I do aerial gunnery in a certain way. I don't shoot at the plane, I shoot at the pilot. Or I shoot where

I think he is, according to my feeling about it, which is like guessing, but not quite. You know that the pilot is halfway between his guns on most fighters, and right behind them on the others, and you just estimate that. When he fires at you from his pursuit curve, his guns have a relation to each other, a tilt, an angle, so that you can more or less tell how fast he's coming down the string. You feel, you guess, and then you fire. If he fires a little before you, you try to nail him between his guns, but when he's in close range, I try not to let him do that. I shoot before he does, by guess and by God. But all the time I'm going for the pilot, not the plane. The thing inside that I shoot by—guess or God or whatever you might want to call it—tells me when I'm on. The four confirmed kills that I had were hit that way; there was no blowing of the tanks, no fire. They were confirmed because they were going down out of control, and the people on my crew could see them, and some of the crews on the other ships could, too. I nailed the other three at night the same way, but the planes didn't explode, nobody saw them go down, and I didn't get credit. But they went, same as the others. I led them in; they came to me, came right down my throat. I fired on that split second, and they were gone. Long gone, I'm telling you. I know what I'm talking about.

At the new altitude we went into the bomb run. The bombardier, Lieutenant Madison, took over the plane, and we steadied on through the run, getting off the two-thousand-pounders and the payload of incendiaries we had, maybe as a warmup for the big raid the Colonel had been talking about. It's always a relief when you get the bombs off the racks and out of the plane. Major Sorbo circled us without drawing flak or any more fighters, and I could see two fires, one a lot bigger than the other, where we had hit the city, or the other planes had. It was an easy enough run so far. We were supposed to have dropped some two-thousand-pounders, some incendiaries, and some frag bombs on the Kiba area of Tokyo, the waterfront, and we had, and now we could pick up the home heading and get out of there.

The next thing was not fire, though later I realized that it had to do with fire, had fire in it, but it did not seem like fire that was separate from us, or that could have been to one side of us, or above or below us. No, it was like the inside of the plane had exploded and we, each one of us, had exploded. It was like we were *inside* an explosion, or maybe we had exploded from inside ourselves. That's as close as I can come to saying it. Major Sorbo was just coming out of the turn for home when it happened.

When I could think, I saw that I was over the butts of my guns. The wind was knocked out of me, but I could move all right, and I held on to the strap of my seat harness and turned around.

The plane leaned up on one wing like it was going into a turn, but it kept leaning. Nobody could have been controlling it and making it go any such way. Then the nose went down, and I knew we were completely gone; everybody on the flight deck was probably dead. One of the waist gunners, I think it might have been the Florida boy, was stretched out right in the middle of the air, his arms and legs going wild trying to fetch up against something solid, to get hold of a chest chute. Then he was gone—on the floor, on the wall, the ceiling, I couldn't tell. Equipment was flying all over the inside of the plane. You couldn't tell what anything was, except that I saw a chest chute bounce off one wall and a hand reach out for it and miss, and the chute was not there, or the hand. We were nose-down now, spinning, the wings going around the airplane.

"Man, I am here," I heard myself say, and it didn't surprise me too much. I unbuckled from the seat, and just as soon as I did I banged against a wall. But I was holding on to the seat-strap web, and I kept holding on to it, and worked my feet forward into the plane. I got banged around a lot, swinging like a clapper in a bell, but I caught on to another web strap—it must have been one of the ones for storage—and pulled on toward where the chutes had been, and the hatch was.

The chute I had taped was still taped, the only one there, and I pulled it loose, and, one hand after the other, holding to the strap with one hand and buckling with the other, I snapped the chute to my chest, over the emergency kit, everything going round and round, faster and faster.

The hatch was only a few feet farther on, and I scrambled and twisted along to it, and pulled the pins. The hatch stayed. And then the only lucky thing of the night happened. The ship yawed like it had been hit again, and swung me on the strap away from the hatch, so that I could get my feet around. When the plane swung back the other way, it swung me, too, and I hit the hatch with both feet, with everything I had.

It was gone. I could see the sky whirling outside the hole in the plane. The air would knock your teeth loose, but it was outside air. I had my door to the open, and I went out through it, and had the whole thing, the whole sky.

The first thing was the cold, but like I said, not the right cold. I was tumbling—sometimes I saw stars and sometimes I didn't see anything, anything but black—and the wind seemed to whip the air out of my nose sideways. But I could see enough to tell that I had some altitude, enough to open the chute, and I waited a little to figure the best way to do it. You're supposed to be facing the ground, with your head a little lower than your feet, when you pull the chute, so that when the lines pay out and the chute opens, the risers will swing you under, and you won't get that terrific grab up through the crotch, that might be bad in a lot of ways. I spread out my arms to try to stabilize, and it was as easy as something in a dream. It crossed my mind how out of control the plane had been, there at the last, and how easy it was to control the way I was falling, and for a second it seemed to me that a man ought to be able to fly without an airplane.

But that was dangerous: I could have held on to the notion too long. I felt for the handle, and took hold of it with my right hand, though I hated to pull my arms back in; I was half believing they were wings. Dangerous, like I say. Then I put my left forearm across my face, because with a chest pack the risers whip right across your face when they come out, and pulled.

Something stuck. I pulled again, and it still stuck. I pulled again, hard as I could, and the handle came away. It felt like I had thrown loose my whole arm, thrown my arm away, but I was still falling, turning over from the position they'd taught me. What the hell, I thought; that's all I can do.

I was shot, through the armpits and between both legs. There'd been a loud pop, a crack like a rifle, and I was sure I had been hit. My face had taken a lick, too; I felt of it, and it was wet on one side.

But the chute was open. I looked up at it, and started to make my thinking include it, and the reason for the cracking sound, and the new hurt under my arms and between my legs. The chute. It was the chute. I was in a very big, quiet place in the middle of the air, and not shot. Not shot. I couldn't get rid of the idea that I had been.

I looked around from my float, from my big wide calm place in the middle of things. Swaying back and forth, I concentrated on the situation. It was the first time I had ever tried to concentrate and sway at the same time, and it was not a bad feeling, though I wouldn't want to do it every day.

Right under me was dark, but to my left was a lot of silver, very beautiful, too. Water, sure enough. It went way out, out into the moonlight as far as I could see. I was not far from all that silver, and I started to wonder about where I would hit. Breaking a leg was not part of my plan, but you can always do that in the dark, and I couldn't see anything right under me at all. I felt for the risers, because I knew I could control where I hit, or control it to a certain extent. But I didn't have anything to sight on except the water. I think I could have slipped the chute enough to land in the water, just barely, but what would have been the good of that? I didn't need to be wet, I needed to be on the ground with no broken bones, dry and figuring.

Even though I couldn't see where I was going to come down, I was not near enough to the ground so that I couldn't spill part of the chute and make a move, a little move, in any direction I wanted, but it was the dark or the water, no matter what, and the more I thought about it, the more I wanted the land. How close to the water, though? How close to the docks, or whatever was there? I didn't want to land on top of a building that I couldn't get down from, or on somebody's roof, if I could help it.

I was getting closer. I could hear a siren, a lot like the ones the Air Force has. I looked inland toward the fires. The smoke came past me, and there was cordite in it from some of our bombs. About a half mile from me there was a lot of stuff burning, and I hoped that would keep people away from where I was going to hit.

I was still high enough to get a fairly good view. I could see the docks now, and the ocean spreading out in another way from the first way. Between me and the water there were some big shadows, tall, thin, and bent, and I could see through them, see the ocean, like silver cloth that's been slung out and ruffled and sewed together with black thread: all that, on the side toward the moon.

Quicker than I would have thought it could be done to me, there was a terrific clutch up between my legs. Under my shoulders, too. My shoulders stopped where they were, and so did I, jigging up and down in the harness, wondering what the hell. I must have still been fifty feet off the ground, and I was hanging. Not hurting, but hanging, and could have swung myself if I'd had a mind.

I looked up at the risers. The chute was collapsed and hung up on something, one of the things that made the long shadows, maybe, or were the long shadows themselves. Though there were not any lights, I could make out the space between the buildings and the water, and I couldn't see anything that looked like a man. If I could get down without anybody seeing me, I could go on to whatever might be next, on my own.

But I couldn't just hang there in the smoke, which was colored with red and seemed to have some kind of wind that came with it, shifting back and forth, turning one way, then back the other. I felt down in it with my feet, felt around on all sides, twisting in the harness, trying to make contact, but there was not anything there for me. I pulled on the risers to see how my strength was, and I had some. I started up the lines, arming it out, hand over hand. When I reached the bottom of the nylon, like a sheet half off a bed, I went past it to where the chute was caught, and felt for what it was caught on.

It was a gantry, a loading crane, I was on, and at least fifty feet from the ground. Holding to the metal, I unsnapped the chute and was a lot freer, just in a second. I worked up the crane and out the arm to where the chute was caught, and cut it loose. A backswirl of the crazy smoke-wind caught it, and it disappeared, collapsing, toward the buildings back from the docks. I housed the knife, crawled head-first back along the arm, and started down the main body of the crane, not hurrying, but little by little, watching and listening all-out. The crosspieces of the thing hurt my feet pretty bad when I put both of them in the same place, and on one section I just had to slide down one of the main beams—shinny, kind of—but I did it. Getting to the ground was something I could tell I was going to be able to do, by now. When I got to the top of the cab, I turned loose all the beams and struts and looked around, and there still wasn't anybody there.

I saw a ladder on the cab, and I used it. The ground was level cement, and full of power. I leaned against the wheel of the cab, in the shadow away from the moon. The smoke was still blowing, though maybe not so much, and somewhere in it, down the dock from where I was, I heard voices, and they were coming. I hit a stillness, a new stillness like a marmot's, and two little men came by, shorter than me even, almost transparent with smoke, talking right into each other's face. I hadn't had time to find the chute, and I hoped they wouldn't notice it, wherever it was. I had my hand on my knife but didn't even crack the blade to light, to any sort of light. I didn't want to give light a chance at it, even though I was in the shadow of the crane. They went past till I couldn't hear them.

Using every bit of cover on the dock, I went looking for the chute, and finally found it spread and crumpled over some barrels and boxes, like it was making a display. I bundled it up and shoved it under the boxes, piled some other boxes and crates on it, then walked back a ways toward the crane—it was friendly—and tried to size up the situation, decide what to do. I really didn't have any notion just then; just a feeling something like the one I got when the guns of the fighter sparkled and I knew he was on the pursuit curve; a feeling that was a kind of guess but not completely; a guess with another thing added to it, something I didn't have a name for. I didn't want a name. It was not words.

What did I need? Where the bombs had hit had been concentrated in one place, I had seen from the chute, but the smoke was fading off now and I couldn't hear any more sirens. In other words, I couldn't bank on people having to deal with the fire. And the bomb drop was only in a small part of Tokyo. Since I hadn't seen any night watchmen on the ocean side of the docks, I thought I might have a look down the streets between the dock buildings and try to find out what they went into. I edged out past the corner of the warehouse nearest to the crane, looked as far as I could toward the city, and then started down that way, in the fullest and longest shadows I could find. If I saw a single person, I would turn back and try something else.

I got almost to the end of the building, and could see a little way into the blacked-out blocks, when I heard voices—not one or two but a lot. A whole crowd went by the end of my truck alley, talking fast. There was no light but moonlight, but I could make them out against the cement of the street and the light-colored buildings on the other side. I couldn't have dealt with them. I had no odds going for me.

Using the same shadows, I went back to the dock and to the crane. What had bored me before, the words of the Colonel at the briefing, all his talk about fire, came up in my head, and all over me. Fire was what I needed, fire from my own side. I needed a whole city in panic, a lot of confusion, as much as there could be, and things would be different. I didn't know when the raid would come, but I knew that it would be soon. Soon. Maybe a day, another night. I would find a way to wait it out.

In the first shadows again, working from one crane to the other, I made it to the end of the dock and just stood paying attention, all the attention I had, to what was there, to what was only a step or two away, or might have been in a few more. Where the docks and the warehouses gave out there were more docks, more warehouses. But I was interested in the field between, and what happened when it came together with the water.

There was no ladder down. I couldn't tell exactly, but I judged it was not far to the ground, though. I hung by my hands off the edge of the concrete, and dropped.

I hit almost right away. The field, whatever kind of ground it was, was slanted toward the water, and I didn't count on that, and hit wrong and fell. I rolled and had my knife out and ready to come up, but there was nobody around. Since it was out, I took the satisfaction of watching the blade flash off the moon. I looked around and did it again, and the satisfaction was as much as anybody could have wanted.

I could see a lot better, too, and I won't say that it wasn't because of the knife flash. Steel that good, and the ocean, that big silver light full of thread—well, you can't tell what might happen. Like I tell you, I believe in things like that. It don't matter why.

The field was set against the water by a kind of wall, cement—a breakwater, I think somebody called it. I inched along the top of it on my belly, like a lizard, running my hand, trying to feel if there might be some kind of hole in it, some place I might be able to wedge into. It took a long time to do it, and I really hadn't come all that ways from the docks when I felt into something, something not concrete, but hard and wet. I smelt of my fingers and knew where they'd been. Using one of my matches, letting it burn nearly all the way down to my fingers, I got a good notion of what was there: a sewer pipe that fell off into the ocean, big enough to hold a man; not running too much, but some. I let myself down and put my feet in.

The smell put my eyes out. I mean, it hit my eyeballs like the worst light, and one that would never quit. My eyes, you know, and that was not meant to be. But it was a hole, and I could go on into it if I wanted to. I took out another match and lit it, though I knew that sewers could blow up. That would be something else, I said to myself, to get out of a B-29 on fire and blow yourself up with shit gas. But nothing blew, and I went on up amongst the squishing shit and other stuff, to where there was a turn, where I was damn sure nobody would come. To do it, they'd have to come the same way I had, and I couldn't think of anybody who'd do that, not even the Japs, no matter what. For one day, maybe for a day and a night, I had shit and safety. What else, I asked myself, what else have you got a right to ask for in the enemy's own damn country, his main city? What else?

I broke back out, and the big air was good, I tell you. The moon was higher, and the stars were so strong they seemed to be blasting light at me, like studs or screw heads that had that kind of power. I broke off a stalk of something from the field and marked the sewer, and started back along the breakwater, this time standing up. So far, things were working. The whole thing was working, right where I stood, where I walked along the silver ocean of the Japs and looked out over the big sewed-together bay.

When I got back to the crane I had a sudden thought: how quick could I get to the pipe? I looked at my watch and took off, running light as I could along the front of the warehouses, my moon shadow in front of me. When I hit the end of the dock I took off, right into the air over the field, like I was trying to jump from the cement loading slabs of my dock toward the other one off as far as I could see, and I hung up there over the field-dark for the longest time, almost like being in the chute again, except that this time it was just me instead of a lot of harness and nylon, and when I hit this time I didn't fall. I found the stalk of stuff I'd left at the edge and let myself down into the hole and swung in, my eyes stinging.

I came out again and went back to the crane, listening for night watchmen but not all that much. It was two-thirty in the morning. I didn't have any notion of sleeping in the shit pipe, so I climbed into the cab. It cut off the wind and had a big seat, big enough for two people. I took the control handles, set them off from the seat, and stretched out. I didn't know when they went to work on the docks in Tokyo, but I figured I could get at least a couple of hours of fresh-air sleep before anybody came. Before that, I would hit for the pipe.

I wanted to sleep in control, and not just like some desperate guy with no chance. There were certain things I had, and I knelt down on the floor of the cab and went over them, holding the matches down below the windows.

My knife I knew about, and left it alone this time. I laid out my .45 and two clips. There was no telling where I might use them, but it would have to be either in a place where nobody could hear or in a situation with so much noise and confusion that nobody'd care, or even notice. I thought about the Colonel's fire, and decided that I would wait a day or two in the whole concentrated stink of Tokyo, crammed into a little pipe, for them to bring the fire: for them to bring the fire, and make a situation where I could operate.

I needed to get outfitted, and that meant I needed some clothes different from a wired-up combat rig, a flight suit underneath it, and GI brogans. I couldn't last long in Tokyo, either in daylight or at night, in what I had on. If the fire came—*when* the fire came—I would go out with the .45 and get what I needed.

I broke open my emergency kit and spread the stuff on the seat, wondering what situations might come up where I'd use it—use this thing and then that thing. There was a little knife that I could use for little doings, like cutting string or scaling fish. There was a packet of fishhooks and some twine. There was a silk map of part of Japan, like a handkerchief printed with a topo layout of Japan up to the strait between Honshu and Hokkaido, and another piece of silk that had an American flag on it, and writing in five or six different languages; the intelligence officers told us that Japanese was one of them. I couldn't read them, but all the crews had had to memorize what they said: *I am an American aviator. My aircraft is destroyed. I am an enemy of the Japanese. Please take me to the nearest American authorities. The government of my country will pay you.* Like I say, I couldn't read any of this stuff, but I looked at all that writing, in Annamese, Burmese, Thai (it said), French, and Japanese, and I struck a blank wall on whether I should keep it. I looked by the match light, before the match went out, and tried to make a decision. But it was funny, anyway, and I think I laughed right there in the cab, and real loud, too.

It was quiet there. I sat on the floor of the cab with my things on the seat:

gun, bullets, fishhooks, map, blood chit with all the languages, and leaned back against the metal of the wall. Nothing, nobody, could be more out of luck.

Muldrow's First Murder (excerpt)

Even in the situation I was in, I couldn't get over the smoke, the way the smoke acted. In a low red light that was over everything before I even realized it was there, the smoke would all of a sudden stir itself, whirl around, and cut one way or the other. It would jog and slant, and settle, then jump and swirl again and go the other way, or come right at me. The incendiaries were hitting everywhere, in front of me and on both sides, but nothing else behind me; there was no more heat on my back. Now, though, as I got closer to the streets, whenever the smoke would blast one way or the other with the bombs—it was hard to believe those quick jumps and jogs were not something the smoke was doing to itself—I could see fire, low fire, buildings and not just white phosphorus twisting in the air, down the street I would be on if I kept running and came off the field and didn't turn.

Through the blasts of smoke I got into the crowd, making the turn to be in their direction and slowing down to their pace, which was a kind of fast shuffle. I couldn't tell much about the people, even the ones who were right next to me, except that they were women, a couple of them with babies. There was one old man bent over like a squirrel. I just caught a glimpse of him, and then he went down under all of us, and we went on over him, on past him.

The smoke in front of us stopped, stopped dead, and then came back and hit us square, face-on. Then I was on top of somebody on the ground, and there was another one on me, or maybe two. I rolled a woman—I'm sure—to one side and got my feet under me. The others were getting up, and it bothered me that I might have stood up too quick and would show my difference, even in all the confusion. The new fire was right in front of us, on both sides of the street, and all of a sudden I looked down, because something was wrong. The zipper of my flight suit caught the light, and caught it strong just for a second, and without any pain I had the notion that I had been gutted, ripped right down the middle by fire, by lightning maybe, and that I was dead from it; that I had come out on the other side alive with another kind of life, still holding the print. I bent down again, and got up slow with the others. Nobody had noticed a thing. We started, and turned off into another street, the smoke jumping and slanting with the bombs. The sound of the crowd around me was made up of high yells, all you could put up with, but around them all was the low sound, which must have been coming from the whole city. How all those high screams could have added up to that one low tone, like a glacier when it first begins to calve off, was not something I could explain. It must have had something to do with the buildings—echoes—all those voices beating back and forth off the walls. Maybe, but I don't know.

On the second street the smoke was bad, even worse than on the other one, and for the first time I noticed how terrific the heat was, and steady, not just near the fires we could see. I kept as close as I could to the woman in front of me—for a while it was the same one—so that my zipper wouldn't show in the flames, but I knew I had better do something about my clothes while I could. I looked around as much as I was able, and I started to figure, in there shuffling with the rest of them, sweating like a thaw, and adding up what I had with me.

I was sure glad I was a great believer in tape. My bread knife was riding down my leg, almost a part of me, just as much in place as it had been in the Quonset hut back at Tinian, and the emergency kit was square in the middle of my chest, breathing with me, and ready to do all the things it could do, from cutting wire to stripping down vines and cleaning fish. I had my .45 and one extra clip, and that was something I could use in what I needed to do; wanted to do, you might even say. It was one of those kind of times. And there was a war on, too, as the Colonel and everybody else used to tell us. That was all right with me.

In the building we were going by there were plenty of doors, some that shut on the street and some that went back a ways. I was interested in the deep ones, and I looked along the left for what I wanted. There was hardly any sidewalk, and I could be in one of the doorways in two pushes and one big step, or two at the most. There were a couple of men in the crowd now, on the side I was edging toward. They were ahead of me, but one of them was about my size, and I figured that there would be more than one to come along later, when I was ready. And I had noticed something else. A lot of people, even the babies, had things, some kind of bandages, over their noses and mouths, like doctors in hospitals; like some of the ones at the base hospital at Buckingham Field, when I was in there for the trench mouth I got from eating GI food; I used to see them go by the ward. That would help, not only now but later on. The officers in indoctrination, in the course we had to take called The Nature of the Enemy, told us that a lot of Japanese wore those things all the time, even when they were not in an air raid. And, again, I knew that would help, and that there was more advantage I could give myself once I had picked out the door.

And there it was, so deep it might have been an alley. I slid and slanted and jumbled over through the women, and then made my two steps, one big and the other more or less ordinary, and I was in. I backed up some more to get the shadow, and got it all, all I could use. There was plenty of time now. Plenty of time, and good conditions.

I felt my face. I had shaved before the mission as I always did, because the oxygen mask fits a lot better that way, and my beard hadn't even begun to grow out. But that was not what I was thinking. I ran my fingers along the wood next to me and looked at them, and the tips were black; the smoke had sooted up everything. I took a good smear of soot off the boards and went across my forehead with it, then more down my cheeks and nose and around my mouth. As the color of my face disappeared and went to another color, there was something inside me that changed, too. It moved, and then sat still. In my mind there was a shape I couldn't exactly make out, but it seemed to be in a crouch, pulled up into itself and ready, and that was the feeling I got from the soot, the stronger the more I put on. I did the back of my hands the same way, and then concentrated on the crowd going by, screaming and moaning, and not one of them even giving a flicker of a look toward me. Millions of them could have gone by, and none of them would have seen me. I was dark now, the same as the shadow I was in. Some of the people were pretty smudged up, too, but I had not made myself like them in any way; it was just that now I wouldn't stand out. I was not like them, I say again; like something else.

I had another thought. Working with little moves, I pulled out the blood chit, the silk handkerchief with the American flag on it, and all the languages—Japanese was one of them, which I couldn't get over—that said that my aircraft was destroyed, I was an enemy of the Japanese, that my government would pay anybody who'd help me. I turned the flag and the writing to the inside and tied it around the lower part of my face. Almost everybody I saw had on a mask or cloth, and now I had mine.

It was time. I zipped down the flight suit and took the .45 out of the holster. I hit the clip with the heel of my other hand to make sure it was seated, and then let the safety off and charged it, and at the same time I brought the crouching shape up front in my mind, and had what it wanted me to have. There was not a flicker of light on the gun barrel. I put my free hand on the wood next to me to get steady, and all at once it jumped and shook. I figured the second story had caught fire, or somewhere up above me had, but I couldn't see for the smoke. On the other side of the street the fire had already come down to the ground floor; I could tell by the crowd edging toward me. In there amongst the people, and close to me, I looked for my size.

About five yards from me a man, I think, went down. The crowd went over him. He tried to get up, but before he could make it to his feet somebody else tripped over him, and this time neither one got up. Out of the smoke another man stumbled, and in a second I knew he was about right, about what I needed. For some reason the two that should have been on the ground were not there, maybe had been shoved off to one side by all that panic, all that pressure, but the one I had my eye on was still stumbling where they had been, correcting, you might say, trying to get his feet all the way under him, and I let him have a couple more steps. He came right to me, like every animal or bird I'd ever shot, or like the Nip fighters sliding down the string of the pursuit curve. If you want to kill something, have it coming toward you. If it comes without knowing you're there, it's the best way of all. I stood up in the doorway and came up with the .45 and shot him right straight into the face, at the same level as mine. I didn't want any blood on the clothes, or any holes. The sound of the gun was hardly any louder than the general noise, and the muzzle flame was just one more little bit of fire, exactly like all the rest of it, and gone quicker than you could think.

The blast knocked him back, the shock—a .45 at close range is like a hand-held 30.06—and he went down, with the two or three other people behind him. I doubled into a crouch, watching hard. The others scrambled back into the crowd and left him, all but one guy who pulled him to the side, and then moved with the others again. The clothes I wanted were lying about half under the feet of the people on my side of the street. He had been dragged a yard or two by his feet, and I couldn't see his head; the others were swarming all over him, to get on. Nobody turned back.

I holstered the .45, stepped out, and then went down on my knees amongst all those feet; they were going by me like they were going by the dead man. I took him by an arm and a leg and hiked him up on my shoulders, like I was maybe going to carry him on with the rest of the crowd, wherever they were going. But all I did was take two or three steps and lurch back into my door, then rolled him off and rolled down beside him.

I stayed there still as I could, then reached a hand. The building was roaring over us, and pieces of wood, some of them big and heavy, were falling faster and faster, and I thought that maybe the whole thing was going to come down on us in the next few seconds. I hoisted up to my knees and took hold of the middle of myself, under the throat, pulled down the zipper in one sweep, came out of the flight suit in a couple of moves, and started pulling off the dead guy's coat and shirt. They were all right by feel; even wearing them over my dungarees was not too tight. The pants were good enough, too, but the shoes were too short. I couldn't come near getting one of them on, sitting in the door frame now like I was doing, not too much different from the way I would have back in the Quonset hut.

I stood up and took one last look at the guy. The top half of his head was gone, but with the fire flickering on him and the ground smoke swirling in and out of the door, he didn't look too bad right then. His hat had been blown off with his head, so I would have to do without it, but I had a crew cut anyway, and my hair is black, so it didn't make all that much difference. It would not be a bad idea to have a hat later on, and some other shoes, but I knew I couldn't stay where I was any longer. The building was going to go any second, I was sure. I balled my flight suit up and flung it into the fire. Nobody was going to look at my feet. Breathing through the blood chit, the American flag, I stepped out.

It didn't take me long to pick up the kind of shuffle-stumble the crowd was moving with, screaming and moaning. For some reason all of us turned a corner, away from the docks, and just as we did there was a crash inside all the other noises—a terrific crash inside the big moaning sound the whole city must have been making—and a building fell in. Whether it was the one I had been in I can't say, and it doesn't make any difference, but I think it probably was. People kept shoving in from the side streets, and we were pushed closer and closer together. It was hard enough to breathe through the smoke, but all that being pressed on made it a lot harder. For a spell there I didn't have any doubt that I could raise my feet up off the ground and the rest of them would just carry me along. It would be better for me to work myself out to the near edge, on the side I had come in from, but still stay amongst them, and not separate myself out, even if I'd been able to.

From Crux (unpublished novel)

The novel that Dickey began during the last years of his life, Crux, *was intended to be* Alnilam's *sequel. Because of his illness, he worked erratically and only completed about thirty pages of the manuscript. In* Alnilam *Dickey dwelled on his hopes, disappointments, and fantasies of revenge surrounding his failed bid to become a combat pilot during World War II. At the beginning of* Crux *he focused on his experiences after washing out of Primary Flight Training in Camden, South Carolina, and being reclassified as a radar observer.*

The characters in Crux *first appeared in* Alnilam, *but now Dickey uses them to trace his own quixotic journey from training base to training base—aerial gunnery in Fort Myers, Florida, to radar instruction in Boca Raton, Florida, to radar practice in Fresno, California—before boarding a transport ship for the war-ravaged Philippines. His plan was to show how the Alnilam group took over the whole Pacific night air war. The drama of the novel, he said, would arise from the conflict experienced by the Alnilam group in serving two masters: Joel Cahill and the U.S. Army Air Corps.*

Journey to War

Where they had been; where they would be. Or almost.

Harbelis fined down the ocean to the place alongside; he did not need the rest of it. Rise and be with, he might have said, had been saying to himself since they fell and went under the first time. Break out and fly again. They came, rose enough for themselves, a thousand fish skimmed on air as they could. For a moment or two their space moved with the ship. Harbelis looked more closely, and, liking this, more involvedly from the gun-stanchion he was backed against; this might be the one time. How is it possible they could do this, and not gain altitude if they wanted to? They must leave the water on their speed, he thought. Just speed and slant. Then what? Now they were gone again, and Harbelis began to wait for them to break out once more, as he had been doing for the last two hours. On a troop-ship there was nothing else to do except try to make sense out of whatever you could see; to watch it, and think about it. He believed, he could not help believing, that their fins must be something like feathers, though the membranes did not flutter, or do anything to keep them up. He wished he could see their faces, especially when they left the water, and when they were ready to fall. It would not be bad, either, to see them while they were in flight, two inches airborne, free, all in formation.

They broke; there just enough. Now he would add one thing to them, each time they rose. One thing. They flattened into their pattern, the sun catching everywhere on it, one spark to a fish. Or it could be a contest of some kind: not to get somewhere first but to go farthest, stay, hold out for most time in the air? Was the same one always in front? Yes, it must be, it must be that way, Harbelis thought. Why not? Joel had said that you fly in the stuff you breathe. He would have got the parallel quicker than I did, Harbelis was sure. Thousands of fish not made, really, for flying, but they did it. They fly like we do, who are not made for it either. Don't breathe it but fly in it. He remembered what had been said about the B-26, the Martin Marauder, which on the drawing-board was not supposed to be able to fly; wing-loading too out of proportion. But it did fly and it does fly; 26's are all right, *Stars and Stripes* said; the crews swear by them. In Italy, especially, they were doing good. Word gets around.

Not fly. Quasimodo would not fly, but it did. The Hammer Field flight line at Fresno was long, the other end out of sight if you stood north and looked south. Down there, though, past even the parachute shack and Ordnance Supply, the dusty and patch-painted P-61 sat, awkward, put-together-looking, like an oversize P-38 Lightning that had lost its clean predatory lines, the twin tail-booms wretchedly large, the rudders a mistaken oblong, as if the shape had been invented to be useless. Most of the replacement crews had wandered down to it, often groups of them; the only relief came when somebody who had been to college explained that the name meant half-made, or more-or-less made. Anyone could understand that; all he had to do was look. "Who'd want to go up in that thing?" an RO had asked. "Don't worry," Hultgren told him. "It'll never get off the ground." Then added, "It's experimental." "Back to the drawing-board," another said, and walked off. There was not any reassurance in knowing that the P-61—"Black Widow," yet—was the first American aircraft developed specifically for night fighter work, and that all combat units were now in transition to be equipped with it. None of them had ever been in a P-61, or seen it fly. The thing had wings, though, and two big Pratt and Whitney R-2800 engines. And 720 radar, too, the RO's kept pointing out: a screen; no time-base line. You could see the target move and come in; you could talk it in, call it to you. That would be power. Call, and it would come, right down the web. Black Widow was maybe a better name than a lot of people thought. Overseas the 61 would be different from this model; it would have to be.

"Quasimodo," Harbelis said aloud to himself. A Radar Observer is a half-made pilot; or half-ass. We've been at the controls, though, at least a little. Blazek is my pilot, my full-ass pilot. Good; you bet. He went back to the fish. They were up, acres of shimmer; each had its sun, then quenched it.

The same thing will take you only just so far, he thought next; those fish could fly me clear to New Guinea, and I wouldn't know any more than I found out when they first hit the light. But if they brought Quasimodo with them, and the flight-line at Hammer Field they can go backward as well as forward; they can fly me from New Guinea to Fresno.

Lieutenant Aaron Adler was at the rail, looking at the ocean. He had been there for a while; Harbelis had known it and not known it. Now he came downship to the stanchion, still watching far out.

"What color is it?" Adler asked.

"Is what?"

"All you can see."

"Flying fish?" He took a second. "Brown or green-brown."

"No," Adler pressed. "The ocean. The ocean, right here in the South Pacific. All around. All over."

"Well," Harbelis said slowly, "it's hard to say."

"No, it isn't. There are a couple of Australians on board. They clued me in."

"Well, what'd they tell you?"

"Tar. Creosote." He held up a finger. "That's not all. That's mine. This is theirs."

"What is 'all'?"

"Creosote-colored fuck-all, is all. 'Fuck-all' is the Australian part. Means nothing: nothing that matters."

Harbelis looked at him. "To begin with," he said, "tar is too dark. Too dark for this." He moved his hand outward. "Creosote is too dark: almost black; blue-black."

"What would you say, then?"

"Blueing."

"Never heard of it."

"Where are you from, Adler?"

"Albany, New York. No blueing."

"People use it for getting sheets and pillowcases white. Stuff like that. My mother used to fill big tubs of it in the basement, in Pittsburgh. Gets the job done. It looks exactly like this ocean. *Exactly,* not just something like. That's what the ocean is, if you want to know. One big tub of blueing. It'll make you white; pure. We'd be pure warriors. Airborne, like those fish."

"Funny that colors should come up."

"Why?"

"Maybe creosote is not right, but it did make me think."

"Creosote is for telephone poles."

"It's what they used to put Joel in, back in Primary. For that skin thing he had."

"So," Harbelis said, "I remember. Never did cure him, though. It went down into the fire with him."

"Maybe it'll come out with him, when he comes."

"I notice nobody says 'if.'"

"They don't." He glanced at Harbelis. "I don't. Do you?"

"No, I don't. All this will come out, in time. It'll happen."

"Enough of that," Adler said. "Enough about resurrection, or whatever."

"It is," Harbelis replied, settling. "Watch the blueing."

Once more the fish slanted, all reaching the air so cleanly that there was no touch of foam anywhere; not a ripple except those the sea made from itself.

"Up," Adler urged, kidding but not quite completely. "Red alert, boys. Bells, sirens. Scramble. Go get 'em."

Their eyes traveled with the spread of small fires until they disappeared into the dark blue, the cobalt, as if merging, as if blanking the ocean.

Adler came back. "What about Shears?" he asked.

"What about him? We're together. We're bound; that's all."

"You didn't answer my question."

"I can't, any more than you can."

"He was Joel's pick."

"I know."

"What was the basis? Do you have any idea? Do you remember anything it could have been?"

"No. That's just the way it is." He pointed. "Now you look out there, Eagle. They're airborne again."

"Fuck the fish. You tell me about Malcolm Shears."

"He's got confidence. He was first in his class with us at Luke. He was ahead of Blazek, and that sure takes some doing. Blazek I'm trusting my life to."

"Would you trust it to Malcolm Shears?"

"Would you?"

"You bet I would. He was Joel's man. That's enough for me. He may even have some of what Joel had."

"I said confidence, not magic."

"Magic's a loaded word."

"What would you call it?"

"I'd say Shears has some, whatever it is."

"You know better than that. What Joel Cahill had, Shears couldn't get out of a million flights, a million missions. Joel is Joel. Magic comes out of the fire."

"I thought we'd talked this out. All the way out."

"I did. I did say so. Let it go for a while. Watch the fish. Look how the sun takes to them. Every one of them. That's magic. Magic has to do with gold."

"I agree. A lot of the time it does."

"O.K. So, we've now got ourselves to thinking gold, Lieutenant."

"You mean, on the fish?"

"Yes. There and somewhere else."

"Where?"

"Sweeping across." Harbelis moved his open hand across the ocean. "Sweeping and sweeping. Across and across."

"You got to tell me."

"On the seven-twenty. Wouldn't you call that gold?"

"More or less; I never looked at it that way. But it is gold; kind of yellow-gold, anyway. Soft or bright; whatever you want." He twisted a dial. "The seven-twenty sweeps good, as long as the spinner holds up."

"The target's in there. There are a lot of them in the Pacific, they tell me. All waiting; all in their positions. All shining. On fire. *In* fire."

"We'll get 'em."

"Strange. It sweeps and paints. Fire paints."

"Paints-in."

"Very strange. The enemy tells you where he is, what his position is, in the fire. He can't help it. He's got to."

Adler pushed his cap back on his forehead. "How do we rate all this?"

"War. War can do anything. Many new miracles, we got. Radar, we got. I don't believe it, but it works. The Japs are not going to believe it, either, until it hits them."

"The U.S. laid it in our hands; it did. That gold, these positions. Like you say, war can do what it wants to. It puts us here, on this ship. That ought to tell you something."

"Everybody in the army asks that question, that one question: how did I get here?"

"Right. How in God's name, how in hell did *I* get here?"

The fish came up in their enormous breadth of scan, the sun through a thousand needle-eyes touching-down on them, traveling. Rise and be with.

How had he got here, from Fresno to the fish? Harbelis wanted no more sound. Or before Fresno?

First by washing out of pilot training. He had been held back in Primary because of the destruction of the aircraft that Joel had ordered, and that he, Shears and the others had carried out. That, and the investigation that followed, which had not found out a thing, or done anything, except to transfer the Commanding Officer, Colonel Hoccleve, to another base and bust one cadet. None of the Alnilam group had given information that did anything but confuse the Board. The blind man, Joel's father, had come back, this time without a dog, and had faced them all down with his green-eyed glasses, which could not see anything but could see through, or you would think so. The two women had testified: Lucille, from Supply, who denied her affair with the Colonel, and the little mill girl from town, who was so weak you could hardly hear what she said. The whole demolition-derby of airplanes, there in the Parking Area on graduation day, had been charged off to inexperience and panic. The cadet who had started the panic, Willis, had been washed out, and that was it.

After that, nobody knew what to do. The strip was closed while the Corps of Engineers hauled away the fuselages, wings, engines, props, tails and other plane parts; the cadets, when not in ground school, wandered around looking at the trees and sandy ground trashed with snow, at the clouds, at the air; the flight instructors went home. After three weeks another Commanding Officer, Colonel Pietz, came in and tried to get things organized, more Stearman PT-17s were railroaded in, or trucked in or flown in, the classes were reorganized, the quotas re-tallied, and the cadets who were supposed to have graduated when the planes crashed, that had all their time in, finally shipped out to Basic, and Harbelis and a few others were held back for their lack of progress, for more air time, and the base little by little began to function again as well as it ever had, or almost.

But Harbelis had not shipped out, at least not to Basic. His problem still was time: in the end not too little of it but too much. A month after the holdback he had been check-ridden, and the Captain—Hollingsworth was his name—had decided that Harbelis could not fly well enough for the time he had logged, and he had joined the eliminees. It did not bother him. Primary had brought him to Joel Cahill, he was a first echelon member of Alnilam, and that was good enough for him; better than good. The air was his, as it was Alnilam's but he did not want to do in it what Joel had done. Joel was the pilot, the only one possible; the rest, like Shears and Neilson, like Blazek even, were pilots far down the ladder; they were in the air but not of it. Adler was eliminated, too, for the same reason as Harbelis. Neither had qualified for Navigator or Bombardier, but he had been offered by the new Commanding Officer a chance to join "an experimental program." Not much was known about it, but if they qualified they would still be air-crew, and would graduate as officers. Gunnery school as enlisted men was a prerequisite. They had accepted. They wanted to fly, to be in the air, no matter what it took.

Gunnery school was in Florida, and started with shotguns. Harbelis had never fired one before, but to be on a skeet range on Army time was an odd good luck he couldn't have foreseen. He did well enough, and went on to the jeep range, where the trainees stood in steel rings in moving vehicles, firing at clay platters sprung from the nondescript fields at unexpected angles; hard to get on to at first. But Harbelis got on, and Adler also; the motion of the jeep became part of them, and when the discs rose from the weeds they did it with a new intimacy and grace that included the gunners. Harbelis stood in the circle of metal with strong confidence, his instincts feeding into the shotgun from the fields. The right lead came to be almost instantaneously his, for each angle and distance, and toward the end he missed few shots, and was actually sorry when he and the others left the range and began to fire air-to-air.

They piled into B-17s. Most of the day before the training mission was spent in preparing, in some of the hardest work Harbelis had ever done: loading cruelly heavy boxes of ammunition hour after hour, and long belts of raw .50-calibre shells, replacing walk-around oxygen canisters, installing and securing the guns. After a while Harbelis took to asking himself questions. Which color would he fire? Red, blue, green, black, orange? The noses of the cartridges were painted to register hits on the target sleeve. I hope blue, he said to himself through his teeth, hauling a box of blue bullets up through the loading-well. Come on, blue. There doesn't have to be a reason. Blue, blue, blue.

He fired black. Black was the standard color for the top turret. ("Orientation only. Waistguns are for score.") For some reason Harbelis was first up. Following the tugs and hand motions of the instructor he climbed the metal rungs, got seated and looked out. "You don't have to worry about shooting off the tail," the instructor had said. "The PGI will take care of that. If it wadn't for the PGI there'd be lots of Forts flying around without tails." They had all been briefed on the Profile Gunfire Interruptor, which cut the guns off when they were aimed at the tail, but Harbelis was not so sure, and swung the twin fifties through the big stiff shape without firing a preliminary burst, then waited at an angle for the sleeve. Before it came, before the tow-plane even showed, there was the huge scrape of blue-green ocean, the Gulf of Mexico, and the tail riding through it. He wanted to believe the tail did not belong where it was, but it was so supernatural in its beauty, strangeness and unreality that he accepted it, finally, for what it added.

The tow-plane showed to the left of the aircraft, passing slowly. It was a Martin B-26, and there was nothing about it that suggested that it had ever had any difficulty either in design or performance. Behind it a black, unbellying thread paid out, so long that it seemed to be dragging the target-sleeve up over the horizon, and Harbelis waited for it to come to him.

"All mine," he said, when the target stopped moving forward, and he saw it ripple with bullets from the waistguns. He brought the sight in and down and rested its rings on the air between the front and middle of the sleeve. There was no reason not to fire, but he had to wait to get the idea of leads out of his mind. Almost all of gunnery school, up to now, had been about leads: when to fire ahead of the target and how much, and when to loose off behind it, as when parallel and overtaking. But never, except for one position on the jeep range, had he shot directly at what he was trying to hit. This was one of those times, though: parallel at the same speed; the bullets would be carried forward at the same speed as the target and the aircraft. You learned it from this phase, this turret, these bullets. Harbelis loosed off, and held for a three count. He did the same thing again, and again, the outside guns hardly pulsing in his hands in their remote position. He was sure he was on target. The sleeve rode on, full of new black holes, he believed, he had fired into it like wishing.

The instructor pulled at him by the pants-leg. He stayed a moment, even so, looking out at what was behind him; be aware: be aware *enough*. A privilege: Goddamn if it's not. The ocean spread with no compromise, a fishing boat drawn steadily away from him, a timed formation of pelicans crossing diagonally, higher than they usually would have been, most likely. Alnilam. This may just be Joel's great field, his great distance-colored field, though it was not late enough in the day for it to be purple. It may be where we will be living, in something as big and empty as that, as beautiful, nihilism and music part of it. What we use will run on electricity and not anything else. Electricity, because all the explanations of it are not good enough; because it is a mystery no one can solve, but works. We must find the electricity; Joel's. It is somewhere; he told us. Some other use; something new. Coming down from the guns, Harbelis admitted with daring and joy that the whole thing—Alnilam, the great field, himself, Shears, Adler, Blazek, Neilson and the others—were all misleading or misled; they were fooling themselves and each other, were maybe a little insane in a certain way; living or dead Joel was the other side of anything you could call sane. But—as his foot reached the floor of the aircraft—he also knew another thing, his mind said freely, given power. Alnilam is more sane than the army is; the least thing about it makes more sense than anything in the Air Corps. And there was surely nobody in the Air Corps like Joel Cahill. I will follow him no matter where he takes me, and so will the others. Precision mysticism: the indwell of the engine not the engine, the young charioteers, the keen stars, music, nihilism, the great field, the new electricity. Rather that than this, rather the Great Field than Buckingham Field, rather Shears than Colonel Hoccleve; rather Joel than me.

He worked back to the waist and bent over the starboard .50 calibre on its post, with blue-smeared rounds feeding in.

"Fire down. Fire at the ocean. Hold for two, then fire again at the same place," the instructor yelled in his ear.

Harbelis thought he heard him, but looked straight across, eye-to-eye with the tow-target. He did not understand; nobody had explained this.

"Splash-firing," the instructor yelled, pointing, jabbing downward. "Fire, hold, and fire again. Watch the pattern."

Harbelis tilted the gun, sighted on the clear ocean, let off a quick burst, stopped, waited, and fired again. Below, dropping back at their own pace, two delicate-feathered prints of whiteness, farther apart than he would have guessed, were going, now gone. He would remember.

He would. He checked the instructor's face and, when it nodded, turned to the target, lined up on the forepart of the sleeve and fired eye-to-eye; fired and fired, one three-second burst after another. There was a fascination in it, in the rhythm, in the fact that he was doing what he was, and at the indifference of the long target, moving as though an escort, unswerving, unflinching. The training plane slowed and increased speed, and he was back into leads again: forward leads, overtaking leads, tracking leads. During one of the tracking runs he was amazed that he could actually see the bullets in the air: a blink, a hinted gold, but definitely copper-jackets, sun-touched between him and the target.

They landed, finally. Following the Sergeants the trainees gathered around the target stretched on the ground, now full of colored holes.

"Who fired blue?" the waist sergeant asked, one finger on the sleeve.

"I did."

"Come look here."

Harbelis crouched forward. Blue was scattered all through the colors; orange and green were in one place or another, there was some red, a little yellow and much black, but blue roamed among all these, picked out, picked at by various fingers.

"That's an afternoon for you," the sergeant said. "That's quite an afternoon, blue boy. What's your name?"

"Private Harbelis, sir."

"Well, Harbelis, you really got together with it. That's the best I've seen yet in eighteen classes."

"And all that black from the turret," another instructor said. "That's probably his, too."

"I couldn't say." Harbelis paused. "Maybe not at all. My scores on skeet were not real good. Or on the jeep range, either."

"Air to air. Air to air, Private. Only in the air, and that's good enough; that's what we want," the sergeant said with satisfaction. He smiled. He turned back to the target and knelt again. "Look here. It even looks like you might shoot some kind of a pattern," he joked. "Did you mean to do this?" moving his finger from hole to hole. "If you connected all these hits with lines, like the kids do in the funny papers, it might make a tree. Or maybe even a pine tree."

"What the hell you talkin' about, Mike?" somebody said. "You ain't gettin' paid for this. You must have the DT's. I wouldn't put it past you."

"DT's, nothin'," the turret sergeant said. "I see what you mean. It could be a tree, or a bush. Or maybe a piece of fire."

"Good God," one of the trainees said. "Is this what I came to gunnery school for?"

"Break up, boys. Let's crawl on back to the barracks." With his hand on Harbelis's shoulder the instructor said, "Keep doin' what you're doin', Private. Do it to the Japs, and do it some more here. You're makin' us all look good. I didn't, but tell 'em I showed you how. Then all I'll have to come up with is the score."

He came forward in memory, still listening to the gunnery sergeant's voice, to the desk where he was. The fish were airborne, the sun justly and secretly on them, empowering equally.

"Did you like gunnery?" he asked Adler. "That never came up when we were doing it."

"It was not too bad. Some of it was fun. I liked the pursuit curve and the bend of the bullets. All they showed us on the graphs, and really turned out to be true."

"What do you remember *mainly,* though?"

Adler straightened his back and leaned the side of his head against the stanchion. "About three days after the first mission we flew, the other B-17 pranged into the Gulf. I knew some of the guys. I did, you did."

"Sure. After the Fort went down, a couple or three of us were walking through the barracks, and when we passed one of the bunks there was an officer's uniform hanging on the rack. Somebody sure thought he'd make it, going through gunnery as a cadet."

"Bars, wings, everything. Never was worn."

"Would I know his name?"

"Massey, was his name."

"What kind of wings were they?"

"I don't know; I didn't pay enough attention. Anyway, it was all that led up to, was where gunnery came in. Where we went afterward."

Boca Raton, Florida. Mouth of the rat. A strip, a few hangars, AT-9 and AT-11 trainers. The barracks were in a scattered pine grove, with duckboards between them over the hot grayish sand. And one cinderblock building; that's where the secrets were. Or the secret. The trainees were searched and marched in, glancing at the barbed wire rolling over the blocks. They went into bare classrooms and were handed notebooks and pencils. No one had any idea what was coming, what they were doing there.

The instructor began to put diagrams and numbers on a blackboard. Harbelis was not interested in mathematics, and had never taken a course in physics. When the three hours of instruction for the first day were finished the trainees were given a period in which to memorize the diagrams and formulas. Without understanding much of what he was dealing with except that it had something to do with electricity, he had memorized the material, given it back to the instructor, and filed out; the building was shut down and locked. The individual notebooks were kept in the building, and returned the next day. As the ground-school phase of instruction went on, Harbelis was prepared to memorize figures and formulas until the final exam, and was resigned to comprehend very little of what the instructor said. He had a good memory, and felt that this would get him through until they began flying. To his surprise, though, he found that he was able to fit fragments of instruction together, and to make the mathematics work with the diagrams. All of it was concerned with the measuring of distances from one object to another, with the sending out of electronic signals and getting them back, so that the location and position of another object could be determined by the source of the signals. The instructor was very painstaking, and Harbelis did not want to discourage him by not being able to follow his lead. There were a good many examples and analogies, particularly concerning signals and bats, which apparently give out sounds that only they can hear; they pick up the echoes and fly; they can fly through mazes of wire. Is that true? Yes; it's true; we can show you film. Two words that came up often were "pulse" and "echo," and it was probably this as much as anything that helped Harbelis do as well as he did. His grades were good, and it was heartening to know that he owned qualities that he had never used before. He credited the army, was glad to do it, and wondered what else it might find.

Perhaps in the last weeks of ground school, which led to the air. There was not much use in the notebooks any more; they were locked away or burned;

forgotten. In cinderblock cubicles, on which a light sweat stood and in places ran, Harbelis and the others were hooded, and in as much dark as could be made, faced a glass circle, where, in uncertain sideways grass, danced the secret, the green-ghostly wings that could not be believed, but must be; they were the enemy's. The scope was in two parts, one round and the other oblong. Down the center of the round one stood a solid bar, a darker green than the shattered-looking persistent flicker on both sides; this was the time-base line; the sidelong flickering was ground-return. Two shadowy triangles, almost invisible, would appear, one of them usually longer than the other. They represented the targeted aircraft, and the trainee, the RO, was intended to talk his pilot into firing range from various positions. When the wings on the screen were equal in length the pursuit aircraft was directly behind the target. If the left, or port, wing was longer the target was to the left, and the opposite was true when the target was on the right, or starboard. The commands were simple, but had to be exact; naval terms were used so that there could be no mistake in the meaning. The RO worked the controls of the set—the bias, the gain or intensity of the image—while he talked the pilot in to the attack. He controlled the speed and relative position of the pursuit ship, planned the attack and gave, at least theoretically, the correct instructions for closure, position, and kill. Hour after hour under the hoods, in the compacted dark, the trainees sweated like the walls, sometimes overshooting, thus making themselves the target, which gave the enemy an instant advantage, sometimes losing the faint wings of the image, often confusing the unseen pilot with the wrong commands, now and again running a successful interception. As the course proceeded the problems became more and more difficult. When the target took evasive action the interplay between RO and pilot could become so rapid that it was impossible for the pilot to obey or even understand what he was supposed to do. But as the action became more complicated and dangerous the excitement also grew, and when Harbelis made a good move, a rate of closure consistent with his attack-plan, a turn that could actually see the target ship, he felt an exhilaration that nothing before had ever given him. Little by little and then with more and more emphasis and conviction, he saw himself as unique, the pursuer in a dream rather than the pursued: far from earth, master, in total darkness, of the ultimate hunt.

Time did not exist in the cubicles. Only the observer mattered there, the time-base line, the hair-like green off the sides of it, shuddering near extinction, and fewer and fewer words from the instructor. Harbelis heard his own commands, saw the frail wings of the target pass from one side of the line to the other, saw them work toward the bottom of the screen, where the interception would end. He lost target after target, sometimes overshooting, and often when the other aircraft went into evasive action, but little by little, not thinking of the cubicle as an aircraft but as a fragment of night air within an infinite darkness his commands, his confidence, grew. The voice of the spectral pilot answered, obeying, and the other-worldly wings on the screen evened out, came closer.

Gently port.

Gently port, Roger.

Harder port.

Harder in the port turn.

Ease off.

Easing off.

Steady.

Straight and steady.

Gently starboard.

Gently starboard.

Steady, pilot.

Steady.

Increase ten.

Increasing ten.

Target stable, two hundred yards, dead ahead, ten degrees above. Do you have visual?

Affirm visual.

Closing set.

Attack attitude. Gun switch on.

Set off.

Could this be done? They walked in blazing sun, meridian sun, toward the aircraft, AT-11s. At the ships they stepped up into darkness. Someone dogged-down the access door; Harbelis and the instructor were left facing two sets. Remember, Harbelis thought. Remember. Remember. The set did not pulse, and he felt with his hands for the on-button, the gain, the bias, the range. A hand went across his.

"Don't do that," the instructor said. "Put your head-set on, and the mike. I'll tell you what to do, when it's time; when it *is.*"

The engines kicked, and they were rolling. Harbelis buckled up by feel, knowing in his hands where the set controls were.

Silent with engine noise, they were dandled, airborne, and, by the drawing-together feel in his ears, climbing. Harbelis swallowed, sucked on his tongue and cleared them. A level came, after a while. Everything waited. A riding dark is like no other dark. What might be under? Only the controls he could not touch were there; he yearned for the set, the time-base line, the bodiless grass of the target. Maybe I can do this, he said into the un-manned mike; to his throat. Maybe it really works.

"Set."

Harbelis leaned, for the voice had not come through the earphones. He prized his right ear loose.

"What?" he asked with his real voice.

A hand was on his wrist, again warm and startling. "Turn on the set."

He reached where he thought to; pressed. Both his scopes stood with grass, incredibly delicate, fuzzed right and left on one screen, on the other up and down.

"See him?" the instructor asked. "He's at four thousand."

Harbelis peered: peered like a man truly *peering*, almost like an actor. At the top of the range-and-azimuth scope were wings, almost invisible, but side-triangles that could be made out, the right longer than the left.

"He's all yours," the instructor said. "Go get him. Bring him in."

Harbelis stabilized his attention with everything he had, then pressed the intercom switch.

RO to pilot.

Roger, RO. I read you.

I have contact. Target starboard, four thousand feet.

I read you R-5 F-5. Four thousand.

Increase twenty.

Increasing twenty.

A new force drew on them, slowly urgent, coming from the world.

Gently starboard.

Gently starboard.

The wing-shapes began to even out, flicker downward.

Steady.

Steady. Straight and level.

Down the central pole the wings crept, clearer; the left one widened.

Gently port.

(Immediately) *Gently port.*

Steady. Hold speed.

Holding, one forty-five knots, and stable.

Climb.

(Brief uncertainty) *How?*

Gently. (Pause: odd conviction; new) Climb gently.

Gently, Podner. Increasing altitude.

(A time. More.)

Level off.

Level.

Range twenty-five hundred feet. Hold speed.

Holding.

Looks good, pilot, he said, remembering he had never seen the other.

Keep him coming.

Roger, pilot. Two thousand feet, ten degrees above. Throttle back five.

Back five.

A little pressure—presence—left them. Suddenly the target was at a thousand feet, then seven-fifty, then five hundred.

Throttle back, Harbelis's voice rose. Hard as possible. Throttle back.

The time-base line stood free; the wings were gone. Before he could say anything more, the instructor cut in, over peaceful engines.

Instructor to pilot.

Loud and clear.

Mission completed. Let's go home.

Roger wilco. Turning base.

Harbelis and the instructor sat in a loose tent on folding chairs, opposite one another across an issue table slant in sand.

"You overshot," the instructor said. "Or undershot."

Harbelis knew it; resigned, he felt also in a way confirmed.

"The target throttled back, and you went right under him. You lost your aircraft. You got you and your pilot killed. All the other plane had to do was drop his nose, put his guns on you, and fire." He made a slow erasure on air. "Scratch one U.S. night fighter."

"I saw it," Harbelis said. "Then I didn't see it. The target just went off the scope. Wasn't anywhere. Damned if I knew what to do. I tried to catch it."

"Too late. Not a little too late; a lot."

Harbelis lifted his hands, exaggeratedly helpless. "I guess I busted the ride, then. Scratch one training mission. Maybe one RO."

The instructor looked up, at the same time trying to straighten the table. "No," he said with some actual surprise. "You didn't. You passed. Everything else was real good. Your pickup was first rate; you got right into the interception. You were really *in* it, part of it, controlling it, and that's what we want, what we look for." He went on, touching his note-pad and ticking off points with his other hand. "Your sense of the relations was outstanding. You always knew where he was, and you knew where you were in relation to him. Your calls were excellent, just right; the pilot said so; said that part of it was the best first ride he's ever flown. What it takes a lot of these new guys weeks to find out you already knew: that pilot needs confidence, and you've got to give it to him. He has to believe you know exactly what you're doing." He smiled openly. "Good; more good than bad. Good on you, as the Aussies say."

"Well, I'll be fucked. I really will."

"I hope you really will, Cadet. Try *east* West Palm Beach."

"Well, but . . ." Harbelis hesitated.

"Let me finish. Your turns were good, too. Just enough and not too much. You got right in there on him."

Emboldened, Harbelis tried again. Now he did not want any of the mission left out, no matter what. "Look here, though . . . believe me, I don't want to . . ."

"I'm coming to that." The instructor framed what he would say. "You did what you did in relation to the target. But something was wrong. What was it?"

"Well, what do you mean? I overshot. The target was gone. Everything went."

"Why? How?"

"You said the other plane throttled back."

"Right." The instructor leaned one elbow on the table, slanting it again. "You figured what you were doing. You didn't figure on what *he* might do; what he did. And he shot you down. So . . ." He got up and bent toward Harbelis.

"When you get in there, close to the target like that, just before attacking, and he's still on the scope, that's crucial." He straightened. "That's *crucial* crucial. If he cuts that throttle you better cut right with him, or as quick as you can, and throttle back full. Hold that target on the screen."

"Okay," Harbelis said, throttling back with both hands. "I'll do my best."

"Don't give away *anything* to the target. He's not just going to sit there and let you shoot him. If he's got any notion you're around, he'll gain altitude, he'll lose. He'll turn all sorts of ways. He's going to jink and he's going to jank. So be ready. Be one ahead of him. Always. Every second. Think like he does. *Be* him." He paused at the tent flap. "And you'll live. So will your pilot. And like the kids say when they play 'Put Your Right Foot In' on skates at the birthday party, that's what it's all about."

Criticism

From Babel to Byzantium

During the 1950s and 1960s Dickey wrote dozens of reviews in which he assessed other poets with the sort of insight and wit of his model Randall Jarrell. He also wrote essays to define his stance as a poet and as a Southerner during the social upheavals of the period. He collected many of these in The Suspect in Poetry, *which Robert Bly published in 1964 at the Sixties Press. Subsequently, Dickey gathered together new reviews and essays for* Babel to Byzantium, *which Farrar, Straus & Giroux published in 1968.*

Barnstorming for Poetry

It is a winter night in the Midwest, and a man is lying alone in a strange room. On the dresser, beside the complicated clock-radio that is supposed to wake him, there is an untidy bundle of railroad, bus, and airline schedules marked with a red pencil, and various notes to himself about how to get to bus and train stations and airports. He keeps opening his eyes in his sleep—or what amounts to it—and looks at his watch, turning it one way and another so that its thin hands can catch the cold light coming in across the snowy campus from the chapel tower. There is only one bus out of town, and it leaves at 4:30 in the morning.

It is time. He gets out of bed and stumbles toward the alarm; just as he reaches it, rock-and-roll music bursts into his face. Rather than fool with trying to shut it off, he pulls out the plug, feeling that he has had his revenge. He turns on the light and dresses, not quite able to believe he is where he is: some place in Wisconsin, where he has given a poetry reading at a small college; he is, in fact, in the middle of a tour of such readings.

So far—considering he is not Robert Frost or Dylan Thomas—he has had nothing to complain of as to the size and response of his audiences. Actually, they have been responsive to a degree he has come to think of as excessive and even manic, but he suspects that attendance at these affairs may be mandatory in some cases. Then, too, many of the schools, like this one, are far back in the country and there is nothing much to do. Still, he is pleasantly gratified at the turnouts, at the students who gather round him afterward, asking questions, pressing their manuscripts into his hands, telling him what is wrong with such and such a poem he has read, such and such a line, such and such a concept. He has never been lionized by anyone, not even his immediate family; but these small, repeated tastes of local notoriety are definitely agreeable, and he does his best to live up to them.

That, in fact, is his problem: the living-up-to, the giving them what they want, or might be expected to feel entitled to from a poet aside from the poems themselves. "Just be yourself," he told himself in the beginning. Ah, but *what* self? The self he has become on this trip bears but little relation to the self he left at home in the mind, say, of his wife. He has taken to doing some curious things. For example, he has acquired a guitar, which he carries about with him as though he were Carl Sandburg. He has not played the guitar for years, but he feels immediately all sorts of new and presumably poetic things happen to him each time he carries it to another campus. At the inevitable parties given after his readings, he plays one or two songs and then scuttles back into conversation, satisfied that he has done the something idiosyncratic that people are expecting and that, much more dangerous to psychological stability, he expects of himself.

He has several disadvantages to overcome. He is middle-aged, beginning to lose teeth and hair. He is ordinarily mild-mannered and agreeable, and secretly thinks of himself as rather colorless and uninteresting. He has written poems for years because he liked to write them, but he has never thought of them as participating in a public act, a kind of literary vaudeville. At the outset of the trip he had thought that the poems themselves would be enough; if they were good, and he read them well, he could collect his money at each stop with a clear conscience. But it is he who is not satisfied with *just* reading; it is not only poetry that is involved: it is the poet as well.

A strange madness took hold of him when he discovered at the first reading that everything he said was noted and commented upon. Too, he *thinks* he heard a bearded student mutter something discontented about "lack of fire" (or was it lack of flair?), and at that moment the image of his great predecessor, the only predecessor, Dylan Thomas, blazed up humiliatingly in the front of his mind. The result of this was that he deliberately drank twice as much liquor as he is accustomed to at the party after the reading, waved his arms wildly about, said anything and everything that came into his head, insulted somebody—merciful heavens, who on earth was it?—and had a terrible hangover the next day.

Yet he has in some obscure way been a good deal better satisfied with himself, has drunk very nearly as much at all the six or eight schools following that one, and is now looking forward to acquiring the courage to get drunk *before* the reading. He is exhausted and exalted as he has never been, and now, standing in the center of a new reality—in this case a cold, sleepless room—he looks at these things for the last time, picks up his bag and manuscripts and his symbolic guitar, and goes out into the white darkness.

There are few lights on the campus, and he is uncertain about the instructions designed to get him to the bus station. Crossing the campus on the one path he knows, he keeps reminding himself of what he is doing in this hamlet, lost somewhere in the snows of northern Wisconsin: he is—eternal strangeness!—a wandering singer, an American poet. When at last he reaches the station, he discovers he is too early by twenty minutes. He sits down, closes his eyes. Time is annihilated; the bus driver opens the door. He stumbles aboard the panting bus and collapses.

When he wakes up, the bus is in the terminal in the next city. He gets out and looks around for whoever is supposed to meet him. There is no one but a priest, and finally it dawns on him that the college he is to read at that night is denominational. He goes up to the priest, who has in fact been sent to drive him out to the college. "I couldn't believe you'd be the one I was looking for," the poet says in his new frankness. "I couldn't believe that you were, either," says the priest with equal candor.

In a station wagon they drive forty miles into the forest. At the college he is given a room in a cavernous building and told that he has an hour or two before dinner. He lies down on the bed, then gets up and paces back and forth. There is a skull on the table, and suddenly, at the sight of this *memento mori*, the great themes of poetry hit him squarely: the possibility of love and the inevitability of death. He has tried for years to formulate his relationship to these things and to say something about them. He takes out his three volumes of poetry and his manuscript of a fourth book, and, ever cognizant of his bodiless, staring audience and of the skull beneath his own skin, rearranges his evening's program around the themes of love and death.

He gives the best reading of his life, the one that all subsequent performances will have to be judged by. Realizing that all role-playing is shameful beside the feeling he experiences now, he has the sensation that his words are being received almost as things, and toward the end he comes to think that the things have the quality of gifts: disturbing gifts, perhaps, inept, inadequate gifts, but gifts just the same: he feels that he is giving something. And the grave, slightly puzzled, sympathetic faces take on expressions he is grateful for, indicating a particular favor conferred upon a stranger they will never see again, one who last night was not gracefully but disgracefully drunk and out of his element, and who now is half in another world with fatigue; one who has spent the most satisfying part of a long trip alone in a room with a skull.

In this reading, for once in his life, he *feels* a correct balance between what is on the page, put there by him at odd, beyond-himself moments, and . . . and the faces. In the middle of a phrase the losses endured by everyone every day—the negation of possibility that occurs each time we pass another human being in the street, in a bar (ah yes, he needs a drink badly), on the stairs of a building and never know him—come home. Who is that thin, serious boy with the crew cut? What is his life like? Where will he die? Who is the nun giving him a calm sense of purposeful life through her thick glasses? He finishes, stands staring for a moment, establishing them in his mind, and steps down.

The next morning he catches the bus at a reasonable hour and rides calmly back to the city. With a certain flair, now, he pulls out the packet of schedules. Something is wrong: he has forgotten that his one afternoon reading of the tour is to take place that day, and he has four hours to go seventy-five miles. The college seems to be all but inaccessible, there being no buses or trains until after the time of the reading. From the airless, close-packed, winter bus station he tries to call his contact at the college, but cannot reach him. He hails a cab and asks the fare to the town he is going to. It is more than he wants to pay, and, caught up by a daring all-or-nothing plan, he tells the driver to take him to the highway. He pays and gets out, scarcely knowing what he is doing, but feeling a little better at being pointed in the right direction. He is standing alone in the snow in a strange state, hitchhiking at the age of forty-five.

An hour goes by. He considers various alternatives, but they are all as absurd as the wish to grow wings. Besides, another kind of exhilaration has come over him, and he sings with white breath to the passing cars, thinking of the open road, the dear love of comrades, the hoboes of Hart Crane's *The Bridge*. Finally someone stops, a farmer, and takes him twenty miles down the road. The farmer turns off the highway and leaves him, and this time he really is in a deserted landscape, with dead corn in the fields, an inept scarecrow, and a few big birds hunched and puffed on the telephone wires. He is happy and grinning; he feels resourceful, foolish, and lucky. "America," he says aloud with powerful vagueness. "Poetry." A car stops. It is driven by a student at the college he is going to.

At the college he reads, sleeps. The next morning he takes a walk around the campus with a young student who is interested in Yeats's occult preoccupations, a curious subject to discuss in the healthy, farmerish atmosphere of this particular college.

Much rested, he gets on a train and rides a deserted parlor car to his next stop, where he is met as arranged and housed with a young professor who writes poems himself and is enthusiastic and companionable. He reads, has a drink at a faculty party, and goes to bed. He dreams he is a scarecrow in a field, and writes poems in his head all night. Some few phrases stay with him when he wakes. He notes them down and moves on to his next stop via local airline.

This is a girls' college, also far off in the country. He finds it a little ominous that the only other large institution in the town is the state insane asylum. Since he has forgotten to telegraph his arrival, no one meets him at the airport. He phones the head of the English department, is picked up. He is taken to a room in one of the girls' dormitories, which gives him an odd sensation indeed, only partially alleviated when he learns that he is next door to the house mother.

He eats dinner with the English department and the Writing Club in the student dining hall, in an unwearying, pulsing tide of female voices. There are many furtive amused glances at him, and he replies in kind. But he is uncomfortable, even desperate; he is sure he has not written any poetry that would appeal to girls, and he even entertains the idea of sneaking back to his room and dashing off a couple of things modeled on Walter Benton's *This Is My Belovèd.*

Perhaps, though, some recent poems about his children will do. He reads these quietly and has a distinct sense of quitting while he is ahead. The applause is long and loud, and when he steps down from the stage into a wave of feathery, sweatered girls, a memorable thing happens to him. One of them, not the one he would have picked to do such a thing, or picked at all, asks suddenly, "May I kiss you?" He agrees without thinking, and she does it with startling ardor.

The next place is a branch of a state university located in the industrial district of a large city. Though he is met at the bus station, it is plain that no one is much interested in his being there. Walking across campus, he hears a loud continuous noise as of revolutions and student demonstrations combined with assembly lines and riveting. To his astonishment, directly in front of the auditorium a lanky student is standing on the hood of a 1953 Buick with a John-Henry-type hammer in his hands, and, having bashed out the windows, is now engaged in beating in the top of the car with inaccurate gusto and many loud grunts. A crowd of muffled students cheers him on; it is a fund-raising scheme for some club or other.

All through the reading the hammering goes on. When an especially loud cheer comes in from outside he looks up, thinking momentarily that it is for him, but no: it is for an exhausted hammerer, or for a new one relieving him. He learns to time his words and lines to the hammer-strokes, and before he is finished he finds his poems, usually rather loose in rhythm, taking on a thumping, thundering kind of metric as he adjusts his delivery more and more to the inevitable banging. Privately he resolves to see if he can work something out in his poetry on this basis later on. What the hell, he thinks, this may be a major technical breakthrough for me. The accompaniment continues, he bellows louder and louder, and the flinching audience is with him to the end. In all, it is a strangely good occasion.

He leaves that night for another city where he has a friend he can stay with for a day or so. He flies in, watching the lights of the city.

The friend will drive him to the next engagement, which is the last. They start out, and take a wrong turn somewhere. On a highway complex as big as this one it is hard to get turned around. It begins to snow: traffic slows all around them for miles. Finally a lucky turn gets them off the freeway; they are not so far from the college as they thought, but he is already half an hour late for the reading. They reach the college, then the building. A crowd of students just coming from the auditorium sees him approaching with his ragged books and manuscripts. One whispers to another. Though he is a little afraid to, he admits who he is, and is instantly surrounded. Someone points him in a direction and he begins walking with students trailing him as though he were a messiah or a Beatle. He reaches a stage, mounts, looks at the last of all clocks with a certain condescending benevolence, and begins.

It is over. He relaxes with the friend in the city for a day and a night before flying home. He sees the people who sponsored his tour—editors of a venerable poetry magazine—has dinner with them, recounts some of his adventures. Everyone seems pleased by the way things have gone; there have even been some letters of appreciation from the schools. But he is still bothered by the difference between his touring self and his usual self. He has definitely been another person on this trip: more excitable and emotional, more harried, more impulsive. Yet he knows that these qualities will die out upon his arrival home and he is more than a little glad of it; they are too wearying, too hard on the nerves. He might live more vividly in this condition, but he cannot write in it. He must calm down and work. But on the aircraft aimed at last at his home, he feels also that such nervous excitement, such over-responsiveness to things, is probably the poet's part. Intensity, he murmurs, where have you been all my life.

He settles down for the sleep that will annihilate the miles, becoming an older and more dependable self, yet remembering the skull in the room, a plain girl's unexpected kiss, the student with the nine-pound hammer. For better or worse, he has been moving and speaking among his kind.

Notes on the Decline of Outrage

i

To be a white Southerner in the mid-twentieth century is to realize the full bafflement and complexity of the human condition. It is not only to see parts of one's world fall irrevocably away, but to feel some of them, tenaciously remaining, take on an accusing cast that one would not have thought possible, and long-familiar situations assume a fathomless, symbolic, and threatening weight. It is also to feel the resentment, the old sense of outrage rise up again toward all those who are not Southerners—against those who would change the world which one's people have made, insisting that it conform to a number of principles with which no one could possibly argue, but which the social situation as it exists must be radically altered to fit. To the "average" Southerner, who, like the average person anywhere, does not think much about issues in the abstract—though abstractions are everywhere implicit in his conduct—the continuing and increasing pressure being brought upon the white South to "do something" about the Negro is felt simply as a return of the indignation that attended Reconstruction—a resolve that the white Southerner shall continue to exercise autonomy in his own affairs and shall resist conforming to the dictates (for that is how he conceives them) of others living in other parts of the country.

This resolve is indicated by any number of private and public rationalizations, but these in themselves are not as important as what they connote: the Southerner's belief that his self-determination is being sapped and bled away by forces that have neither his interests in mind nor an adequate knowledge of his basic situation in its day-to-day reality. Negroes, who heretofore had seemed to occupy a place in the social structure which was, as far as many white Southerners were concerned, as good as ordained by God, have now taken on an entirely new dimension, and it is especially troubling that this new dimension is simply that of their ordinary humanity, long deferred by a series of historical circumstances reaching back for hundreds of years and rooted in the greed and callousness of men long dead. It is also beginning to be shockingly apparent that, in the simplest, easiest, and most obvious way in the world, generations of men later than the slave traders and plantation owners have kept human beings essentially like themselves in a state of economic and social bondage scarcely to be believed, and have done so with absolutely no qualms or even any notice of what was in fact taking place, lulled within a kind of suspended judgment with respect to the Negro's humanity, which allowed him to exist only in a special way, limiting his experience and even his being to areas where they conformed, not only to the ideas about Negroes most congenial to the white Southerner's preconceptions about race, but to the white man's opinion of himself.

It is an even more terrible paradox that the very quality that has been obscured all this time—the Negro's ordinary, everyday humanness—is obscured even more thoroughly, now that he has become a symbol which concretizes the historical uneasiness of an entire people, pointing up, as nothing else in this country has ever done before, the fearful consequences of systematic and heedless oppression for both the oppressed and the oppressor, who cannot continue to bear such a burden without becoming himself diminished, and in the end debased, by such secret and cruel ways that he is never really sure of what is happening. No act of redress is possible for the thousands who have been spiritually maimed, to say nothing of the countless lives wasted on the hardest and most unrewarding kind of labor, amidst the most degrading and soul-breaking life situations that have ever existed in America.

All these things are now in the minds of Southerners; they are charged with hidden significance whose true import comes from history's inadvertent and almost poetic power of revelation; and they in turn charge innumerable personal relations—thousands of them each day—with the chagrin, the helplessness, and the indwelling terror that come from centuries of wrongdoing that those who began and fostered them never, incredibly, conceived as wrong, or at least not wrong enough to do anything about. This is absurd, one thinks. How could anyone fail to see the Southern Negro's situation as wrong, as completely, blindingly, hauntingly wrong? The point is that Southerners did not, or that they refused to see the life the Negro has been given for what it actually is, pleading historical causes, jackleg theories of race, economic considerations, and a good many other things—none of which, not even the cotton empire or the age-old power of money to purchase labor, has any permanent meaning before the fact that millions of people have served in utter hopelessness through no fault but that of their birth, and for no reason but that others, differently born, should benefit.

It is a problem which, to many, admits of no solution, but toward a solution of either a merely painful or a starkly terrible kind it appears to be moving. It is not too much to say that in the "Negro problem" lies the problem of the South itself. Because of it, people are wondering now, as never since the 1860's, "What does it mean to be a Southerner? What does the social and economic and cultural history of this part of the country mean to *me,* to my life?" Above all they ask, "What will happen now, and *how* will it happen?" Rather than deal in generalities, it is better to go back to the individual as he exists in a predicament in which these questions come implicitly into play, and to attempt to understand the manner in which he asks them, not of others, but of himself.

ii

On a downtown corner of a Southern city in midsummer, a man, a youngish though not quite young man, is waiting for a bus. He is not used to riding on buses, as he has his own car: in truth, he dislikes buses now more than ever, for he is aware that they have recently become a great deal more than the groaning, clumsy vehicles they have always seemed to be. They have been transformed into small, uncomfortable rolling arenas wherein the forces hidden for a hundred years in the structure of his society threaten to break loose and play themselves out each time a bus pulls away from a corner. Here, a city injunction has just been passed permitting Negroes to occupy any empty seat they prefer. The bus that appears, however, is not tossing with conflict or running blood from the windows. As usual, the Negroes are sitting well toward the back, and, as usual, our man prepares to pick a seat toward the front, as much toward the front as possible, perhaps next to a thin man in a flowered sports shirt and steel-rimmed glasses.

But suddenly he realizes that quite another thing is now possible. Seized by a desperate logic and a daring he cannot and does not want to account for, he walks past this man and on into the section occupied by Negroes. As he passes the last of the whites he has a powerful sense of pure transgression which gives way immediately to a kind of guilty, clandestine joy even more powerful. It is the sense of crossing a boundary beyond which there will be no going back, and it has all the exhilaration and fear, all the intimations of possibility and danger that might be occasioned by passing a real frontier into a strange land, perhaps even into the country of an enemy.

But *what* enemy? And why an enemy? He sees only two immense Negro women, a man in overalls and a painter's cap, a mulatto girl in a white uniform, ten or twelve others of both sexes, so familiar as to be indistinguishable from each other, and a plump, tea-colored young man who holds a small, even lighter colored boy on his lap. None of these people seems to wish him ill, or to hold anything against him; yet he is more conscious of his own color at this moment than he ever remembers being, for he recognizes it in the light in which he is told the rest of the world regards it: the color of the unjust man, more damning than the whiteness of the leper. In spite of this, or more likely because of it, he takes a firm grip on the rail of the lurching bus and slides into the seat beside the plump man and his son. After all, has not the city edict, has not the Emancipation Proclamation, freed *him* as well as the Negro? He realizes only too well his intense self-consciousness about the meaning of his gesture; for it is purely that. At the same time, through an awesome silence, he hears his mind repeat every cliché about Negroes he has ever heard: "Would you want one living next door to you?" Or, coming not so much from himself as out of the very air he breathes, out of the tremendous sunlight itself: "Would you want your sister to marry one?"

Though he has heard these questions asked rhetorically all his life, he has never before entertained them at any real depth of interest. His sister has not married "one," and it is highly unlikely that a Negro will move in next door to him, for thus far zoning laws in his neighborhood have been rigidly maintained. Yet over and above the information asked for and the responses demanded by these questions, he is aware of a far more significant thing: the spirit of outrage that surrounds the words, the assumption that even to *ask* the question is outrageous, and that such a transgression is to be set right only with the collaboration of the questioned, whose most violent denial is needed to place things in their customary perspective again. He cannot imagine answering such questions in the affirmative; or, if he can barely imagine it, he is at the same time conscious of the withering climate of indignation that would attend the answers, an indignation more killing than any other he can think of, because it would include, in addition to that of his contemporaries, the infinitely more terrible condemnation of his own past.

At this moment he is very much aware of himself as a Southerner, and that he is in some way betraying someone or something, even though the impulse which brought him to his present seat on the bus may have been completely laudable, *sub specie aeternitatis*. Oddly enough, he cannot help feeling also a sharp upswing of defiant joy at remembering that he *is* a Southerner, a joy that in no way wishes to distinguish approval from disapproval, right from wrong, good from evil. He is of the people from whom the Army of the Confederacy was drawn, and this is and has always been a source of intimate personal strength to him. The lives of both his grandfathers are with him, he believes, whenever they need to be, and help him understand what men may mean to each other in a common cause, regardless of whether or not history labels the cause worthy of their effort. Yet nothing like Pickett's Charge, nothing like the Shenandoah campaigns of Stonewall Jackson exists, any longer, to give Southernness an atmosphere of accomplishment, destiny, and glory. Of the spirit that caught up the Confederate Army and made Jackson, Lee, and Jeb Stuart the demigods of his people, almost none remains, and what of it does still exist has no adequate channel through which to flow. Southern autonomy, qua Southern, now tends instead to come out in petty, vindictive acts of ill will toward the Negro, and he wants no part of that.

All this he knows, but at the same time he recognizes the fact that the South still stands for . . . for something. He has read W. J. Cash, and so has been told the "truth" about the much-advertised codes of Southern honor, the cult of Southern womanhood, the Southerner's characteristic extroversion and his "habit of command," the cultural shallowness of the nineteenth-century South, and so on. He knows the verdict of history on his people. He knows one more thing about history too: that it has trapped the Southern white just as securely in his complex of racial attitudes as it has trapped the Southern Negro in his deplorable social, physical, and psychological environment. And he knows that with the increase of industry and "business," with their attendant influx of thousands of people each month from other parts of the country, the "solidarity" of the South, in manners as well as in attitudes about race, is breaking down more and more rapidly, and that when the older patterns of behavior are gone, there will be nothing to put in their place save the empty money-grubbing and soul-killing competitive drives of the Northern industrial concerns. He knows that, as a Southerner, he has only a few things left to him: the intonation of his voice, an appetite for certain kinds of cooking, a vague familiarity with a few quaint folkways far off in the mountains, and his received attitude toward the Negro; and that of these the only one important as a rallying point for his Southernness, as an effective factor in producing sectional assent, as a motivating force in political action, is the last.

It is abundantly apparent that his people do not want their sense of being Southerners to die. This may be the reason that there is, all around him, a tremendous, futile yearning back toward the time of the Civil War, when something concrete could be done, when a man could pick up a gun and *shoot* at something, in a setting of purpose and meaning. In the light of the Supreme Court ruling on segregation, the Civil War has come to seem no longer a defense of slavery and of states' rights, as Southerners had reluctantly begun to admit, but of the South against the encroachment of Others, and so heroic—the battle for one's home and one's mind against the invaders. Perhaps because of this his own brother is obsessed by the Civil War in a particularly curious way. He is a collector of relics. Accompanying his brother to the battlefield sites that surround the city, as well as to some others farther off in the country, he has walked slowly through farms, climbed over breastworks, waded through stream beds in the fraught, stammering heat of August, swinging the flat metal plate of his brother's mine detector over acres of weeds and brush in search of the war buried here for a hundred years a few inches beneath the pine straw. He has heard the lifeless and desperate cry of rusted metal, and dug with a totally inexplicable enthusiasm and dread, perhaps unearthing a piece of a parrot shell, a Minié ball, part of a canister container, a belt buckle, a branding iron, a corroded mess tin, and once even a sword transformed by the earth and time into a long, warped shape like a huge burned matchstick, whose brass handle, under polishing, later took on its soft, fiery, original sheen. But looking at the decrepit guns on the walls of his brother's house, at the golden, breadlike patina of rust on the thousand fragmentary metals of destruction, and pondering on the unearthly, leper-white Minié balls and canister shot, he knows that the continuing power of the Civil War is not in these things but in its ability to dramatize and perpetuate a feeling about a way of life. It is actually a symbol of his people's defense of their right to be Southerners, and as such is more effective now than it has been at any other time during his own life.

As he sits at the present moment, however, he is not a Confederate soldier in whose hands these weapons are new and bright. He is merely a man moving slowly in a public conveyance through a heat-shimmering city built on land where such swords and bayonets have lain underground for a century. May he not take this fact itself as a new beginning place for self-definition? Why may he not simply be a man, like and unlike others, living from day to day as best he can? Yet as he asks this question he is struck by a peculiarly terrifying thought. Can the past so easily be denied? Whether the past has been right or wrong, intelligent or mindless, good or evil, it is still the past, the only one, and it cannot change. Because of it, he is who he is; of the subjects occasioned by his reverie, every one wells up out of history—the history of his people as Southerners. Yet may there not be feelings, states of being which underlie and do not depend exclusively upon the past?

On the pretext of looking out the window, he glances at his companions. The young Negro father has got over his initial self-consciousness, which, to tell the truth, was not even in the beginning very pronounced. He has set his light porkpie hat on the back of his head and is playing with his tiny son, who, to the other man in the seat, looks exactly like every other small Negro boy he has ever seen, except for being dressed in a white shirt and short, dark blue wool pants with halters, and very bright black shoes. The man is now sticking out his wide pink tongue at his son, who swipes at it. They are both laughing. Well, what does one do next, if one is obviously looking, not out the window at all, but at another person no more than a foot away? "That's a fine boy you've got there," the young man does in fact say, and for the first time the Negro looks at him, a little shyly but squarely. In his gaze there is, thank God, no real mistrust, though he ends his reply with "sir." And there the conversation ends.

But something has happened, and it brings with it a new flood of questions more demanding than any others the young man has asked himself. What, actually, is his attitude toward Negroes, over and above gestures, over and above received opinions? And how does he really feel about the South—

the actual South he lives in, that is, stand as it may in the shadow of that other, dead, undead, imagined, magnificent, and tragic South? And how are these questions related? For it is certain that they *are* related in some profound and fundamental way. He must admit immediately that he has always concurred, or as good as concurred, in the assumptions about Negroes that his forebears and contemporaries have had, and have. The unspoken rationale underlying these assumptions is that, inexplicably but in perfect keeping with the natural order of things, Negroes have been endowed with human shape and certain rudimentary approximations of human attitudes, but that they possess these only in a kind of secondary or inferior way, and, to the end of having this be readily recognizable, have also been given a skin pigmentation and a facial bone structure which make their entire status apparent at a glance, and even from a very great distance. Spoken or unspoken, these are the beliefs that have assigned every Negro, from the lowest hod carrier up through the ministry and the medical profession, his place in the Southern scheme of things.

The notion that the Negro must be "acclimated" slowly to the Caucasian world, now advanced among some Southerners as a genteel refinement on the above idea, is in reality not nearly so honest an appraisal of an actual state of mind as the more fundamental assumption from which it proceeds. As a result of the practices rather than the "theories" concerning the Negro, the worst possibility, the most fearful dream the white Southerner can have—or at least that the young man can imagine himself as having—is to have been born a Southern Negro. As he is, as he has existed among the circumstances of his life, he has always rather liked Negroes, in an offhand, noncommittal way, though it is certain that he has never formed a deep man-to-man (or, for that matter, man-to-woman) relation with one. Yet he realizes that he has just as surely always participated in the popular belief that the Negro is more or less a child, happy and easily diverted, or, more properly, somewhere between a child, a pet, and a beast of burden, but prone to flare up, especially among his own kind, into a terrible jungle violence. The Negro is also commonly thought to be the victim of a lust so powerful that before it all laws, all social codes and restrictions are as nothing, and during these seizures may leap from a sheltering fringe of bushes, like a wild shadow cast from Africa, and attack a solitary white woman working in a field, a girl on her way home from high school. He knows that there is enough misconstruction placed upon certain aspects of the Negro's life in his past and present environment to give these assumptions the outward cast or appearance of an entire truth, and that any isolated instance of Negro-white rape, for example, is enough to corroborate and intensify this feeling, and the others which attend it, all over the South, and to bring halfway to the surface disturbing dreams of all-out racial conflict and an intolerable sense of impending anarchy which must at all costs be put down.

But where does he, the questioner, stand in these matters? What *does* he believe? Does he believe that Negroes are essentially children? No; he does not. He believes that the Negro is a man like any other, woefully stunted and crippled by his circumstances but with amazing reserves of tolerance and humor, and a resilience that should eventually take its place among the most remarkable shows of human adaptability in history. Does he then believe in denying the Negro the social and economic concomitants of his humanity? No; he does not. There is no possible justification of such a denial. Yet why then does he *act* as if he believed, exactly to the extent that the veriest redneck or country politician rabble-rouser believes, *all* these admittedly indefensible ideas? Well, because . . . because he is a Southerner, and these attitudes are part of his past, of his "heritage" as a Southerner, and he suspects that if he relinquishes them, he also gives up his ancestry, to say nothing of severing an essential bond between himself and his contemporaries, all of whom are struggling in various ways to preserve segregation.

At present, with an impersonal materialism visiting its final ravages on the only place on earth he has ever really belonged, he does not want the *sense* of this place, the continuity of time as it has been lived, the capacity of the past to influence and if possible to assist him in thought and action, to disappear entirely. With others of his generation, he has wandered a great deal, and now, staring forward into the comfortable abyss of middle age, he wants, *really* wants, to regrow his roots, if such a thing is yet possible, in the soil from which he sprang. He does not believe the South to be merely a matter of climate and fried chicken; he understands it as a place where certain modes of thought are mutually held without the necessity of constant analysis and definition. One of these, and increasingly the main one, is the white Southerner's attitude toward the Negro, as the Negro exists in *his* "place." What that place is, however, he does not yet want to examine. Setting aside momentarily the "Negro question," what of the South itself, the South that he remembers? In what ways has it made him what he is?

Of the world in which he grew up, he can honestly recall only a very few things which he would identify as characteristically Southern, but these are powerfully centered in his consciousness. He has lived elsewhere in the

United States, for example, and he can think of no other region where the family, on out through distant cousins, nephews, great-uncles and aunts, has such actual solidity and warmth as it does in the South. It is not that members of Northern and Midwestern families care for each other any the less, so much as it is that there seems to be in the South (or seemed in those years to be) a more vivid and significant belief that blood ties underlie and bolster the human affections in a way not to be explained by either logic or environment. There seemed, there still seems to him, something indisputably right about this. Though he has many relatives for whom he does not greatly care, he has always valued even those as part of the family association, the great chain of being that attached him truly, by ties surpassing in power anything the mere mind of man can invent, to other human beings in a group.

Something of this feeling extends outside the circle of kinship, also. A good deal of snobbery notwithstanding, it is hard for a Southerner to feel anything but a sense of basic comradeship with other Southerners, regardless of their relative social status. And this too seems valuable. To be told, with all the authority of the United States Supreme Court, that some of the beliefs proceeding from this community are wrong, and have been wrong from the beginning, for all the time the community has been alive, seems not only monstrous but preposterous as well, and appears to have more than a tinge of the *hubris* of man trying to set himself up against the existing nature of things, and to dictate by abstractions rather than by the realities in which people live. The sense of community and belonging is probably the most important single good that a society can bestow; it has been strong in the South, though including, as it manifestly does, a number of grievous injustices; it has been strong, and now it is fast disappearing; and he is dismayed and even frightened to see it go. He remembers something, long since thought forgotten, he once read in a book in France, laboriously puzzling out the sentences with the aid of a glossary. Perhaps it was in one of the *Journals* of Julien Green, himself of American Southern parentage: "The South did not really lose the Civil War until around 1920, when it consented to follow the lead of the North." With this statement he heartily concurs. That is, he concurs emotionally. As soon as he examines what might have happened, and probably would have happened, if the South had *not* consented to follow the lead of the North, he sees that the present trend of industrialism and business was not only more or less inevitable, but probably even for the best, dreadful as some of its results have been.

Could the South, in fact, have remained a farming region? With machines doing more and more of the farm labor and consequently decreasing the number of agrarian jobs, how could a population consisting entirely of farmers have been supported? Or should the South deliberately have turned its back on the machine, and insisted upon using the modes of labor, transportation, and distribution of a hundred, of a hundred and fifty years ago? Can one forget that a machine, the cotton gin, helped to create and maintain the infinitely rich cotton empire of the Old South? How then have the machine and not have it? How change and not change? How in all conscientiousness deny advances in medicine, public health, education, to say nothing of agriculture? Should the South have willfully turned itself into an enclave of clannish, half-educated farmers, hopelessly outmoded in every phase of contemporary life, even in the one profession which they knew and lived by?

Obviously not. To insist upon such artificial means to preserve a few admittedly desirable features of family and community life is to ignore everything in the human makeup that moves and wants to improve itself and the conditions among which it exists. There is no compromise between the old modes of Southern life and "progress," a word which no one likes, but which one must inevitably use. With the machine, and the shifting and mixing of populations it encourages, the sense of place is attenuated, and with it the sense of belonging by right to a given segment of the earth, held in common with other human beings to whom one is tied by the immense force of the past, by the lives of forebears who knew and in their time lived on the same part of the earth, who fought for it, who are buried in it, and who, somehow, seem still to be brooding over and watching the ground which they possessed in a profundity now become unattainable to their heirs.

Nowhere else in this country, not even in New England, is the ancestor held in so much real reverence as he is in the South—his opinions, his acts, his idiosyncrasies, his *being*. Consequently, nowhere else is his spirit, his ghost, so powerful, disturbing, and influential. "Why, your grandfather Tom would turn over in his grave if he thought . . ." or, "What would your dead mother think, if she could see you now?" Questions like this, perhaps more than any the living could ask, require answers. Well, what *would* his dead mother—or, worse still—what would his grandfather Swift think if he *could* see him now, sitting in the same seat in a bus with a Negro? His grandfather's first reaction would be, he is sure, incredulity, and then . . . and then . . . outrage. "What in the world has happened to you, boy?" he would no doubt ask, in a rising, irresistible, and particularly terrible tide of resentment, and a bewilderment even more terrible. He feels a quick, deep flush of shame thinking of this; he has loved and honored his grandfather; he loves and honors him still.

Of the old man he retains several images of tremendous depth and authority. The most important of these is simply a recollection of sitting on the porch of a house in the country, listening to his grandfather tell of his experiences in the troop of General John B. Gordon. For a moment, in speaking of a battle, he had rested his steady and very old hand on the child's shoulder and said, "I wish you could have been there with me." He can still feel the touch of his grandfather's hand. And he has always liked to think that in some way he *was* with his grandfather that day, and that he did not falter, but acted with the unhesitating courage and authority he is sure his grandfather must have displayed, not because the situation required it, but because his life did. Never has he had so much reverence for anyone else as for his grandfather Swift, the kindest, gravest old man he can remember, or would ever want to remember, whose manners proceeded from the most scrupulous consideration for others with whom he came in contact, but even more from a kind of climate of courtesy which belonged to the world that had created him. He remembers also his grandfather's behavior with Negroes: considerate, but admitting of no argument and no redress. So far as he had been able to tell, the Negroes accepted and even welcomed these conditions, and he recalls the uncontrollable grief of many of them as they stood by his grandfather's coffin.

These memories are now intolerably confused. He asks himself if the good of his grandfather's life, and of the kind of life which produced his grandfather's character, were not inextricably entangled with attitudes which, rightly seen, are and have always been indefensible, inhuman, corrupt, and corrupting. It hardly matters that such attitudes have been implicit in human affairs ever since the first primitive man realized that it would be more profitable and considerably easier for him if he could get another to perform certain tasks instead of having to do them himself; he is occupied at the moment mainly with the knowledge that his grandfather's indignation, his *outrage*, could he see his grandson now (and in this land of powerful and eternal ghosts, does he not see?), would be limitless, and would include a betrayed, bewildered, and unbearable sadness. The young man understands himself as the victim of a cruel and fathomless paradox, a dilemma between the horns of which only a god could survive and still retain his identity. But perhaps he has led himself into an absurd train of logic. Is it in fact true that he cannot really be the grandson he wishes to be without seeing Negroes as his grandfather saw them? Can he truly be his grandfather's kinsman, torn as he is by a thousand doubts that never would have troubled those of his grandfather's generation?

To state the issues in this way is undoubtedly to insist upon their extremes, but he knows that sooner or later the public fruit of what is now opinion must ripen, and that in the end he will have to go on record as being of a certain mind, having taken a stand. After the Supreme Court decision on segregation, and with the admission of Negroes to buses and streetcars on an equal footing with whites, with their entry into white residential areas and private clubs and eating places, and, above all, into the public schools, he knows he will have to assert himself one way or the other on the Question. He needs no one to remind him of the consequences of the position he may take; if he sides with Negroes instead of against them, he will have helped as effectively as he could ever hope to do to kill the South and lay it in its grave.

Yet he is, after all, not his grandfather. He recognizes only too well the distance of his fall, the gulf between his grandfather's character and his own. Still he does not in all honesty believe that he can by an effort of will, even for the sake of retaining his identity as a "Southerner," take opinions and attitudes for his own which are not his, and against which his whole nature as a sentient and rational man rebels. He cannot, either, regard himself as a "neutral," to be which is an ultimate impossibility. Then where, exactly, *does* he belong?

As nearly as he can tell, he sees his position, and the South's, more in terms of an image, a vision or daydream, than in a logical formulation. It is a banal image, but for him at least it is endowed with the capacity to define the situation in just such a set of clear-cut and dramatic opposites as a subtler, more considered approach might fail to furnish. It is the image of a wall, an old, high, crumbling but still massive wall along the top of which are set sharp, rusty spikes and broken bottles. He has actually seen such a wall, not in the southern United States, but somewhere in Europe. However, in his mind he sees himself, his family, and his ancestors living on one side of the wall. He lives on the side he does because his forebears have lived there, because he has been joined to them by the divine accident of birth, and because they built the wall. On the other side, there because they were once brought and purchased like beasts, in indescribable poverty and humiliation which they have learned by their own means to turn into a kind of virtue accessible to none but them, live Negroes. This is the Negro's "place," the place in which he must stay to be allowed his identity by those who determine the forms and limits which that identity may take.

Through the closely guarded door in the wall come certain Negroes, under all but constant surveillance of whites. Through it, in point of fact, and under this constant scrutiny, come very nearly all Negroes at one time or another, and most of them every day—the men to work at menial, badly paid jobs, tearing up and laying down railroad track, driving trucks, lifting heavy weights, running elevators, digging, piling, sweating, grunting, and heaving, with amazing musculature and unquestioning patience; the women to wash clothes, to look after white children, to serve the tables and clean the houses of the whites. At night they return through the wall, and the door is closed. Behind the wall, what happens, when the Negro is once again inside the one poor world he can call his: when he is "in his place"?

The young man has never had more than a fragmentary and inadequate notion of what lay behind the wall, in the easily violated world of the American Southern Negro, but he feels continually the human force trapped and maimed there. He knows that the Negro's place is squalid, dark, and huddled, and he suspects it is filled with an undercurrent of violence scarcely to be borne. When in high school, and drawn there by some obscure, compulsive reason, he spent part of a Saturday night in the emergency ward of a city hospital, and watched the attendants bring in the victims of that violence, shot in the belly at close range with shotguns, slashed with razors, gored and spitted and gouged with ice picks and pocketknives, beaten with pokers, bleeding, unconscious, or moaning slowly and hopelessly, accompanied by women, relatives, and even children. Somewhere among this background, among the locked-together, filthy shacks and the unseen menace of Saturday night and its duels with straight razors and bread knives, the man sitting next to him is attempting to raise a family in decency, and, yes, in love.

Upon what tremendous power does this man draw, to be able to play with his child here in perfect unselfconsciousness, with no apparent resentment toward anyone, content in his own being and in the small fact of his son? Or is the Negro, in this light, simply the victim of another's self-abasing sentimentality? Is there and has there been at the very heart of the South, all these years, such a source of unused intelligence, unwanted friendship, thwarted and never-defeated affection as would make one catch one's breath even to think of? Yes; and nothing has thwarted these possibilities so much as the zealous guardianship of Southern uniqueness and identity, admittedly in some ways a good, but not *the* good. The South, once crippled beyond humiliation and now clinging to its prejudices as the last vestige of its autonomy, its irreplaceable sense of destiny and glory, is a South he does not believe should be preserved at all costs—that is, at the cost of condemning millions more like the man beside him to lives of the most brutal and hopeless degradation.

For all these reflections, he himself is not any the less a Southerner than he has always been. He is by no means sure that traces of what he has been raised to look upon as his "natural" advantages over Negroes will not remain with him for the rest of his life, do what he will to get rid of them. Not for a moment does he entertain the notion that these prejudices are just, fitting, or reasonable. But neither can he deny that they belong to him by inheritance, as they belong to other Southerners. Yet this does not mean that they cannot be seen for what they are, that they cannot be appraised and understood. The greatest danger, he believes, resides in the assumption that there is no reason to struggle against such prejudices, since they have been closely woven into the very fabric of Southern reality for at least a hundred and seventy-five years. Again, where does this leave him? He is quite convinced that it is just as wrong to love a man solely because he is black as it is to hate him solely because he is black. If there is a solution to the South's dilemma it must come from the individual, or rather from a number of personal relationships, each composed of a Negro and a white who have discovered (the Negro as well as the white, for he has much to learn of the white in any role other than that of master) the common basis for their lives as men, a thing more fundamental than any environment or set of social customs could supply.

With the practical means by which this kind of relationship might be fostered he is as yet unconcerned. It may begin with as simple a thing as a conversation on a bus. In order for this to come about, of course, it is first necessary that it be made possible for the Negro and white in question to sit together on a bus. The basis for such legislation as would bring this about, it is to be hoped, is that by such means both Negro and white can begin to comprehend their likenesses as men more readily, and that their differences may begin to lose the importance that they have had. Yet legislation is completely self-defeating if such is not the outcome, and if "civil rights" simply set the Negro up as an out-and-out enemy, to be despised, flouted, and openly disdained, where hitherto he had been tolerated, so long as he remained "in his place." Legislation is undoubtedly involved in the answer, but legislation is of no value whatever without goodwill and the part that must be played by the real and not the advertised heart.

He is glad that he is not amazed by his own feelings at this moment, and that the thought of his grandfather's outrage is not so saddening and terrible as it had seemed at first. He is glad that he has communicated on a human level, though briefly and as though across an immense gulf, with the young Negro man and his son. To extend his private emotions into a social panacea is not within his strength, and he has no wish to do so, especially since such an attempt might well destroy the personal and so the only value of those emotions. He believes, however, that if such feelings are possible to him, they are to others also. He laughs a little ruefully as he discovers that all the time he has been thinking he has been murmuring to himself, as a semi-unconscious accompaniment, "The past is dead, the past is dead."

But even as he realizes what he is saying, he knows that it is not true. The past is never entirely dead, nor should it be disowned or forgotten. His powerful and perhaps foolish pride in the military effort of the Confederacy is not dead, nor is the memory of his grandfather. The human insufficiency of the Southern "cause" in no way diminishes the steady courage and devotion to each other of his forebears, nor do the racial beliefs of his grandfather destroy his kindness, his seriousness, his quaint and marvelous honesty, courtesy, and directness. Perhaps his grandfather would have been an even better man had he gone among the Negro slaves like Christ, preaching the gospel of freedom, but as it is, he has been good enough; he has been a far better man than his grandson in every way but this. And is the grandson's behavior, even here, superior? If so, how? It is probably true that he will retain at least to some degree some of the attitudes he has inherited with his way of life. But he can now separate them and attain a partial objectivity, and so a partial mastery over them, which his grandfather had never seen any reason to do. If he cannot quite envision a cocktail party composed of Southern Negroes and whites, all enjoying each other's company as if they were all white, or all Negro, and if he still flinches at the idea of Negro-white intermarriage, he can at least begin to recognize the common humanity of himself and the young man sitting beside him, though their differences, both as to racial heritage and countenance, may still appear, and be, enormous.

When the Negro and his son get up to leave the bus, the young man, no more self-consciously than might be expected, raises his hand in good-bye, and the Negro smiles, no more self-consciously than might be expected. A few blocks farther on, the young man gets off and enters his office building, harboring a bargain with himself that he knows he cannot possibly keep in all its implications. But the core of what he has come to believe is not an illusion, he suspects. He tells no one about it, for he correctly assumes that such things must be entirely personal and freely arrived at to be valuable. He goes in to work for a firm almost all of whom are Northerners, the products of forces other than those which have shaped him and brought about his reverie. He knows in a way they do not even suspect that most of the uniquely Southern traditions and characteristics he loves (and that they, occasionally, joke with him about in a vague, uninvolved fashion) cannot continue to exist without the social milieu, the entire complex of attitudes and mutually held opinions that nourished them, since social customs are not subject to the tampering of sociologists in their efforts to promote the desirable aspect of mores and eliminate the undesirable. The best he can do, he reflects, is to go outward toward persons whom he respects, admires, and likes, "regardless of race, color, or creed."

In his case, given his time, his background, and the temper of unrest that exists in the South, this may well be as destructive a thing as he could do, for whatever Negroes he may wish to know as well as for himself. But he must believe that in the end it will not be destructive, and so he must take the consequences, also, of believing that in this place where he was born and where he will probably die, where the Negro must become either a permanent enemy or an equal, where in one form, one body, unsteadily balanced, live the ex-slave, the possible foe, and the unknown brother, it can be a greater thing than the South has ever done to see that the last of these does not die without showing his face.

Robert Frost

"Belovèd" is a term that must always be mistrusted when applied to artists, and particularly to poets. Poets are likely to be belovèd for only a few of the right reasons, and for almost all the wrong ones: for saying things we want to hear, for furnishing us with an image of ourselves that we enjoy believing in, even for living for a long time in the public eye and pronouncing sagely on current affairs. Robert Frost has been long admired for all these things, and is consequently one of the most misread writers in the whole of American literature.

In Frost's case the reputation has come, at least to some extent, from the powerful additive of the Robert Frost Story, a secular myth of surprising power and tenacity: an image that has eaten into the rock of the American psyche and engraved Frost's very engravable face as in a kind of Mount Rushmore of the nation's consciousness. The "Frost Story" would, in fact, make quite an acceptable film script, even allowing for the notorious difficulty Hollywood has in dealing with writers. We enjoy wandering off, mentally, into a scenario of this sort, partly because we know that the main facts of the Frost Story, leaving aside the interpretation that has been put upon them, *are* facts, and also because the Story is and has long been something we believe in with the conviction accorded only to people and events in which we want to believe and will have no other way. Frost is unassailable, a national treasure, a remnant of the frontier and the Thoreauistic virtues of shrewd Yankeedom, the hero of the dozing American daydream of self-reliance and experience-won wisdom we feel guilty about betraying every time we eat a TV dinner or punch a computer. The Frost Story stands over against all that we have become, and hints with mysterious and canny authority that it all might have been otherwise—even that it might yet be so.

It is a dream, of course. To us a dream, surely, but also a kind of dream to Frost, and despite the authenticity of whatever settings the film might choose for its backgrounds, despite the rugged physical presence of Frost himself, any film made of such elements would have to partake of nostalgic visions. It might open, for example, with a sequence showing Frost moving among his Properties—apple trees, birch trees, stone fences, dark woods with snow falling into them, ax handles, shovels, woodpiles, ladders, New England brooks, taciturn neighbors—and then modulate into a conversation with Frost for that cryptic, homely, devious, *delightful* way of making sense out of life—any aspect of it—that the public so loved him for: his way of reducing all generalities to local fact so that they become not only understandable but controllable.

If one wanted to include chronology one might have a little difficulty in making Frost's life in England interesting, for aside from showing some of the places he lived in and visited and photographs of some of the people he knew, like Ezra Pound, Edward Thomas, and Lascelles Abercrombie, it would be hard to do much more than suggest his experiences there. Most of this part would probably have to be carried by voice-over narration, and might deal with Frost manfully being his Own Man, resisting being exploited and misinterpreted by Ezra Pound ("that great intellect abloom in hair"), and with his being a kind of literary Ben Franklin in Georgian England, uncorrupted and wary, delighting the jaded and oversophisticated with, well, his authenticity.

One might then work forward by easy stages into what everybody knows is coming: the great Recognitions of the final years, the readings, the lectures and interviews, the conferences with students and the press—thus affording more time for the Frost Talk—the voyage to Russia and the meeting with Khrushchev, and so on, all culminating in the Ultimate Reading, the Kennedy Inaugural and its little drama of the sunlight, Vice President Johnson's top hat, and the details familiar to those who watch great as well as small events on television. Another poet, Galway Kinnell, has written of this occasion:

> And as the Presidents
> Also on the platform
> Began flashing nervously
> Their Presidential smiles
> For the harmless old guy,
> And poets watching on the TV
> Started thinking, Well that's
> The end of *that* tradition,
>
> And the managers of the event
> Said, Boys this is it,
> This sonofabitch poet
> Is gonna croak,
> Putting the paper aside
> You drew forth
> From your great faithful heart
> The poem.

That drawing forth of the poem from "the great faithful heart" would be the end—how could you top it?—and everyone could leave the theater surer than ever that he had inherited something, some way of responding and speaking as an American, that matters.

To move from this drama of public appearances to Lawrance Thompson's *Robert Frost: The Early Years** is to move, if not wholly out of the myth—for

* *Robert Frost: The Early Years* by Lawrance Thompson. New York, Holt, Rinehart and Winston.

Thompson is very much in its thrall, despite all that he knows of Frost's actual life and personality—then rather into the area of its making, and the reasons for its making. One cannot inhabit Dr. Thompson's book, even under the influence of the Story (or the film, for legends are probably all films of one kind or another), without ceasing to be comfortable in one's prior assumptions. As partial as it is, Dr. Thompson's account is yet the fully documented record of what Frost was like when he was not belovèd: when he was, in fact, a fanatically selfish, egocentric, and at times dangerous man; was, from the evidence, one of the least lovable figures in American literature. What we get from Dr. Thompson is the much less cinematic narrative (and yet, what if someone tried to film *this* Frost Story?) of the construction of a complex mask, a *persona*, an invented personality that the world, following the man, was pleased, was overjoyed, finally, to take as an authentic identity, and whose main interest, biographically and humanly, comes from the fact that the mask is almost the diametrical opposite of the personality that lived in and motivated the man all his life. Most of *Robert Frost: The Early Years*, which takes Frost up through his period in England, is concerned with the twined alternatives of fear and *hubris*: with Frost's desperate efforts to establish and maintain his self-image in the face of every conceivable discouragement, the period when he would quit any job—he quit a good many—go back on any commitment, throw over any trust or personal relationship which did not accord him the deference he persuaded himself he deserved. Dr. Thompson talks persuasively—though not, I think, conclusively—of Frost's need to protect his sensibility from crasser natures and desensitizing work, but one never really believes that this justified Frost's arrogance and callousness on the many occasions when they were the most observable things about him. These were the years of Frost's hating and turning on anyone who helped or cared for him, from his friends like Carl Burell, who worked his poultry farm for him while he nursed his ego, to his grandfather, whose generous legacy Frost insisted on interpreting as a way of "writing off" the poet and "sending him out to die" on a farm that the grandfather actually purchased to give Frost a livelihood and a profession.

The fact that this is the "official" biography keeps coming back to one as one reads, and with this a recognition of the burden that must surely have been on Dr. Thompson's shoulders in writing it: the difficulty in dovetailing the author's bias in favor of his subject—for it is abundantly apparent that Thompson really does deeply care for Frost's work and also for Frost himself—and the necessity to tell what did in reality occur on various occasions.

Dr. Thompson has large numbers of facts, and the first task of the biographer is to make facts *seem* facts, stand up as facts before any interpretation is made from them. One of the ways to do this is to be pedestrian, for the world's facts are pedestrian, and most of the time simply sit there saying over and over again, I am here, I am true, I happened, without any particular emphasis. Consequently there is a good deal of material like "at this stage the Frosts had an unexpected visitor, none other than Edmund J. Harwood, from whom Frost's grandfather had bought the Derry farm" and "another acquaintance was made that evening, a burly red-faced country squire named John C. Chase, the modestly well-to-do owner of a local wood-working factory, which turned out a variety of products including tongue-depressors and similarly shaped tags for marking trees and shrubs in nurseries." This makes for a certain monotony, but one is inclined to go along with it partly because it is the truth—the man's name *was* John *C.* Chase, and he *did* make tongue depressors—but mainly because it is a necessary background for the second and far more important of the biographer's tasks, that of interpretation. That part is primarily psychological, and if the protagonist has not chosen to tell either the biographer or someone else why he said or did something on a given occasion—and one must be constantly wary of taking him at his word—one must surmise. Dr. Thompson is very good at this, most of the time, but also at some points unconsciously funny.

> During her sophomore year, Jeanie [Frost's sister] suffered through moods of depression much like those which had beset her, intermittently, since her childhood days in San Francisco. Her spells of tears, hysteria, ravings, which caused her to miss more and more days of school, puzzled her mother increasingly. In the midst of one spell Jeanie was making so much noise that Mrs. Frost turned desperately to her son for help. Enraged, he stormed into Jeanie's bedroom, found her lying face down on the bed, turned her over, and slapped her across the face with the flat of his hand. Just for a moment the one blow had the desired effect: Jeanie grew silent, stopped crying completely, and sat up. She stared at her brother and then said, scornfully, "You cad, you coward." That was not Rob's only use of violence when trying to help his sister.

When other incidents indicate clearly that brother and sister absolutely detested each other, one has a certain hesitation in identifying "Rob's" motive as helpfulness. Yet it seems to me that Dr. Thompson's deductions are right a great deal more than they are wrong, and that is really all we can ask of a mortal biographer.

Frost was born in San Francisco in 1874. We watch him live through the decline and death of his alcoholic, ambitious father, follow him as he is shunted around New England as a poor relation, supported by his gentle, mystical mother's pathetically inept attempts to be a teacher. We see him develop, as compensation, a fanatical and paranoiac self-esteem with its attendant devils of humiliation, jealousy, and frustration. He considers suicide, tries poultry farming, loses a child, settles on poetry as a way of salvation—something, at last, that he *can* do, at least to some extent—borrows money and fails to pay it back, perseveres with a great deal of tenacity and courage but also with a sullen self-righteousness with which one can have but very little sympathy.

He wanted, and from his early days—Dr. Thompson makes much of his "idealism," learned from his mother—to be "great," distinctive, different, a law unto himself, admired but not restricted by those who admired him. He did well in high school when he found that good marks earned him a distinction he had never had before, but he was continually hampered by his arrogance and his jealousy of others, and after graduation seems to have been able to do little else but insult the people who tried to help him and accept and quit one humiliating job after another with as bad grace as possible.

During all this time, however, his writing developed, and in a remarkably straight line. He had, almost from the beginning, a flair for straightforward, uncomplicated versification of the traditional kind, and a stubborn belief that poetry should sound "like talk." He also apparently fastened very early on the notion that to hint is better than to say, and the idea that there are ways of saying, of seeming to say, both more and less than one seems to be saying.

Determining all questions of technique was his conception of the imaginative faculty as being essentially *protection*, self-protection, armor for the self-image. Looking back on Frost through the lens of Dr. Thompson's book, one finds it obvious that the mode, the manner in which a man lies, and what he lies about—these things, and the *form* of his lies—are the main things to investigate in a poet's life and work. The events of Frost's life, events similar to those experienced by a great many people, are not nearly so important as the interpretation he put upon them. The *persona* of the Frost Story was made year by year, poem by poem, of elements of the actual life

Frost lived, reinterpreted by the exigencies of the *persona*. He had, for example, some knowledge of farming, though he was never a farmer by anything but default. Physically he was a lazy man, which is perhaps why images of work figure so strongly in his poems. Through these figures in his most famous pieces, probably his best poems—haying, apple-picking, mowing, cleaning springs, and mending walls—he indulged in what with him was the only effective mode of self-defense he had been able to devise: the capacity to claim competence at the menial tasks he habitually shirked, and to assert, from that claim, authority, "earned truth," and a wisdom elusive, personal, and yet final.

At his simplest, his most rhythmical and cryptic, Frost is a remarkable poet. In deceptively "straight" syntax and in rhymes that are like the first rhymes one thinks of when one thinks of rhymes, Frost found his particular way of making mysteries and moral judgments start up from the ground under the reader's feet, come out of the work one did in order to survive and the environment in which both the work and the survival prolonged themselves, leap into the mind from a tuft of flowers, an ax handle suddenly become sin itself, as when "the snake stood up for evil in the garden." This individualizing and localizing way of getting generalities to reveal themselves—original sin, universal Design, love, death, fate, large meanings of all kinds—is a major factor in Frost's approach, and is his most original and valuable contribution to poetry. Like most procedures, it has both its triumphs and its self-belittlements, and there are both good Frost poems and awful ones, not as dissimilar as one might think, to bear this out.

The trouble, of course, is that Frost had but little idea of when he was in a position to make an effective ("earned") judgment and when he was not. In the beginning he was cautious about this, but when the public spurred him on, he was perfectly willing to pronounce on anything and everything, in poems or out of them. This resulted in the odd mixture of buffoonery and common sense (but hardly ever more than that) of his last years.

And yet at his best, which we must do him the service of identifying as his most characteristic, he is perfectly amazing. We have all harbored at odd times a suspicion that the key to large Significances lay close at hand, could we but find it. Frost understood how this feeling could be made to serve as the backbone of a kind of poetry that was not only profound but humanly convincing as well, as most poetry, panting and sweating to be linguistically interesting, is not. One *believes* the Frost voice. That itself is a technical triumph, and of the highest kind. It enables the poems to come without being challenged into places in the consciousness of the "average" reader that have been very little visited before, and almost never by poems.

Yet it is well to remember, for all the uplifting force that it has legitimately, and illegitimately, been in so many lives, for all the conclusion-drawing and generalizing that the public has esteemed and rewarded it for, that the emotions of pain, fear, and confusion are the roots of Frost's poetry. Lionel Trilling, with his usual perceptiveness, has seen this, and seen it better than anyone else, perhaps even including Frost, ever saw it. Trilling's Frost of darkness and terror is more nearly the real Frost, the Frost permanently valuable as a poet, than any other, and it is in poems where these emotions fuse with his methods—poems like "Design"—that he moves us most.

What he accomplished, in the end, was what he became. Not what he became as a public figure, forgotten as quickly as other public figures are, but what he became as a poet. He survives in what he made his own invented being say. His main achievement, it seems to me, is the creation of a particular kind of poetry-speaking voice. He, as much as any American poet, brought convincingness of tone into poetry, and made of it a gauge against which all poetry would inevitably have to be tried. This voice endures in a few powerful and utterly original poems: "After Apple-Picking," "Provide, Provide," "To Earthward."

Dr. Thompson's authoritative and loving book makes clear that Frost's way was the only one open to him, and also the fact that, among other things, his poems were a tremendous *physical* feat, a lifelong muscular striving after survival. Though tragically hard on the people who loved him, put up with him, and suffered because of him, Frost's courage and stubbornness are plain, and they are impressive. But no one who reads this book will ever again believe in the Frost Story, the Frost myth, which includes the premises that Frost the man was kindly, forbearing, energetic, hardworking, good-neighborly, or anything but the small-minded, vindictive, ill-tempered, egotistic, cruel, and unforgiving man he was until the world deigned to accept at face value his estimate of himself. What price art, indeed? Dr. Thompson's biography has, or should have, the effect of leading us all into a private place—the grave of judgment, or the beginning of it—where we ponder long and long the nature "of life and art," their connections and interconnections, and the appalling risk, the cost in lives and minds not only of putting rhythmical symbols of ink on a white page, but of encountering, of reading them as well.

Marianne Moore

Though her new *Reader** contains a generous sampling of all the forms her writing has taken, her poems are, of course, Marianne Moore's main work. They depend largely upon her voluminous memory of things she has read in an unimaginable variety of places, from highly technical reference books on animal species to the daily columns of sports writers, on her ability to draw judgments from these and to make points which the culled items themselves would never have thought of, and on her own power of description, which is dazzling:

> The barnacles which encrust the side
> of the wave, cannot hide
> there for the submerged shafts of the
>
> sun
> split like spun
> glass, move themselves with spotlight swiftness
> into the crevices—

Surely few poets have had so keen and so *right* an eye for the ways in which one thing resembles another, or one aspect of a thing suggests an aspect of another. Her capacity for finding, fastening onto, and transmuting the wayward, the peculiarly apt, the odd and the interesting fact, the little known and the universally known is constantly astonishing, and so is her faculty for making these dovetail into a careful, reticently revealing assessment of what, together, they illustrate or seem to prove. Few poets, either, have shown how endlessly various, how ingenious and idiosyncratic and inexplicably fascinating, how sheerly *interesting* the world is in its multifarious aspects, many if not all of which are constantly modifying the beings and meanings of others in secret and half-glimpsable ways: have shown how the world is always becoming more and more absorbing, divulging to the imagination behind the practiced, practical eye a continual metamorphosis of illuminating correspondences and potentialities, some of which were always there, only waiting to be discovered, and others which have just come into being, from the outcome of a baseball game played yesterday, a new statement by a physicist,

* *A Marianne Moore Reader*. New York, The Viking Press.

a new treatise on rare animals or on the fur trade in the Hudson Bay area in the 1880's. Though there are notes to some of these poems, the poems are readily graspable without them, and are in no sense like the sterile paste-ups of William Empson and Charles Madge. Though Miss Moore is learned and sometimes devious, her poems have a way of coming wonderfully clear in the end, for their details are first lived before they are written into their forms of language, and she cares about communicating.

The dangers that Miss Moore's method runs are two. First, there is the risk of her disappearing behind her quotations, and of the essential second-handedness of this part of her approach becoming obtrusive and therefore self-defeating. The second danger is that, in a universe of correspondences such as she posits, the resemblances and cross-fertilizations of her selected items will, if inspiration fails, seem simply fortuitous or "yoked by violence," a danger somewhat alleviated by Miss Moore's use of syllabic meters, whose slow, sober matter-of-factness can be made to *seem* to carry anything and makes even the ridiculously diverse appear not only to belong together, but to *want* to belong together. Miss Moore's task as she has set it is to bring forth only the best and most humanly useful, the most telling, the *essential* parallels: out of the infinitude of possibilities of comparison and illustration, only those we most need. In firm tones, ever the half-prose substructure of syllabic verse, Miss Moore has only to say "Like the . . ." and anything could be admissible. It is perhaps not the least tribute one could pay to her work to say that anything is definitely *not* admissible, and that her exquisite tact and insight into her materials enable her to surmount both these dangers—though she is never very far from them—with a quiet and responsible assurance that amounts to triumph. Surely there has not been such imaginative and evocative precision since the Hopkins of the *Note-books*, and one can only regret, here, the exclusion of so many of the other poems Miss Moore has written, for nothing that she has touched is unprofitable, and we should welcome all the contact we can get with her watchful, spoken songs, with her way of putting the world together.

Her essays are as particularizing, judicious, modest, and incisive as her poems, and one realizes in reading them that in a sense the poems are inspired verse essays which make use of the daring leaps in logic and sequence which poetry permits more readily than prose. Except for the obvious omission of Miss Moore's metrical patterns and her cunning rhyme schemes, the essays are not greatly different from the poems; the packing of the text with quotations is still very much in evidence, as is her method of weaving together the thing being said from a number of other sources. Miss Moore's piece on Ezra Pound, for example, is the best on Pound that I can remember, and this is largely because it is Pound writing on himself as he should have written; it is hardly more than an extremely discriminating choice of citations from Pound's verse and prose, but these are arranged in a manner which reveals strikingly what his principles and his practice offer in their essences; even though Miss Moore seems hardly to permit herself to get a word in edgewise, we see Pound a great deal more clearly than before. That, I take it, is what is meant by interpretive criticism at its best.

Miss Moore also includes a number of translations from La Fontaine's *Fables*, published and much discussed several years ago. Howard Nemerov and others have shown that her French is not quite certain, and that she positively misreads more than a few passages, all of which adds up to demonstrating, I suppose, that her *Fables* are more Moore than they are La Fontaine. That is all right with me. Though I don't know La Fontaine except through Miss Moore, I suspect her of being the same kind of translator that Pound is, in, say, his renderings from the Chinese: being, even at his wrongest, somehow righter than right. If La Fontaine sounds like Miss Moore, he's lucky. Few writers are, this many years after death.

The one thing I most strongly regret about *A Marianne Moore Reader* is the inclusion of the so-called Ford Letters: the correspondence in which, at the instigation of Robert B. Young, of Ford's Marketing Research Department, Miss Moore undertook to find a salesworthy name for a new automobile. What I dislike most intensely in the whole affair is the assumption on the part of Mr. Young and his associates that there must be, might be, *some* practical good to be got from poets, who after all use words, just as copywriters do, but conceivably a little better; I keep imagining one executive at Dearborn saying to another, "Why, if poets can sell cars, let's use 'em." I have had considerable experience with this viewpoint myself, and I admire the perspicacity with which Miss Moore handles Mr. Young and his ghostwriter and/or stooge Mr. David Wallace, and the characteristic tenacity with which, without knowing anything whatever of advertising methods, she attempts to discover a usable trade name. But it is distressing, too, to see her struggling, with all her good faith and the same painstakingness that produced her poems, to come up with either the first thing that a junior copywriter would know enough to discard ("The Ford Silver Sword") or names so recherché and esoteric that they must have made the members of Ford's marketing team smile in amazed disbelief, as they did me, as I tried to imagine the company's money being paid out to publicize something called the "Triskelion," the "Turcotingo," or the "Utopian Turtletop." But I have also a vicious and continuing delight in recalling that the car, eventually named the "Edsel," was on all counts the biggest failure in recent automotive history, and must have been a financial disaster as well. Miss Moore's part in the whole thing was honorable and mistaken, and I hate to have such evidence of her exploited naïveté included in the only comprehensive selection that has been made of her work. It is a small price to have to pay, though, for the amassed riches of her *Reader*. To use her words, which are better than mine, her writing is a prime example of the "intensified particularity" of which we must be capable in order to get all the way *into* life, into the world both as it is and as it can be when we have achieved the "simplicity that is not the product of a simple mind but of a single eye." One relishes saying of Miss Moore, as one passes her book along, what she says of Paul Rosenfeld: "When everything has its price, and more than price, and anyone is venal, what a thing is the interested mind with the disinterested motive. Here it is."

Heaven is a vision, and so is earth; or at least it can be. Of one of these we know something; about the other we have to speculate. A question: What poet would we most like to have construct a Heaven for us, out of the things we already have? Construct it from his way of being, his particular method of putting the world together and endowing it with consequence? And what would we end up with, picking one rather than another? Would we prefer to inherit the cowled, ecclesiastical, distantly murmuring twilight of Eliot? Should the angels sing in a mixture of Provençal, Greek and frontier American, presided over by the perfect Confucian governor, as Ezra Pound might have it? Or would Paradise be the Artificial one of Baudelaire, a place like nocturnal Paris: a Heaven which—the maker might argue—contains those elements of Hell without which our joy could not exist?

If the question were put to me, I would choose Marianne Moore. And I suspect that this is so because of her persuasiveness in getting the things of this world to live together as if they truly belonged that way, and because the communal vividness of her poems suggests to me order of an ideal kind. In a way, she has spent her life in remaking—or making—our world from particulars that we have never adequately understood on our own.

Well, what kind of Heaven would Miss Moore's be? Much, most probably, like the earth as it is, but refined by responsiveness and intellect into a state very far from the present one; a state of utter consequentiality. For what is Heaven, anyway, but the power of dwelling eternally among objects and actions of consequence? Miss Moore's Heaven would have a means of recording such objects and actions; it would have a history, and a way of preserving its discoveries and happenings: it would have books. But it would be, first of all, a realm of Facts: it would include an enormous amount of matter for there to be opinions about, and so it would make possible vivid and creative and personal parallels between things, and conclusions unforeseeable until they were made. It would take forever from Fact the deadness of being *only* fact, for it would endow what Is with the joyous conjunctions that only a personality itself profoundly creative, profoundly accessible to experience—a personality called a soul—can find among them. Truly, would we have it otherwise in the Eternal City?

This is how Miss Moore might do it. Or, more truthfully, how she has done it, by taking—literally—everything as her province, as the province of her poems. Her Heaven would be not only an artist's Heaven—though it would be that with a magnificent authority—but a Heaven to show the angels what they have missed. Missed, for example, by not knowing, or caring *enough*, about the story in Meyer Berger's "Brooklyn Bridge: Fact and Symbol" of the young reporter of the 1870's who, drawn by some unknown imperative, climbed one of the cables of the bridge, became spellbound to the extent that he couldn't come down, and simply hung there all night. Who ever knew this but Mr. Berger, the reporter, and Miss Moore? Miss Moore knew it not only because she encountered it, but because she *cared* to encounter it, and then came to possess it, first by knowing it and then by using it.

Each of her poems employs items that Miss Moore similarly encountered and to which she gave a new, Mooreian existence in a new cosmos of consequential relationships. What seems to me to be the most valuable point about Miss Moore is that such receptivity as hers—though it reaches perhaps its highest degree in her example—is not Miss Moore's exclusive property. Every poem of hers lifts us toward our own discovery-prone lives. It does not state, in effect, that I am more intelligent than you, more creative because I found this item and used it and you didn't. It seems to say, rather, I found this, and what did you find? Or, better, what *can* you find?

Miss Moore's critical intelligence is not destructive, as criticism is almost always taken to be, but positive in the richest and best sense. As a result of its use, who knows better than she how sheerly *experienceable* the world is, and in how many ways and on how many levels? She has asked, and the world has answered, for it understands, in all its billions of parts, how to answer when questions are rightly put.

This is Miss Moore's first book of poems since 1959,* and it is probably the finest of them all. It is, of course, much like her others, for she is not the kind of writer who goes through phases, but rather one who deepens down into what she already was: a poet of surprising particulars that also happen to be true. Here, some of her particulars are large, like the Brooklyn Bridge, and some are small, like the bear in the old Frank Buck animal-trapping film she saw. (And, come to think of it, "Bring 'Em Back Alive" is not an unrevealing way to characterize Miss Moore's poetic method, either.) What you find out from these new poems is what Miss Moore has learned from in the last seven years: what she has read, what ball-players she has watched, what museums and zoos she has gone to, what people she has talked to.

In one poem, for example, she juxtaposes a quotation from Sir Kenneth Clark's "Leonardo da Vinci," another from da Vinci's own notebooks, and a statement by da Vinci that Henry Noss, a history professor at New York University, cited in a television lecture. These become entities which strike whole showers of fresh sparks from each other, and one feels that their conjunction is possible only because Miss Moore so thoroughly understands, by an act of the acutest intelligence, these quotations in all their expressive possibilities, and not simply in the contexts in which they originally occurred: she knows what they are *all* about, instead of merely what they think they are all about.

Informing Miss Moore's work is a lovely, discriminating, and enthusiastic involvement with the way things are: *are*. In her poem to the Brooklyn Bridge, it is part of her involvement to know as much as she can learn about the engineer who built the bridge, and also something of the purely technical problems of its construction: to know what a "catenary curve" is. As it turns out, this "curve formed by a rope or cable hanging freely between two fixed points of support" is not only interesting in itself, but it becomes a poetic as well as an engineering term: the next time you ride by it or on it or see a picture of it, feel how the bridge deepens not only its structural Thereness for you, but its range of suggestiveness as well, being now a construction as much like a poem as a bridge, and requiring on both levels its own laws, its own initiates.

In her "burning desire to be explicit," Miss Moore tells us that facts make

* *Tell Me, Tell Me* by Marianne Moore. New York, The Viking Press.

her feel "profoundly grateful." This is because knowledge, for her, is not power but love, and in loving it is important to know *what* you love, as widely and as deeply and as well as possible. In paying so very much attention to the things of this earth that she encounters, or that encounter her, Miss Moore urges us to do the same, and thus gives us back, in strict syllables, the selves that we had contrived to lose. She persuades us that the human mind is nothing more or less than an organ for loving things in both complicated and blindingly simple ways, and is organized so as to be able to love in an unlimited number of fashions and for an unlimited number of reasons. This seems to me to constitute the correct poetic attitude, which is essentially a life-attitude, for it stands forever against the notion that the earth is an apathetic limbo lost in space.

Who knows of Heaven? It may be only the convenient fiction of a reviewer, after all. But whatever her labors in the realm of the celestial—and I personally would never discount the possibility of their existence—one thing is certain: Miss Moore is making our earth.

From Sorties

Doubleday published Sorties, *a collection of journal entries and essays, in 1971. As in* Babel to Byzantium, *in* Sorties *Dickey expressed his controversial views of his contemporaries and also developed his ideas about the poet's need for a mask or persona. Dickey maintained that the writer should be a superb liar. He had to develop new selves and project them convincingly in his work. With this in mind, Dickey sometimes resorted to a kind of* ad hominem *criticism, rebuking poets like Theodore Roethke and Robert Frost for what he perceived to be a lack of creativity in their mask-making.*

The Self as Agent

i

Every poem written—and particularly those which make use of a figure designated in the poem as "I"—is both an exploration and an invention of identity. Because the poem is not the actual world of tactile sensations and relations, but must be represented as such by the agreed-upon meanings and the privately symbolic values of words, the person who is so identified often bears only a questionable and fugitive resemblance to the poet who sits outside the poem, not so much putting his I-figure through an action but attempting to find out what the I-figure will do, under these circumstances as they develop and round themselves out. The poem is admittedly a fiction; its properties are all fictional even if they are based on fact, and its devices are those of consciously manipulated artifice. The poem is created by what is said in it, and the *persona* of the I-figure is correspondingly conditioned far more by the demands of the poem as a formal linguistic structure than by those of the literal incident upon which it may be based. Therefore the notion of a poem-self identifiable with the author's real one, and consistent from poem to poem, is a misreading of the possibilities of poetic composition.

What is the motive on the part of the poet, in this regard? Why does he assign to "himself," as he appears in his own poems, such and such traits, such and such actions? In other words, why does he make himself act the way he does in his poems? This question could of course be answered in the most obvious way, by saying that there is bound to be some degree of wish-fulfillment present in the poet's practice, and undoubtedly there would be truth in the assertion. But more important than that, the I-figure's actions and meanings, and indeed his very being, are determined by the poet's rational or instinctive grasp of the dramatic possibilities in the scene or situation into which he has placed himself as one of the elements. To put it another way, he sees the creative possibilities of the lie. He comes to understand that he is not after the "truth" at all but something that he considers better. He understands that he is not trying to tell the truth but to *make* it, so that the vision of the poem will impose itself on the reader as more memorable and value-laden than the actuality it is taken from. In the work of many a poet, therefore, the most significant creation of the poet is his fictional self. The identity that is created by the devices and procedures of the poem has made him into an agent fitted more or less well, more or less perfectly, to the realm of the poem. The personality that the I-figure has therein may never recur, and the external poet, the writing poet, is under no obligation to make him do so. Likewise the *author's* personality as it changes from poem to poem is not itself assignable to any single poem. A certain Protean quality is one of the poet's most valuable assets. Therefore he is almost invariably embarrassed at the question he is bound to be asked about his poems: "Did you really *do* that?" He can only ask in turn: "Did *who* do it?"

From poem to poem the invented self is metamorphosed into whatever it is to become in the poem. Though language itself is the condition that makes the poem possible, there are a great number of other factors that make this particular *use* of language possible and, with luck, desirable. To use an analogy, the poem is a kind of local weather, and what creates it is the light that words in certain conjunctions play upon each other. It is a place of delicate shades as well as of sudden blindnesses, and, while it is in the process of being made, it is impossible for its creator to tell what the total light of the completed poem will be like. But no matter whatever else it may be likened to, the poem is a realm that is being created around the I-figure as he is being created within it. The poet knows that his figure will be taken for him; he knows that "this is supposed to be me," but the conditions by which he is limited and delimited in the poem are, in fact, nothing like the same ones that shape his actual life. During the writing of the poem, the poet comes to feel that he is releasing into its proper field of response a portion of himself that he has never really understood.

As for the I-figure himself, he is at first nebulous, ectoplasmic, wavering in and out of several different kinds of possible identity. He is a stranger in a half-chaotic place that may with fortune and time become familiar. Though by the time the poem is completed he may have come solid, dominant, and even godlike, he is tentative indeed at the beginning of the poet's labors. The poet in his turn exercises an expectant vigilance, always ready to do what the agent-self inside the poem requests him to; he will do what he can to make his agent act, if not convincingly, then at least dramatically, tellingly, memorably. The questions he must answer in this respect come to the poet in forms not so much like "What did I do then?" but rather "What might I have done?" or "What would it be interesting for me to do, given the situation as I am giving it?" Or perhaps, if the poet is prone to speak in this way, "What can I make my agent do that will truly *find* the poem: that will focus it on or around a human action and deliver a sense of finality and consequence, and maybe even that aura of strangeness that Bacon said every 'excellent beauty' must possess?"

As we know, it is part of the way in which the human being makes identifications to take the *persona* of the poem for the poet himself: to make him personally accountable not only for the poem's form and its insights but for the events which the poem describes, translated back into the world of real human beings and non-mental objects. Who does not, for example, identify Prufrock as Eliot? It is hard not to do this, even when the I-figure is designated in the title or by other means as a *persona*, as in Browning's "The

Bishop Orders His Tomb at Saint Praxed's Church." In reflecting on such matters, one realizes the implications, both artistic and personal, that reside in Proust's injunction to Gide to the effect that one can "say anything, so long as one doesn't say 'I.'"

ii

What does the poet begin with in attempting to create a personage in a poem who will bear the name "I"? With an individual in a time and at a place, or reflecting in a kind of timeless and placeless mental limbo. The poet usually gives him some overt or implied reason for speaking, and for reacting in a certain way to the events in which he finds himself or those that he thinks about. What he reacts to, for example, may be a condition or a person he knows well, or one he knows to some degree, or it may be something that acts upon him with the wonderful or uncertain or dreadful shock of newness. Now the poet believes that he understands his *persona* only to the extent that he understands himself. But that is not quite the case. For some unfathomable reason, the poet may find his "self" acting in quite an inexplicable way, often doing things that the poet never knew either of them knew. So the poem becomes not so much a matter of the poet's employing a familiar kind of understanding but rather a matter of aesthetic and personal curiosity: the placing of a part of himself into certain conditions to see what will come of it in terms of the kind of interaction between personality and situation he has envisioned from the beginning. He must of course then empathize, he must think himself into the character, but he must realize that his character also possesses the power to think itself into him and to some extent to dictate what he writes. For the poet's part, one of the most interesting things to note is that the poet is just as likely to attribute to his character traits that are diametrically opposed to those that the poet displays during his day-to-day existence. For this reason as well as for others, it is possible for psychologists to make a very great deal out of poems, as Ernest Jones does with *Hamlet*, to take one of the most obvious cases. But the poem, though it may be useful or instructive in this way, does not exist exclusively or even primarily for this reason, as we know. It is not because of its psychologically revelatory qualities that the poem interests us; it is its capacity to release to us—and release us to—insights that we otherwise assuredly would not have, giving these by means of the peculiar and inimitable formal devices of a practiced art.

As a poet, I have done a good deal of speculating on the kinds of ways certain poets might be presumed to make themselves think, act, and speak in their poems. And in my own work I have wrestled with the problem in my own way. For example, should the poet cause his I-figure to speak in a manner in which he might be expected to speak, but which *feels* wrong to the poet? And are the advantage and perils of first-person narration the same for poems as they are for novels and stories? Some of the best of our fiction writers—Henry James comes to mind—have called the first-person device a limited and even "barbarous" method. But for poetry as well as for fiction it has one quite simply incomparable characteristic, and that is credibility. When the poet says "I" to us—or, as Whitman does, "I was the man, I suffer'd, I was there"—we must either believe him completely or tell him in effect that he's a damned liar if his poem betrays him, by reason of one kind of failure or another, into presenting himself as a character in whom we either cannot or do not wish to believe. Because of its seeming verisimilitude, some recent writers have so overused the first person that they are designated—and rightly—as "confessional." And, though all poetry is in a sense confessional, no really good poetry is ever completely so, for "confessing" means "telling the truth and nothing but the truth," and, setting aside the question of whether that is really possible to any creature lower than the angels, it is evident that for any imaginative poet there are too many good opportunities outside of and beyond the mere facts to pass up; in most instances these are the opportunities that, when utilized and realized in the poem, make it more telling dramatically—and "truthful" as well. What the poet wishes to discover or invent is a way of depicting an action in a manner that will give at the same time the illusion of a truth-beyond-truth and the sense of a unique imaginative vision. The real poet invariably opts for the truth of the poem as against the truth of fact, the truth of truth.

And so the poet is aware, more than he is aware of anything else, of the expressive possibilities of his use of himself: that agent in the poem whom he calls "I." He feels a strange freedom and a new set of restrictions when he realizes that he can call into play—can energize—any aspect of himself he wishes to, even if he doesn't yet know what it is to be: any self that the poem calls for. He exults in his "negative capability" and can, as Keats says, take as much delight in creating an Iago as an Imogen. His personality is fluid and becomes what it is most poetically profitable for it to become, in the specific poem in which it comes to exist. Poems are points in time when the I-figure congeals and takes on a definite identity and ascertainable qualities, and the poet is able to appear, for the space of the poem, as a coherent and stabilizing part of the presentation, observing, acting, and serving as a nucleus of the unities and means and revelations of the poem, a kind of living focal point—or perhaps it would be better to say that he finds himself *living* the focal point. The better the poet is—Shakespeare, Browning—the more mercurial he will be, and, paradoxically, the more convincing each of his *personae* will be, for he can commit himself to each independently and, as it were, completely. The better the poet is, the more personalities he will have, and the more surely he will find the right forms to give each of them its being, its time and place, and its voice. A true poet can write with utter convincingness about "his" career as a sex murderer, and then in the next poem with equal conviction about tenderness and children and self-sacrifice. As Keats says, it is simply that the poet "has no personality." I would say, rather, that he has a personality large enough to encompass and explore each of the separate, sometimes related, sometimes unrelated, personalities that inhabit him, as they inhabit us all. He is capable of inventing or of bringing to light out of himself a very large number of I-figures to serve in different poems, none of them obligated to act in conformity with the others.

To speak personally, this has always seemed to me to constitute the chief glory and excitement of writing poetry: that the activity gives the poet a chance to confront and dramatize parts of himself that otherwise would not have surfaced. The poem is a window opening not on truth but on possibility: on the possibility for dramatic expression that may well come to *be* what we think of as truth, but not truth suffering the deadening inertia of what we regard as "actuality," but flowing with energy, meaning, and human feeling. I am quite sure that I myself, for example, owe to the activity of writing poetry my growing conviction that truth is not at all a passive entity, merely lying around somewhere waiting to be found out. I conceive it as something that changes in accordance with the way in which it is seen and more especially with the way it is communicated. And if the poem in which the poet's I-figure serves as an agent concretizes and conveys this sensation of emotional truth, a humanly dramatic and formally satisfying truth, then the literal truth has given birth to a thing more lasting than itself, and by which it will inevitably come to be remembered and judged.

It has always seemed to me that Plato's "The poets lie too much" should be construed as an insult of quite another kind than Plato intended. To be most genuinely damaging to the poets, the philosopher might better have said, "Our poets do not lie creatively enough; I prefer the real world untouched by their fabrications based upon it." For it is within the authentic magic of fabrication (a making-up as a making) that the I-figure moves, for as he receives his kind of reality—both an imposed and a *discovered* reality—from the poet and from language, so his being, his memorability, and his *effect* increase, and his place in his only world is more nearly assured.

The reader, on the other hand, knows that the thing he is dealing with is a *poem*, and not a news bulletin; therefore he can enjoy the luxury of submitting to it; that is, of abandoning his preconceptions about reality and entering into the poem's, for whatever there might be in it for him.

It is quite possible that I am oversimplifying, and drawing the lines too sharply. If the personality and being of the I-figure and the poet himself were *entirely* separate from each other, it would be much easier to discuss the two. But, of course, that is not—and could not be—the case. What happens is that the poet comes on a part of himself inadvertently; he surprises this part and then uses it, and, as he uses it, he more fully discovers it. For instance, suppose that one imagined himself as questioning Wordsworth about the composition of "Tintern Abbey." And suppose the poet answered, as he might well have done, "Yes, I *did* once find myself in just such a situation, and I did, as I recollect (in tranquillity!), feel very much as the poem says I did." And yet the point to note here is that the emotion could not possibly have presented itself, at the time of which it speaks, in the particular images and rhythms of the completed poem; these were factors that were added and worked in later, much after the fact, in an attempt to give the incident some kind of objectifying scheme of reference: to present it by means of a linguistic construction which could, by virtue of the fact that men may communicate verbally in several ways including the poetic, make the experience in at least some ways generally available. Put another way, Wordsworth might conclude of the devices and form of his poem, "They *might be said* to convey something like what I think I remember about that day, and how I felt about it, now that I have thought of it in this way."

Let me take a more recent example—Bernard Spencer's "Ill":

> Expectant at the country gate the lantern. On the night
> Its silks of light strained. Lighted upper window.
> "Is it you sent for me?" The two go in
> To where the woman lies ill, upstairs, out of sight.
>
> I hear sky softly smother to earth in rain,
> As I sit by the controls and the car's burning dials.

And always the main-road traffic searching, searching the
horizons.
Then those sounds knifed by the woman's Ah! of pain.

Who dreamed this; the dark folding murderer's hands
round the lamps?
The rain blowing growth to rot? Lives passed beneath a
ritual
That tears men's ghosts and bodies; the few healers
With their weak charms, moving here and there among
the lamps?

Now one cannot say with certainty whether Spencer ever *did* anything like this or not, though such is the persuasiveness of the poem that one is more likely than not to believe he did. But what is certain is that he reinvented himself in order to write the poem. He put himself in a car in the dark outside a country house, and he gave this figure of himself a way of thinking, a set of images and rhythms, and above all a way of speaking that he believed were right to body forth the scene in his particular way of being a poet. We are in the poem because he is, at a definite place and time, and we experience the invisible doctor and sick woman through his reactions. What he thinks and feels are what a reflective and imaginative mind has *found* to say about the incident between the time it happened or was invented and the time the poem was completed.

The I-figure does not live in the real world of fact but in a kind of magical abstraction, an emotion- and thought-charged personal version of it. Rather than in a place where objects and people have the taciturn and indisputable tangibility, the stolid solidity, of fact, the poetic agent inhabits a realm more rich and strange and a good deal "thicker" than reality, for it gathers to itself all the analogies and associations—either obvious or far-fetched—that the poetic mind as it ranges through the time and space of its existence can bring to the subject. Constrained only by the laws imposed on him by the situation of any and all types, from the most matter-of-fact sort of reporting to the wildest phantasmagoria, he can be whatever his poem needs him to be. It is by virtue of his having his existence in just such a specialized kind of linguistic fiction that the I-figure—and in another way the poet—becomes what he is: a man subject to the permutations and combinations of words, to the vicissitudes of denotation and connotation. Both are creatures trapped by grammar, and also at the mercy of its expressive possibilities and those of all the particulars and means of the poem. The poet is also a man who has a new or insufficiently known part of himself released by these means. He is set free, for he is more inclusive than before; he is greater than he was.

Metaphor as Pure Adventure

The longer I continue to write, the more it seems to me that the most exciting thing about poetry is its sense of imminent and practical discovery. With this in mind, and also in view of the fact that I am the one giving the lecture this evening, it might be interesting to look for a little while at the kinds of discoveries that poetry, with luck, makes possible and at what happens when the poet asks parts of creation to get together, not with the consent of the Almighty, but simply because he asks them to.

Let me begin with a passage from a favorite novel of mine, *The Time of Man*, by Elizabeth Madox Roberts. This is the first paragraph of the book.

> Ellen wrote her name in the air with her finger, *Ellen Chesser*, leaning forward and writing on the horizontal plane. Beside her in the wagon her mother huddled under an old shawl to keep herself from the damp, complaining, "We ought to be a-goen on."

This is a primitive—but to me very moving—way of self-definition and could stand for the kind of thing every poet is attempting to do: write his name on the air. But in the case of poets the important thing to notice is that self-definition is not a matter of formulaic or any other permanent kind of restrictive attitude but is rather a thing of the moment: as though, if one were to understand the self of the moment, one might thereby understand something of the essential self. One may never apprehend the whole of the self, as if the self might be uncovered in its entirety, bit by bit, as one strips the trivia away. The relation of poetry—and of metaphor—to the self is not like this at all. It is a matter of moments, and of the conjunctions that may be born of the moment, and illuminate the moment, and then come to stand for one of the ways in which the moment may strike to the heart of time itself. As Blake said, "Eternity is in love with the productions of time."

The deliberate conjunction of disparate items which we call metaphor is not so much a way of understanding the world but a perpetually exciting way of recreating it from its own parts, as though God—who admittedly did it right the first time—had by no means exhausted the possibilities. It is a way of causing the items of the real world to act upon each other, to recombine, to suffer and learn from the mysterious value systems, or value-making systems, of the individual, both in his socially conditioned and in his inmost, wild, and untutored mind. It is a way of putting the world together according to rules which one never fully understands, but which are as powerfully compelling as anything in the whole human makeup. Making metaphors is like operating according to dictates—and even here I am reasoning by "likes" as one will do—which are imperatives, but which are not fully comprehended, but mainly felt; imperatives which simply *present* themselves, not in the form of codified *dicta*, but as modes of action in *that* particular context: "Put *this* word with that one rather than the other one. It is *these* two things that you want to compare, not those two."

I conceive of poetry not so much as a matter of serene and disinterested choice but of action, and the very *heat* of choice, I think of the poem as a kind of action in which, if the poet can participate *enough*, other people cannot help participating as well. I am against all marmoreal, closed, to-be-contemplated kinds of poems and conceive of the poem as a minute part of the Heraclitean flux, and of the object of the poem as not to slow or fix or limit the flux at all but to try as it can to preserve and implement the "fluxness," the flow, and show this moving through the poem, coming in at the beginning and going back out, after the end, into the larger, nonverbal universe whence it came, I am everywhere aware of relation, connection, with one object shedding a light—a more or less strong, a more or less interesting light—on another. It is at least fairly interesting to say, "Stages—ah, stages and . . . and *mountains!*" Or better still, plateaus! There is a certain similarity of form: people in the Bible are always making speeches from mountains; there are lots of stage-precedents and mountain-precedents that one can, if one is an Eliotic traditionalist . . . But no, that is not really very interesting, after all. When carried away in this kind of vein, it is best to heed the warning implicit in the great story of the Argentinian writer Jorge Luis Borges, "The Handwriting of God." Borges asks you to note that each single thing implies the whole universe. If you think of the jaguar, you also imply the herds of deer on which the jaguar fed, the grass that nourished those herds, the rain that fell on the grass, and finally the whole eternal process that caused the jaguar, the single jaguar, to be. The poetic method of connecting things, however, cannot really be this broad. To be satisfactory to the poet, metaphor must connect items according to a more rigorous and profoundly personal way than mere arbitrary juxtaposition. The question is, in *what* way?

I have pondered this question a good while because it interests me, and because I thought that if perhaps I clarified the issue somewhat in my own mind, I could move with less obvious waste. One evening, while pondering "weak and weary" over many a volume of theoretical lore, I came on the following statement by the modern French poet, Pierre Reverdy:

> Insofar as the juxtaposition of entities be separated by the greater distance, and yet be just, the metaphor will be thereby stronger.

Now, that struck me as being something like what I feel about the metaphorical relationship—something *very* like. If we could figure out, and *apply*, one word in this just-sounding aphorism, we would be a lot nearer knowing how the poetic metaphor lives. The word is "juste"—just, or apt. It is obvious that it is not awfully hard to tell when the two terms of a metaphor, the two things that are being compared or asked to live together, are far apart, as the world or the ordinary man judges. But it is not always easy to tell when the comparison between them is "juste." This is where we get back to imponderables and individual reactions, for what may be just to me may very well be unjust, or even absurd, to you. I am willing, however, to leave it at that, because the individual sense of justness—or poetic justice—is in any given case the poetic sense itself, or at least so far as comparison or metaphor is concerned. I should state here, more or less parenthetically, that I am not here concerned with textbook definitions of metaphor, with metaphor as distinguished from simile, or anything of that kind. I take metaphor in the broad sense, as denoting any kind of comparison as a basis for the kind of illumination we call poetic. It would require a mind like Paul Valéry's or Wallace Stevens' to follow such questions as these into territories where they would begin to yield the results they deserve to yield, and I must stress what you already know: that I am not a philosopher, or even a philosophical poet. My purpose here is simply to call attention to the proclivity—nay, the compulsion—of the human mind to make comparisons, partly as a way to real or fancied knowledge or control of the subjects involved—and thus as a kind of primitive magic and personal science—but also for the sheer thrill of ingenuity, the puzzlemaking, resolving, and aesthetic excitement of the activity itself. When sportswriter Jim Murray of the *Los Angeles Times* tells me, for example, that quarterback John Brodie of the San Francisco Forty-Niners is "slower than fourth-class mail," I am delighted beyond measure, not because I am gloating over Mr. Brodie's heaviness of foot but because the mind that made the comparison delights me with its energy, ingenuity, and quickness. When a movie critic says—or said, years ago—of Shirley Temple's first husband, the mercifully forgotten John Agar, that "he acts as though the idea of acting was not his in the first place," I am equally delighted and in an entirely different way, dependent not so much on watching John Brodie run on Sunday-afternoon TV as on watching old movies even later in the evening, such as Mr. Agar's opus *Ride a Crooked Mile*. As I say, I take pleasure from the aptness of these examples because I have seen the principals act out, each in his way, the metaphors. But they would be good metaphors even without John Brodie and John Agar because there will always be slow athletes and handsome, inept actors. Yea, and until the end of time!

The masters of metaphor are not, however, sportswriters and movie reviewers, but poets. The greatest, the most enduring, metaphors have been made by them. And it is fascinating, in our Age of Investigation, to see how various poets put the world together in their particular and idiosyncratic ways. There are many learned treatises on the fashions in which various poets do this, and one can go to the files of the universities in Syracuse and Buffalo and of Washington University in St. Louis—and to the files of the Library of Congress—and pore over the draft sheets and worksheets of poets to see how they have changed, patched and shaded, discarded, found, have searched thesauruses and dictionaries, have compared and contrasted, have called into play everything, literally, in the world, to help them write their poems. Sometimes you can't make much of these sheets, the poet's working habits being too private. But sometimes you can tell a good deal, though never *quite* enough. Dylan Thomas will have, say, a selection of words, one of which he may end up using in a certain place in a line, or none of which he may use. And it is fun—and instructive—to arrive at various ways of agreeing with the poet (for who would disagree with Dylan Thomas where his own work is concerned?) as to why he chose this word and discarded the others. And yet the list of words *itself* is, with Thomas, the most mysterious and provocative list ever seen and is likely to be taken by the unwary for a Thomas poem in its own right. If we could tell why Thomas selected *those* words out of which to choose (or not to choose), the poetic process, at least in the case of Thomas, would be a great deal clearer to us than it is now. But how the list came to Thomas' mind in the first place is something we shall never know; it is part of the poetic mystery, and I for one am glad that it is.

Despite the great area of the Unknowable in which poems are born and live, there are a few very broad generalizations we can make about kinds of metaphor. There is surely a generic difference, for example, between the *merely* ingenious kind of conjunction and the kind that has both the strangeness and the inevitability of poetry. When Marshall McLuhan says that the electric light bulb is "pure information," we can see what he means, but it is the sort of formulation in which the straining to be original is much more evident than the originality. Of course it is possible to look at the light bulb from the standpoint of its being "pure information," but that is not, at least to my view, particularly enlightening. The comparison of light bulb and information has the obviousness-with-a-twist that we think of, in every age, as the mark of the minor talent. When Robert Duncan says something to the effect that "the sky is not sure it is not an elephant," we feel the same sense of strain and would-be about the figure. But when D. H. Lawrence refers to a fish as a "gray, monotonous soul in the water," quite another thing happens. At first one is troubled by Lawrence's calling the fish a "soul," but then he remembers that this poet's way of looking at existence is essentially that of a personal animism. And fish *do* look gray under water. But it is the "monotonous" that is the truly poetic word. There is that wavering of the fish through the water, like a ghost and like a soul that seems almost on the point of disappearing but will not go, and perhaps *cannot* go, moving with perfect silence in his heavy, half-transparent purgatory. The mind of the reader dilates around the image of the fish when it is presented in this way; all kinds of imaginatively profitable and creative connections come in. As in the case of all good poetic figures, there are the connections that we all make in more or less the same ways and those that are utterly private and personal. But again, what made Lawrence see the pike as a "gray, monotonous soul in the water" may be guessed at, after the fact, but never really known.

The ways in which the mind associates, and the particular *materia mater* out of which the associations come—the *materia mater* that is available to the mind in toto, and the mysterious way in which bits and pieces of this come up at a certain time, as though there were an element of fate involved—we know almost nothing of, and *can* know but very little. If I were going to write about a fish, for instance, what happens in my brain? Do all the fish I have ever seen in my life swim to the surface for possible use? No; at best, only a few of them come. Why those? I can't say, beyond supposing that these must be the ones that impressed me the most, for one reason or another. But impressed me in what way? I simply must accept them as the most fishy fish, the most archetypal fish I have in my mind, the Platonic fish that will have to stand for all the rest.

That, however, is only the beginning. In my own case, to cite the example closest to hand, the only poem I have ever devoted to a fish, a long one called "The Shark's Parlor," is not about anything I have ever done or any actual fish I ever saw. A shark has been made out of the few hammerheads I have ever seen in the water, those I have seen hanging up at docks, and one I found dead on a beach. It is not quite that these sharks combined into one in my mind but that the dead one on the shore drew into himself, as my strongest mental hammerhead, all the others, so that the others became him and contributed to him in my mind, where I then attempted to place him in another kind of sea, in a poem, and cause him to live and act there. But my apprehension of my shark was conditioned, as it must inevitably be, by what experiences, including pictures in books and dreams, I have had in other places and other times—and perhaps other lives—with sharks. The poem was also influenced, in what ways it is hard for me to tell, by a movie called *The Shark Fighters*, which starred, if I remember correctly, Victor Mature. All of these things came together into the passionate and mysterious aura of association that this kind of fish had for *me*. And from these mixed sources I made a poem about an imaginary incident.

The pure adventurousness of making metaphors and poems is a condition that must be felt to be believed. I remember how tremendously excited I was when I first formulated to myself the proposition that the poet is not to be limited by the literal truth: that he is not trying to *tell* the truth: he is trying to *make* it. Therefore he is absolutely free, in the sense of the definition of creativity as the capacity to act according to laws of one's own devising. When one grasps this, the feeling of liberation and the attendant devotion to one's own vision are so exciting that the dedication of a life to following these things wherever they may lead seems a small enough endeavor, the least that one can do. For what the poet is trying to accomplish is to discover relationships that give life: mental, physical, and imaginative life, the fullest and most electric sense of being.

One begins with the sensible world, which in its entirety is a gift, and a gift also in each of its parts. As far as I am concerned, that is as good a definition as can be given of a poet: that he is one who feels the world as a gift. But there is a second gift that you give yourself, based on the world's great gift. I often wonder how Adam felt—or the earliest man felt—when he closed his eyes and saw that the world was still there, inside his head. That is the most miraculous thing in the whole of existence to me: those pictures of the world inside one's head; pictures made of the real world, but pictures that one *owns*, that one infuses with one's own personality. They are fragments of the world that live, not with the world's life, but with ours.

But I am not here, so my announced subject tells me, to talk about the image, as much as I would like to, but to talk about comparisons of one thing to another and about the part that language plays in the kinds of comparisons that we call poetic metaphors. But almost all metaphors begin with pictures in the head. Now these pictures, these entities, are, first of all, possessions of ours. We have paid nothing for them, but we *have* them, in the magic CinemaScope of the mind; we have them because they are there, and no one can banish them except ourselves—and even that is doubtful, for when we attempt to banish them, we may very well simply be making them obsessive.

If we are poets—that is, *conscious* poets—we are interested in three things concerning these fragments of the world as they have come to us. First, we wish to find threads of continuity running through them, threads of consequence and meaning which may work out into a narrative or dramatic action or at least into a distinct relationship that the items have obtained, not from their position and interrelationship in the "real" world, but purely from us. The second thing we look for (or perhaps I should say *I* look for) is a way to recombine these elements so that they undergo a fruitful interchange of qualities, a transference of energies, an informing of each other. The greatest poets have the greatest power to do this, as when Gerard Manley Hopkins compares the longest flame of a bonfire to a whip, or speaks of thunder rolling its *floors* of sound. Without Hopkins there would never have been any particularly illuminating connection between thunder and floors, but *with* Hopkins there is a startling connection: one sees and hears the justness of the comparison immediately, though each apprehends it in his own way, depending upon what thunders (and floors) he has known. The third thing the poet tries to do is to introduce his vital, necessary, and incomparable element, language, into this thread-discovering and -connecting process that he is engaged in. And here the difficulties are very great and the excitement and sense of adventure correspondingly intense. For when the poet is, as W. S. Graham beautifully says, "trusted on the language," he is both submitting to and consciously working with a medium he prefers, much as the partners in lovemaking are both submitting to and working with each other. The poet is committing himself to making his discoveries in *this* way: the way of words in a certain order, and with a certain informing spirit which he hopes will be his; for if it is not his, it is nothing.

Now when things are compared linguistically, they are never quite what they were in isolation from each other or in the non-verbal context of the world. As we all know, words are signs for things, but they have at least two ranges of signification. When the poet says "tree," for example, we all presumably see a tree, somewhere in the head. But the second range of signification is not universal but personal and private: we don't all see the same tree. In fact, *none* of us sees the same tree. This is one thing about poetic imagery that has bothered some people, for they wish to submit, or reduce, the poetic act to a condition based upon which "scientific" or universal judgments may be made about it and about the individual poems that it produces. It has bothered some people, but I don't believe it has ever bothered any poet; or at any rate any real poet. For, as John Keats says, "What shocks the virtuous philosopher, delights the chameleon poet." Poets think it a kind of double good fortune that they may ask each of their readers, not to see the poet's tree, but to supply one from his own life, and to bring it—as a gift—into the poem.

The making of poetic metaphors is an intrinsic process: a continual process of transfiguring reality. For example, having encountered Hopkins' thunder as the rolling of "great floors of sound," I am neither in the presence exclusively of either thunder, or floors, or sounds, nor yet of rolling, as isolated entities or actions. I cease to experience the thunder alone (either real thunder or mental thunder), or the floors alone, but I enter into a magical secondary state, an enriched reality made possible by the conjunction of these items, by the comparison where thunder, floors, sounds, and rolling are, so to speak, together in a new kinship made possible by a special use of language, but having, also, a sort of kinship in the mind which seems to me to be extra-linguistic as well, having to do only with the things themselves. When I have apprehended this new relationship, have brought my own thunders and my own floors to it, my mind then roams round and about this new relationship in a different world from one I can open my eyes and see, or unstuff my ears and hear, and all this is qualified and amplified by the pleasure I take in the newness and aptness of Hopkins' figure of speech and the feeling of extension that it provokes in me. It is another emotional dimension that I have been given—a present—and my main attitude toward it is simple gratitude.

For these reasons, and many others, the ways of making comparisons, metaphors, figures of speech, and so on, are subject to none but the very broadest of rules, and even these must be liberally interpreted. If we could codify the metaphor-making process, we would all be able to write like Hopkins—or indeed anybody else we wanted to. It is because of the utter impossibility of codifying and making generally available an authentically poetic way of comparing, of making genuinely original metaphors, that poetry is and will always be entirely different from science. Again, the aura of association about specific words differs greatly from person to person. The particular kind of getting-together-of-things that I characterize as poetic results in a variety of insight that is, though not scientific, nonetheless of very great value to those equipped to receive it. I don't want to turn this evening into a "Defence of Poesie," for poetry can defend itself quite well enough, but I *would* like to lay down the few generalizations about metaphor that I have been able to glean from the years.

First, the terms of a metaphor are almost always concrete and *one* of them *is* always concrete; that is, the terms are parts of the given world. A correspondence is established between already created things.

Second, this correspondence carries an emotional charge, or rather two of them: a general one which anyone might be expected to respond to, and another one to which any individual, in his particular life situation, is free to respond out of those specific conditions which have resulted in his being who he is.

Third, the true metaphor orients the mind toward freedom and novelty; it encourages the mind to be daring. And at the same time the metaphor furnishes the mind with at least the illusion of a new kind of relational necessity, as well as giving it the joy—the pure joy—of employing faculties that are not used in conceptual language.

If I may go a little further into abstraction, I would also say that metaphor permits one to experience at the same time the perpetual and the instantaneous, the paired objects both in the world they came from and in their linguistic relationship in the poem.

But it is not really my purpose to generalize, in the manner of the seminar room, about a subject as mysterious as metaphor. I had rather simply talk about the very great delight in making metaphorical relations at any level at all. And delight it *is*. That is why poets don't want to go to Heaven: they are already there the day they are born as earthly creatures. I remember with affection the words of the all-but-forgotten American painter Charles Burchfield, who was asked, a few months before he died, how he felt about "eternal life." He said, "I don't know anything about it. But I hope there is painting there."

As for poets, I don't believe it is possible for men to conceive—or for God to conceive—of a better universe for poets and poetry than the one we have. But the natural order of things *is* the natural order. A river is not a stone, and a tree is not a star; nor is a woman a tigress (that is, not *literally*). But poets believe, with a high secret glee, that precisely because God made these things as they are (the star, the tree, the woman), because He made them so much themselves that they can be nothing *but* themselves, someone else—someone like a poet, say—can come along and compare a star to a woman, or to a tree, and accomplish something valuable by it. Poets believe that the things of this world are capable of making connections between each other that not God but men see, and they say so. Stars, stones, and trees have no emotional charge in themselves, but a very powerful one for men. To Matthew Arnold, to the ancient Greek tragedians, and to many other human beings the sound of the sea on pebbles brings "the eternal note of sadness in." And it is in the language of metaphor charged with specific emotions that the poet makes his statement and creates, out of the world as it is, the world that he must, because he is what he is, bring to birth. Much has been written of the agonies of creation, but to at least one poet it seems the most delightful, exciting, and natural act in the world, a kind of perpetual and pure adventure.

For the world without the play of the mind over it is a dull place indeed. After all, rocks are only inert matter, trees are only stolid wood that sways a little in the air according to the natural law of the wind. Stars are only burning chemicals, and a woman is only a collocation of animal cells formed into the female humanity-reproducing beast. It is the mind itself, in its quick and intimate and original presence, that turns the universe into a magical arena, or, as Keats called it, "a vale of soul-making." If I had only one point to make this evening, it would be in favor of imaginative participation in the cosmos. As D. H. Lawrence says in *Apocalypse*, "We have lost the cosmos." What I take this to mean is that Lawrence believes we no longer have any vital relationship to the universe, and he is very likely right. He thinks, also, that we can only possess the cosmos by an act of worship. This seems to me to be perfectly true. And if we believe, with Kafka, that "all writing is a form of prayer," then we would have to agree that the poets have been praying the longest, although perhaps not the loudest. The poet's form of worship is both descriptive and relational; he imbues the cosmos so strongly with his own emotions that he believes that, in return, the cosmos allows him to recombine its elements in his own way, largely for the sheer delight of it—for the adventure.

As I said earlier, it is lovely to engage in the relational adventure at any level, from the serviceman's or fraternity boy's search—a very real one—to describe sexual intercourse (there *have* been some good tries), or from the whole male sex's eternal quest to find a truly adequate name for the female sex organ, at which we have failed abjectly, through the rather ordinary quips in *Reader's Digest* ("He had a face like an unmade bed"), up through the superhumanly brilliant epic similes and metaphors of Homer and Virgil and Lucretius and Dante and Milton. If I had time, I'd like to make for you a little anthology of my favorite metaphors and tell you just what I like about them (though of course I don't know *completely*, in any given case, why I like what I like). I can't do that, of course, but neither can I resist giving you a few of the best. And my fondest hope is that you will begin collecting comparisons, as I have done all my life, and I hope also that you will never accept any but the best ones: the ones that have it, as the hippies say, for *you*. These are some that have it—*it*—for me.

When William Strode, who lived just after Shakespeare, says

> Nor snow when falling from the sky
> Hovers in its virginity

he has made a connection between a fact of nature and humanity that counts.

When Milton says of the angel Raphael that he

> Comes this way moving; seems another morn
> Risen on mid-noon

you have seen, as Adam did, an angel come to you. How could an angel come in any other way, at noon?

When Edgar Allan Poe—yes, even Edgar Allan Poe—refers to the sea as

> That wilderness of glass

something has truly changed in your perception and experience of the sea—and also in your perception and experience of glass, and of wildernesses.

When Tennyson speaks of the sea into which the sea-buried corpse is flung, and says that the shotted body

> Drops in its vast and wandering grave

you know something else again, about the sea, about the poor human body, and about death.

And when the blues singer, Scrapper Blackwell, invites someone to

> Put your arms around me like a circle round the sun

you never want to love in any other way.

Well, these are just a few instances of individual aptness of perception having to do with parts of the world in a new relation made possible by seeing and saying them in a particular way.

Let me reiterate: find your own metaphors. Or better still, *make* your own. Just to get you started, let me give you a problem to work on. See if you can find the combination of things and words, the objective and unobjective correlatives, to get this scene said. (I expect to get some mail on this, I conjure you!)

This is a kind of scene out of early adolescence: mine. I was walking along a beach in south Georgia, and for some reason or other I had half a loaf of stale bread in my hand. It was low tide. The sea was flat and low, a "wilderness of glass," in fact. There was a sandbar about a hundred yards from where I was, and I walked out through the water toward it, through schools of minnows. Now, I don't know how all this grabs you, but it's had hold of *me* for years, especially lately, for it is so obviously a Dickey kind of subject: a large scene from nature, forms of alien life, fish, sun, silence, and—a loaf of bread. Can you do anything with that? It's a Dickey poem, but Dickey can't seem to write it.

Anyway, I got out to the sandbar and tore off a piece of bread and gave it to a sea gull. He rose and hovered and came back, and for a while I kept throwing pieces of bread into the air, and he'd sweep by and catch them. Then he reproduced himself in mid-air—ah! maybe we could use *that!*—what I mean is that there were two of him, then five, then dozens, then hundreds. One of him hit me in the back of the head like a sledgehammer—no; we need a better comparison here: there *must* be one!—and I suddenly realized that if I didn't do something to protect myself I'd be likely to lose an eye or two. At least I ought to give up the rest of the bread. But I didn't. I stood there on the sandbar covered with wings and beaks, and kept pitching up the bread in smaller and smaller pieces until it was all gone, and the birds reluctantly, slowly dispersed, and I was there alone, shook up and happy, with a moderately bloody head.

Now, I've never been able to get any kind of metaphorical meaning out of this incident, or indeed any kind of meaning that seemed to have poetic possibilities. But it strikes me now that it could be a metaphor for metaphor itself: the gulls may—*may*—be likened to fragments of the world which come at the poet from all sides—the world's beautiful and dangerous gifts—sometimes threatening him, not in themselves caring for him, but bearing their presences in on him just the same. The poet is the man with the bread—that is, with the means of attracting them to himself, the bread being the imagination that calls them and feeds them. Again, maybe calling the gulls was my own way of writing on the air: of writing my name on the air, with bread, blood, and wings.

And yet I am not satisfied with that, quite. It is a little too pat, too serviceable, too one-dimensional. As I say, I'm not satisfied with it; it is merely the best I have been able to do. And I expect that things will remain so, in regard to this particular unwritten poem. That is, until I hear from you.

Spinning the Crystal Ball

Somehow or other, poets always find themselves at bay: before critics, before other poets, before well-meaning ladies at cocktail parties, before talk-show MCs and publishers and wives and friends and novelists. In fact, poets *like* to be at bay: it is sort of their natural habitat. They are always at the edge, and what they do there, besides writing poems, is express their opinions. These present remarks are offered not so much from the vantage of any particular height, but merely from an involvement in the situation from which the future must inevitably come, whether it comes from my part of, or part in, the situation or not. It is a kind of speech which will try to combine a certain more or less hopefully shrewd guesswork and blindly emotional prejudice; that is, it will be partly about what I think might happen in American poetry and what I hope *will* happen. And if the speech turns out to be clairvoyant, I will be more surprised than any of you.

Well, first of all, how does one usually predict? From empirical evidence, mainly. One tries to say what will be from an examination of what has been, as it operates on what is now, and as these two examinable bodies of evidence seem to indicate a continuation of one through the other: a kind of vector that points in a certain direction. But again, before I plunge into the weird world of assessments and predictions, let me stress once more the purely personal nature of these remarks; if certain affinities and allegiances color what I say, I would like to believe that these may be taken simply as evidence of involvement, of caring.

To proceed from the available evidence, rather than from preference, we can look first at the "confessional" school, or what I should be tempted to call "the poetry of personal complaint." The most prominent figure of this group is Robert Lowell, but his work is already so well known in this and other regards that it would be better, here, to look at some of its results: at how his influence operates in the work of those who are seeking to continue it and extend it. When one reads W. D. Snodgrass, Anne Sexton, and, most particularly, Sylvia Plath, one thing strikes one before anything else does. The impulse behind the poetry appears to be—and no doubt is—essentially therapeutic: one variation or another of the famous statement of D. H. Lawrence's, "One sheds one's sicknesses in books." The material is pretty much the same as that which furnishes the conversation of the psychoanalytical encounter and the desperate phone call to the best friend whom the caller simply will not—cannot—let go until he or she has poured out the whole awful truth, with all the physical details of humiliation, and the rest. The notion here, no new one to either analyst or bartender, or, in fact to anyone else, is that if one can get it out, can share it, that is, *describe* it, one can alleviate the intolerable pain of the condition one describes. An analogy that occurs to me in this connection is, oddly enough, the recent book by William Manchester on the assassination of President Kennedy. The fascination of the book is that it functions as a kind of rite of exorcism. People feel that if the terrible event is known, fully known, down to the least detail of who stood where, what this one wore, and what the other one thought, that day in Dallas will then deliver its secret, the secret that everyone believes it has, *must* have. So with these poets. *My* complaint against the poets of personal complaint is not that they are confessional, in the sense of being engaged in a true encounter with the horrible depths that everyone has, with the compulsive hatreds that tear us apart, but that they are not confessional enough. They are slickly confessional; they are glib. They do not really offer the "real life"—as opposed to "literary life"—they purport to do; they are astonishingly literary—and here I mean literary in the bad sense—despite their insistence on "ordinary life." Here are a few excerpts from a poem by Sylvia Plath, called "Fever 103."

> Pure? What does it mean?
> The tongues of hell
>
> Are dull, dull as the triple
> Tongues of dull, fat Cerberus
> Who wheezes at the gate.
> . . .
> the low smokes roll
> From me like Isadora's scarves . . .

—Isadora Duncan, and her bizarre death—

> Greasing the bodies of adulterers
> Like Hiroshima ash . . .

—one must get that in, some way—

> The sheets grow heavy as a lecher's kiss.

And so on. The main feeling that one has—or at least that *I* have—is of an attempt to be clever; and if there is one thing that I find intolerable in either literature or in the world, it is slick, knowing patter about suffering and guilt, particularly about one's own.

This is a limited and solipsistic approach to poetry, luxuriating in and hiding behind the supposition on the reader's part that the poet has actually suffered what the poem describes. One can surely sympathize with that part of it, as one would sympathize with the person whether a poet or not. It is the *way* in which the suffering is presented which so falsifies it, and which the reader will not easily forgive. The more he believes the personal situation, the less he believes the poem. I think, though, that the confessional poem, as a kind of poem, is near the end of its tenure. Who could outdo Robert Lowell at this? One must, in the end, be more than a follower, if one is a true poet.

The confessional poets believe in Life, in *their* life, rather than in Art. Out on the West Coast, at that bastion of American neoclassicism, Stanford University, they believe in Art; they believe in "the mind" and in its capacity to make sense of experience and to embody that sense in verse which proceeds by means of the rational faculties. They are poets of classical serenity and a surprising degree of wit. They are not chaotic, nor arbitrary, and if they despair, they despair in extremely educated ways. This is part of a sequence by J. V. Cunningham:

> It was in Vegas. Celibate and able
> I left the silver dollars on the table
> And tried the show. The black-out, baggy pants,
> Of course, and then this answer to romance:
> Her ass twitching as if it had the fits,
> Her gold crotch grinding, her athletic tits,
> One clock, the other counter clockwise twirling.
> It was enough to stop a man from girling.

One like this! The true horror of the educated, sensitive man is to confront something like the gold crotch of Las Vegas: it is exactly the kind of encounter that the neoclassic wit needs, that calls forth his best powers, including his powers of versification and rhyme. Verse is here a medium of control rather than of confession, but it is no less an exorcism than the poems of Lowell. The exorcism is in the control, as McLuhan might say, but I don't think has yet said. We might make a point or two here about the interaction of literary technique and personality, which had always interested me very much. It seems to me that literary techniques not only express but alter the personality fully as much as the personality determines the techniques. "As he *is*, so he writes," as Coleridge said. To write as Cunningham does requires a special use of the intelligence, a great deal of schooling, a belief in the poem as a conserver rather than as a releaser of energies and insights, and it often requires also a classical education. For example, this is a translation by Cunningham of a poem by the Latin poet Janus Vitalis Panormitanus, whom I'd never heard of before, much less tried to pronounce. It is called "Rome." Think of this, ye tourists!

> You that a stranger in mid-Rome seek Rome
> And can find nothing in mid-Rome of Rome,
> Behold this mass of walls, these abrupt rocks,

> Where the vast theatre lies overwhelmed.
> Here, here is Rome! Look how the very corpse
> Of greatness still imperiously breathes threats!
> The world she conquered, strove herself to conquer,
> Conquered that nothing be unconquered by her.
> Now conqueror Rome's interred in conquered Rome,
> And the same Rome conquered and conqueror.
> Still Tiber stays, witness of Roman fame
> Still Tiber flows on swift waves to the sea.
> Learn hence what Fortune can: the unmoved falls,
> And the ever-moving will remain forever.

That is cool, beautiful, and final, and the shifts and sleights of meaning that occur from one use to the other of the verbs and nouns having to do with conquest are quite beyond the conception of any but an extremely subtle and skillful intelligence (and I would hazard a guess that they are also beyond the powers of the original Latin poet as well). Poems of this sort come out of an essentially humanistic attitude, an attitude which admits to the limitedness and perhaps vanity of human knowledge. And yet, when we read the other, mostly younger, practitioners of this approach to the poem, how dry and pedantic they seem! There are not many Cunninghams among them. Many seem to be without any kind of significant subject matter, though they know the conventions of verse perhaps better than they are known in most other schools. But as a kind of practice having possibilities of influencing the future, this approach is not a good bet. It requires more reading, more delicacy of nuance, more control, than most other kinds. Furthermore, it also appears that more and more gifts are expended to bring forth less and less obviously valuable results. It seems to me that the neoclassicists are a minority group and will remain so. It may be that people are tired of too much conscious manipulation in poems; skill, particularly of the obviously mannered sort, becomes boring, so that even a magnificent poet like Gerard Manley Hopkins palls a bit, because his poems are so obviously *poems*, literature. Most of the better young poets on both sides of the Atlantic tend to reject this kind of mannerism—including what many of them regard as the mannerism of rhyme—as not only unnecessary but in a certain sense misleading, even immoral. For example, one of the very best of the new poets, the Canadian David Wevill, who now lives and writes in England, had this to say, in answer to some questions asked him on the BBC Third Programme concerning the traditional formal disciplines of English poetry:

> I respect them, but I don't feel drawn to employ them. I think because by experience I've learnt that they don't really suit my needs and that I'd much rather pay greater attention to individual words and phrases and cadences, and that the moment I strait-jacket myself with a strict form or metre I'm not free to say what I want to say. This doesn't mean that one writes in a completely undisciplined way, but you've then got to impose your own set of rules and that's a very personal thing.

Now this is an important point, this "very personal thing," this way of substituting one's own cadences for more predictable or traditional ones, and insisting on them to the extent of excluding received modes of writing. Wevill is a real poet, and his individuality as a writer is evident and at the same time is available only to himself. I suspect that this is as it should be. The American writers who want to break with tradition, however—as one might have predicted—want to lay down manifestoes of one kind or another and form "groups," publish their own magazines, and go through the whole familiar "bit" of organizing things. This is the case with the group of poets led by Charles Olson and including writers like Robert Creeley, Edward Dorn, and, to some extent, Denise Levertov. Olson's theories are more interesting than his verse or most of that of his followers. One is never sure that one understands it! He has all kinds of notions about the relationship of "the line" to breathing and other bodily processes, and he uses a curious and perhaps private vocabulary to talk about them. Here is an example, as well known as any other:

> A poem is energy transferred from where the poet got it
> (he will have some several causations), by way of the
> poem itself to, all the way over to, the reader.

Well, at this point, the reader agrees: Okay, okay, but so what? Olson then says:

> Then the poem itself must, at all points, be a high
> energy-construct and, at all points, an energy-discharge.

This seems to me to display a certain degree of naivete. When Olson uses a term like "energy-construct," he supposes himself to be using a scientific vocabulary, but what he is in fact using is a layman's idea of scientific lingo, or jargon. Who would not want to believe, for example, that poetry is "energy" in this sense, or indeed in any other? But Olson's is a specialized and prejudicial use of the term, and it is, semantically, absolutely meaningless. What this kind of usage represents is the effort—perhaps inadvertent, but symptomatic nonetheless—of a basically unscientific mind to "dignify" or at least make acceptable to his science-cowed followers and readers a thing (poetry) which is not scientific at all, that is, not subject to empirical "proof," but which is intimate and personal, subjective. If it be argued that subjectivity itself is subject to scientific investigation, one would then have to come up with the means of measuring or assessing the kind of "energy"—some sort of psychic or imaginative energy, I suppose—which Olson posits, and it is not difficult to see the absurdity of this.

But the test of all theories of poetry is the kind of poetry they produce, and this is where Olson and his followers seem to me to fail all but abjectly. Their work has absolutely no personal rhythm to it; it all comes out of the tiresome and predictable prosiness of William Carlos Williams. It is the sort of thing—as Randall Jarrell once remarked—that you use to illustrate to a class the fact that the sports page of the daily paper can be rendered into accentual-syllabic verse by cutting it into "lines."

The other "movement" around is the one headed up by Robert Bly, out of Madison, Minnesota. As professional soldiers say of the particular war they're fighting in at the time, "It ain't much, but it's the only one we got." Bly believes that the salvation of English poetry is to be found in non-English poetry, particularly in Spanish and French and German, understood as badly as possible. One does translations, taking as many liberties as one wants to take with the original, it being understood that this enables one somehow to approach the "spirit" of the poet one is translating. If I had time I would talk some about surrealism, for the French and Spanish surrealist poets are very much the bellwethers of the Bly faction. But it might be better to quote a couple of things to show you the end results. This is Bly's "Approaching Winter."

i

September. Clouds. The first day for wearing jackets.
The corn is wandering in dark corridors,
Near the well and the whisper of tombs.

ii

I sit alone surrounded by dry corn,
Near the second growth of the pigweeds,
And hear the corn leaves scrape their feet on the wind.

iii

Fallen ears are lying on the dusty earth.
The useful ears will lie dry in cribs, but the others, missed
By the picker, will lie here touching the ground the whole winter.

iv

Snow will come, and cover the husks of the fallen ears
With flakes infinitely delicate, like jewels of a murdered Gothic prince
Which were lost centuries ago during a great battle.

Here is another poem, called "Thinking of Robert Bly and James Wright on the First Hot Day in April After Having Stayed up Late All Night Drinking and Singing With a Gang of Old Norwegian Trolls." (Bly is Norwegian.)

Whenever I think of you,
Tiny white horses gallop away in darkness.
I am lulled by the sound of old guitars
Strummed by ghostly fingers of the wind.

Your gentleness is like beautiful white snow
Drifting down on ancient homesteads
Over lonely prairies in Tennessee;
And you are falling, falling softly down.

America is falling also
Into dark cathedrals of the sea.
But what is that to me?
I am oblivious to missile siloes in Minnesota.

I lie here in the holy darkness
Listening to cornstalks creaking,
Thinking I have ruined myself
Climbing over a pale barbed-wire fence.

Now, though this latter poem is a conscious parody—it came to me in the mail the other day—the writer said he turned it out, without changing a word, as fast as he could type. Though, as I say, it is a parody, it really isn't, for it is completely undistinguishable from the seriously intended poems it models itself on. It has the same particular faults and characteristics as its models: the sentimentality, the attempt to link up all sorts of disparate items—snow, corn, jewels of murdered princes, missile siloes, and so on—in a kind of loose emotional mental drifting having a bogus, unearned conclusion. The parody is as good and as bad as the original. Above all, it is as arbitrary. This is essentially a derivative, imitative, extremely lazy, unimaginative poetry: small, static, and very easy to write. It lacks *necessity* of statement; it cannot sustain narrative. If the salvation of American poetry is to write imitation Spanish poems, even that will have to be done better than this. But no such salvation is indicated, even if it were possible. We have a lot more going for us than that.

Up to now, I have been sort of taking inventory of the extant poetries: the movements, the kinds of writing that we have among us now. As may be evident, I don't care much for any of these. I've been dwelling among the empirical evidence up to now, with some admiration but mainly indifference and some distaste. Let me now go on and develop what I think should happen, and with luck, *will* happen.

First of all, let me read something. It is by Randall Jarrell, who is going to be—if indeed he isn't already—a hero to us.

> Moving from Cheer to Joy, from Joy to All,
> I take a box
> And add it to my wild rice, my Cornish game hens.
> The slacked or shorted, basketed, identical
> Food-gathering flocks
> Are selves I overlook. Wisdom, said William James,
>
> Is learning what to overlook. And I am wise
> If that is wisdom.
> Yet somehow, as I buy All from these shelves
> And the boy takes it to my station wagon,
> What I've become
> Troubles me even if I shut my eyes.
>
> When I was young and miserable and pretty
> And poor, I'd wish
> What all girls wish: to have a husband,
> A house and children. Now that I'm old, my wish

Is womanish:
That the boy putting groceries in my car

See me. It bewilders me he doesn't see me.

Now this has its faults. Like much of Jarrell's work, it is somewhat flat. But it does have the quality that I'd like to see become dominant in the poetry that is forthcoming: It is convincing as speech before it is convincing—or even felt—as "Art," as poetry. One *believes* it, and therefore the poem can act either as human communication or poetry, or both, without the reader's having to kill off one side of his receptiveness so that the other can operate. Further, this passage has what I can only describe as a kind of *folk* quality to it. Some of Jarrell's work is folk—or folksy—in the bad sense, for it is self-consciously so, but the best of it is not. And oddly enough, even in our computerized age, this offers a direction of which we have never—but should have—thought. For what do we mean by folk, leaving aside for the moment considerations of the connections between a folk idiom and the cultural environment from which it arises? Do we not mean a body of linguistic forms, of music, of crafts, customs, and so on, immediately accessible to the sensibilities of those from whom they arise? Recognizable as the language one speaks? And in poetry and balladry, for example, that language heightened but still recognizable as ours? Now this is very general, so far, but when we apply it to, say, a particular locality, it begins to make sense.

This is a short poem by Eleanor Ross Taylor, a Southern poet, and it is called "Motherhood, 1880."

When Dave got up and struck a light
We'd neither of us slept all night.
We kept the fire and watched by May,
Sick for fear she might

Go off like little Tom. . . . They say
"Don't fret . . . another on the way. . . ."
They know I favor this least child.

No use to cry. But while
I made a fire in the kitchen stove

I heard a pesky mourning dove.
Lor! What's he calling "O-love" for?

And here is the last stanza of a poem called "After the Late Lynching" by Katherine Hoskins, a poet usually cited for her difficulty, but one also capable of speaking with utter directness.

Nor not from whitest light of foreign poems
Hope help;
But from her native woe
Who took that black head in her hands
And felt,
"A sack of little bones";
Whose arms for the last time round him knew,
"All down one side no ribs
But broken things that moved."

Now these two poems are by highly sophisticated women, but it seems to me that they have been able to get back through the sophistication to something that sophistication does not usually afford: to a sense of the absolute basics of life, and for these the language of Eliot and Empson is not right. For this kind of poetry needs nothing more nor less than the simple language of necessity, such as would be conveyed if one caveman said to another one, "We have meat." This is not to say that poetry of this sort is incapable of more than one meaning; it is simply to say that multiplicity of reference and "richness of ambiguity" are no longer going to be the criteria by which the value of poetry is measured.

This kind of simplicity, which Mr. McLuhan might call "tribal"—and if he wouldn't, I would—takes a great many forms. The interesting thing about it to me is that the essential folk quality—sometimes attached to a region and sometimes not—doesn't seem to encroach on the individual poets' particular kinds of vision at all. Here, for example, is a stanza from "In Medias Res" by William Stafford, who is basically a Midwesterner, though he lives in Oregon.

On Main one night when they sounded the chimes
my father was ahead in shadow, my son
behind coming into the streetlight, on each side

a brother and a sister; and overhead
the chimes went arching for the perfect sound.
There was a one-stride god on Main that night,
all walkers in a cloud.

An interesting variation of this developing approach is a kind of poetry of what I'd be tempted to call the "domestic imagination," or the poetry of the everyday nightmare, the quotidian. Allen Tate once remarked that he thought of his poems as comments on those human situations from which there is no escape. Well, there is no escape from the toothbrush and the rug that is wearing thin, or from the mirror in the hall and the dripping faucet. The best of these poets is a youngish fellow named Vern Rutsala, and I'll read one of his poems because I think you ought to know something about him. This is called "Sunday."

Up early while everyone else sleeps,
I wander through the house,
pondering the eloquence
of vacant furniture, listening
to birdsong peeling
the cover off the day.

I think everyone I know
is sleeping now. Sidewalks
are cool, waiting for
roller skates and wagons.
Skate keys are covered
with dew; bicycles look
broken, abandoned on the lawns—
no balance left in them,
awkward as wounded
animals. I am the last
man and this is my
last day; I can't think
of anything to do. Somewhere
over my shoulder a jet
explores a crease
in the cloudy sky;

I sit on the porch
waiting for things to happen.

O fat god of Sunday
and chocolate bars, watcher
over picnics and visits to the zoo,
will anyone wake up today?

It has been argued for years that ours is a complex age, and a complex age calls for—no, demands—a complex poetry. This seems to me to display what logicians call the analogical error. I think that the poetry of the future is going to go back the other way, back toward basic things and basic-sounding statements about them, in an effort, perhaps a desperate one, to get back wholeness of being, to respond fullheartedly and fullbodiedly to experience, aware all the time that certain constants must be affirmed, or not much of life will be worth anything. The great thing about poetry has always been that it can speak to people deeply about matters of genuine concern. Some of this feeling has been lost since the ascendancy of Pound and Eliot, and the poem has become a kind of high-cult *objet d'art*, a "superior amusement" as Eliot once termed it. I believe that the true poets of the future will repudiate that notion absolutely, and try to operate in that place where, as Katherine Anne Porter says, one lives "deeply and consistently in that undistracted center of being where the will does not intrude, and the sense of time passing is lost, or has no power over the imagination." And if we are lucky in this search, and believe in it enough, we shall at least arrive at a condition of emotional primitivism, of undivided response, a condition where we can connect with whatever draws us. Walter Pater, of all people, wrote something about Wordsworth that bears on what I am saying.

> And so it came about that this sense of a life, a living soul, in natural objects, which in most poetry is but a rhetorical artifice, is with Wordsworth the assertion of what for him is almost literal fact. To him every natural object seemed to possess more or less of a moral or spiritual life—to be capable of a companionship with humanity full of expression, of inexplicable affinities, and delicacies of intercourse. An emanation, a particular spirit, belonged not to the moving leaves or water only, but to the distant peak arising suddenly, by some change of perspective, above the nearer horizon of the hills, to

> the passing space of light across the plain, to the lichened Druidic stone even, for a certain weird fellowship in it with the moods of men. It was like a survival, in the peculiar intellectual temperament of a man of letters at the end of the eighteenth century, of that primitive condition which some philosophers have traced in the general history of human culture, in which all outward objects alike, including even the works of men's hands, were believed to be endowed with animation, and the world seemed "full of souls."

Now, we don't live in Wordsworth's age, or Pater's, but an attitude of mind—a kind of *being*—like Wordsworth's is no more impossible to us than it was to him. Theodore Roethke, the greatest poet we have ever had in this country, is a marvelous proof of this.

> I, who came back from the depths laughing too loudly,
> Became another thing;
> My eyes extend beyond the farthest bloom of the waves;
> I lose and find myself in the long water;
> I am gathered together once more;
> I embrace the world.

That is what we want: to be gathered together once more, to be able to enter in, to participate in experience, to possess our lives. I think that the new poetry will be a poetry of the dazzlingly simple statement, the statement that is clairvoyantly and stunningly simple but not simple in the manner of, say, greeting cards: a stark, warm simplicity of vision: the simplicity that opens out deeper into the world and carries us with it. For we are not condemned to division within ourselves by the world we have made for ourselves. We have one self that is conditioned, all right. But there is another self that has never heard of an automobile or a telephone. This is the one that connects most readily with the flow of rivers and the light coming from the sun; it is in this second (or first) and infinitely older being that we can be transfigured by eyes and recreated by flesh. We can participate in a "survival" (in Pater's terms), a certain animism. As Camus says as he eats a peach (he *does* dare to eat a peach!):

> My teeth close on the peach. I hear the great strokes of my blood rise into my ears. I look with all of my eyesight. On the sea is the enor-

> mous silence of noon. Every beautiful being and thing has the natural pride of its beauty, and the world today lets its pride leak away everywhere. But before this world, why should I deny myself the joy of being alive, even if I can't close this joy up and keep it? There is no shame in being happy. But today the imbecile is king, and I call the imbecile that man who is afraid of joy.

It can begin—a poem, a true life—with something that simple. We need that worse than we need anything else: not sensation, but feeling; mainly the feeling of ourselves. And any poetry that I want to read in the future will find its own way of conveying this basic, this irreducible sense of being.

And—who knows? Maybe at some undetermined time in the future, encompassed around by Marshall McLuhan's world of telemetry and computers, his "instantaneous world" of electric circuitry, in that place he calls "the global village" and "the retribalized society," we shall again have a purely tribal poetry, something naive and utterly convincing, immediately accessible, animistic, communal, dancelike, entered into, participated in. We are not Eskimos or Bantus, and our "global village" is immeasurably different from one composed of igloos or thatched huts, but if McLuhan is right—and I think he is more right than wrong—and if *I* am right, we may live to see the day that our poetry has the simplicity, though not the subject matter, of this, from an un-McLuhan-type tribe of Eskimos in northern Canada:

> Glorious it is
> To see long-haired winter caribou
> Returning to the forests.
> Fearfully they watch
> For the little people.
> While the herd follows the ebb-mark of the sea
> With a storm of clattering hooves.
> Glorious it is
> When wandering time is come.

And with this "second being"—the part of us that the light of the sun moves without our having thoughts of "harnessing its energy" or using it in any way—we will write the poetry that I want most to read and hear. As Richard Jefferies so magnificently says:

> The mind must acknowledge its ignorance; all the learning and lore of so many eras must be erased from it as an encumbrance. It is not from past or present knowledge, science or faith, that it is to be drawn. Erase these altogether as they are erased under the fierce heat of the focus before me. Begin wholly afresh. Go straight to the sun, the immense forces of the universe, to the Entity unknown; go higher than a god; deeper than prayer; and open a new day.

And finally it may be, if this is indeed a real trend I describe, that we shall get back even farther than the poetry of the tribe and reach all the way to the very root-beginnings, back to the state of mind of the first man himself, who stood on the shore and opened his arms to the world, that he and the world might possess each other. Let me end by quoting part of a wonderful poem by Brewster Ghiselin called "The Vision of Adam." As Adam swims in the sea to try to discover his origin, he discovers instead the divine sensuality of the world, where the spirit of each of us hides and waits for each of us to come.

> And over the empty ocean the rose and amber
> Paled slowly and without sorrow, and ever more faintly gleamed
> About the increase of a western star. Adam swimming
> In the chill water loved the cold and the menace.
> He felt vast depth beneath him, and looking back
> Saw the faint shore and heard far off the murmur of anger beginning
> On the benighted sand, under wind and falling foam.
> "It is not vision, but life, I want," said Adam,
> "The power of the sea." A wave filled his mouth
> With keen-salt. The wind of evening gathered the wide billows beyond the last kelp
> Into mounds with soft ripples crowning delicately
> The long slopes with the sweetness of water released from the parent urge.
> And Adam ceased swimming, and floated over darkness beyond the kelp
> Which makes a seamark for swimmers, and watched how the stars

Came to the open pool of the central azure.
And he thought not at all, but felt the incalculable power
 of the ocean
Cradled upon the foundations of the world, and moving to
 the unspeaking moon.

Adam idly, in the black water, turned and swam shoreward
Past the place where the sea stars are lonelier
Than the stars of the land. He swam on his back
Through thick kelp: sea-shine clinging
On the long leaves ground fire against motion.
Then, swimming through clear water, he looked up
And saw the seaward stars:
The Scorpion in bright anguish coiled on a bed of sea mist,
And where the split sky-stream divided light above the ocean,
Sagittarius, the Archer, the dancing rider, in a faint snow
 of stars. And still he swam
And was not as nothing beneath the tyranny of all that
 splendor,
Nor poured out like starlight in wonder along the ocean.
 Yet the mystery of the stars,
Darker than night wind in spring, and more strange with
 secrets,
Was present as he swam, and was like a wind
Freshening the world.

The Greatest American Poet: Roethke

Once there were three men in the living room of an apartment in Seattle. Two of them were present in body, watching each other with the wariness of new acquaintance, and the other was there by telephone. The two in Carolyn Kizer's apartment were Theodore Roethke and I, and the voice was Allan Seager in Michigan. All three had been drinking, I the most, Roethke the next most, and Seager, apparently, the least. After a long-distance joke about people I had never heard of, Roethke said, "Allan, I want you to meet a friend of mine. He's a great admirer of yours, by the way."

I picked up the phone and said, according to conviction and opportunity, "This is Charles Berry."

"This is *who?*"

"Your son, Amos. Charles Berry, the poet."

"The *hell* it is!"

"I thought you might like to know what happened to Charles after the end of the novel. In one way or the other, he became me. My name is James Dickey."

"Well, thanks for telling me. But I had other plans for Charles. Maybe even using him in another novel. I think he did finally become a poet. But not you."

"No, no; it's a joke."

"I had it figured. But it ain't funny."

"Sorry," I said. "I meant it as a kind of tribute, I guess."

"Well, thanks, I guess."

"Joke or not, I think your book *Amos Berry* is a great novel."

"I do too, but nobody else does. It's out of print, with the rest of my stuff."

"Listen," I said, trying to get into the phone, "I doubt if I'd've tried to be a poet if it weren't for Charles Berry. There was no call for poetry in my background, any more than there was in his. But he wanted to try, and he kept on with it. So I did, too."

"How about Amos? What did you think of him?"

"I like to think he's possible. My God! A middle-aged businessman trying to kick off all of industrial society! Get rid of the whole of Western civilization and go it on his own!"

"Yeah, but he failed."

"He failed, but it was a failure that mattered. And the scenes after the rebellious poet-son meets the rebellious father who's just killed his employer and gotten away with it—well, that's a *meeting!* And Amos turns out to be proud of his boy, who's doing this equally insane thing of writing poetry. Right?"

"Sure. Sure he's proud. Like many another, when the son has guts and does something strange and true to what he is. Say, is Ted Roethke still around there?"

"Yes. He's right here. Want to speak to him?"

"No; but he's another one. He's one of those sons. But his father didn't live long enough to know it."

That was my introduction to Allan Seager, a remarkable man and a writer whose works—*Equinox, The Inheritance, Amos Berry, Hilda Manning, The Old Man of the Mountain, The Death of Anger, a Frieze of Girls*—will, as Henry James said of his own, "kick off their tombstones" time after time, in our time and after. His last book and his only biography, *The Glass House* (McGraw-Hill, $6.95), is this life of Roethke, who is in my opinion the greatest poet this country has yet produced.

During his life and after his death in 1963, people interested in poetry heard a great many rumors about Roethke. Most of these had to do with his eccentricities, his periodic insanity, his drinking, his outbursts of violence, his unpredictability. He came to be seen as a self-destructive American genius somewhat in the pattern of Dylan Thomas. Roethke had a terrifying half-tragic, half-low-comedy life out of which he lifted, by the strangest and most unlikely means, and by endless labors and innumerable false starts, the poetry that all of us owe it to ourselves to know and cherish. If Beethoven said, "He who truly understands my music can never know unhappiness again," Roethke's best work says with equal authority, "He who truly opens himself to my poems will never again conceive his earthly life as worthless."

The Glass House is the record—no, the story, for Seager's novelistic talents give it that kind of compellingness—of how such poetry as Roethke's came to exist. It was written by a man who battled for his whole adult life against public indifference to novels and stories he knew were good, and fought to his last conscious hour to finish this book. Some time after meeting him by telephone, which was in the spring of 1963, I came to know him better, and two summers ago spent a week with him in Tecumseh, Michigan. Most of that time we talked about the biography and about Roethke, and went over the sections he had completed. From the first few words Seager read me, I could tell that this was no *mere* literary biography; there was too much of a sense of personal identification between author and subject to allow for mereness. Seager said to me, in substance, what he had written to a friend some time before this:

> Beatrice Roethke, the widow of Theodore Roethke, has asked me to write the authorized life of her husband. I was in college with him and knew him fairly intimately the rest of his life. It is a book I'd like to do. Quite aside from trying to evoke the character that made the poetry, there are a good many things to say about the abrasion of the

> artist in America that he exemplifies. We were both born in Michigan, he in Saginaw, I in Adrian. We both came from the same social stratum. Much of his life I have acted out myself.

Though Seager did not witness the whole process of Roethke's development, not having known the poet in his childhood, he did see a great deal of it, and he told me that he had seen what happened to Roethke happen "in an evolutionary way." More than once he said, "Ted started out as a phony and became genuine, like Yeats." And, "I had no idea that he'd end up as fine a poet as he did. No one knew that in the early days, Ted least of all. We all knew he *wanted* to be a great poet or a great something, but to a lot of us that didn't seem enough. I could have told you, though, that his self-destructiveness would get worse. I could have told you that awful things were going to happen to him. He was headed that way; at times he seemed eager to speed up the process."

I saw Roethke only twice myself. I saw only a sad fat man who talked continually of joy, and although I liked him well enough for such a short acquaintance, came away from him each time with a distinct sense of relief. Like everyone else who knew him even faintly, I was pressed into service in the cause of his ego, which reeled and tottered pathetically at all hours and under all circumstances, and required not only props, but the *right* props. What did I think of Robert Lowell, Randall Jarrell, and "the Eastern literary gang"? What did I think of the "gutless Limey reviewers" in the *Times Literary Supplement*? I spent an afternoon with him trying to answer such questions, before giving a reading at the University of Washington. Carolyn Kizer, an old friend and former student of Roethke's, had given a party the day before the reading, and I was introduced to Roethke there. Though I had heard various things about him, ranging from the need to be honest with him to the absolute need *not* to be honest, I was hardly prepared for the way in which, as Southerners used to say, he "carried on." I was identified in his mind only as the man who had said (in the *Virginia Quarterly Review*, to be exact) that he was the greatest poet then writing in English. He kept getting another drink and bringing me one and starting the conversation over from that point, leading (more or less naturally for him, I soon discovered) into a detailed and meticulously quoted list of what other poets and critics had said about him. I got the impression that my name was added to those of Auden, Stanley Kunitz, Louise Bogan, and Rolfe Humphries not because I was in any way as distinguished in Roethke's mind as they were, but because I had provided him with a kind of *climactic* comment: something he needed that these others hadn't quite managed to say, at least in print. And later, when he introduced me at the reading, he began with the comment, and talked for eight or ten minutes about himself, occasionally mentioning me as though by afterthought. I did not resent this, though I found it curious, and I bring it up now only to call attention to qualities that must have astonished and confounded others besides myself.

Why should a poet of Roethke's stature conduct himself in this childish and embarrassing way? Why all this insistence on being the best, the acknowledged best, the *written-up* best? Wasn't the poetry itself enough? And why the really appalling pettiness about other writers, like Lowell, who were not poets to him but rivals merely? There was never a moment that I was with Roethke when I was not conscious of something like this going on in his mind; never a moment when he did not have the look of a man fighting for his life in some way known only to him. The strain was in the very air around him; his broad, babyish face had an expression of constant bewilderment and betrayal, a continuing agony of doubt. He seemed to cringe and brace himself at the same time. He would glare from the corners of his eyes and turn wordlessly away. Then he would enter into a long involved story about himself. "I used to spar with Steve Hamas," he would say. I remember trying to remember who Steve Hamas was, and by the time I had faintly conjured up an American heavyweight who was knocked out by Max Schmeling, Roethke was glaring at me anxiously. "What the hell's wrong?" he said. "You think I'm a damned liar?"

I did indeed, but until he asked me, I thought he was just rambling on in the way of a man who did not intend for others to take him seriously. He *seemed* serious enough, for he developed the stories at great length, as though he had told them, to others or to himself, a good many times before. Such a situation puts a stranger in rather a tough spot. If he suspects that the story is a lie, he must either pretend to go along with it, or hopefully enter a tacit conspiracy with the speaker in assuming that the whole thing is a joke, a put-on. Unfortunately I chose the latter, and I could not have done worse for either of us. He sank, or fell, rather, into a steep and bitter silence—we were driving around Seattle at the time—and there was no more said on that or any other subject until we reached his house on John Street. I must have been awfully slow to catch on to what he wanted of me, for in retrospect it seems quite clear that he wished me to help protect him from his sense of inadequacy, his dissatisfaction with what he was as a man.

My own disappointment, however, was not at all in the *fact* that Roethke lied, but in the obviousness and uncreativeness of the manner in which he did it. Lying of an inspired, habitual, inventive kind, given a personality, a form, and a rhythm, is mainly what poetry *is*, I have always believed. All art, as Picasso is reported to have said, is a lie that makes us see the truth. There are innumerable empirical "truths" in the world—billions a day, an hour, a minute—but only a few poems that surpass and transfigure them: only a few structures of words which do not so much tell the truth as *make* it. I would have found Roethke's lies a good deal more memorable if they had had some of the qualities of his best poems, and had not been simply the productions of the grown-up baby that he resembled physically. Since that time I have much regretted that Roethke did not write his prizefighting poems, his gangster poems and tycoon poems, committing his art to these as fully as he committed himself to them in conversation. This might have given his work the range and variety of subject matter that it so badly needed, particularly toward the end of his life, when he was beginning to repeat himself: they might have been the themes to make of him a poet of the stature of Yeats or Rilke.

Yet this is only speculation; his poems are as we have them, and many of them will be read as long as words retain the power to evoke a world and to relate the reader, through that world, to a more intense and meaningful version of his own. There is no poetry anywhere that is so valuably conscious of the human body as Roethke's; no poetry that can place the body in an *environment*—wind, seascape, greenhouse, forest, desert, mountainside, among animals or insects or stones—so vividly and evocatively, waking unheard of exchanges between the place and human responsiveness at its most creative. He more than any other is a poet of pure being. He is a great poet not because he tells you how it is with *him*—as, for example, the "confessional" poets endlessly do—but how it can be with you. When you read him, you realize with a great surge of astonishment and joy that, truly, you are not yet dead.

Roethke came to possess this ability slowly. *The Glass House* is like a long letter by a friend, telling how he came to have it. The friend's concern and occasional bewilderment about the subject are apparent, and also some of the impatience that Roethke's self-indulgent conduct often aroused even in those closest to him. But the main thrust of his life, his emergence from Saginaw, Michigan (of all places), into the heroic role of an artist working against the terrible odds of himself for a new vision, is always clear; clearer than it ever was to Roethke, who aspired to self-transcendence but continually despaired of attaining it.

Heroic Roethke certainly was; he struggled against more than most men are aware is possible. His guilt and panic never left him. No amount of praise could ever have been enough to reassure him or put down his sense of chagrin and bafflement over his relationship to his father, the florist Otto Roethke, who died early in Roethke's life and so placed himself beyond reconciliation. None of his lies—of being a nationally ranked tennis player, of having an "in" with the Detroit "Purple Gang," of having all kinds of high-powered business interests and hundreds of women in love with him—would ever have shriven him completely, but these lures and ruses and deceptions did enable him to exist, though painfully, and to write; they were the paraphernalia of the wounded artist who cannot survive without them.

These things Seager deals with incisively and sympathetically. He is wonderful on the genesis of the poetry, and his accounts of Roethke's greatest breakthrough, the achievement of what Kenneth Burke calls his "greenhouse line," are moving indeed, and show in astonishing detail the extent to which Roethke lived his poems and identified his bodily existence with them in one animistic rite after another.

> On days when he was not teaching, he moped around Shingle Cottage alone, scribbling lines in his notebooks, sometimes, he told me, drinking a lot as a deliberate stimulus (later he came to see alcohol as a depressant and used to curb his manic states), popping out of his clothes, wandering around the cottage naked for a while, then dressing slowly, four or five times a day. There are some complex "birthday-suit" meanings here, the ritual of starting clean like a baby, casting one's skin like a snake, and then donning the skin again. It was not exhibitionism. No one saw. It was all a kind of magic.

He broke through to what had always been there; he discovered his childhood in a new way, and found the way to tell it, not "like it was" but as it might have been if it included all its own meanings, rhythms, and symbolic extensions. He found, in other words, the form for it: *his* form. Few writers are so obviously rooted (and in Roethke's case the word has special connotations because the poet has so magnificently put them there) in their childhood as Roethke, and Seager shows us in just what ways this was so: the authoritarian Prussian father and his specialized and exotic (especially in frozen, logged-out Saginaw) vocation of florist, the greenhouse, the "far field" behind it, the game park, the strange, irreducible life of stems and worms, the protection of fragile blooms by steam pipes, by eternal vigilance, and by getting "in there" with the plants and working with them as they not only required but seemed to want. Later there are the early efforts to write, the drinking, the first manic states, the terrible depressions, the marriage to Beatrice O'Connell (a former student of his at Bennington), the successive books, the prizes, the recognitions, the travels, the death at fifty-six.

I doubt very much if Roethke will ever have another biography as good as this one. And yet something is wrong here, even so. One senses too much of an effort to mitigate certain traits of Roethke's, particularly in regard to his relations with women. It may be argued that a number of people's feelings and privacy are being spared, and that may be, as has been adjudged in other cases, reason enough to be reticent. And yet a whole—and very important—dimension of the subject has thereby been left out of account, and one cannot help believing that a writer of Seager's ability and fierce honesty would have found a way to deal with it if he had not been constrained. To his credit, however, he does his best to suggest what he cannot overtly say. For it is no good to assert, as some have done, that Roethke was a big lovable clumsy affectionate bear who just incidentally wrote wonderful poems. It is no good to insist that Seager show "the good times as well as the bad" in anything like equal proportions; these are not the proportions of the man's life. The driving force of him was agony, and to know him we must know all the forms it took. The names of people may be concealed, but the incidents we must know. It is far worse to leave these matters to rumor than to entrust them to a man of Seager's integrity.

Mrs. Roethke, in especial, must be blamed for this wavering of purpose, this evasiveness that was so far from Seager's nature as to seem to belong to someone else. It may be that she has come to regard herself as the sole repository of the "truth" of Roethke, which is understandable as a human—particularly a wifely—attitude, but it is not pardonable in one who commissions a biography from a serious writer. Allan Seager was not a lesser man than Roethke, someone to be sacrificed to another writer's already overguarded reputation. As a human being he was altogether more admirable than his subject. He was a hard and devoted worker, and he believed deeply in this book; as he said, he had acted out much of it himself. If he hadn't spent the last years of his life on *The Glass House*, he might have been able to finish the big novel he had been working on for years. As it was —thanks again to Mrs. Roethke, who, in addition to other obstacles she placed in Seager's way, even refused him permission to quote her husband's poems—he died without knowing whether all the obstacles had been removed.

Certainly this is a dreadful misplacement of loyalty, for Roethke deserves the monument that this book could have been. He had, almost exclusively by his art, all but won out over his babydom, of which this constant overprotectiveness on the part of other people was the most pernicious part. He deserved to be treated, at last, as a man as well as a great poet. And it should be in the *exact* documentation of this triumph—this heroism—that we ought to see him stand forth with no excuses made, no whitewash needed. Seager had all the gifts: the devotion to his subject, the personal knowledge of it, the talent and the patience and the honesty, and everything but the time and the cooperation, and above all, the recognition of his own stature as an artist with a great personal stake in the enterprise. He died of lung cancer last May.

Since I was close to the book for some time, I am bound to be prejudiced; I am glad to be. Even allowing for prejudice, however, I can still say that this is the best biography of an American poet I have read since Philip Horton's *Hart Crane*, and that it is like no other. God knows what it would have been if Allan Seager had had his way, had been able to do the job he envisioned, even as he lay dying.

From Night Hurdling

In Night Hurdling, *which Bruccoli Clark published in 1983, Dickey collected an assortment of poems, interviews, reminiscences, essays, lectures, commencement addresses, and reviews. His lecture on Ezra Pound, whom he had met at St. Elizabeth's Hospital in 1955, was an attempt to come to terms with the politics and poetics of one of the greatest tutelary spirits in twentieth-century poetry. In "The G.I. Can of Beets" Dickey discussed the different poetic styles, which, like Pound's, influenced his own. His "Bare Bones: Afterword to a Film," which reveals some of the disagreements Dickey had with John Boorman over* Deliverance, *originally appeared as the introduction to the screenplay published by Southern Illinois University Press in 1982.*

The Water-Bug's Mittens

*Ezra Pound: What We Can Use**

Since I have chosen to deal with those aspects of Ezra Pound's work and influence that appear to me to be profitable, to provide a continuing direction, a kind of enchanted vector for present and future poets, these remarks must of necessity deal with specific writers and demonstrable debts as well as the ideas and theories that produced certain poems. Pound's enormous, scattered, dismayingly wrongheaded and dazzlingly right-headed learning is of course very much a part of his literary attitude, which in his case is to say a life-attitude, and can plainly be seen, dismayingly and dazzlingly, in the work of the Welsh-English writer David Jones, whose mythographizing novel of World War I, *In Parenthesis*, and long poem, *The Anathémata,* have been extravagantly praised by T. S. Eliot, W. H. Auden, and others of authority.

> "I have made a heap of all that I could find." So wrote Nennius, or whoever composed the introductory matter to the *Historica Britonnum.* He speaks of an "inward wound" which was caused by the fact that certain things dear to him "should be like smoke dissipated." Further, he says, "not trusting my own learning, which is none at all, but partly from writings and monuments of the ancient inhabitants of Britain . . . I have lispingly put together this . . . about past transactions, that this material might not be trodden under foot."
>
> Part of my task [says Jones, in reference to his poem *The Anathémata*] has been to allow myself to be directed by motifs gathered together from such sources as have by accident been available to me and to make a work out of those mixed data. This, you will say, is, in a sense, the task of any artist in any material, seeing that whatever he makes must necessarily show forth what is his by this or that inheritance. True, but since, as Joyce is reported to have said, "practical life or 'art' . . . comprehends all our activities from boatbuilding to poetry," the degrees and kinds of complexities of this

*This essay was originally given as the 1979 Ezra Pound lecture, administered by the University of Idaho. During the process of organizing and writing the lecture, I found the enterprise turning into a search in which, almost without my knowing it, I sought to clarify my own feelings about Pound's work, and to ascertain and evaluate the aspects of it which might implement the poetry I would presumably write, as well as pay homage to Pound for his influence—shadowy but vast—on my earlier verse. What I feel about Pound's example is given here and I believe that my opinion has solidified to a degree that will make any further changes of attitude on my part unlikely if not impossible.—J.D.

> showing forth of our inheritance must vary to an almost limitless extent.[1]

And so, in the works of both Pound and David Jones, it is so: "the degrees and kinds of complexities of this showing forth of our inheritance [varies] to an almost limitless extent." The preponderance of Pound's original work has been conceived in accordance with this assumption, and all of Jones's has. Since it is beyond the intent of this occasion to attempt anything even approaching a full-scale assessment of Pound's achievement or place in literary history, I shall limit myself to a necessarily biased and fiercely personal summation of those qualities in Pound that I have found of imaginative and above all of practical value in writing the poetry that I have written and am trying to write. Pound's presence is so pervasive that a contemporary poet cannot put down a single word, cannot hear, even far off or far back in his head, a cadence, a rhythm, without the suspicion that Pound has either suggested it or is in the process of causing him to accept it or reject it. Pound's influence is both direct and insidious; I believe it on the whole to have been—no; to *be*—not only beneficial but releasing and exhilarating, and I believe also that it will continue to possess these qualities for as long as human language is capable of exciting in disparate sensibilities the joys and revelations that certain words in conjunction with other words can afford.

There are four Ezra Pounds, or at least four main ones. The first is the Pound of ideas, discoveries and rediscoveries, the Pound of preferences. Simply to make a personal, fragmentary survey, I would never have heard of Guido Cavalcanti and Arnaut Daniel, or indeed of Provençal verse, or the curious culture of woman-worship, warfare and poetry that produced it, had it not been for Pound. I have never shared Pound's *all-out* enthusiasm for those poets, that culture, or for medieval Italy, or for Roman poetry, but I am grateful to know something of them, and what I know is due to Pound. And I am grateful past the telling of it to know the poetry of Tristan Corbière, whose use of local idiom and argot—in his case the Breton—has taught me with delight what *not* to do with the Southern country-talk of my native Georgia.

But for Pound I would not have in my memory—that is to say, in my mind, my blood and nerves and the rest of me—Lionel Johnson's beautiful line: "Clear lie the fields, and fade into blue air."[2] No; I would not see fields that way, though of course I did all the time. The point is that I did not have those *words* with which to see them, though the fields—in Georgia or Idaho or China or anywhere—are the same. The line is Lionel Johnson's, but the finding of it, the perception of its beauty and the *qualities* of its beauty, the relation of word to world, and, following all this, the insistence on the validity of the perception, the wording or *voicing* of the perception, come from one's simplest and most spontaneous reaction to a fragment of what existence has momentarily made available: these Pound has made available.

Again, in a poem of one of Pound's closest followers, there is the question:

> Have you seen a falcon stoop
> accurate, unforseen
> and absolute, between
> wind-ripples over harvest?[3]

The image of the bird over harvest-ripples is in itself very strong as an image, but with the qualifying words "accurate," "unforseen," and "absolute" stooping with it, that bird becomes *necessary*; all other birds—real birds—will have to learn to fly like that. In fact, those three words of Basil Bunting's could with equal justice be applied as criteria for the kind of untrammeled and primitive observation and careful, simple wording that the best of Pound's own poetry exemplifies and encourages: "The water-bug's mittens show on the bright rock below him."[4] Ah, yes! Those mittens! *Mittens!* The *water-bug's* mittens! How curious, and how exactly, exactingly, observably and unforeseeably right! For that is what the water-bug's invisible tracks—his feet, his fingers—look like, transformed by the sun and water and rock into shadow. It is an amazing picture, an amazing image, and I for one would not want to do without it. Next winter, when I wear mittens, I shall certainly believe that I can walk on water. Why not?

"The central act of the mind, in the 'Imagist' poems Pound was writing about 1913," as Hugh Kenner points out, "is a leaping that interprets one thing clearly seen with the aid of another seen in the mind's eye."[5] This triple conjunction—of associating mind, thing observed, and thing remembered—is fundamental to Pound's practice insofar as the imagery of his poems is concerned, and the encouragement toward its widespread and idiosyncratic employment is the best tool he has put into our hands. Randall Jarrell says somewhere that Imagism failed as a school because none of the Imagists could write poetry, and, though there are a few observations still retaining a kind of half-life in F. S. Flint and H.D., Jarrell's harsh judgment is largely true. But the principles of direct unclouded observation and Occam's law of parsimony as applied to the *number* of words in a poem are still useful, and would not have come to such obvious good in the works of Basil Bunting and David Jones—to say nothing of those of T. S. Eliot—if Pound had not formulated them. The characteristic that raises Pound's images far above those of H.D., Richard Aldington, Flint, Amy Lowell and the rest of the programmatic Imagists is no more than the highly personal and imaginative distinctiveness that Pound brought to them; no more, and that is everything. Pound was more adventurous, more trusting of his senses, more verbally daring than the others, and the faculty that presented and then chose among his linguistic options was both wider and more discriminating than theirs. The French poet, Pierre Reverdy (whom, incidentally, Pound knew) says that "Plus les rapports des deux réalités rapprochées seront lointains et justes, plus l'image sera forte, plus elle aura de puissance émotive et de réalité poétique."[6] Let me run that back to you through English, very roughly: "The farther-removed the points of similarity of two realities taken in conjunction with each other are, and at the same time the more just they are, the stronger the image will be, and the more emotive power and poetic reality it will have." The principle that underlies the application of the word *justes* in this context is that of the hitherto unnoted, the hidden similarity, the farfetched comparison that may be seen to have some measure of demonstrable or *felt* reasonableness about it: some measure of the "accurate, the unforseen," which then becomes, or seems to become, "the absolute."

Pound has always insisted on this kind of distinctiveness; his watchword, his battle-banner, his national anthem is "Make It New." He has put forth daring observation, plain diction, and strong unhesitant rhythm as desirable elements in the memorable presentation of an insight, and his stressing of these factors has resulted in a poetry far more exciting, more intellectually invigorating, and above all more humanly resonant than we would have had without it. More than any other single writer, Pound has stripped poetry of unnecessary ornamentation, of linguistic fat, and given the things of the world back to people in terms they could actually see and feel, unashamed of responding to their simplicity, their existence as they were or seemed to the observer to be. Pound has destroyed the false distinction between poetic and nonpoetic subject matter (a distinction that cruelly damaged the work of John Keats, for example) and opened up the whole universe of real and imagined subjects for contemplation, communication-in-depth and "significant form." The inspired image-maker, the answer to his own Platonic dream-image of the ideal Imagist poet, is the second Pound. Without him we would probably not have the arresting disturbances (arresting, once you look at them) on the New York martini, described by John Updike: "Ringlets of vibration, fine as watch springs, oscillated on the surface of his Gibson."[7]

The impact of this second, Imagistic Pound has been variously felt, over the past seventy-five or so years, by a great many poets, and it is probably fair to say that the Imagistic practice has resulted in poems (and poets) that were better for Imagism than they would have been without it. It has been an excellent influence in the work of Eliot, and in that of Basil Bunting and David Jones. It has created the poems and reputations of writers whom I consider only moderately good, such as William Carlos Williams, Louis Zukofsky, Denise Levertov and Robert Creeley, and has been disastrously misused and even unconsciously parodied by talentless writers like Charles Olson and Robert Duncan. Pound's "keep your eye on the object" injunction is not a panacea, but a useful tool in the unearthing of talent where talent already existed. The power of eye is still individual power, and trivialization of the object is always the Longinian "pitfall" awaiting the Imagist poet without insight as well as biological sight.

This lack of a personal vision, for example, brings all the poetry of William Carlos Williams to the same dead level of commonplaceness: commonplaceness of fact and commonplaceness of apprehension of the fact. Perhaps it is idle to speculate on whether or not Williams's writing would have been better if it had been couched in the almost ludicrously "literary" diction of Pound's early poems—all "haths," "thees," "thous," "mids," "yeas," and "nays": all this Pre-Raphaelitism from the subsequent champion of plain speech, "living language"—or whether the observing-the-nailhead-and-saying-that-it-is-a-nailhead, the matter-of-fact recording of a literal part of mutually observed reality, is better. Idle speculation, almost surely. And yet one does it anyway, and if that one is myself, and is forced to choose, I would opt for the Williams that we have: the Williams of the red wheelbarrow and the rose frozen in the cake of ice in front of the plumber's shop. But the case of Pound's influence, even in one of its more salutary directions, does not really rest there, either. A universe of brute facts and *uninspired* notations about them is a very dull universe: if I had to choose between seeing the rose in the cake of ice and reading about it in Williams's "shredded prose" offered as poetry, I would choose to look at the rose, if I could find the right plumber. Or I would go back to the verbal rose on Rilke's tombstone: ". . . pure contradiction, / To be no one's sleep / Under so many lids." Yes, I would do that, and then go to a real rose with the understanding—and love—of it that only a real poet could have given me. I don't wish to berate Williams, for he was a brave, an unselfish, a dedicated and truthful man. But a real poet, in any sense in which I can understand the term, he was not. His work exhibits, as

Henry James said of Whitman's, "the effort of an essentially prosaic mind to lift itself, by a prolonged muscular strain, into poetry."[8] This effort, insisted on and championed by Pound and resulting in the work of Williams, Zukofsky, Olson, Rexroth (a ludicrous example of ineptitude), Duncan, Levertov, Jonathan Williams, and almost *any*body who went to Black Mountain College in North Carolina in the fifties, can now be seen as an interesting but decidedly small factor in the imaginative literature that followed Pound's general insistence on the mind-object relationship and the word's plain-speaking of it. Even though some of the truly creative poets that came after Pound owed something to this aspect of him, Theodore Roethke, John Berryman, James Wright, Margaret Atwood, Ann Stanford, Jane Cooper, and Wendell Berry owed more to their subjective selves than they did to Pound's objective method, and that is the main reason that the future will be theirs, if I am any judge.

The third Pound, after the promotional and proselytizing Pound and the direct-observation and plain-statement Pound, is, unfortunately, the Pound that both the literate and illiterate portions of humanity have identified as the main Ezra: this might be called the culture-plundering Pound, the complex-associational Pound, the riddling Pound: the Pound that Yvor Winters refers to as "a barbarian on the loose in a museum."[9] Winters says that Mr. Pound resembles "a village loafer who sees much and understands little." When I go through Pound's major poem, his lifelong effort, *The Cantos*, I feel that I see a good deal, too, but that, despite the help of predecessors in the Pound lectureship like Hugh Kenner and Marshall McLuhan, I, too, understand very little. What hope for me from Pound, indeed? What help from Kenner and McLuhan, if Randall Jarrell is right when he says "*The Cantos* are less a 'poem containing history' than a poem containing history recollections, free associations, obsessions"?[10] Jarrell says also that:

> A great deal of *The Cantos* is interesting in the way an original soul's indiscriminate notes on books and people, countries and centuries, are interesting; all these fragmentary citations and allusions remind you that if you had read exactly the books Pound has read, known exactly the people Pound has known, and felt about them as Pound has felt, you could understand *The Cantos* pretty well. Gertrude Stein was most unjust when she called that ecumenical alluder a village explainer: he can hardly *tell* you about anything (unless you know it already), much less explain it. He makes notes on the mar-

gin of the universe; to tell you how just or unjust a note is, you must know that portion of the text itself.

This third Pound, the one that attempts to make a kind of rebirth ritual of everything Pound has ever run across or been impressed by in one way or another, is a curious and despairing darkness to me, though when light flashes through, it is exceptionally bright, pure, and clear: or—a word that recurs to me again and again in connection with these moments: *clean*.

> Maelid and bassarid among the lynxes;
>   how many? There are more under the oak trees,
> We are here waiting the sunrise
>   and the next sunrise
> for three nights amid lynxes. For three nights
>   of the oak-wood
> and the vines are thick in their branches
>   no vine lacking flower,
> no lynx lacking a flower rope
>   no Maelid minus a wine jar
>   this forest is named Melagrana
>
>   O lynx, keep the edge on my cider
>   Keep it clear without cloud . . .[11]

When I read these lines I am charmed first by their ceremonial tone, for I have always liked rituals involving animals, especially predators that are beautiful—as most predators are—but I am not sure that I want any more from the passage than that: that and the fine, forceful, authoritative sound of it. The supposition that the lynx has or can have something to do with keeping the edge—the *edge*—on someone's cider is enthralling, and I would put up a fight rather than have someone bring in a complex mythology—a *literature*, books—to explain it. What I like in Pound is exactly the opposite of what the world has taken him to represent. I like the maker (the *fabbro*) of the clean phrase and the hard-edged, imaginative image, and am tempted to let most of the rest of Pound go.

And yet I know I should not, and will not. There is a great deal more to Pound than I have been able to appropriate for my own conscious uses. What of his approach to translation, for example, and his own translations (particularly from the Chinese) that are more original poems than translations, and are better poetry than *their* originals?

> March has come to the bridge head,
> Peach boughs and apricot boughs hang over a thousand gates,
> At morning there are flowers to cut the heart,
> And evening drives them on the eastward-flowing waters.
> Petals are on the gone waters and on the going,
> And on the back-swirling eddies . . .[12]

When one has come to that passage, when one has come to that rhythm, when one encounters these things, when one stays with them, especially the fifth of these lines: "Petals are on the gone waters and on the going," then a permanent value has been added to a grateful and growing sensibility: water is alive with inevitable and beautiful movement, the words that bear the flowers bear it like a river, and the whole heartbreaking marvel of time—time and seasons long past and time but recently past, time at this very moment passing but still, *now*, trembling with its own pastness not yet come, but passing into, passing—the gone waters and the going . . . well, I must break off, for my words are no match, and above all, no substitute, for Pound's. Neither Li Po nor Rihaku (Li Po's Japanese name), nor the scholar Ernest Fenollosa nor indeed the whole of Oriental culture itself ever wrote so well, or at least so well *Orientally*, in English as this, so that we can not only see but *feel* it: what the East's way of sensing and experiencing existence has been, is, and must be. The sheer *excitement* inherent in the cross-fertilization of languages, cultures, writers has been made ours by Pound. I shall never forget the first wild rush of possibility that flooded me when I had finally learned a few hundred words of French and at the same time began to read Pound, and I realized that the second language constituted a kind of magic in which all kinds of new writers existed, new insights and images awaited me. I have never since stopped dwelling in that adolescent raptness, for, after all, Pound never did, and his example has been before me ever since that time, always opening new doors, giving me new writers, new lines, new sources of imaginative joy, new access to the stealing of the fundamental Promethean fire, the living flame of poetic insight: the true spark, no matter in what language, what place or writer or work.

When I came to *The Cantos* after reading the *Cathay* poems I was certainly stumped. I would have liked, at that time, to have had my confusion not only aided and abetted but in a measure justified by something Katherine Anne Porter wrote, reviewing Pound's *Letters* in 1950, a year after I had finished at Vanderbilt:

> The temptation in writing about *The Letters of Ezra Pound: 1907–1941* is to get down to individual letters, to quote endlessly, to lapse into gossip, to go into long dissertations on the state of society; the strange confusions of the human mind; music, sculpture, painting, war, economics; the menace of the American University; the weakness of having a private life; and finally the hell on earth it is to be at once a poet and a man of perfect judgment in all matters relating to art in a world of the deaf, dumb, and blind, of nitwits, numbskulls, and outright villains.[13]

The temptation "to quote endlessly, to lapse into gossip, etc." is not only Miss Porter's; it is Pound's as well. One might say with some justice that *The Cantos* are composed almost entirely of quotations—often seemingly endless, though fragmentary—of gossip, and above all of dissertations. Some of these are on subjects which entertain Pound's interest only slightly, but others, as we know, such as economics and the virulent nature of credit, are nothing less than obsessions, not to say manias. As a college boy I wondered, and I still wonder at the mind that could take itself with such humorless and utter seriousness, and at such patience-consuming length, as the mind which rambles through *The Cantos* in at least seven languages, ranting obscurely, lulling into poignant and piercing lyricism, leaping from one historical figure, one era, one event to another, seeming to draw all kinds of inferences but making none clear, never out of breath and, though claiming to be, never really conclusive. Yet I had this comfort: moments like those in the *Cathay* poems appear all through *The Cantos*; they are there; you just have to dig for them. And I keep believing, with this fact as a base, that little by little, line by line, reference by reference, culture-image by culture-image, I may be able to come into possession of more of Pound than I have now: that he will keep opening things up for me: things I would never have known without him. After all, he has not really failed me yet, though confuse me he certainly has.

Pound's practice of quotation and cultural cross-reference has had a profound and far-reaching effect on the composition and reception of poetry, but I believe that effect to be lessening. The use of the out-of-context quotation is supremely effective in the work of T. S. Eliot and Marianne Moore and perhaps that of David Jones and the black American M. B. Tolson, but it is disastrously bookish and hit-or-miss in the *Maximus Poems* of Charles Olson, in William Carlos Williams's *Paterson*, and in the lyrics of Robert Duncan. *The Cantos* and *The Waste Land*, by authority of the weight of commentary made upon them, have made the quotation-haunted, cross-pollenized poem the only kind of structural organization that poets have allowed themselves to employ in forms longer than the brief lyric. Compared to the layers of reference of *The Cantos*, say, the straight narrative verse-novel, such as any of those by Edwin Arlington Robinson, seems pathetically thin and one-dimensional. Delmore Schwartz comments on *The Cantos*:

> Taking this long poem in itself, we must of necessity see it not as an integral part of a literary period, but in the company of other long poems of like ambition. The first lack to be noticed from this standpoint is the absence of a narrative framework such as sustains every long poem which has become a portion of the whole corpus of poetry. Pound himself has declared that it is above all by its story that a literary work gains its lasting interest, and it is difficult to see what basis for unity in an extended poem would be superior to that of plot . . .
>
> . . . The Cantos have no plot, although as the poem continues, the repetition of key phrases, characters and situations, makes more and more clear the kind of unity which the Cantos do have, a wholeness based upon certain obsessions or preoccupations, deriving itself from the character of Pound's mind, and displaying itself not in conjunction with the numerical order of the Cantos, but, so to speak, against the grain of continuity, which itself seems to be determined by the requirements of musical order, *melopoeia*, as Pound calls it. Or to put the whole issue differently, here we have a long poem without a hero, such as Achilles or Odysseus or *Virgilio mio*, or Agamemnon or Hamlet. Or if there is a hero, it is not Thomas Jefferson, Sigismondo Malatesta and the other letter writers, but it is, in fact, Pound himself, the taste of Pound, above all his literary taste, that is to say, his likes and dislikes among books and the men who in some way have had to do with books or documents of some kind.
>
> And when we examine the texture of the verse, we find lacking, amid such beauty of language and observation other elements which have been characteristic of great poetry. The Cantos, as others have noted, consist of many surfaces, presented with great exactitude,

> but with nothing behind them. We get what is upon the surface, whether the idiom of a text which Pound is translating or the particular quality of sunlight upon the water which Pound is describing; but we do not get anything more than this.[14]

It is at this point that I take issue with Mr. Schwartz, as brilliant and useful a critic as he is, and perhaps with Pound as well, for it is in just these "surfaces, presented with great exactitude," that I find the Ezra Pound that I can most truly, effectively and permanently use. Certain of these passages have had for me what amounts not so much to a "shock of recognition" but a shock of *possibility*: the possibility of catching an observable or imaginable part of the world in fresh, clean language that would be simple without being thin and ordinary: that would have the forthrightness of assertion, and be given in language having a strongly marked rhythmical pulse, somewhere near the Anglo-Saxon, and consequently the sound of a voice saying something both simple and extraordinary, the tone of a thing *meant*, which is also the tone—the *tone*—of a delivered truth:

> Blue dun; number 2 in most rivers
> for dark days, when it is cold
> A starling's wing will give you the colour
> or duck widgeon, if you take feather from under the wing
> Let the body be of blue fox fur, or a water rat's
> or grey squirrel's. Take this with a portion of mohair
> and a cock's hackle for legs.
> 12th of March to 2nd of April
> Hen pheasant's feather does for a fly,
> green tail, the wings flat on the body
> Dark fur from a hare's ear for a body
> a green shaded partridge feather
> grizzled yellow cock's hackle
> green wax; harl from a peacock's tail
> bright lower body; about the size of pin
> the head should be. can be fished from seven a.m.
> till eleven; at which time the brown marsh fly comes on.
> As long as the brown continues, no fish will take Granham
>
> That hath the light of the doer, as it were
> a form cleaving to it.[15]

Now that's *fishing*! That's not Renaissance Italy, or Jefferson's or Mussolini's political theories or the economic theories of Major Douglas. The passage is from the fifty-first Canto, in the midst of one of Pound's otherwise inchoate and violent fulminations against usury. It occurs as an illustration of one of Pound's favorite doctrines, that of dedicated and loving and above all *personal* craftsmanship: the activity performed well, the object made well, because of dedicated expertise employed for the love and honor of the thing performed, the thing made. The quality that makes Pound a good and sometimes great poet is that, though he is a great, buffoonish hater, he is not so great a hater as he is a lover. His love of what he deems excellence in all its manifestations he has ever encountered amounts very nearly to paranoia, and, though as strong and overriding as that love is, it cannot help seeming to the reader of *The Cantos* that Pound is attempting to place him under a species of cultural house arrest: that the poet is forcibly enlisting him in a totalitarianism of the excellent, as Pound defines it. The profit I have had from reading *The Cantos*—profit as a human being and a poet—has come largely from picking through those heavy-laden and earnest pages for startling, isolated shocks of possibility: conjunctions of words that opened up my own rather unbookish but very word-sensitive mentality to what I might come upon in my own memory and set forth with a corresponding imaginative forthrightness, strong rhythm—rhythm using rather more double-stresses, spondees, than is usual—and an unhesitant sound of authority, a tone of truthfulness and "no nonsense": a tone of "this is it, and don't argue." I like that kind of assertiveness, especially when it is personal and imaginative as well as assertive, and Pound's example has been of immense help to me in formulating passages in which these qualities were dominant.

All this is an admission, of course, that I do not really *know The Cantos*, and that I am missing most of their real intent, the real totality of the poem. Searching for Pound's best shots—his best shocks—of insight, I have been able to come closer to that totality than I was when I first started, and I have in the main disliked what I have found. Once more to quote Delmore Schwartz, and argue with him:

> The obscurity of the Cantos, their dependence upon quantities of information which are not readily available is at once another definition of the poem, and yet not at all as important a handicap and burden as some suppose. The amount of learning necessary in order to understand the manifold allusions of the Cantos can easily be exaggerated, and could quite simply be put together in one sup-

> plementary volume such as has already been provided for Joyce's *Ulysses*. Pound is not as learned as he seems to be—the scattered impression of his learning leads to the mistaken impression—and at any rate the amount of information which must be acquired is nothing compared to what must be done in order to read *The Divine Comedy*, or the effort we make when we learn a foreign language. It is curious, of course, that a writer of our own time and language should require so much external help, but the only question is: is the poem good enough? It is.[16]

Well, Delmore, it is and it isn't. One of the main troubles with it is its lack of actual concern with people. Every person that Pound brings to our attention is an *example* of something: that is to say, a symbol, an effigy, a stand-in for an abstraction: good government, bad government, artistic excellence, economic right-mindedness, and so on. Even the anecdotes about people Pound has known, such as the famous one about Henry James, are more *illustrations* than they are anything else; there is no true human encounter. Perhaps this is not a valid criticism; I don't know. But there does seem to me, despite Pound's hectoring enthusiasm—or love, as I choose to call it, though of an often forbidding kind—that there is a distressing erector-set mechanicalness about *The Cantos*, a complex in-group snobbery, a very off-putting air of contemptuous intellectual superiority, and I'm afraid one part of me will never get over it. There are various kinds of bullheadedness in literary criticism, of course. One kind is Pound's and another kind is J. B. Priestley's:

> For all his long and deep concern for the art, [Pound] has been a bad influence on modern poetry. It is he more than anybody else who has encouraged an unnecessary obscurity, not arising from the flashing broken images of passion, but too often from a cold cleverness working away at compression. For a line can be so loaded with meaning that it can only be understood if the reader regards it as part of an exceptionally difficult crossword puzzle; but at what moment, in this puzzle-solving atmosphere, does aesthetic experience arrive, when does poetry begin? It is he who has encouraged too many younger poets to collect savory and rare ingredients, but then to ruin the dish because the oven, the poetic feeling, is too low to cook it properly. Following his example, they have offered us too many recondite allusions, too many scraps of other languages (for a poem is a per-

> formance on one instrument, not one of those "musical acts" in vaudeville), and too many of these cold flat statements, filled with polysyllabic abstractions, that read like quotations from legal documents. What may have originally been conceived in passionate intensity too often somehow loses, through too much concentration and cool brainwork, real poetic feeling, and ends by suggesting an over-self-conscious intellectual sneering and showing off.[17]

There is that side, too: the clean, sharp, hard-edged and forthright statement-in-depth, the insight voiced with strong and compelling weight and memorable rhythm is buried in ill-digested philosophy, economics, history and politics: that is a simplistic statement, but it seems to me to be exactly true. The Hugh Kenners and Donald Davies of the world, the professors, will continue to find great profit in their studies of *The Cantos*; Pound is already an industry in academia, and will be more and more of one in the future, comparable in the volume of its products, perhaps, to Milton, Melville and Kafka, to say nothing of Joyce and Eliot. Meanwhile I will continue to hunt through Pound's work for those isolated but indispensable shocks of verbal possibility that only his example affords me, and to honor his effort to make the *paradiso/terrestre* for which he so strenuously wished and worked in all his doctrines and poems but most particularly in *The Cantos*. "I have made a heap of all that I could find." So says Nennius, so says the author of the *Historia Britonnum* if it wasn't Nennius, so says Pound's disciple David Jones, and so says Ezra Pound, by implication and example.

An extraordinary heap. Pound's wish was always for more insight, more understanding, more consequentiality: in a word, more *life* for us. What he wanted for each of us, and for all human culture, was highly relevant personal experience: the guarantee of this within ourselves and our culture's guarantee that such experience should be ours. A sense of the consequentiality of things, actions, men, ideas and civilizations is what we most want, and what we most sorely lack. Pound was on the right side of the question, as confused and confusing as he often was and is, and as elitist as his stance is. "What thou lovest well remains." It does. What remains to me as a working poet are the water-bug's mittens, there in live observation from a living world, in believable, extraordinarily releasing, clean, powerful statement: those shadow-garments, but of marvelous shadow: the everyday hand-garments of children now indicating the invisible, water-walking feet of miraculous, real creatures, the world of nature observed and lived and recorded and transfigured for oneself as the sun transfigures the position of the water-bug: those shadow-feet, those mittens, on the beautiful fact, the bright rock.

Notes

1. David Jones, *The Anathemata* (London: Faber & Faber, 1952), p. 9.
2. Lionel Johnson, cited by Ezra Pound in *Literary Essays of Ezra Pound*, edited by T. S. Eliot (New York: New Directions, 1968), p. 362.
3. Basil Bunting, *Collected Poems* (Oxford: Oxford University Press, 1978), p. 31.
4. Ezra Pound, *The Cantos of Ezra Pound* (New York: New Directions, 1970), p. 800.
5. Hugh Kenner, "Pound, Ezra (Weston Loomis)," in *Contemporary Poets of the English Language*, edited by Rosalie Murphy (Chicago: St. James Press, 1970), p. 872.
6. Pierre Reverdy, *Le Gant de crin* (Paris: Librairie Plon, 1927), p. 32.
7. John Updike, cited by Stanley Edgar Hyman in *The Critic's Credentials* (New York: Atheneum, 1978), p. 111.
8. Henry James, *The Portable Henry James*, edited by Morton Dauwen Zabel (New York: Viking, 1951), p. 426.
9. Yvor Winters, *In Defense of Reason* (New York: Swallow Press / Morrow, 1947), p. 480.
10. Randall Jarrell, *The Third Book of Criticism* (New York: Farrar, Straus & Giroux, 1965), p. 304.
11. Pound, *The Cantos*, p. 491.
12. Pound, *Personae* (New York: New Directions, 1949), p. 131.
13. Katherine Anne Porter, *The Collected Essays* (New York: Delacorte, 1970), p. 40.
14. Delmore Schwartz, *Selected Essays*, edited by Donald A. Dike and David H. Zucker (Chicago: University of Chicago Press, 1970), pp. 109–110.
15. Pound, *The Cantos*, p. 251.
16. Schwartz, p. 111.
17. J. B. Priestley, *Literature and Western Man* (New York: Harper, 1960), pp. 406–407.

The G.I. Can of Beets, the Fox in the Wave, and the Hammers over Open Ground*

I have always liked to be caught up in questions for which there have always been, are, and always will be a great many answers but never *the* answer, such as the true meaning of Moby Dick's deformed jaw, or the reliability of the repair service for the telephone in Kafka's *Castle*. One of the most perennially interesting and unanswerable of these questions, of course, has to do with the nature of poetry, and I enjoy—have for years enjoyed—rooting around in myself and others for such a definition, because many of those offered, many of those that wake one up at 4:30 in the morning, are provocative, and above a certain level one is (almost) as good as another. There are ingenuities, plausibilities and fantasies all over the place; one can pluck them out of the air, in a library or anywhere else, and after throwing out all those patently foolish and trying-for-it tries, such as Sandburg's "poetry is a combination of hyacinths and biscuits," one inhabits, doing this, a very heady realm with a good many of the finest minds ever produced by the human race floating—free-floating—around in it with you and the lesser heads. A definition of poetry: no, impossible. If Plato can't make a definition stick forever, if Aristotle can't hammer something together that can't be questioned or pulled apart, if Hume and Locke and Berkeley and Whitehead and Heidegger among the commentators can't, and Wordsworth and Coleridge and Shelley and Frost and Wallace Stevens and Lorca and Rilke and Valery and Pasternak and Kenneth Burke can't blow all the others away, *I* can't hope to blow them away, and of course wouldn't want to if I could. Nevertheless, there are certain speculations that may lead somewhere, and I like to follow those I either pull out of myself, or extend from someone else's idea that strikes me. As for my own unaided pursuit of a notion, I abandon myself to Hofmannsthal's epigram about the composition of poetry, that "perilous, terrible art": "This thread I spin out of my body/ And at the same time the thread serves as my path through the air." Sometimes that kind of path is good, but at times I come on things from another mind that are better than the thread, and sometimes the threadbare ozone, my own search has given me, and I'm more than happy to take off from them.

It would seem on the face of it that an attempt to say anything of significance or even of interest about poetry from the standpoint of the *intent* be-

*South Atlantic Modern Language Association, Atlanta, 1982

hind it—the intent that produced the poetry—would be even more impossible to bring to any sort of successful or usable conclusion than the effort to establish a definitive description of poetry itself. And yet I do think on these things, and I believe with some benefit, at least to myself and my own practice. There is, for example, an entry in the *Notebooks* of Winfield Townley Scott, an American poet who committed suicide in 1968—a fine poet and a great loss to us—that furnishes me the ground on which I now stand, down for once out of my own wandering atmosphere onto a place I think of some solidity and substance, a real launch-pad for speculation, a base that needs to be here. Scott says this:

> There are two kinds of poetry. One, the kind represented by Crane's line: "The seal's wide spindrift gaze toward paradise," the other represented by Robinson's: "And he was all alone there when he died." One is a magic gesture of language, the other a commentary on human life so concentrated as to give off considerable pressure. The greatest poets combine the two; Shakespeare frequently; Robinson himself now and then. If I have to choose, I choose the second: I go, in other words, for Wordsworth, for Hardy, in preference to Poe, to Rimbaud. . . . This is all an oversimplification, I know; but I think the flat assertion of the two kinds indicates two very great touchstones.

So do I. Quickly—instantaneously—it is apparent that in the Crane line, "The seal's wide spindrift gaze toward paradise," the word "spindrift" calls immediate attention to itself. It must, for the "reality-world"—as opposed to the word-world—is not well served by this word, in this line, this image. "Spindrift" is sea-foam, wave-foam, usually wind-blown along beaches, and, though the seal's eyes may be wide, and his gaze toward Paradise, "spindrift" is really not, cannot be, part of his vision: the word is word only, associational word, and in its way beautiful, but word. And it came hard; one remembers Hart Crane's search for it, day by day through dictionaries (note: *dictionaries*) on his lunch hours, when he was working on Sweet's Advertising Catalogue. The Robinson line, on the other hand, is simply factual. There are only plain words in it: a statement. Plain words in ordinary order; nothing unusual, much less exotic. The line puts the reader into contemplation of something that happened to someone, and the condition of the happening: it is the clear pane of glass that does not call attention to itself, but gives clearly and cleanly on a circumstance; that is the approach, the poetry.

Having gone this far, one is provoked to test the applicability of Scott's statement in other lines, other poets: lines and poets all over the place, in fact. Immediately, when one tries the statement out, all the poetry that one has ever read, to say nothing of the poetry one has tried to write, falls one way or the other; the poets pile up on each other like cord-wood, on either side of the fence. A partial list of the Commentary-On-Life party, the Human-Conditioners who might be called, in some sense—in many different senses—"literalists," would include Homer, Frost, Robinson, Lee Masters, Thomas Hardy, Francis Ponge and Guillevic in France, the early Gottfried Benn in Germany, Philip Larkin and R. S. Thomas in England, and my prime example, Randall Jarrell, of Nashville, Tennessee.

Magic-Language exemplars would be Gerard Manley Hopkins, Hart Crane, Wallace Stevens, John Berryman, Stephane Mallarmé, Paul Valéry, and almost any surrealist or surrealist-influenced poet: Paul Éluard, Federico Garcia Lorca, Octavio Paz, and dozens of others, these days, in almost every Western language.

So what we have here to play with is in the nature of a set of two fundamentally different approaches that exchange and interplay in thousands of mysterious, frustrating, lucky and unlucky ways. For the Magicians, language itself must be paramount: language and the connotative aura it gives off; one remembers, here, Mallarmé's injunction to "give the initiative to *words*." The words are seen as illuminations mainly of one another; their light of meaning plays back and forth between them, and, though it must by nature refer beyond, outside itself, shimmers back off the external world in a way whereby the world—or objective reality, or just Reality—serves as a kind of secondary necessity, a non-verbal backdrop to highlight the dance of words and their bemused interplay.

> Let me pass by that gate
> where Eve gnaws the ant
> and Adam impregnates a dazzle of fish.
> Give way to me, horned little man, let me pass . . .

One is quite whirled away by the possibilities of suggestion here, for a thing has been stated—*stated*—such as never happened on earth, or could happen, but can be *said*; it can be made to happen in the mind by means of words, and with this concept a whole universe of chance-taking and craziness—of freedom—opens up. If Lorca can say these things, we, too, can say them; can say, in fact, quite unimpeded, anything we want to. But freedom, too, has its rules, more mysterious than any others. Why is it that some combinations of words are in some manner more moving and acting-upon—acting upon each other, and even, tangentially, on the world—than others? Why is the startling conjunction of Adam and dazzlement and impregnation and fish as daring and truly striking as it is: an assertion that has the power of a true spell, and surely had the power to get the poet past, as he implores or orders, the "horned little man"—who may indeed be conventional reason, and the guardian of the traditional ways of poetic thinking—more memorable, more *successful* than something like André Breton's "My wife with the sex of a mining-placer and of a platypus/ My wife with a sex of seaweed and ancient sweetmeat," which is merely silly, and operates according to no secret law of conjunction, no hidden magnetism that in the true poet draws the right things together, even though initially they may be far apart, and known only to the one imagination? Why is Lorca memorable and Breton ridiculous?

Let me lay on you here, as they say, a kind of imaginative problem, or puzzle of the imagination. It has to do with individual response, and no one can really be more right than anyone else. It was said by Van Wyck Brooks that an author can be most deeply characterized by the one word around which all his work gathers; or, as I would designate it, his "boss word." Faulkner's, for example, would be something like "doom" or "fate." The historian Francis Parkman's is "manly." Jack London's was "wolf," and Lewis Mumford's is "renewal." To digress momentarily, it was Brooks's pointing this out to me that led me to read a writer whom I previously had never felt I had cause to seek out. Willa Cather's favorite word was "splendor," and immediately I found this out, I sought *her* out. Where do you find splendor any more, with existence getting more and more crowded and inconsequential, more rat-like every day? In Miss Cather there is actual real splendor, and distance, and space, and serenity. I went where she went, in those marvellous novels, and I am still there, out on those Kansas and Nebraska prairies. But I am getting ahead of where I want to be, which is with linguistic self-sufficiency and magic-making.

Words. There are not only boss words, but boss metaphors, and of no kind of writer is this more true—with a truth tantamount to absolute—than of poets. See how you respond to a few of these, for out of any of them can be raised an infinite number of metaphorical connections not supervised by existing logic, though of course these controlling figures could also be used by the poets I have called "literalists," as well. Nevertheless, the poets I have chosen are all magic-makers, the erectors of systems of language, the central metaphors of which are the following. See which ones take you; let your own imaginations dilate around these, one by one, as though the edifice of language proceeding from the central figure might possibly become your own. Without naming the poets, I'll give you their controlling images. The first is the sheaf of wheat. God knows what one might evolve out of *that*! The second is the net. The third, simply wind, the movement of air. The fourth is the military disaster on the road. The fifth is the universal void. The sixth is the snake, whatever he may stand for, whatever words may arise from him. For one of these poets, the essential metaphor is the creek running through grass; for the last of them, it is the cry in the ravine.

Here, as I said earlier, no one can be righter than anyone else, though for my own money it would be hard to beat, among those, the cry in the ravine; simply because I am the way I am, the elements of uncertainty, fear and incipient (or possible) action appeal to me.

And of course thereby I tip my hand, for I am not of the party of the magic-language practitioners, though some of them I admire extremely, and would inhibit their freedom not to the slightest extent, for the best of them say wonderful things, and renew the imagination and the language in ways that the more earthbound and literal-minded poets cannot do, because the approach to the use of language is radically different, being more inclusive. Though there is overlap between the two practices, poems still come out, ultimately, to be more of one persuasion, one intent, than the other. The difference is still between Mallarmé and Frost, between Hart Crane and Edwin Arlington Robinson, between Vachel Lindsay and Edgar Lee Masters, between Paul Éluard and Guillevic, and, in the end, between John Berryman and Randall Jarrell. The literalists, some of them almost inventive enough and far-out enough to move into the other place, the Magic Circle, have a powerful say among us, and can't—can never be—written-off or forgotten, for the world is a powerful ally, and not a bad poet itself, as God will tell you. The Frosts and Jarrells will always be with us, even though the man of the wheat-sheaf speaks of "eyes more dangerous than moving sand," and the man with the net tells a painter friend that he must not wish that his forms "be softened by the changing cotton of an unforeseen cloud"; though the man in the wind tells us that "the most powerful lungs among us have reached true space," and the military surrealist admits that, despite his not speaking of storms, "nor of great steers skinned alive, nor windmills sugared to death on the plain," he still is fascinated by the setting where it all takes place: "behind the grayhaired conquerors, I continue to see nothing on earth/ But a road on fire." The poet who lives in the void is possibly the most delicate, for against the void he has only love, sexual love, and "it is there that vertigo/ folds on itself like a bird." These are remarkable insights, and so are many others so conceived. The poet whose chief image is the snake says "deported from the yoke and from the nuptials, I strike the iron of invisible hinges." He of the net, again, says "lobsters that sing are Americans," and the watcher of peaceful water in meadows says to the "soul submitted to the mysteries of movement,/ Pass, carried by your last wide-open look:/ pass, transient soul no night can stop, neither in your/ passion, nor your smile, nor your ascension." The poet who hears the cry in the ravine has the same tone, for he is the same man who watches the creek: "a bat/ is lost in daylight,/ lost every day, torn apart by his black/ wings. . . ."

In World War II Randall Jarrell was in the Air Force, and, though he was never overseas, his human empathy and compassion and his dedication to the world, to a Reality which can only be hinted at but never really reached by language—being what it is and sufficient to itself—made of him one of the very best interpreters of warfare ever to write, able to fix unerringly on the most truthful and revealing observations and insights of other men, of combatants, and of war reporters like Ernie Pyle. But for Jarrell's singling out this episode, I would never have known something about the helplessness, and at the same time, of the grotesque resources, of the human spirit in warfare, that now, forty years later, I think it not only desirable but necessary for me to know.

> I stooped over the form of one youngster whom I thought dead. But when I looked down I saw that he was only sleeping. He was very young, and very tired. He lay on one elbow, his hand suspended in the air about six inches from the ground. And in the palm of his hand he held a large, smooth rock.
>
> I stood and looked at him for a long time. He seemed in his sleep to hold that rock lovingly, as though it were his last link with a vanishing world . . .

That rock *is* the world, is the universe, is the earth of living creatures and their existences, and Randall Jarrell held to it as unthinkingly and as lovingly and as desperately as that sleeping boy was doing after the Normandy beachhead. If it is over-weighting the scales on the side of the Human-Condition poets for me to quote Jarrell as much as I do here, I am not apologetic, for I intend my remarks as a kind of tribute to Randall, from whom I believe I learned more about what really matters in poetry and in literature than from anyone else I have known. As a poet, he might have tried a little harder for the magic, for the inescapable oddness of an idiom perhaps not based so entirely on what he thought to be the actual patterns of American speech. It is rare that you remember the actual words in which he says a thing. There are exceptions to this, however: wonderful exceptions in which language, in Randall's use, catches both the commonplace and the unusual, the inevitable, the miraculously necessary, all in a few words, a kind of blind blurted list in which, just the same, there is a rueful incisiveness. He invokes Woman, "Before the world's eyes narrowed in desire,"

> Now, naked on my doorstep, in the sun,
> Gold-armed, white-breasted, pink-cheeked, and black-furred . . .

Now *there* is the touch of the world! We men have known such creatures! Each of us has known at least one, and she is truly, as Randall says, "the last human power."

Here, then, are two extreme extremes, almost as though the proponents of either were using different media rather than the same medium. One orientation is bent on generating, for whatever sake, the proliferation and dance of words themselves, among themselves; the fascination is in the sometimes selective, often highly unselective action of words upon each other, for whatever meaning or sensation they may throw off, evoke. The other faction, of which Jarrell seems to me the most eloquent and persuasive defender of my time, believes in words as agents which illuminate events and situations that are part of an already given continuum and which are only *designated* by means of words. According to this view, this practice, the poem is something overseen, *supervised* by life: by what, as Jarrell would say, we all know, we all have felt. The ultimate critic, which is to say not only the ultimate judge of value and interpreter after the fact, but the ultimate Virgil or Dantean truth-guide as the poem is composed, is its relation to lived actuality. If the reader is tempted to ask "lived by whom?" I would answer, defending as much as outlining the point, by all of us insofar as mutual human emotions and reactions are concerned: those, like fear and hunger, rooted in our common animal nature, and those like greed, and causeless anxiety, that are uniquely human. This is the world of "flesh-and-blood objects and their flesh-and-blood relations, the very world, which is the world/ Of all of us,—the place where, in the end,/ We find our happiness or not at all."

Poetry thus conceived is largely though not invariably scenic: scenic and "thing-y."

These are transient barracks, at an Air Force Base, in 1944.

> Summer. Sunset. Someone is playing
> The ocarina in the latrine:
> You Are My Sunshine. A man shaving
> Sees—past the day-room, past the night K.P.'s
> Bent over a G.I. can of beets
> In the yard of the mess—the red and green
> Lights of a runway full of '24's.
> The first night flight goes over with a roar
> And disappears, a star, among mountains.
>
> The day-room radio, switched on next door,
> Says, "The thing about you is, you're *real*."
> The man sees his own face, black against lather,
> In the steamed, starred mirror: it is real.
> And the others—the boy in underwear
> Hunting for something in his barracks-bags
>
> With a money-belt around his middle—
> The voice from the doorway: "Where's the C.Q.?"
> "Who wants to know?" "He's gone to the movies."
> "Tell him Red wants him to sign his clearance"—
> These are. Are what? Are.

It's real, all right; the poem is set as solidly in the details of an actual situation as it can be by means of a simple listing and connection of the items that make up a time and place. If you believe in the G.I. can of beets, you believe in everything that is mentioned; there is no need to lie, for the man who set down these items, who composed this scene out of a very real memory, would not lie, because he believes that the poem and the Truth it refers to are not separable from each other: if there had not been that scene, there would not be this poem; the poem refers us to a part of what has happened to someone—to what, in 1944, happened to many. Is this reference to reality, to things as they are, to things as they have been, to things that seem so much to be what they are that they cannot be anything else, entitled to be the limiting factor for all imaginative use of language? The Magicians say no; that there *are* no limits, or that the limits are defined only by personality, only by the individual poet's creative reach, only by the laws he makes for himself, and by means of which he operates. Speaking of contemporary painting, abstract expressionism, Jarrell says that "much of the world—much, too, of the complication and contradiction, the size and depth of the essential process of earlier painting—is inaccessible to Pollock. It has been made inaccessible by the provincialism that is one of the marks of our age." Then he says to us, later in the essay, as he says to his wife, "'What a pity we didn't live in an age when painters were still interested in the world.'" And yet, here too is a kind of provincialism, and it seems to me that very good poets of a certain kind cannot for long be held by it, will not allow their imaginations and their metaphor-making hungers to be confined, limited, and finally judged and condemned, exalted or forgotten by the ordinariness—or even the strangeness—of the strictly observable part of existence, either anybody's or everybody's. Empiricism, as others than Jarrell have noted, yields—no, *is* itself a kind of poetry, but it is not the only source and the only strength.

Recently I have tried, as the athletes say, to work out with the magical side of language: to break away from an approach that I felt was tending toward the anecdote, and depending too much upon it for whatever value this dependency might give it. Perhaps, in the latest poems I have done, this has been a mistake, but even if it has, I can still say that by the attempt I have been made aware of ranges of expression, of possibilities, of departures, of "new thresholds, new anatomies," that I previously had no idea existed, or certainly had no idea that I might explore. Excitement over the new is the life-blood, the guts of any kind of creativity: something, some way as yet untried.

I have shared this excitement with a good many poets of my time, some a little older, some the same age, but most, younger than I. A great deal of translation work has been undertaken during my lifetime, and at least since the success of Ezra Pound's *Cathay* poems there have not been the restrictions on translation that had, previously, demanded certain fixed standards, such as fidelity to the original text, and—despite Pope and Dryden and Homer and Virgil and the heroic couplet—something approximating the metrical and linear form of the original. Pound's renderings changed all that, as, for better or worse, Pound changed a lot of things. If you go to a quite good popular anthology of Chinese poetry, like, say, Robert Payne's *The White Pony*, you may find there a quite respectable poem by Li Po called "A Song of Chang Kan." Most of us don't read Chinese, but if we read Payne's translation we are likely to feel that it is a good, feeling poem that projects a human situation with modesty and a certain power. I won't text-creep here, won't compare—but I expect you would agree with me that Payne's transliteration has produced something readable and even moving. "A Song of

Chang Kan," before us in this way, is definitely a good poem. But Ezra Pound's version, made possible to some degree by Ernest Fenollosa's research but mainly by Pound's intuition, tact, resourcefulness, and daring, is not a good poem; it is a *great* poem, up there with the best our time has produced: utterly clear, tonally just right: a depiction of female love in deep and modest language that must be with us as part of us, from the very first encounter. But, as any good Sinologist would tell you—if he likes scholarship better than poetry, tell you gladly—Pound's version is not strictly accurate; in fact, to scholarly scrutiny, it is not accurate at all; even the name of the village is wrong. Much has been left out of the original, and words, lines, images have been changed. Where does this leave Li Po, long dead, some say, from getting drunk and trying to embrace the moon in the Yellow River? Long dead, but the writer of the poem? What happens to the English-tongue greatness of the poem, as it emerged forever from passing through Ezra Pound's hands? It is a great poem. Whose is it?

I can no more hope to solve the problem of what constitutes a true, just, accurate and at the same time poetically-valuable translation than I can solve the one I started with: what poetry itself, is. I am convinced, however, that any given translated poem should be a good poem in its own right in the second language. It need not be a better poem, and can even be a worse poem, but the experience of poetry itself, as the beholder of it takes it in, is similar in all cultures, I suspect, and among all people: it must be a real poem, and not some classic or contemporary author in another language embalmed or petrified: or, to use a phrase I like, to describe *some* translations—doubtless accurate and scholarly—as "laid-out in English." Whatever your opinion, and whatever my opinion, it is a fact that translation—accurate translation, inaccurate translation, half-translation, half-assed translation, "imitation," free-form "improvisation from," pseudo-translation, intuitive translation, having-nothing-at-all-to-do-with-the-original writing—which should not be called translation at all—and many, many other forms of poetic mediation between languages—is now probably the paramount influence on poetry in English. Americans do more of it, but the English do plenty, and the Irish, some. What amounts to an international style is emerging from this. The cohesive poem, the structured poem, the classically-overseen poem, the reasoned-out and yielding-to-reason poem, the poem of scholarship and wit, the ironic poem, the New Criticism-ed poem, the satirical poem—which depends on a line of argument—the light-verse poem (except for the *New Yorker*!), the narrative poem, all these are rare; you will find few of them in the magazines, or in the hundreds of books of poetry, of would-be or aspiring-to-be poetry, that come out each year. What, instead, do we find?

We find writing which is largely, in each poem, and from poem to poem, discontinuous, alogical, and arbitrary. For example, this is the kind of writing aimed at; it happens to be German, and is by Paul Celan, and called "Flower." The translation is by Michael Hamburger, who is very accurate indeed, having German as much to hand as English. This is what Celan says.

> The stone.
> The stone in the air, which I followed.
> Your eye, as blind as the stone.
>
> We were
> hands,
> we baled the darkness empty, we found
> the word that ascended summer:
> flower.
>
> Flower—a blind man's word.
> Your eye and mine:
> they see
> to water.
>
> Growth.
> Heart wall upon heart wall
> adds petals to it.
>
> One more word like this, and the hammers
> will swing over open ground.

The poem, even so, is not rendered with *exact* fidelity, for Celan merely says that at the word—the one word "like this"—"the hammers will swing free." Hamburger, a fine poet himself, could not resist the "over open ground," which for my money is the best thing in the poem. Once again we are brought up against the Pound problem: among so many, the Pound problem of translation: what liberties may be taken in the interest of producing good poems based on other poems in another tongue? The more pressing question is, though, what principle should determine the items of a poem? Should their relationship to each other be strong or weak? Or should any principle of connection exist at all? The current international style in English brings in items from all over, and frequently their relationship is either so tenuous that it cannot be grasped, or it is nonexistent, the references of the poem being so discrete and arbitrary that one cannot comprehend—or worse, cannot *feel*—the poem in any unifying or impacting way except as a succession of details, some of them remarkable and a good many ranging downward from the "nice try" variety to silliness and the self-parody that is neither funny nor parody of the first-rate examples of the genre they attempt, but of the fourth- and fifth-rate: in short, of others like them.

The arbitrariness of the method, the approach, the intent, the practice, is what bothers me most. That and the fact that there is no characteristicalness, no real author, no imprint of personality in individual poems, or indeed in whole collections. It would be no trouble to take lines, phrases and images and transplant them from one poem to another without loss or gain; the same process could be employed within the same poem, with the same result. The end is a kind of poetry of interchangeable parts, sometimes interesting, but only scrappily, only point-to-point in individual observations and phrases, but not experienceable as whole poems, for all sense of progression, to say nothing of an inevitable-thing-having-been-said, has been impossible to the poem since the poet began to write it from these particular assumptions. "The essential fault of surrealism," Wallace Stevens says, "is that it invents without discovering. To make a clam play an accordion is to invent not to discover. The observation of the unconscious, so far as it can be observed, should reveal things of which we have previously been unconscious, not the familiar things of which we have been conscious plus imagination." Moreover, *drama*, here, is not so much dead; it never had a chance. This is why there has never been a great surrealist poem, as there has never been a great poem in English conceived entirely in this way; and in my opinion, there will never be. It is arguable that there have been great surrealist *poets*—some of the French would say that Éluard is one and most of them would argue that Rimbaud is one, but *Le Bâteau Ivre* is imminently logical and can be shown to be; the logic is unconventional, with elements of hallucination, but it is logic just the same: the man, or boy in the boat, or the poet seen as the boat itself, undergoes a voyage, and in it—some things before, some things after—events follow each other. Even stretching a point and categorizing Rimbaud as a surrealist, although "pre," we can still assert that aside from him, there are no great—truly great—surrealist poets, for great poets must write great poems, and surrealist poems cannot be great because they cannot *build*, and neither can the poems of the new international style. They have no armature: of narrative, of logic, of idea-development and/or idea-succession or change, or transformation; they are not thematic, or at least the theme is most of the time not publicly available. This is why, when they are not darkly mysterious or frivolous, or on-putting, the titles of international-style poems are important, for otherwise no theme could make even a weak gesture at claiming the items of the poem. In the Celan piece earlier quoted, for example, and entitled "Flower," except for the title, a repetition of it, and the one word, "petals" near the end, it could be about anything at all. "Blindness" would be a better title, or something like "Search," or even "Quarry." "Flower—a blind man's word./ Your eye and mine:/ they see/ to water." Why *water*? What necessity has this? What aptness? Why not fire? Why not cloud? Why not diamond? Why not murder? Why not goose-grease? All of these would yield different "meanings," but not to a general theme, a central situation; not to flowers. It seems to me that there is a terrible inconsequentiality about poems of this kind, for the *world* is lacking, and the buzz of language and hit-or-miss-metaphor-generation is everything; the poem itself is nothing; or only a collection of fragments.

And yet, as Mr. Eliot remarked, the bottom is a great way down. Dylan Thomas would have been impossible without this approach, or something like it; as he said, he allowed one image to breed another, and the two to breed a third, to these "a fourth contradictory image, and let them all, within my imposed formal limits, conflict." His imposed *formal* limits . . . or, his *imposed* formal limits. His work too, in quite a different way from Rimbaud's, is logical, though the logic is principally that of a quasi-private symbolism held together by a magnificent and thunderously rhetorical prosody.

> For as long as forever is
> and the fast sky quakes in the web, as the fox in the wave,
> with heels of birds & the plumed eyes . . .

This has what I would call the right kind of seeming arbitrariness—what is a fox doing in a *wave* anyway?—which is Dylan Thomas's sort; the figure is not pulled, with great assertiveness and little personal sense of selection, out of an air from which one can select any two things and put them together, nor is the language, delivered as chopped-up prose with no rhythmical continuity, or what I would call "surge," shovelled off the top of the midden-heap or multicultured dump of a current style. Even though the poem with the fox in the wave was never used except for one line of a later poem, it is thematic, and has to do with the lives of hunted creatures, the passage of time, in which human beings, in their fear and the inevitability of their fate, suffer, live and die with the animals: "For as long as forever is . . . forever the hunted world at a snail's gallop goes." The fox was pulled out of the great world and put into an unexpected and untoward place. I am glad he is there, for he is part of a wonderful image: not only wonderful in itself but wonderful where it occurs, in this poem unpublished until Paul Ferris's biography. Dylan Thomas, I would argue, would not have been possible without the unlimited freedom that came into writing at the time of the surrealist poets, whether he drew on them or not. The point is that he used the freedom, the risk of the *merely* arbitrary, the range of his mind and imagination over everything available to him, everything he could reach or conjure up, and discovered or made—again *within his imposed formal limits*, and using *rhythm* as only he could use it—an English-speaking poetry unparalleled in our time or in any, for originality, inimitability and indispensability.

So where are we? With Jarrell and the G.I. can of beets, with the fox in the wave, or with Paul Celan's hammers over open ground? I side with the world; as Kafka said, "in the contest between yourself and the world, back the world." I do, but I also want its support, *at* my back. I want, as Randall wanted, "poems in which there are real people with their real speech and real thought and real emotions."

I admit, though, to being profoundly interested in what might be the yield of absolute freedom, and hope, in practice, to be able to make metaphors I have never yet been able to achieve, bound into one poetic situation, one scene, one event after the other. The hammers swinging over the ground, detached as they are, out of nowhere and anywhere, have strong appeal to me. *What* hammers, *what* open ground? Perhaps, as some of the new poets say, it doesn't matter. But maybe it could be made to matter, in the sense that Thomas's fox in the wave matters. There may be unsuspected fortune in an approach that offers, literally, even to a literalist, any metaphorical connection that his mind can make, that offers to literature any connection that *anybody's* mind can make. What hammers, indeed? What open ground? Reality . . . World . . . what an *image*!

Bare Bones: Afterword to a Film

When it was first resolved that *Deliverance* would be made into a film, I was engaged to do the screenplay. Outside of two small documentaries I had written for the government when I lived in California, I had no experience of film writing, and certainly none in the area of "novel-into-film" that, together with much horrifying evidence, I had been led to believe was a kind of ossuary or elephants' graveyard of the integrity, trust, and efforts of a good many novelists, some of whom I knew.

To begin with, I had no idea of format, and I asked the functionaries of Warner Brothers to send me some sample scripts, which they did. Among these I remember *A Clockwork Orange*, which seemed unduly skimpy and altogether too easy; this sort of thing was not at all in line with what I had in mind to do. On the other hand I had been told that James Agee turned in—preliminary to the final shooting script from which the films were made—long, almost excruciatingly-detailed "treatments," which were "as good as literature." That was more like it, I thought, so I got hold of *Agee on Film*, volume 2, and read the treatments very carefully. I came up somewhat confused, though with much more of an idea of the procedure I wanted than I had had. I could not see any reason why the film script, or the treatment, should not be a valid art form in itself; I did not then and I still do not. Since the writer of screenplays, particularly in the earlier stages of the development of material, is quite literally not limited by anything, he is free to visualize in ideal terms the story as he would like to see it: that is, *his* ideals as they have always existed in connection with the story, or as they develop from instant to instant as he works. With this in mind, and with the eye of imagination making the movie I would like to see come up on the screen shot for shot, I opened my novel and began. There was no reason to suppose that the sequence of events in the book needed to be altered in any way from what it was on the page; the main concern was the transference of the essential story from one medium to another, and so the writing of the treatment became an intense and extremely stimulating sort of game in which, with a camera in the hands of God rather than those of any mortal cinematographer, I wrote the scenes one after the other as I would like to have them be, all things considered *sub specie aeternitatis*, and with completely unrestricted resources, some from the actual world and some from my mind, imagination, fancy, or somewhere else private but accessible. The story had been with me for such a long time, and I felt that I knew each detail of it with such intimacy, that nothing anyone else could do could bring a dimension of understanding to it that I could not easily better. Perhaps this sort of egomania is necessary to creation in any form, but one is particularly susceptible to it when turning one's own material from a medium which may reach a few thousand into another which may reach millions. The only thing to do, I thought, was to go ahead with the treatment on my own terms and see what happened. But the idea of creating a work in the medium of the film treatment that would stand on its own as a work of art, utilizing the techniques and qualities of the medium, underlay my intent from beginning to end. An audience capable of both reading the novel and seeing the movie was being offered two versions of the same story, and I hoped that, with luck lasting, these would strengthen, enhance, and deepen each other, so that the overall experience of *Deliverance* would be just that for the beholder or participant, and would say certain things to him. For this reason I tried to visualize every nuance, every flicker of light of every scene. I left almost nothing to the actors—to whatever actors there would be—to the director, to the cinematographer, to the sound technicians, or even to the safety crew on the river. I had Platonic, ideal working conditions, and no one to tell me what I had done wrong. I had a thousand ideas I thought not only workable but positively inspired for every scene, every camera angle, every movement, every transition, every fortissimo or diminuendo of sound, every change of chord in music, every birdcall. When I sent the completed initial screenplay to Warner Brothers, I was convinced I had put down on paper what I wanted to have happen on the screen, no matter who the director was, or the actors, or any of the rest of the crew. After all, it was my story, and no one else on earth could know it as I did.

The various details of what transpired between my starry-eyed completion of the screenplay and the actual 105 minutes of running time of the released version is not the intention of this Afterword to record. But I feel I should say what a good many other writers must have felt and some perhaps have said. The writer quickly discovers that, well-intentioned as he is, as intimately involved as he may be with his own story, or whatever commitment either artistic or emotional he may have in the transference of his material to the screen, his opinion, after a certain quickly-reached point, will not count for much. The first thing he is told by any number of people is that, though his story is "film material," and though he is supposed to have credit—or *a* credit—for the script, he himself does not "know film." Sadly this is true; he does not know film and he realizes little by little and then more by more that he is not going to learn film, either, to his or anyone else's satisfaction during the time that his story is being made.

The essentials of the writer's situation are these. First of all, he has sold his material to the film medium, and consequently and presumably to those who "know film." It is useless for him to speak of his ideas for a scene; an opening scene, say. For such and such a reason, he is told, such an idea is unfeasible. He is told that specific scenes cannot be filmed as he wishes them to be because of considerations known to the makers but unknown to him, and these are never sufficiently explained, or at least not plausibly. By the time the film begins to move into the actual production process, the writer has begun to feel like the pig in Randall Jarrell's parable of the Poet and the Critic. The filmmaker, like the Critic, like the judge of pork at the county fair, says to the pig-poet-novelist-screenwriter as he pokes him contemptuously in the ribs, "Huh! What do *you* know about pork?" Though he *is*, unfortunately, pork, the novelist can in fact find little by the way of answer. The director first, then the actors, then the technicians and other functionaries set things up to be filmed in a way which is congruent with the director's version of the dramatic and scenic possibilities of the story and whether or not this is consistent with the writer's is strictly immaterial, irrelevant, and in the end something of an embarrassment, at least to the writer. Details are changed, whole sequences are changed, dialogue is altered or improvised until, though something which resembles the original idea of the story remains, the texture, the field of nuance, the details, characterizations, dramatic buildup and resolution as originally conceived, are lost; nothing but the bones are left. The writer wanders around the set, among the bones, wondering with vague but fascinated impotence what is going to be filmed that day, what compromise or invention will be deemed necessary. There is a certain amount of interest accruing to this position, but eventually the role of faintly-embarrassing specter gets as old, predictable, and tiresome as any other, and after some time spent in this unprofitable way and after seeing his own opinions, suggestions, ideas, convictions, his notions of psychological and dramatic propriety as the first considerations to be dismissed in favor of approaches he believes not only hopelessly but even laughably inadequate, and after being given every encouragement to leave the location and the making of the picture, the writer indeed does leave and simply sits back to wait until the film plays his own local theater, where he can watch it with only a little more of an inside knowledge than those anonymous creatures of public darkness around him.

And yet I don't want to end this on such a funereal note, for as it turns out, the director, John Boorman, the actors, and the crew did, I think, their honest best to come up with what they believe is a credible film version of the novel *Deliverance*. All of them ran considerable risks, and qualify as brave and dedicated men. But the movie, enormously successful as it was and with a longevity given to few films to achieve, is not the film as I would have it. That version is still only in the wide screen of my head, and in these pages; it is still Platonic and possible; it is still in the making. And I like to think that someday, long after I have departed this and all other scenes, it will be made, with the full implications of the story restored, the delineation of character as I have indicated it, the dialogue as I have written it, and the dramatic emphases as I have placed them. I like to think that any reader or viewer who encounters this treatment of the story will enter into Plato's cave with me, will show it in the wide-screen theater of his mind, and will compare it with the version he has seen in actual theaters, or on television.

The main entity the two versions will necessarily have in common is the river itself, and here I do not believe that my imagination or anyone else's could improve on the Chattooga River used in the film, or on cinematographer Vilmos Zsigmond's handling of it. The river in the film is fully the equal of the river in the book, and the sweep and amplitude of the actual running current, the slow stretches, the cliffs, the stones, the rapids, and the force of the water are everything, in Zsigmond's handling, that I could have wished. But the psychological orientation—the *being*—of the characters, their interrelations, their talk with each other, the true dramatic progression, are only hinted at here and there. If these things were to be realized in another version of *Deliverance*, my later, true ghost—not the one that wandered apologetically and impotently through the thickets and over the clifftops of the sets of the movie—would be pleased. For anyone who wishes to imagine or "see" the film as the author wished it to be experienced, it is in the words of the original screenplay and in the imagination.

Chronology

1923 February 2, James Lafayette Dickey born to Eugene Dickey and Maibelle Swift Dickey.

1941 Graduates from Atlanta's North Fulton High School, where he participated on football and track teams, and enters Darlington School in Rome, Georgia.

1942 Graduates from Darlington and enters Clemson A&M College, where he plays on freshman football team. Enlists in Army Air Corps.

1943 Trains to be a pilot but washes out in Camden, South Carolina. Reclassified as radar observer.

1945 Flies thirty-eight missions with 418th Night Fighter Squadron in Philippines and Japan.

1946 Enrolls at Vanderbilt University, where he majors in English. Publishes poems in *The Gadfly,* the university literary journal.

1948 November 4, marries Maxine Syerson.

1949 B.A. in English, magna cum laude, Phi Beta Kappa, from Vanderbilt.

1950 M.A. in English from Vanderbilt for thesis on Melville's poetry. Teaches fall term at Rice Institute in Houston, Texas. Recalled to Air Force during Korean War to teach radar operation at bases in Mississippi and Texas.

1951 First son, Christopher, born.

1952 Returns to Rice Institute.

1954	Receives *Sewanee Review* fellowship sponsored by Rockefeller Foundation. Leaves Rice in summer for Europe, where he travels and writes.
1955	Teaches at University of Florida but quits during spring term in 1956 after being reprimanded for reading poem, "The Father's Body," to group of local Pen Women.
1956	Trains to be advertising copywriter for McCann-Erickson in New York, then works on Coca-Cola account for McCann-Erickson in Atlanta.
1958	Second son, Kevin, born. Awarded Union League Civic and Arts Foundation Prize by *Poetry* (Chicago) for poem "Dover: Believing in Kings."
1959	Wins Longview Foundation Award and Vachel Lindsay Prize.
1960	Publication of *Into the Stone and Other Poems* in *Poets of Today VII.*
1961	Receives Guggenheim Fellowship to travel and write in Europe. Fired from advertising firm Burke Dowling Adams.
1962	Publication of *Drowning with Others*. Travels in Europe.
1963	Poet-in-residence, Reed College, Oregon.
1964	Poet-in-residence, San Fernando Valley State College, California. Publication of *Helmets, The Suspect in Poetry,* and *Two Poems of the Air*.
1965	Publication of *Buckdancer's Choice.*
1966	Receives National Book Award for *Buckdancer's Choice,* the Poetry Society of America's Melville Cane Award, and an award from the National Institute of Arts and Letters. Poet-in-residence at University of Wisconsin at Madison. Begins Poetry Consultantship at Library of Congress in September.

1967 Publication of *Poems 1957–1967* and *Spinning the Crystal Ball.*

1968 Publication of *Babel to Byzantium: Poets & Poetry Now* and *Metaphor as Pure Adventure.* Teaches fall semester at Georgia Tech.

1969 Poet-in-residence and Professor of English, University of South Carolina.

1970 Publication of *Deliverance; The Eye-Beaters, Blood, Victory, Madness, Buckhead and Mercy;* and *Self-Interviews.* Writes screenplay of *Deliverance.*

1971 Publication of *Sorties* and *Exchanges.* Awarded France's Prix Medicis for *Deliverance.*

1972 John Boorman's film, *Deliverance,* released. Inducted into National Institute of Arts and Letters.

1974 Publication of *Jericho: The South Beheld.*

1976 Screenplay of Jack London's *Call of the Wild* made into television movie. Publication of *The Zodiac.* First wife, Maxine, dies. Marries Deborah Dodson.

1977 Reads "The Strength of Fields" at President Jimmy Carter's Kennedy Center inaugural celebration. Publication of *The Owl King* and *God's Images.*

1978 Publication of *Tucky the Hunter, Veteran Birth, In Pursuit of the Grey Soul, The Enemy from Eden,* and *Head-Deep in Strange Sounds.*

1979 Publication of *The Strength of Fields.*

1980 Publication of *Scion.*

1981 Daughter, Bronwen, born.

1982 Publication of *Puella, Deliverance* screenplay, and *Varmland.*

1983 Publication of *Night Hurdling: Poems, Essays, Conversations, Commencements, and Afterwords* and *False Youth: Four Seasons*.

1986 Publication of *Bronwen, the Traw, and the Shape-Shifter*.

1987 Publication of *Alnilam*.

1988 Inducted into American Academy and Institute of Arts and Letters. Publication of *Wayfarer: A Voice from the Southern Mountains*.

1990 Publication of *The Eagle's Mile*.

1991 Publication of *Southern Light*.

1992 Publication of *The Whole Motion, Collected Poems 1945–1992*.

1993 Publication of *To the White Sea*.

1994 Suffers near-fatal case of jaundice.

1996 Awarded Harriet Monroe Poetry Award. Suffers fibrosis of the lungs.

1997 Dies January 19.

Permissions

"The Vegetable King," "The Performance," "The Other," "Walking on Water," "Into the Stone" from *Into the Stone*; "The Lifeguard," "The Heaven of Animals," "A Birth," "Fog Envelops the Animals," "Between Two Prisoners,""Hunting Civil War Relics at Nimblewill Creek," "The Hospital Window" from *Drowning with Others*; "At Darien Bridge," "Chenille," "Springer Mountain," "Cherrylog Road," "The Scarred Girl" from *Helmets*; "The Firebombing," "Buckdancer's Choice," "Pursuit from Under," "Sled Burial, Dream Ceremony," "The Fiend" from *Buckdancer's Choice*; "Falling," "The Sheep Child," "Power and Light," "Adultery," "Encounter in the Cage Country," "May Day Sermon to the Women of Gilmer County, Georgia, by a Woman Preacher Leaving the Baptist Church" from *Falling, May Day Sermon, and Other Poems*; "Daughter," "The Olympian," "For a Time and Place" from *The Eagle's Mile*; "Reading *Genesis* to a Blind Child" from *The Whole Motion* used by permission of Wesleyan University Press/New England University Press.

"The Eye-Beaters" from *The Eye-Beaters, Blood, Victory, Madness, Buckhead and Mercy*. Copyright © 1968, 1969, 1970 by James Dickey; excerpts from *The Zodiac*. Copyright © 1976 by James Dickey; "The Strength of Fields," "The Voyage of the Needle" from *The Strength of Fields*. Copyright © 1979 by James Dickey; "Deborah Burning a Doll Made of House-wood," "Deborah and Deirdre as Drunk Bridesmaids Foot-racing at Daybreak" from *Puella*. Copyright © 1982 by James Dickey; "The Self as Agent," "Metaphor as Pure Adventure," "Spinning the Crystal Ball," "The Greatest American Poet: Roethke" from *Sorties*. Copyright © 1971 by James Dickey, used by permission of Doubleday, a division of Random House, Inc.

"The Shark at the Window" first published in *The Sewanee Review*, vol. 59, no. 2, Spring 1951. Copyright © 1951 by the University of the South. Reprinted with the permission of the editor.

"Joel Cahill Dead" first published in *The Beloit Poetry Journal*, Summer 1958. Reprinted with the permission of *The Beloit Poetry Journal*.

Excerpt from *Deliverance*. Copyright © 1970 by James Dickey. Reprinted by permission of Houghton Mifflin Co. All rights reserved.

Excerpts from *To the White Sea*. Copyright © 1993 by James Dickey. Reprinted by permission of Houghton Mifflin Co. All rights reserved.

Excerpts from *Alnilam*; "The Wish to Be Buried Where One Has Made Love," "The Wheelchair Drunk" from *Striking In*; excerpt from unpublished, unfinished last novel *Crux*; "The Water-Bug's Mittens: Ezra Pound: What We Can Use," "The G.I. Can of Beets, the Fox in the Wave, and the Hammers over Open Ground," "Bare Bones: Afterword to a Film" from *Night Hurdling* by permission of the Estate of James L. Dickey III.

"Barnstorming for Poetry," "Robert Frost," "Marianne Moore" from *Babel to Byzantium: Poets & Poetry Now* used by permission of Farrar, Straus & Giroux, Inc.

"Notes on the Decline of Outrage" from *Babel to Byzantium: Poets & Poetry Now* used by permission of *South*.